Ghosts of Rosewood Asylum
by Stephen Prosapio

Otherworld Publications, LLC
4949 Old Brownsboro Rd. Suite 113
Louisville, Kentucky 40222
www.otherworldpublications.com

Interior design and typesetting by Lynn Calvert and Stephen
Prosapio
Cover design by Irina Ivanova
Author photo courtesy of Robert Rossi

Paperback ISBN: 978-1-936593-10-1
Hard Cover ISBN: 978-1-936593-09-5

In memory of Mark Crisman, whose passing during the writing of this novel reminded me what's truly important.

"But if anyone causes one of these little ones who believe in me to sin, it would be better for him to have a large millstone hung around his neck and to be drowned in the depths of the sea."
-- The Gospel of Matthew 18:6

Ghosts of Rosewood Asylum

Prologue

July 4, 1900

Amelia Lovecroft continued to pretend that the evening's firework show was important to her. Other girls her age were likely eager for the festivities—busying themselves with trivial affairs, such as wondering if their hair ribbons matched their dresses, or if their mothers might let them finally wear a corset. Those issues didn't matter to Amelia. At least today they didn't. At dusk, Amelia was supposed to rendezvous with Boy.

She looked out the window from the administrative building of Rosewood Hospital. Her mother, still wearing black since Father had died, worked at Rosewood as a nurse. Amelia didn't understand how the patients were sick—they didn't look sick. She saw them strolling through the gardens from time to time, but Mother said those weren't the really troubled ones.

"Mother, these clouds won't hide the fireworks will they?" Amelia said looking skyward with a frown.

"Well aren't you the little patriot? A girl your age so interested in celebrating our country's birthday."

"Tell me, Mother!"

"Don't be getting your head full of bees," Mother said. "You know I'll answer by the by."

Mother had been in a foul mood all afternoon. Despite the Independence Day holiday, she had been tasked to stencil room numbers onto small placards. Mother had taken offense and had groused to the doctor in charge, Dr. Johansson, that she was not a maid.

She set down room number 217 on the table and looked out the window. "Perhaps the clouds will drop, but I'd be surprised if they obscure the fireworks."

Amelia made a gleeful clap that caused her mother to smile. But her real worry was that she would miss Boy. She only saw him at Rosewood and only during twilight hours. Last time, he had promised they would see each other more often. She edged toward the door.

"Hallo, where are you going?"

"May I walk?" Amelia held her breath as Mother produced a timepiece from her pocket and examined it.

"Well, the patients are locked in their quarters," she said. "But I want you returning before it's fully dark."

Amelia bolted for the door.

"And stay out of the dirt," Mother called after her. "I don't want you looking all a ragamuffin tonight."

"Yes ma'am." She passed through the doorway and rushed down the garden path toward the pond. Lined with heavenly white roses, lilies and carnations that blocked her view on both sides, they exuded a heavy floral scent that made Amelia feel a bit giddy.

"Boy? Are you here, Boy?" Amelia called out. She had reached their meeting point out beyond the gardens. "Boy?"

He'd never told her his name. At first, she thought it a secret, but once when she had asked, it seemed as though he himself could not recall it. Amelia thought that very odd, but Mother always said, "Keep your breath to cool your porridge. Others can manage their affairs without the help of a meddlesome girl."

Amelia did not want to be rude to Boy, so she had not broached the topic again.

She ventured off the path and nearer the tree line — the woods that walled in the hospital's eastern border. So as not to soil her dress, she stepped carefully. "Boy?"

"I'm here."

She whirled about. There he was, standing in the path from whence she'd just come.

"How do you do that, Boy?"

"Never you mind," he said with a smile.

Boy was near her age, perhaps a year or two younger, but he could do things that Amelia only wished she could do. He always seemed to know when an adult was nearby and how to navigate through the bushes and trees to avoid discovery so that they could explore on their own.

"Let's walk in the woods," he said.

"But I mustn't get dirty tonight."

Boy shuffled ahead of her. He took his steps gingerly as though both of his feet were painful to walk on. Boy's clothes were not ragged, but they looked old-fashioned. His hair was cut short, in a way she had seen in old-time photographs. Amelia followed him.

"Boy, is it your mother or your father who works here at Rosewood?"

He grabbed for the green sprig of a plant, but it didn't move. "No. Neither."

Amelia focused on Boy as she followed him deeper into the woods, but she soon noticed her inattention to the path had caused her to step in a tiny puddle of mud. Her shoe would come clean, but she'd also soiled her hemline. Mother would almost certainly scold her. Boy continued to limp ahead of her on the path. Rather than try to clean her dress, she scampered after him.

"If neither works here, then why do you come?"

"I'm looking for helpers."

"To help you with what?" she called out.

He turned and faced her. There was something about his expression, or perhaps the look in his eyes, that made him appear older and certainly less innocent. "I'm different."

"Oh, I know," she said.

Amelia tried to act nonchalant. She swatted at the branch of a sapling and pretended not to pay Boy any attention, but she could feel him staring at her. Her stomach quivered with an unusual excitement and she could no longer contain her curiosity. "How did you get this way?"

His voice came out deeper. "I did something special that made me this way."

Boy smiled and gazed into her eyes. It made her feel lightheaded—not dizzy but tingly. Amelia had seen older girls act silly and scatterbrained around boys, but she was determined not to let that happen to her.

"Would you like to be special too?" he asked.

"What did you do, Boy?"

Before he could answer, a howl arose from somewhere further down the path that could not have been made by mere wind. Its tone changed, and the shrill pitch hurt Amelia's ears. She plugged them with her fingertips. Above her, the treetops swayed mightily.

The noise stopped and the air became icy cold, prickly against Amelia's skin in contrast to the warm July evening.

"No," Boy said, looking up into the tree branches, "this is my place."

Just off the path from where Amelia and Boy stood, a hazy vapor began to form. Amelia blinked, as she saw it change from a swirling outline of smoke and light into the shape of a young woman with delicate features. Her shoulder-length blonde hair fluttered in the breeze, looking every bit as real as Amelia's own curly hair.

"My place," he repeated at the woman.

"It is *not* your place," the woman said. Her stern voice contained an odd echoic quality.

Amelia trusted Boy to protect her and she took a few steps toward him, shivering. He remained motionless. His face expressed both petulance and fear.

"Boy," Amelia whispered, "who is she?" Her knees trembled but her feet felt locked to the path beside him.

"I'm not strong enough yet," Boy said to her. "Go. I'll find you."

Amelia looked back at the woman. Her beautiful complexion began to transform into charred, black flesh. Her shimmering hair burned away leaving ragged, uneven stalks. Clumps of it peeled from her skull. Her dress smoldered. Amelia smelled the rank odor of soot.

The woman pointed a blackened finger at Amelia, who stood rigid with fright. "Get away from this place."

"B-but I c-can't..." Amelia stammered.

"Get away!"

Amelia desperately wanted to run, but how could she desert Boy? And her legs still wouldn't move. This feeling reminded her of the day Father died. When Amelia had heard the news, she'd felt woozy and unbalanced, yet frozen. The doctor had called it shock. She hadn't been able to feel anything, even sadness, until the next day. But this kind of shock was already wearing off. The numbness being replaced by something worse; something both electrifying and foul. She remained frozen, but her insides felt like everything was trembling.

"Well then," the woman said, her lips forming a sardonic grin, "you can watch what I do to him."

Boy flinched at the woman's words, but held his ground.

Slowly the woman evaporated back into a swirling mist. White plumes silently swept toward Boy. Upon contact with his skin, the mist, or Boy's flesh, sizzled. His mouth opened emitting a noise that seemed to be comprised of many cries. Amelia once again found herself forcefully plugging her ears. It was as if his throat contained a dozen discordant voices. Amelia had learned about hell in church, but she had never conceived of tortured wails so disturbing. Screams that must have originated someplace far away from Pullman, Illinois.

Boy's mouth seemed to stretch and pull as the wails continued to escape. Then they stopped. Boy was gone.

In the place where he'd stood, the woman's apparition reappeared. Her charred face scowled. Black sockets stared out where eyes had once been.

"Do you wish to be next?"

Amelia turned back toward Rosewood and began running, not caring about soiling her shoes or dress. As she ran, she could sense the woman approaching silently from behind. She inhaled deeply. "Mamma, help! Help me!"

Amelia reached the tree line, but fell. Above her, a cold mist swirled about kicking up dirt and mud onto her dress. Would the ghastly woman do to her what she'd done to Boy?

Lightheaded, Amelia struggled to regain her footing. She attempted another step toward safety, but it was no use. The charred woman now blocked her way.

Alone on a desolate path, Amelia Lovecroft blacked out.

Chapter One

The fifty-sixth floor of the Willis Tower provided a majestic view of downtown Chicago. Skyscraper shadows stretched out toward Lake Michigan on the autumn afternoon, as though reaching vainly for the distant shores on the other side. Known for its first thirty-six years as the Sears Tower, it had been the tallest building in the world. It was also home to the corporate offices of Sci-D TV.

For the umpteenth time, Zach Kalusky brushed imaginary creases off his slacks and used his palms to press his jacket and tie—as though a wrinkle-free appearance would ensure a successful outcome to the upcoming meeting. His black sports coat contrasted his pale complexion but matched his wavy hair. The tie was coal gray with emerald flecks, which, Sara said, brought out the green in his hazel eyes.

"They'll be just a moment," an elderly secretary said through a virtual fog of perfume.

"Okay. Thanks, Cheryl," Zach said. "Wait, did you say '*they'll* be just a moment?'"

"Yes, Dr. Benz and Ms. Chen."

Sara Chen, his show's producer, often quelled his anxiety before network meetings. She hadn't mentioned she was seeing the president prior to their audience with him, and she'd been unusually evasive about the purpose for this little conclave. For all Zach knew, the show was being canceled. Losing the source of his tuition's funding would be bad—as in "reverting back to being *Stellazzio's* best pizza chef" bad. Making pepperoni pies wasn't going to fund his PhD studies. Fortunately, regardless of the day's result and to negate any temptation to jump, the windows on the fifty-sixth floor were permanently sealed.

"Zach, come on back." Sara had emerged from the hallway leading to Dr. Benz's office.

He approached her. "This is what you mean by 'meeting me here'?"

"Hey," she said, "I was told not to tell you anything in advance."

Despite standing approximately five-feet-zero-inches tall, a foot shorter than Zach, Sara could still intimidate him.

"Oh. Great."

"Don't worry so much, Zach. We might be getting a ninety-minute special."

"Really?"

Her reply was a head-tilt and a gesture for him to follow her. He sighed deeply and trailed Sara down the hallway. Aggressive as she was intelligent, Sara had gotten her start in Hollywood as a reality TV "story editor" for the dating program, *"Yada, Yada or Yada?"* Since reality shows were supposedly "unscripted," no writers could be listed on the credits but, for all intents and purposes, Sara had written many episodes of that show.

In her first role as a supervising producer, Sara had taken a very active role in *Xavier Paranormal Investigators* development and filming. As much as Zach liked to think of it as his creation, and as much as he and Sara often didn't see eye-to-eye on maintaining the purity of the program's paranormal aspects, he had to admit that the show was neither entirely his nor hers. It was a joint-custody baby.

She stopped outside the double doors to the network president's office.

"I thought maybe," Zach said, "the show was getting canceled or something."

"You worry too much. Don't you know stress is bad for your health?" She peered at his suit as though hunting for even a microscopic piece of lint. She brushed a fleck or two of nothing from his shoulder and appeared satisfied. "Anyway, they're talking about giving us a Halloween Special."

"Shucks, I was really hoping for a Christmas Special." He snickered at his own quip.

"Get serious, Zach. It's not time for joking."

When flushed, either with excitement or anger, Sara became even more attractive. Her demure lips and sultry eyes sometimes made it difficult for Zach to keep his hormones from sending his good-Catholic-boy brain a deluge of impure thoughts. And he *was* a practicing Catholic. He wasn't "The Pope Should Rule the World" kind of Catholic, but he tried to follow the Church's doctrine. Tried to—meaning that some rules were easier to obey than others.

The office doors swung open.

"Zach, Sara, come in." Dr. David Benz stood in the doorway, both arms extended. He hardly looked the part of a network president or a scientist. Shaved head and a stocky figure, he looked like a cross between a professional wrestler and a bulldog. Supposedly, Dr. Benz had only been a bench-level scientist for a short time before moving into marketing. At some point, he'd parlayed a government grant into a monstrous sum of money and then founded the cable television network—Sci-D: *The Network for Science-tainment and Discovery!*

Or so the promos went.

"Thank you, Dr. Benz," Sara said.

Zach smiled and received a wide grin and a hearty handshake from Dr. Benz in return. "Zach, great to see you again. Great work with the show. I'm so proud of you. Come. Sit."

His office comprised approximately eight hundred square feet of the northeast corner of the building. It commanded an astounding view of the cobalt blue Lake Michigan, as well as Chicago's skyline.

The plush leather seats squeaked when Zach and Sara sat in them. Benz plopped down in the chair behind his desk and sat casually, propping his right foot onto his opposite knee and leaned back.

"Sara's told you the news then."

Zach cast a furtive glance at her. Should he pretend that she hadn't? Her plastered smile relayed little information.

"Not much."

"Did she mention something about a Halloween Special?"

"Yes," Sara chimed in. "I told him that."

"And the location?" Benz asked.

"I haven't told him about that yet, sir," Sara said.

"Ah. Good."

The room seemed much warmer as they discussed him as though he were a lab experiment. Careful, Zach told himself, can't get too emotional here. God forbid...

Zach wasn't afraid of ghosts. He wasn't afraid neither of heights nor of public speaking. However, at twenty-four years old, Zach lived in near constant anxiety about losing control of his gift and thereby divulging his secret. Under emotionally charged situations like the present one, he knew his apprehension wasn't unfounded.

Benz leaned farther back, put his hands in his lap and propped his feet up on his desk. "Zach, your show's ratings have been good—not great, but good. One thing we've learned over the years is that after the novelty of the first season wears off, either a show takes on a momentum or..."

"Or it dies." Sara slammed the point home.

"Yes." Benz swiftly stomped his feet on the ground and sat at attention. "So Zach—a Friday night, Halloween Special. If there were one place in all the..." Benz cringed as though mentally calculating international flights for the entire cast and crew. "If you could choose any haunted facility within two-hundred miles, which would you investigate?"

"That's a no-brainer, Dr. Benz." Zach's heart raced at the thought. Is this why they'd been so hush-hush? Rosewood Psychiatric Hospital, commonly known as "The Haunted Asylum" was famous not only throughout Chicago, but the entire Midwest. He had been trying to get his team through the State of Illinois bureaucratic red tape all year. Rumor had it that a rival paranormal show, the *Demon Hunters*, was also fighting hard to publicly investigate the infamous asylum.

"Rosewood!" Zach's heart pounded in his chest.

As though on cue, a hint of *Sailor Black* wafted into his nose as a signal – this time, as a warning. There was nothing intrinsically offsetting about pipe smoke, especially *Sailor Black* brand. With subtle cinnamon and faint tangerine scents, the tobacco aroma hinted of leather-bound books in an ornate library more than it did danger on the high seas.

But to Zach, *Sailor Black's* sweet and spicy smell implied danger at the highest level.

Zach focused on breathing and staying in the moment with Sara and Dr. Benz. He knew that they couldn't smell the tobacco, nor would they hear the voice that would inevitably speak unless he controlled himself. And if he accidentally lapsed into an episode, it would end his television career. Something like that—something that bizarre just couldn't be explained away.

Zach blurted out the first thing that came to mind. "The place has been haunted ever since the thing with the nurse's daughter back in 1900. But everyone in Chicago knows about that."

Benz smiled. "Yes. And more recently?"

"Well, they built a strip mall next to Rosewood," he said. "Allegedly, a few months ago, there was an incident. After the *GrocersMart* closed for the night, windows were blown out from the inside. A security camera captured one of the windows breaking completely on its own. The video is all over the internet!"

Sara bit her lip as if to keep from giggling at his excitement.

"So I've heard," Dr. Benz said. "Anyway, the state has agreed to give us unlimited access for forty-eight hours."

"Unlimited access!"

"More or less," Benz said. He shifted in his chair.

The pipe scent intensified. And the voice came.

They're not telling you everything.

The voice rarely lied and, judging by the tense body language of both Sara and Dr. Benz, it wasn't lying this time. As though to confirm his suspicions, Zach spied furtive glances between them. His temples began to throb – subtly at first but, as the pipe smell swirled around him, the room felt hotter.

Zach knew that during an episode his heart rate dropped dramatically. He could feel it steadily slowing—making his fingers tingle. His hands and feet grew numb. If things continued, it would render his arms and legs inoperative. He took a deep breath and looked down at the tiny *Chi Rho* symbols tattooed on the insides of each of his wrists. With his slightly blurred vision, the markings resembled less the symbols of early Christianity and looked more like the *XPI* of his show's logo. Then slowly, as he continued to inhale as much oxygen with every breath that he could, the tattoos calmed him. They centered him. They reminded him of what he was.

"Are you okay, Zach?" Sara asked.

"Yes, yes. I'm just so excited. How did we finally get approval to go in there?"

Dr. Benz grinned like a cat with feathers in his teeth. "Finally pulled the right strings with the right people in Springfield. Apparently, there have been almost ten attempts to convert the place over the past hundred years?" He looked at Sara for verification.

"I think the number is seven," she said. "Seven attempts to renovate it."

"Regardless, they can't tear the place down, it's federally protected land," Benz said. "The entire town of Pullman has landmark status. My hunch is that the state hoping for us to debunk the haunted rumors so that they can use it as an extension of Chicago State University that's just a couple of miles away. Or hell, sell it off."

"There have been numerous fires on the property recently," Sara said, turning to Zach. "They haven't even reported all of them and are trying to keep things hush hush. Apparently, they're hoping for an explanation, a scientific explanation."

They're not interested in science.

Zach ignored the voice and took a deep breath. "When do we begin?

"Right away," Sara said. "We film the case briefing tomorrow and we're onsite the following two days."

"This week? Why the short notice?"

Benz shifted in his chair. "The state was allegedly supposed to have notified us sooner," he said. "But I think they kept this quiet until the last minute so that the news media didn't get wind of it."

"Anyway," Sara interjected. "It's going to be a week of intense focus. We need some good *dramatic* stuff."

They still haven't told you all of it.

"Well, we can't control how dramatic our findings are, but you know I'll give every ounce of effort." Zach fidgeted with the arms of his chair hoping that the meeting had come to an end.

"Now, Zach, we've only been given forty-eight hours to investigate Rosewood. So..." Benz raised a finger in the air as if he were a used car salesman about to throw in the final bargaining chip to close the deal.

Zach sensed Sara tense up beside him.

Benz continued. "Well, our network family has two groups that want the opportunity to investigate Rosewood and, in an effort to minimize our production costs and not compete against each other..."

"As well as get great ratings!" Sara said as though on cue.

No, they were not. No, Zach thought, they are not setting me up to do a show with those lunatics. Not the *Demon Hunters*. His budding headache worsened.

"Yes," Benz said. "As well as provide us great ratings. One team, your team, needs some exposure. The other team could use some additional..." Benz snapped his fingers in rapid succession.

"Legitimacy?" Sara volunteered.

"Thank you, Sara. Yes, legitimacy." Dr. Benz smiled. "Zach, this Halloween Special is a 'can't miss opportunity' for us all. It is my sincere hope that it will combine the best aspects of both *Xavier Paranormal Investigators* and the *Demon Hunters*."

Between the stench of *Sailor Black* tobacco, Zach's throbbing temples and his plummeting heart rate, it was all he could do to not pass over into a full-blown episode.

Chapter Two

The blow to Zach's midsection forced all the air from his body. Zach stumbled backwards and raised a trembling arm as if it would protect him from the burly boxer approaching him again.

"C'mon. C'mon," Ray said pounding his gloves together in succession. "I'm not done."

The musky smell of the gym and the sounds of other boxers jumping rope, hitting bags and lifting weights enhanced Zach's sense of accomplishment for even having been willing to climb in the ring.

"FuggRay..." Zach mumbled through his mouthpiece. "R'you tryin' to kill me?"

Zach offered a few half-hearted bobs that he hoped would substitute for bouncing on his toes. After enduring just two minutes in the ring—and more than a couple of his best friend's punches, Zach could barely move his legs or lift his arms. "There must be ten other guys—"

"C'mon, buddy." Ray "The Railroad" Ross spit out his mouthpiece but kept dancing and weaving around Zach. "This is quality time together."

"I though you weren't s'ppose ta fight souff-paws?"

"My next fight is with a lefty. That makes you the perfect sparring partner, buddy."

The bastard wasn't even out of breath.

Zach nodded and padded closer to Ray. He knew that he'd be little more than punching bag fodder but if he could get one solid punch in, or maybe a flurry, he'd expel the frustration from his earlier meeting with Sara and Dr. Benz.

"C'mon. C'mon. With uhn name like 'Kalusky,'" he said in a poorly done Eastern European accent, "you should be like uhn big Polish fighter."

The name. With his dark hair, hazel eyes and wiry frame, Zach didn't look in the least bit Polish—but at least Sci-D TV had given up trying to convince him to alter "Kalusky" to something more "marketable" for the show.

Poof. Pa-poof. Poof.

A flurry of Ray's punches came up mercifully short of Zach's nose.

"Damn. When you goin' pro?"

"Can't just yet. Ya' know, once I'm pro, I'll have to quit the job."

"Riiiight. BS alert."

"Hey, I might have to punch someone." He looked away. It was the first time he'd taken his eyes off Zach the entire time in the ring. "I might need to toss a customer out on his ear."

Ray worked as a bouncer at a strip club.

"So?"

"So. They might sue me."

"Huh? You got no money to sue for."

Poof. Pa-poof. Poof.

All three punches tapped Zach's headgear. It felt like a warning to change the subject. For a year, Ray had been postponing a leap into his boxing career and apparently, the inflamed spot was becoming sorer.

Two more of Ray's punches landed and pressed Zach into the corner of the ring.

"You're making me do this 'cuz you got twice the videotape last case," Zach said.

Besides being his best friend since high school and tormenter in the boxing ring, Ray, the only member of *Xavier Paranormal Investigators* not a student at Saint Xavier, served as Zach's Video Review Analyst.

"Nah, the more videotape, the more time with Sara."

Zach attempted a jab but Ray deftly dodged it.

"Ya know seriously," Ray said. "I think reviewing those videos helps my boxing eye."

"I'd think," Zach said panting, "it would make you go blind."

Ray grimaced. "That's what my trainer said too."

"I knew I'd find a way to beat you." Zach smiled as best as he could manage through his mouthpiece.

"Smoke and mirrors, my friend," Ray darted back and forth "Smoke and mirrors."

Despite a torso as wide as an oak tree trunk, Ray moved at lightning speed.

"I'll show you smoke," Zach said unleashing a flurry of lefts and rights that, in his mental plan, had been fluid and quick. Instead, the glancing blows to Ray's arm and chest weren't even worth attempting to avoid. Zach wondered if the guys outside the ring might be comparing his awkward forward motion to that of a baby giraffe—as if guys like those watched Sci-D's nature shows.

"So, did ya put in a good word for me yet?" Ray asked.

"With who?"

"Sara. I told you. I think she's hot."

"If I put in a good word to every girl you think is hot..." Zach couldn't talk and move at the same time.

"Yeah?" Ray asked.

"I don't have *that many* good words."

"Keep it up, buddy. They'll be carting you out of here on a stretcher."

"Great." Zach's legs were becoming room-temperature Jell-O. "At least I'll be carried."

"So?" Ray asked. "What *is* my Sara up to?"

"Ugh. She's kissing up to the network." Zach bobbed up and down.

"How so?"

There was no way to keep pace with Ray. Zach gasped for breath; he was rapidly getting lightheaded. "Halloween Special."

"So what's wrong with that?"

"With *Demon Hunters*."

"Oh."

Ray shook his head as though he'd been momentarily stunned by an uppercut to the jaw. Zach could have taken advantage of the distraction and charged in with a flurry of punches, but instead used the opportunity to catch his breath. He really felt useless as a sparring partner, but he and Ray rarely said no to a request of the other.

"So what are you going to do?" Ray asked.

"Same thing as now."

"Dance away like a sissy?"

If Ray was attempting to hide a smirk, he failed.

"Funny. No. Just grin and bear it."

"Hmmm," Ray said, his eyes taking on the intense glare of a predator. "I'll lay you *bare*." He moved in for the kill.

Zach stopped and held both gloves up in a gesture that was more of a protest than surrender. *"No mas. No mas."*

"C'mon. C'mon." Ray unleashed a flurry of punches on a make-believe opponent in the center of the ring. "I'm just getting warmed up." Not only was he not out of breath, he'd barely even broken a sweat.

"Not on me you're not. I've got a television face to protect."

"I've got news for you, buddy," Ray said. "Zac Effron you're not."

While his friend had a point, as *Xavier Paranormal Investigators* had gained popularity, Zach was surprised at the amount of fan mail –much of it love letters –that he received from both young girls and…from older men. Fortunately, none of the show's "clients" had ever made an on-air pass at him, although off the air a few had made it clear that they would more than welcome follow up calls from him. Lonely as he became sometimes, Zach was determined to stay single until he completed his doctoral thesis.

Besides, becoming emotional held a certain unusual and serious consequence for Zach. One that began with whiffs of *Sailor Black* and ended in something Zach could never show to a lover. The first time he'd kissed a girl in junior high he had almost immediately lapsed into an episode.

Zach spit out his mouthpiece. "I'm going to hit the showers, bud."

"You got it, man. Thanks for the workout." Ray approached and stuck both gloves out for Zach to tap. "I'm gonna get a little more work done before I call it a day."

Zach nodded and, as they climbed from the ring, two other boxers eagerly slipped between the ropes. Zach had survived a session in the ring with a professional-level pugilist, but he doubted he'd contributed much to Ray's path to his first paid fight—or maybe he'd pumped up Ray's ego a little.

Zach glanced over his shoulder at his friend slamming his fists to the midriff of a punching bag that, if administered to a real fighter would have landed even heavyweights on their knees.

Ray had actually found an opponent even less mobile than Zach.

"The Haunted Asylum, buddy!" Ray slapped him a shower-moistened high five. "You've been talking about that place as long as I've known you."

Before toweling off, Ray bent over and vehemently shook his head, spraying water droplets from his hair onto Zach the way a dog would after fetching a stick from a lake.

"That's disgusting—come on, you're getting my books all wet!"

"Awwww. Poor Psychology-boy."

Sitting with textbooks spread open in the gym's locker room, Zach must have looked the part. Ray's "little more" workout had lasted over an hour and Zach needed to cram for an Evolutionary Psychology test.

"Anyway," Ray said. "I've heard that every time they're to reopen Rosewood, something stops them. Everything from suicides to fires to sightings of some witch ghost halts all plans. I guess it's happened like twenty different times."

"I think the number is closer to seven," Zach said. "But, yeah."

"Whatever. Still, there are those Evergreen Park High School students who snuck in on a dare to stay overnight. One of them died that night and another of the kids eventually went insane."

"That's such an urban legend."

"It is not. Remember Danny Joyce? His older sister's best friend was one of those girls." Ray applied a generous amount of cologne on his neck and chest.

"Danny Joyce was a moron. I wouldn't believe anything he ever said."

"What about the rest?"

"Well," Zach said, "reports of the female ghost are extremely common, and she's supposedly pretty gruesome. One report alleges that she's even hideous enough to date you."

Ray finished pulling a t-shirt over his bulging muscles and feigned a punch. Zach stuck out his chin daring him to do it.

"So seriously," Ray said. "Those Demon Hunters are hack artists. They use all those quick cuts, silhouettes and dramatic angles, but you can tell that they're just playing up *any* sort of activity they find."

"You sound rather familiar with the show," Zach said. "A closet fan?

"Nope. It's no secret. I'm their biggest admirer." Ray slipped into his jeans.

"You would be."

"Anyway, rumor has it," Ray continued, "they once used an icy beer can to produce a cold spot on their thermal camera. What are you gonna do — try and get out of it?"

"I don't think I can — the network calls the shots. Without the Sci-D TV paycheck, it's back to working nights at the pizza place, and that's not going to pay for my PhD."

Zach's scholastic achievements, even in his favorite subjects, psychology and theology, weren't anywhere near impressive enough to merit a free ride through Saint Xavier's esteemed doctoral program. He'd never been particularly outstanding in math, science, English, or history, for that matter. Therefore, it struck him as ironic that a science television network was paying for his PhD studies because of his interest in ghosts.

"Besides," he continued, "a Halloween Special is enormous for the show. If we can pull this off, the sky's the limit."

"Buddy, c'mon. Who you tryin' to kid? You give a rat's ass about the show. It's just a means to an end."

It seemed Zach could neither run nor hide, in or out of the ring. Ray's comment was true — at least it *had* been true. As an undergraduate, because of his own childhood experiences with the supernatural, Zach had founded *Xavier Paranormal Investigators* to investigate residential haunts. Over the first couple of years, a number of Saint Xavier students lent their skills to make the group successful. Most just worked a case or two and, curiosity satiated, left *XPI*, but a tightly knit core remained. While clients paid a nominal fee, the money collected was barely enough to cover equipment and expenses. Noticing that just about every cable station aired a ghost hunting show, Zach contacted Sci-D TV and proposed *Xavier Paranormal Investigators* as a television program. *Demon Hunters* had already been greenlighted for that season, but Dr. Benz loved the idea of investigating the paranormal by college students with a more scientific angle. The idea took flight from there. Once the show had become a reality, Zach often felt torn between the glamour of a career in show business and a calling to help children who'd experienced trauma, especially paranormal trauma, which was how he hoped to apply his PhD.

"Look," he said to Ray, "this is a huge opportunity. I'll – we'll conduct the best investigation we can. Debunk whatever we can. I think that's what the state is hoping for. The property has protected landmark status both federally and at the state level. They want to sell that property and, between the exposure we provide and the myths we dispel, they might get a shot at selling it off."

"And if instead, we don't debunk?"

"Then, we see if we can get hard data of anything supernatural. My gut tells me that we're going to have enough abnormalities that we won't need to manufacture drama."

"Yeah?" Ray asked sarcastically. "Demon Hunters may just drum up all the drama you need for the rest of your abnormal life, my friend."

Zach had never confided in Ray how abnormal his life really was. There had been a close call—freshman year of high school, when Zach had just begun to gain control of his affliction, but in the end Zach had kept the secret even from his best friend. "Again, you sound way too familiar with the show."

Ray took a scapular from his locker and kissed it before draping the small, Catholic sacramental article over his head and tucking it into his shirt.

"You know that isn't just supposed to be a good luck charm," Zach said. He also wore one of them—he and Ray had gotten them together at their Confirmation ceremony in sixth grade.

"Okay, Mr. Judgmental," Ray said. "You keep your Sundays as you want, and I'll keep mine as I wish." He shoved his sweaty clothes into his gym bag. "So how's your dad getting along?"

"He's okay. Still grieving or maybe still in shock. He and my mom may not have had the best marriage, but they were together for almost thirty years."

Ray stopped packing and stared at him. "And you? How are you with it?"

It was a question that, since the funeral, Zach hadn't asked himself often. Over the years as his mother's condition worsened, more so as her emotional illness worsened, his visits had become less and less frequent. After one unusually intense outburst, his dad suggested, for the benefit of everyone, Zach stop coming by the hospital altogether. That arrangement had lasted six months — until she'd called him to her deathbed.

"I'm okay. I mean, you know. It's hard but..."

"No, I don't know," Ray said, shaking his head. "And I don't even want to imagine how hard it is, but I am here for you, buddy."

"I know. Thanks." They rarely shared moments like this. "Anyway, the biggest thing now is establishing a relationship with Dad again. It's different now."

"I'll bet," Ray said. "Wow. Almost three decades of marriage, huh? That's gotta be some adjustment for him to go from...that to living alone."

"Oh, that reminds me. Dad and I need your help this weekend. The old deck on the house is showing signs of termite damage."

Ray had finished getting dressed. "That rickety ole thing? Yeah, and?"

"And we're going to have to tear it down and haul it away ASAP before those little buggers spread."

"Yeah? *And?*" He smiled.

"Screw you. Are you going to make me beg for help and the use of your precious cargo truck?"

Ray smirked. "Nah, as you know, I would do just about anything for..." He slapped Zach on the shoulder. "...your dad."

Despite his growing apprehension, Zach grinned. Ray was loyal, practically a brother, but Zach could sense his friend's disappointment at having to work with the Demon Hunters. Would the other team members merely be let down, or would they feel betrayed?

Chapter Three

Oak and maple trees dotted the campus of Saint Xavier University. Their orange and red leaves waved in the breeze brushing against their green counterparts as if reminding them that they too would be falling to the ground. Unrelenting autumn would strip the trees naked by the end of the season. A faint musk of decay hung in the air that even a strong breeze couldn't whisk away. Students scurrying from one mundane class to another seemed ambivalent to the subtle alterations that, one after the next, were leading them into winter.

Sara had arranged for Zach to make the announcement of the Halloween Special to *XPI* on the university quad in a circular sitting area near the bronze Our Lady of Mercy statue. She felt filming on campus added a "collegiate flavor" to the show that appealed to a young audience.

The fall afternoon reminded Zach of the day years prior when he founded *Xavier Paranormal Investigators.* He had waited on the quad wondering if anyone would take seriously his posted flyers expressing interest in forming a ghost hunting group. Ray tagged along offering moral support. Little did either of them know that he would one day be an integral part of the team. Shelly Raynor, a Criminal Justice major, was the first to show up. Dark haired and attractive, she confessed that she would join only for a few cases. Once she completed her degree, she claimed, she'd be getting a job as a crime scene investigator. Several years and dozens of cases later, she still remained on *XPI.* Zach suspected that she'd one day work for the federal government. In his mind's eye, he could already picture her dressed in a navy blue suit normally worn by FBI agents.

Rebecca Smythe had been the next to join *XPI,* but she likely wouldn't have said twenty words had it not been for Shelly's delicate interrogation. Short and plain-looking, Rebecca wore wanton brown hair that completely contradicted her personality.

She revealed that she held a strong commitment to the supernatural that had emerged from a personal experience she had declined to share. Because she had researched the paranormal extensively, Zach made her the team Occult Specialist. Their first case, she discovered an ancient Navajo ceremony to release the spirits of infants who were haunting a school that had been converted from a hospital where the babies had died in childbirth. Since then, Rebecca's dedication and research had made her an expert in the supernatural.

Over the years, students joined and left, but the core members of XPI–which included the technical guys who'd been added later, had become a family of sorts. Sometimes it was a dysfunctional one, but a family nonetheless. And now, Zach was going to shock them with two surprises. One, the case at Rosewood, he knew they'd like, but the other, working with the Demon Hunters, had the potential to divide them.

"Okay ladies and gents," Sara said, snapping Zach back to the present. "Is everyone here? Where's Matthew Morgan?"

"I'm here," Matthew said. He was wearing a black t-shirt and a red baseball cap. They'd done twelve episodes and he had made that combination of apparel his signature of sorts. Matthew, a theater production major, was an expert in producing intricate stage sets. His ingenuity carried over into his work on the show. Whenever a contraption needed to be constructed to facilitate lighting or cameras, Matthew was "the man." While he'd earned his reputation for being tardy, he had arrived early and already constructed a makeshift platform for the cameraman to get shots from an elevated position.

It was Mike "Turk" Turko, Ray's audio and video review counterpart, who appeared to be running behind schedule.

"Where the hell is the Turk?" Sara demanded.

Zach cringed as soon as Angel Perez opened his mouth to speak. "He's probably banging the easiest freshman he could find."

As XPI had come to rely more and more on technical equipment, Zach had recruited Angel as their Technical Lead. The pudgy, acne-scarred Mexican-American was not a handsome man, per se, and his antagonism and resentment towards the Turk made him even less attractive.

Sara glowered at Zach as though both Angel's attitude and Turk's lateness were his fault. Zach pulled out his cell phone but, just then, Turk popped out of the glass doors of the brick building nearest them, the cafeteria. His slicked back jet-black hair and sunglasses gave him the slightest hint of movie star quality which he played to the hilt. Chomping on a banana, he hustled over to the group.

"Thanks for showing up, Turko," Angel said. "Nice banana. Don't you usually freeze those and use 'em when you're alone?"

"Hey." Zach squinted at Angel. "You're in mixed company here." He did not intend to continue playing referee between those two. Their history of gamesmanship was obviously not clean.

Most of the *XPI* team cast not-so-subtle glances at Wendy Merrick, their Historical Researcher. Wendy had been added to the *XPI* team immediately prior to filming their debut episode. Thin, blonde and self-conscious, had she refused to date either Angel or Turk, no one would have been uncomfortable. Had she not been girlfriend to *both* of them at various times over the prior summer, the comfort level would have been perfect.

"Okay people, listen up!" Sara's normal energetic demeanor kicked into an even higher gear.

As usual, Ray was standing as close to Sara as he could without literally casting his shadow on her. "I'm listening," he said.

As usual, she ignored him. "We're going to start filming. Zach's going to fill you in on the case details. Give me some honest reactions and no clowning around. Zach's got a couple surprises in store."

She pointed at him, which meant that the high-definition cameraman standing near her was already filming.

"Welcome back, *Xavier Paranormal Investigators.* As most of you have heard, we've been given a high-profile case that will likely be a ninety-minute special to air on Halloween night. What you don't know is that—"

"Wait," Angel said. "Sara, do you want me filming this?" He held up a hand-held video camera which they used in many scenes to give the show a documentary appearance.

A collective grumble went through the group. Turk's groan was predictably louder and longer than the others. Shelly whispered something to Rebecca, and the pair exchanged a smirk and a grin. God only knew how and where Sara would splice that sneaky little shot into the episode.

"Keep rolling," Sara said to the HD cameraman. "Yes, Angel. Start filming."

Zach regrouped. "What most of you don't know is *where* this assignment will take us." He stuck his hands in his pockets, looked at his feet and began pacing. Zach tried not to act overly dramatic while the cameras were running. He felt that sometimes just a slight dramatic effect—like him pacing, improved the show's timing. "There is a place that I've wanted to investigate most of my life. I'd almost given up on ever getting that opportunity."

Shelly raised her hand and whisked dark hair off her face for the camera shot. Zach knew her guess before she even asked it. She had a penchant and passion for investigating female ghosts. "Willowbrook Ballroom?" she asked.

The western suburban dance hall was the second most notable presumed-haunted facility in Chicago. Hundreds of people had reported having seen or experienced a ghost named "Resurrection Mary" on or near the grounds. Shelly had been lobbying him to let *XPI* investigate that spot all year.

Zach stopped pacing, looked up at her and tilted his head. "Nope."

Presumably having guessed the answer, a couple team members gasped, most were just silent.

Thumping her hand to her chest, Wendy was the first to vocalize it. "Rosewood Asylum!"

Again, silence.

Even the normally frenetic quad hushed. Students, who had been allowing a relatively wide berth, slowed or stopped as though in reverent admiration.

"Yes," Zach said. He puffed out his chest and took a step toward the group. He and Sara had discussed, even rehearsed this next speech. Not only would it come off well on TV, but it would ensure that no one in the group could later back out without looking like a total quitter. "And I need to know, here and now, if anyone feels strongly about not investigating this with me. Even if it's just a nagging fear from inside that you won't be able to hold up under the pressure, I won't care now if you come forward and decline this mission."

Only Ray pursed his lips; he already knew what was coming. The others, as though mesmerized, just stared.

"I need to know right now. Are we in this together?" Zach asked. "Are we in this together, no matter what?"

Most nodded slowly. Looking around, Matthew spoke up. "I think we're all behind you, boss."

Zach exhaled deeply and smiled. He glanced at Sara who was already sending a text message to cue the next act of the performance.

The team fired questions at Zach in rapid succession.

"How did we get permission from the state?"

"How much time will we have?"

"When do we start?"

Zach held up one finger and shook his head. "Guys...guys, I still have one major announcement."

The team quieted. The cameraman slowly circled behind Zach discreetly pointing his lens at the faces of the team. Sara held up a handheld video cam at the doors that Turk had earlier emerged from. Ray's smirk had transformed into a rueful grimace.

"Because this is such a major undertaking," Zach continued, "the network has seen fit to provide us some help, some reinforcements, I'd like to call them."

Ray tapped Angel on the shoulder and pointed to the cafeteria exit where the Demon Hunters were emerging. Seeing the stunned looks on his team's faces and knowing they were being captured in high definition, Zach wondered if he'd made a major mistake.

Chapter Four

Led across the quad by their enigmatic host Bryce Finman, the Demon Hunters looked like a pack of Hells Angels who'd ridden their motorcycles through the entire length of a circus train. In their late-twenties to early-thirties, they were grungy, colorful and eclectic in a "rock star" sort of way. The Demon Hunters were tall, and to a person, appeared much thinner than they did on television. Two of the five looked almost emaciated—or maybe it was just an illusion produced by their thick layers of make up.

Clad in a gray overcoat out of *Tombstone*, Bryce strode towards Zach with his arms hanging limp at his sides. His neo-1980s hairstyle was dyed platinum blond.

Zach had never met him in person and had assumed that they'd be about the same height. He was wrong. When Bryce unexpectedly embraced him in a hug, Zach's face met the chest of his counterpart's trademark black and pink striped shirt. His stature had been camouflaged by the height of the other Demon Hunters; Bryce stood at least six-feet, four-inches tall.

"Zachman, we really appreciate you inviting us along on this investigation," Bryce said. Considering his tone, not to mention the fact that he had *not* invited them, Zach found the comment subtly patronizing.

Bryce paused to face the XPI team as a whole, and then pumped a fist in the air with every syllable. "And we shall not let you down!"

In unison, the Demon Hunters pounded their fists together and barked like a pack of wild dogs, as a sign of their agreement and support. Zach had witnessed their signature cheer on every episode of their show.

Not one *Xavier Paranormal Investigators* team member had uttered a word since the appearance of the motley band of rival ghost hunters. Sara however, was grinning as though envisioning an Emmy award on her mantelpiece.

Zach knew he should speak but couldn't find the words.

"To the rest of you in *XPI*, I say this," Bryce droned on, fist still prepared to pump, "please consider us your new friends and your new teammates. We-are-in-this-to-ge-ther!"

Again the Demon Hunters performed their bark and signature fist clunking. Zach was growing tired of the rah-rah; it was time to get down to business.

"Thank you, Bryce," he said, and then turned to the camera. "As you know, Rosewood is *considered* the most haunted place in Chicago. That makes it a prime target for anything from good-natured tricks and pranks, to hoaxes and all out sabotage. If people get wind that our teams are investigating Rosewood, they may look to make a name for themselves. They'll deceive us and then after the show airs, go public with the hoax." Zach took a few steps around the group's outer circle. It provided a dramatic pause. "Therefore, we need to be on the lookout for any evidence of both natural explanations and fraud. The state may be hoping we'll debunk the haunting, but with over one hundred years of reputation, I find it hard to believe we're not going to find ample evidence of paranormal activity at Rosewood."

The Demon Hunters looked to Bryce as if anticipating a signal to cheer, but he subtly shook them off. Shell-shocked glares from the *XPI* team let Zach know that they were inspecting his every move for either evidence of leadership or betrayal. Sara and her cameraman circled around both groups alternating between shots of Zach's speech and the reaction to it.

"We're meeting the Rosewood custodian at the site tomorrow at 9 A.M. We've got forty-eight hours to collect as much data as humanly possible. That means, before we go in there, we need to know as much as we can about the history of Rosewood." Zach pointed. "Wendy, please be prepared to brief both groups at the gates of Rosewood tomorrow morning at 8 A.M."

She nodded.

"We need *extensive* historical research done."

"Yes, sir!"

"Patrizia?" Zach turned to the *Demon Hunters' DemonHistorian*.

In normal terms, Patrizia was a demonologist. On their show, she wasn't involved much with the on-site investigations. Zach thought to call her 'hot' would not only be an understatement, but based on her scowl and icy stare, it might be the last thing uttered by whoever said it. She had long, jet-black hair and was darkly complexioned. Her attire of black leather pants, a black spandex top that exposed her taut midriff and white leather jacket appeared ready for an action film.

"Would you please assist Wendy and focus your research on the modern-day occurrences—especially that incident where the *GrocersMart* surveillance cameras captured video of store windows breaking from the inside? Get to the bottom of that," Zach said. His inflection inadvertently made it sound more like a question than a command.

There was an edge to Patrizia, not her expression so much as her velvet brown eyes which seemed to lose their softness as he stared into them. They flashed indecision but for a second, and then as though forcing any uncertainty beneath the surface, she squinted. "Right."

Zach barely suppressed a shudder. He'd been wrong. She wasn't just hot, she was absolutely gorgeous.

She turned her gaze to Bryce, and Zach looked the other way.

"Tech guys –Angel, Pierre and Matthew, get together and do a tech inventory. We're going to need a lot of equipment and there's no electricity at Rosewood. In addition to plenty of battery packs, we need to get a generator," Zach turned to the camera, "because spirits can sap the power out of batteries."

Angel held out his hand to Pierre, their *TechniHunter*. Pierre was the only *Demon Hunter* with facial hair – an inverted, triangle soul patch on his chin.

"Geeks of the world unite," Angel said.

"A pleasure, mate. I look forward to workin wit'cha."

Zach joined most of his team in a double take. The thick Australian accent shocked him. *Demon Hunters* had edited the show so that Pierre spent plenty of time on camera but had never uttered a word on the air.

Determined to wrap up the introductory meeting before any foul wind steered them into even more uncomfortable waters, Zach spoke. "Sara, Bryce and I are meeting for lunch and will be planning more of the specifics. We'll let you know more tonight or tomorrow. Any questions?"

Matthew spoke without raising his hand. "Since we've got two technical guys with a lot of experience, could I help out in the actual investigations?"

"We've got more investigators than tech guys, Matthew," Zach said more sternly than he'd intended. "As I've told you before, next season we'll get you more investigation time. This certainly isn't the case for it."

A dejected look on his face, Matthew nodded. Zach didn't even need to glance at Sara to know she'd probably gotten a close up of that disappointed expression.

"Anything else?" Zach asked.

The moment Zach saw Sashza, the transvestite Demon Hunters medium, raise her hand, he regretted ever having asked the question.

"Zachary," she called out in her falsetto voice, "before we go our separate ways this afternoon, might we perhaps unite in a circle so that I may bless our undertakings?"

Zach tried to make his face stone-like to avoid showing any emotion on camera, but mentally castigated himself for not suggesting that *he* lead them in prayer. Now, he could not say no without offending her and the Demon Hunters. By his study of their show, Zach gathered that Sashza's "religious beliefs," were an eclectic combination of Buddhism, Native American Paganism and Schizophrenia.

"I guess that would be okay." He made a mental note to lead them in the Lord's Prayer prior to tomorrow's investigation.

"All right everyone," Sashza broadcast loudly. "Please join hands with each other and let's all form a united circle. She extended her left hand toward Rico, the *Demon Hunters* Jersey-accented *Lead InvestiHunter.*

Sashza grasped Ray's hand in her only slightly smaller palm. The glare Ray gave Zach ensured he'd not be stepping into the boxing ring with his best friend again any time soon. Zach suspected Ray's punches to his headgear might not be love taps next time. The rest of *XPI* complied with Sashza's request even without their traditional grumbling. Once hands had been joined, Sashza asked for a moment of silence for all spirits— living, departed and lingering. Zach sighed as his thoughts turned to his recently passed mother. A memory flashed through his mind; one of the few remaining he held of her smiling, really smiling.

When it came, Sashza's alto screech startled everyone. "Gods of the heavens and gods of the stars join us here. From the gods of the earth to the gods in the sea, from the gods in the air to the gods of—"

Sashza gasped. She looked skyward but her eyes were white. "The gods of fire!" She leaned slowly backwards and then lurched forward. Her movement was so violent that it broke Ray's handhold. Sashza fell to the ground face first, her arms not extending to break her fall. Her chest and shoulders hit the earth squarely. Her muscular body thudded on the ground.

One look at Bryce's reaction convinced Zach this was not scripted drama. His new co-host had broken the circle and was rushing to her. It took both Bryce and Ray to flip Sashza over. Someone put a balled-up jacket under her head.

"Sashza?" Bryce lightly slapped her face and caressed her forehead.

From up close, Zach noticed for the first time how much makeup she wore to cover what was not feminine skin. Her eyes rolled around behind closed lids which fluttered a moment before reopening.

"Sashza, what did you see?" Bryce asked.

Her mouth opened and closed, but she didn't speak.

"Can someone get some water?" Zach called out.

Sara and her cameraman swirled about them filming like war reporters on a battlefield.

Sashza bolted upright. "Someone is going to burn for their sins!"

"Shhhhhh. It's okay," Bryce said. "It's only a vision."

"No. No, it's not," she said to him. "I cannot be a part of this. Someone's lies are putting us all in danger."

Zachary's Past—Age Three

Beth Kalusky was halfway through a videotape of Friday's "Tonight Show with Johnny Carson" when keys rattled outside the door of their modest duplex. Gary entered. He turned and made a point of locking the deadbolt before looking in her direction. Beth was not about to let him off the hook easily.

She glared at him as he stood frozen just inside the doorway. "You reek of alcohol and cheap perfume!"

Gary sighed and shook his head. "I absolutely do not."

"Crawling in at nearly three in the morning when you've got a wife and a baby is not acceptable behavior." Beth pointed to the clock.

Gary gritted his teeth and stared at the ceiling the way he did when he was bottling his rage. She wished once, just once, he'd let it out and show her that he cared. Show her the man he was before she'd given birth to his—

"It was my brother's fucking wedding, he said. "You left early." Harsh as they were, the words came out monotone—no feeling in them. No passion.

This isn't the same man I married.

"Brother's wedding or not, you're drunk and irresponsible. How dare you drive like that? How dare you disrespect me and your family that way!"

"My family? My family?"

There was a flicker of anger—quickly suppressed, but where was the passion? She knew with the turn of a screw, she could open him up. "Yeah, yeah, yeah," she said. "I know—sorry darling, you never promised me a rose garden..."

"Goddamn it, Beth, enough with the melodrama. I was with my family tonight. My entire family. You're the one who ran out of there as soon as the clock struck ten."

"Your son had to get home, Gary. Believe it or not, three-year olds need sleep."

"He was fine sleeping on the coats and blankets my sister laid out. You're the one who bailed on family tonight."

"We are your family, Gary." Her voice rose and she took a step toward him. "Zachary and I are your family!"

Before he could respond, if he'd intended on responding at all, the room instantly turned ice cold. The vague scent of pipe wafted by, and not just any pipe smoke: Sailor Black brand. By his facial expression, Gary must have smelled it too. He exhaled. A stream of his breath looked as thick as smoke. Even on the crisp, October night, it wasn't this cold outside.

"What is it?" she asked, staring deeply into Gary's eyes. She believed in the paranormal; he did not.

"Henry. He's here?" He uttered the words as though trying to convince himself that they were true.

Two months prior her eldest brother Henry had died.

The first chime of the clock struck. Its harmonious tones were still ringing when Zachary screamed.

They bolted for his bedroom and arrived before the clock's third chime. The toddler was standing on his bed. His eyes were wide and he reached toward the corner of the ceiling. It may have just been shadows, but the darkness stirred there.

"But," he said. "Don't want come."

With the smell of Sailor Black tobacco thick in the air, for a moment, Beth wondered who had been smoking in the room. She darted for her boy and snatched him in her arms.

Gary flicked on the lights, but the darkness in the corner lingered. Gary blanched.

A voice said, "He is my godson. It must be passed to him."

"Leave my son alone!" Beth said, clutching Zachary.

"No," Zach said, still reaching toward the dark entity. "Stay me. Stay me!"

"Zachary." Beth pulled his arm down. "No!"

He closed and opened his extended hand repeatedly. "Stay!"

He had no sooner uttered the word than the blackness swooped down at him. It disappeared into his mouth and nostrils. Zach collapsed unconscious in her arms.

Just as quickly as the apartment had gone cold, it returned to a normal temperature. Looking at her son, Beth saw the blood.

She screamed.

Chapter Five

"So has she done that before?" Zach asked, after they'd ordered lunch.

Zach had been queasy since the events on the quad, and the aroma of rich Italian food that Zach normally adored, did nothing to settle his stomach. He was conflicted. On one hand, he was nervous that Sashza had somehow sensed the spirit housed inside his body, had somehow discovered his possession. Given her terror at whatever vision she had, Zach suspected she would have bluntly pointed him out had she uncovered his secret. On the other hand, he was anxious because she may not have been referring to his condition—which meant someone else was hiding an even more sinister secret.

"Done what?" Bryce asked.

"What she did at the quad?"

"Oh, yeah, no. Well, she does get intuitions and feelings and suspicions. She's swooned before, but I've never seen her as shaken and scared as she was today."

"She *will* relent and show up tomorrow, won't she?" Sara asked.

Bryce ripped a piece of bread from the loaf on the table and shrugged. "Might work out better for the show if she doesn't. If our fans see that Rosewood is too creepy for Sashza. More dramatic that way." He shoved the bread into his mouth.

"Was that planned?" Zach asked.

"Nnnnt mmmm." Bryce shook his head fiercely.

Zach continued. "I want to be up front here. Just investigating Rosewood should provide us plenty of drama. I don't want anything manufactured."

"Why not?" Bryce asked.

Zach couldn't believe his ears. "Why not?" he echoed.

Sara stuck her hand between them. "Bryce, what I think Zach is saying is let's let this situation play out. We got some great footage today to start. Tomorrow, we'll investigate the haunting and see where it goes from there."

"Whatever."

Blood rising to his face and temples already throbbing, Zach wasn't about to back down an inch. "Not 'whatever.' If we're going to work together, we work together straight up, no tricks and no backstabbing."

Bryce's hands rose. "Halleluiah and Amen! I was kidding. Christ, learn to take a joke. Now, if you're accusing me of something do it, but this isn't a trial and it had better not be a lynch mob."

"What's that supposed to mean?"

"Just as it was said, pal."

Zach had no clue what Bryce's point was. His mounting frustration brought on the scent of *Sailor Black*. The smoke mixed with the smells of Italian cuisine to create an odor Zach guessed would saturate the lair of a mob boss. Although they probably smoked cigars.

"Look," he said, trying to clear his head. "All I'm saying is that on my show, we do things by the book. We have checks and balances to make sure our evidence is authentic. It's reviewed independently."

"Checks and balances," Bryce echoed. "Sure. I've seen how your audio and video reviewers authenticate evidence on *your* show."

"What's wrong with that?"

"What's wrong with it? Dude, that's the difference between *Demon Hunters* and *XPI*. We don't doubt that haunts are real. We trust our clients and help rid them of evil spirits."

"We do pretty much the same thing, Bryce."

"No, you guys walk around all high and mighty acting like you have all the answers. Well, you don't. Point-in-fact? That 'GrocersMart security video' you're all hot and bothered by?" Bryce used two fingers on each hand to make air quotes. "It's a fake, dude. It's nothing more than an Internet hoax."

Surprised, Zach said nothing.

"Yeah, we researched it *ad hominem*." Apparently unaware or unconcerned that he'd used the term incorrectly, Bryce ripped another piece of bread and waved it around as though celebrating a victory. "I didn't want to say anything while the cameras were rolling, but anyone worth his investigative salt would have noticed that the stacks of *Woods Red Firelogs*, which are clearly displayed on the video, weren't ever sold in Chicago stores. Plus, they were discontinued nationally two years ago — long before some poseur claimed that video was from the *GrocersMart* built on former Rosewood property."

Zach ignored the dig. "Okay, cool. One more myth we can debunk on the show."

Bryce sighed. "I told Patrizia to study the architectural blueprints, so we know the ins and outs of all the buildings' layouts."

"And I'm just hearing about this now?" Zach asked. It came out much harsher than he'd intended. The scents of red sauces and sausages were drowned out by *Sailor Black*. His fingertips tingled. Unlike most people in an argument whose heart rates sped up, Zach's slowed, making his thoughts distorted. "Why not first talk about it?"

Calm down, godson.

"Listen, Patrizia works for me — not you." Bryce's voice rose. "I don't need your permission or your advice. I'll be the one who tells *my people* what they will — "

"Boys!" Sara pounded the table hard enough to cause the silverware to jingle. The restaurant hushed and many of the patrons inspected them curiously. "This isn't a contest of whose dick is bigger or smarter."

Zach wasn't shocked at Sara's language. She wasn't opposed to using flat out vulgarities in order to make her point. Bryce stared at her.

"If you guys want me to pull the plug on this special right now, I will," she said. "I'll save the network a whole lot of money and I'll move on to another project. I don't need this shit."

Zach was pretty sure that she was bluffing, but she sure sounded convincing. He wondered if his own face had turned as red as Bryce's had. Nearby patrons had paused their meals, stopped being coy and were just staring at them.

"Or," her diatribe continued, "we can all play nicely. Put aside our egos and give this project two days of intense focus. We need some good stuff. Yes, Zach, some *dramatic* stuff."

"Sara, I told you, we can't control how dramatic our findings are."

"Yes, but you know this place. You've seen the case file— it's ripe with legend and strange activity. People are not going to want to see a Halloween Special that merely debunks urban legends for ninety minutes. Some of the rumors have to come from authentic paranormal activity. How could it not be? The place is a former insane asylum."

"Former *psychiatric hospital.*"

"Zach."

She had a point. This case had more potential for what they called in the business an "intelligent haunting," than any case they'd filmed during their abbreviated first season; the "trial season" as Sara had called it.

"Listen," Bryce said, looking at Sara. "You know that I can be as good of a team player as the next guy. I agreed to use you as our producer rather than our own, and I'm cool with that. I just don't want my team treated as an afterthought."

Sara fixed her steel glare on Bryce, and then alternated it on both him and Zach. "Look guys, I know the potential is here for a phenomenal show. If we do this right, the network may even give both shows two or three year deals. That doesn't include syndication, specials, foreign rights, licensing, etcetera, etcetera – provided neither of you fucks this up."

"I'm willing to let bygones be bygones," Zach said.

Bryce nodded. "Ditto."

Zach held his hand out across the table. Bryce shook hands firmly, but Zach couldn't help but notice that the entire length of the handshake Bryce Finman never made eye contact.

Chapter Six

After the uncomfortable truce, things had gone moderately well at lunch — Zach even agreed to allow Bryce his infamous "BryceCam," a tiny video camera which he wore attached to his belt buckle. It rarely contributed videos of anything except images of chaotic activity, but Zach didn't want to make a stink over something so trivial. After lunch, he had needed to clear his head and had driven east through a few questionable neighborhoods to Pullman.

Zach arrived at Rosewood Psychiatric Hospital just as the sun was setting. The clear autumn sky held captive peach-orange hues and illuminated Rosewood's grounds in a peculiar glow. As Zach peered across the weed-strewn lot at the three-story asylum, he felt as if he was staring at a sepia-toned photograph. He could imagine the property as it might have been a hundred years ago: The inclined path to the brick asylum would have been well kept and welcoming. Two massive oak trees spaced forty feet apart and standing between the pathway and 115th Street may have been mere saplings when Rosewood opened. The asylum's clock tower in the center of the wide angled L-shaped building would be sturdy instead of besieged by the elements. As opposed to having its hands stuck at 12:43, the clock would keep accurate time. Had he stood there a century earlier, the fountain in the middle of the circular driveway in front of the building wouldn't have been cracked or damaged; water would have jettisoned into the fresh country air plummeting down into a basin pool, flowing over into the main receptacle.

A line of trees concealed the back fence, but in Zach's vision, the wooded area extended as far as the eye could see. Visitors, men in derbies and women wearing Victorian hats, strolled along tended garden paths near the south end of the property. Others sat on benches surrounding the orange-brick hospital — relatives hoping their loved ones would regain their sanity. The sun slinked below the horizon, the long shadows vanished, and the happy fantasy faded to gray twilight.

Zach had driven by Rosewood plenty of times. He'd even parked and walked through the historic neighborhood. Blocks away, restoration of both the Market Hall as well as the old Pullman factory was nearly complete. Decades ago, fire had ravaged the historical landmarks. Zach vaguely recalled the incident, but didn't remember the details. Details that, no doubt, Wendy would supply at tomorrow's briefing.

Standing at the chain-link fence that separated him from Rosewood's original wrought iron gate, Zach felt much more anxious than he had on previous walks around Pullman. Soon he would be inside the asylum; in a position to solve the hundred-year mystery of Rosewood's haunting. As dusk slowly claimed Pullman, questions ran through Zach's mind. Would the two teams, *XPI* and *Demon Hunters*, work in harmony? Would they discover natural phenomenon that would scientifically explain and debunk the ghost stories, or would they document proof of the paranormal? Would the infamous female spirit who had scared off people for a century reveal herself to them? To *him*?

The asylum's main entryway had stood sentinel for over a century. Situated on the northeastern edge of the property, set in from the corner of 115th Street and Pine Avenue, a nine-foot fence topped with barbed wire separated Zach from the historic buildings. The fence served as a northern barrier along 115th Street. Past the two oak trees to the west, lay the new strip mall with the *GrocersMart* and a *Muses Coffee House*. The fence also ran southward around a building that had been the hospital's administrative offices and another that had long ago been the asylum's stables.

Although his emotions were in check, Zach swore he caught a hint of *Sailor Black* in the air. Was this a warning to stay away from Rosewood? Was the investigation doomed before it had even begun? When he heard a voice, Zach nearly crawled out of his skin.

"Allo, mate."

Zach spun around. Pierre, the *Demon Hunters' TechniHunter*, stood on the side of Pine Avenue within thirty feet of him. In his right hand was a lit pipe.

"What the heck are you doing here?"

"Prolly just like you, I came t'ava lil Captain Cook."

Zach struggled to make sense of what he was trying to say. "What?"

"Ya' know, an earl tea look."

Zach had read about the colloquial language of Australians, but he'd never met anyone who used the Cockney-like slang.

"Yes, an early look," Zach said. "I, too, wanted to get a lay of the land."

Pierre appeared as confused as Zach felt.

"Right. *Lay of the land*," Pierre repeated. He chuckled and took a puff from his pipe. Not *Sailor Black* but a similar aroma.

"Did you, Angel and Matthew get things squared away for tomorrow?"

The more Zach had considered their task, the more he understood that it was a technical nightmare — it was going to take a lot of generators to power their cameras and lights. Moreover, the cameras and video equipment would require substantial effort to properly situate and set up.

"*Squared away*," Pierre repeated. "I'd say we're squared, mate." He appeared pensive. "Did things go well wif you yanks at lunch?"

"Sure, it was all shits and giggles."

"*Shits and giggles*, eh?" He peered at Zach and then took a purposeful suck on his pipe. "Well, nice chattin' with ya, but I think I might find me a ribbidy dub. I could really do with a kitchen sink."

That one had Zach puzzled. It was becoming quite clear why the *Demon Hunters*, or perhaps the network, had prevented Pierre from speaking on camera. The wrong phrase uttered at the wrong time could ignite World War III.

"You want to get a cup of coffee?" Zach asked, pointing towards *Muses*.

"No coffee for me, mate, but a Germain Greer will really hit the spot."

"A beer?" Zach was starting to get the hang of it. "Not for me. I gotta wake up early."

"A'course, but I can't sleep without my beer." Pierre winked. "Don't worry, I'll slosh back a kitchen sink or two for you. G'nite, mate!"

Zach watched him mosey up the street, but couldn't let the Australian have the last word. "I'll see you tomorrow. Keep your *eyes peeled* for me."

Pierre looked back and nodded.

Out of nowhere, Zach's internal voice spoke.

One may smile and smile and be a villain.

Charming as Pierre was, Zach didn't trust any of the Demon Hunters and found it a bit suspicious that he'd run into him at Rosewood. Then again, maybe Pierre was thinking the same thing about him.

Situated at the east end of the strip mall, *Muses Coffee House*, especially its outdoor patio, offered a good view of Rosewood's back wall. At least fifty yards from the road, the building was beyond the reach of streetlights. As twilight turned to night, the asylum became harder and harder to see. It slowly slipped into brooding darkness. As he sipped a Decaf, Zach wondered if this nightly disappearing act helped account for Rosewood's haunted reputation. He spent a couple hours jotting down notes, impressions and reminders–notably about the houses across the street from Rosewood's grounds.

Beyond an alleyway behind the strip mall were six bungalows. Both corner lots on either side of the cul-de-sac that connected to Lincoln Avenue were vacant. At one time, all the houses, lots and even the entire strip mall had been the property of Rosewood Psychiatric.

Zach looked at his watch, sipped the last of his drink and stood up to leave. From behind him, came a timid voice.

"Mr. Kalusky, is that you?"

"'Mister Kalusky' is my dad," Zach said, turning around.

The voice belonged to a woman much older than he had expected. She wore a simple, off-white dress with a white shawl. She stood there smiling. He guessed her to be almost eighty-years old. Her wrinkled face gave away her age, but there was also a youthful glow, a vibrant aura that exuded from her.

"Oh, hello ma'am. I'm Zach."

"My mother is 'ma'am,' she said. "I'm Evelyn."

"Nice to meet you, Evelyn." Well trained in manners, Zach knew not to extend his hand to a woman, especially an older woman, unless and until she did so first. She did not. "What can I do for you?"

"Perhaps, it's what I can do for you. You are to investigate Rosewood, are you not?"

Her question seemed more a statement of fact. One that took Zach by surprise. "How do you know that?"

She smiled. It was both bashful and knowing. "Well, you are here across the street from Chicago's most infamous place, so I assumed. More importantly however, I have some information for you regarding Rosewood."

"Really? How?"

Her mouth twitched, a sudden and quick nervous tic. "My mother worked there as a nurse. I know things."

"Okay. What can you tell me?"

"Well, Mister Ka—"

"Zach," he reminded her, gently.

"Well, it is a rather sensitive subject," she said, softly. "My mother told me things. She spoke of events that happened there many years ago."

"Painful things?"

It appeared at first as though she didn't know how to respond. "Secret things," she said. "Happenings that, under normal circumstances, should not be brought into the light of day."

"Can I buy you a cup of coffee," Zach asked, glancing inside. When she hesitated, he added, "Or perhaps tea?"

She smiled wistfully as though considering. "No. No thank you. I don't drink coffee or tea anymore."

Zach grinned and shoved his hands into his pockets. "Well then. Tell me what you know about Rosewood. Please."

"Before I begin, I need you to promise that you'll keep what I say in the utmost of confidence. For reasons which will become obvious, you must not disclose where you learned what I am about to reveal."

Zach chuckled. "Okay, you'll be my 'Mark Felt.'"

Her expression remained blank.

"My 'Deep Throat' — like in Watergate."

"Oh yes. Of course."

If Zach didn't know better, he'd have wondered if she'd ever even heard the terms. The old lady might just be nervous. Or have Alzheimer's.

Zach raised his right hand the way he had when he was in Boy Scouts. "Whatever you tell me, I give you my word that I'll not disclose your identity to anyone."

She beamed.

"Then first, you must be very careful. There are forces here the likes of which you may never have before encountered."

"Like?"

She scowled as though tasting something awful. "As in demonic forces."

"How do you know?"

Her mouth twitched as it had before. "My mother told me."

"Okay," Zach said. "How about if you start from the beginning?"

"We don't have time for that now. I need to go, but I will tell you more after you verify what I'm about to tell you is true. Otherwise, it may be too overwhelming. You might think I'm crazy."

"I'd never think you're cr—"

"Listen," she said. "You'll have to investigate all the fires. With only a cursory look, you'll not see it, but they're all connected."

"The fires across the street?" Zach nodded toward Rosewood.

"No. Well, yes and no. The fires there. And the fires over there." She pointed at the dual empty lots near the bungalows. "They're all related to fire here long ago and the fire that destroyed the Pullman Market Hall. Connected even to the fire that burned down the White City."

Zach didn't know what to make of it. "The White City?"

"Yes. They were all started by one man." Her face darkened. "I've told you enough for now. Once you have verified what I've told you is true, we can speak again."

"How will I contact you?"

"We can meet here again. Shall we say tomorrow night?"

"Sure. What time?"

"About this same time," she said, already inching away. "After eleven."

"Wait. Can I walk you to your car? I want to make sure you get home safely, Evelyn." He not only wanted to ensure her safety but to prolong their conversation a few more minutes.

"Oh no," she said, her eyes sparkling. "I'm not going home just yet."

She turned and made her way toward the *GrocersMart* adjacent to the coffee house. Zach looked at his watch again. No wonder that she'd been in a hurry. The store's closing hour was quickly approaching. Apparently the secretive old girl kept some late hours.

Chapter Seven

"Okay," Sara said to him looking no more frazzled than she typically did the first day of shooting. "Are we ready?"

Zach nodded and waited for Sara to get her cameras rolling. There were two HD camera operators and a few members of the production crew holding boom microphones. After a season on the air, Zach thought it funny how easy it was to ignore them swarming around.

When he sensed everyone was situated, he strode to the gates and held his hands out to his sides. "*Xavier Paranormal Investigators* and *Demon Hunters*, welcome to Rosewood Psychiatric Hospital!"

"Woot! Woot! Woot!" The Demon Hunters startled him with the signature cheer normally reserved for Bryce. They thunked their fists together in rapid succession while they barked. Zach's fellow *XPI* members clapped a bit less enthusiastically at first but quickly picked up steam to match their rivals' intensity.

"In just a little while, Rosewood's custodian will be here to open these gates and give us a full guided tour of the grounds. But first, to kick things off today, we're going to have a briefing about the property presented by our phenomenal Historical Researcher, Wendy."

As much as Wendy's selfish dating behavior had been criticized, no one questioned her on-camera awareness and presence. She flashed her photogenic smile, cozied up to Zach and made a point to brush her hand on his forearm as she began speaking.

"Aw. Thanks, Zach." Her tone was seductive. "Our story begins in 1879, just fourteen years after the conclusion of the Civil War and just seven years after the Great Chicago Fire. Industrialist George M. Pullman purchased 4,000 acres of land in this area, and the first American model industrial town was born. In 1889, Hyde Park Township, which included Pullman, was annexed into the

City of Chicago through popular election. Now, the majority of *Pullman* residents voted against annexation. One of the major issues of the time was the City's desire to build an asylum here. Chicago wanted to have a place far enough away from Downtown to send 'undesirables' before the upcoming World's Fair Columbian Exposition."

"Move it along, Wendy," Sara called out.

As sensitive as Wendy often was in real life, on-camera, she was unflappable. Over the course of the first season, Sara had worked with her to eliminate reading, in favor of an extemporaneous speech which could be later edited. Wendy responded by quickly learning to spit out historical facts in sound byte fashion.

"Rosewood Psychiatric opened in 1892."

"Good!" Sara said.

"In 1893, the World's Fair, nicknamed 'The White City,' took place. There was a nationwide depression. Blah, Blah Blah. In 1894, during the Pullman Strike, the White City burns—"

"Wendy!" Sara's tone had taken on the sting of a jockey's whip on a racehorse's backside.

"Sorry. That info was for Zach. Okay..." Wendy smiled for the cameras as if she'd just been awarded an Emmy. She held up a sepia-toned photograph of a two-story building. "In 1898, Rosewood's female quarters burned to the ground. More than a dozen women were incinerated in the fire, and patients first began to report seeing a ghastly female spirit."

Wendy held up a badly faded, black and white photograph of a homely looking woman and a cute little girl. "It wasn't until 1900 that people began lending credence to the ghost stories. A widow, Abigail Lovecroft, who was working as a nurse at Rosewood, and her daughter, Amelia, reported a paranormal event. The daughter witnessed a boy consumed by a powerful female ghost who then threatened her. There was no little boy known to be on the premises that day, so it was assumed he was a ghost as well."

"Good. Keep it moving," Sara shouted.

Wendy took a deep breath. "Abigail Lovecroft was the first Rosewood employee to resign her post because of the haunting, but she certainly would not be the last."

Sara flashed Wendy two thumbs up.

"In fact, by 1902, there had been so many complaints that people began attempting to block relatives from being sent to Rosewood. More patients were committing suicide than were being discharged! Additionally, it became increasingly difficult and eventually impossible to staff the hospital. Like Abigail Lovecroft, nurses often quit abruptly never to return. In 1903, months after the mysterious death of the hospital's administrator, Dr. Louis Johansson, and just eleven years after opening, the hospital shut its doors. Despite several attempts over the last century to open it as a boarding school, hospital or museum, Rosewood has remained closed to the public to this day." She exhaled deeply.

"Thanks, Wendy," Zach said.

"But Zach!" Her eyes widened and she clasped his hand in both of hers. The softness of her skin and her perfume's lilac scent could make it easy to forget that she wasn't his type of girl. "That's when our ghost story really begins."

She pulled away and looked back at the camera. She'd tricked him.

"After World War II, the vacant eastern portion of the property was sold. Roads were put in and homes built. Over the years, several of the homes, especially ones built on the site of the old female quarters, burned down in mysterious fires."

Someone gasped. Members of both teams were riveted.

"I know, right?" Wendy said. "Moreover, the Pullman Market Hall, just blocks away, was destroyed by fire in 1973. Blocks from *there*, in December of 1998, a homeless man torched the main Pullman Factory building. Never having been in trouble for anything else, the one-time arsonist didn't even flee the scene of the crime. When they asked him why he did it, he claimed he heard *voices* that *demanded* he burn it down!"

"Demonic voices?" Bryce asked theatrically.

"Uh, no. Maybe. Anyway, those fires are just the beginning. Yes, friends, Rosewood and Pullman have a long, long history of fires. *Arson* fires. And now, the State of Illinois wants us to investigate mysterious ones burning the property of the oldest, most famous, haunted place in Chicago. You might be asking yourselves, why not just tear it down? Well, legally, they can't! In

1969, Pullman received State of Illinois landmark status. In 1971, the entire town received *National* Historic Landmark designation."

"The whole town? I didn't know that, Wendy," Zach said.

"Wrap it up," Sara called out.

"Lastly, adding to Rosewood's mystique, back in 1983, some high school students snuck onto the property and attempted to stay overnight. They were caught and arrested before completing their adventure. But from that actual event, all sorts of urban legends sprang up. A popular myth claimed one of the kids died that night. Another rumor persists that one of the girls eventually went insane. *None* of those rumors could be, in fact, confirmed."

Zach deftly winked at Ray who subtly flashed his middle finger.

"Regardless, barbed-wire-topped fences were put up and, since then, no one has been able to investigate the property. Until today."

"Awesome job, Wendy. I can't wait to see what else you will uncover with your continued historical research," Zach said, over the rising cheers and barks.

The ritual had gained a couple of converts. Both Matthew and Turk hooted and were pounding their fists together in *Demon Hunter* fashion. To Zach, it didn't appear they had even made the decision consciously. Before he could stew on that thought, Wendy pulled the sleeve of his shirt and moved her mouth toward his ear.

"I left something important out," she said. "I need to tell you as soon as we're alone."

Chapter Eight

Custodian Grant Winkler pulled up in a white, state maintenance pickup truck minutes after 9 AM.

"Where's Zach?" he asked, exiting his van. "Which one of you is Zach Kallinski?"

Dressed in a gray uniform and grungy White Sox cap, he was hardly the tour guide that Zach had expected or ventured that the network had planned on. Considering his sunken cheeks and overall disheveled appearance, Zach thought he looked like a cross between a creepy scarecrow and a — creepy scarecrow.

"I'm Zack Kalusky. Mr. Winkler?" Zach offered his hand.

"Well, I ain't Santa Claus." He appeared reluctant to accept the handshake, but briefly did. "*All* these..." He paused to spit, "people planning on coming in?"

"Yes, sir."

"Looks like a damn field trip."

Sara had moseyed up oozing the charm she saved for the most difficult of people. "Hi Mr. Winkler. I'm Sara Chen. I'm the producer of this show."

"What a joy that must be." He fumbled for his keys and headed toward the chain-link entry. After a few steps, he hollered back over his shoulder. "Where's yer security?"

"Security?" Zach and Sara asked in unison.

Winkler stopped and looked to the sky as if mentally imploring to be beamed up. He turned toward them and cocked his head. "Well, you don't expect me to leave these gates open and unattended all night do you?"

"Oh shit," Sara muttered under her breath. She reached for her cell phone. "My bad. I'll call someone!"

"Or, I could just lock you in all night if you want?" Winkler chortled and dragged himself the rest of the way to the gate.

"Friendly guy," Zach overheard Turk whisper to Rico.

Rico, wearing a black T-shirt with a massive New York Yankee logo, smirked. "It's...Old Man Winkler!"

Turk visibly held back a guffaw. "And I'd have gotten away with it too if it hadn't been for you meddling kids!"

Zach shushed them. No need for spraying lighter fluid into a live cigar butt.

Rico whispered something to Turk, and the pair shared a private joke. From the episodes of *Demon Hunters* that Zach had watched, Rico was a decent paranormal investigator, but the show had aired a few scenes that displayed tension between Rico and Bryce. One episode, the pair had gotten into a shouting match over whether or not a case could be solved due to the client's house having been built on a Native American burial ground. Zach wasn't certain how much of their conflicts had been accurate versus manufactured television drama, but he suspected at some point, Rico would branch off *Demon Hunters* and host his own show.

Grant Winkler unlocked the series of padlocks, removed the chains and opened the entryway of Rosewood to *XPI* cheers and *Demon Hunter* barks.

Winkler had what could only be described as an 'I'll-turn-this-car-around-right-now' look on his face. "If you're coming in, come on in," he said. "I ain't leavin' this gate unlocked until your security guard gets here."

Both groups passed through the gates. Winkler followed them in, wrapped a chain snugly around the metal bars, and clamped a padlock on.

Ray walked up to Zach.

"Nice guide," he muttered low enough that Winkler couldn't hear him. "Relative of yours?"

As though on cue, the custodian pulled a hanky from his pocket, wiped the sweat off his brow and neck, and then blew his nose with it.

Zach leaned close to his friend. "Maybe if you're a good boy, he'll let you borrow that later."

"Yeah, to—"

"Zach?" Sara said. "Can I talk to you a minute?"

"Sure," he said. He turned back to Ray. "I'll see you up there."

Led by Winkler both groups trudged up the incline toward the asylum. Sara stayed behind and gave instructions to the cameramen. "Get some low angle movement shots walking toward the front doors. You know the kind."

They nodded and went off.

"What's up?" Zach asked Sara when they were alone.

"Don't you think you should," she said and paused. In his head, Zach translated it to mean "I think you had better..."

"What?"

"Well, I wonder if we should have you with Bryce on camera most of the time during the tour. I mean, you and Ray can pal around any time, but the viewers are going to want to see you and Bryce investigating this together."

After the prior day's lunch, Zach would have preferred spending time with a foul-breathed Neo-Nazi. He had, to that point, avoided Bryce most of the morning, but from an entertainment perspective, she had a point.

"Fine. Anything else?"

"No, that's it."

Rather than wait and walk up with her, he trotted toward the group that was approaching the hospital's entryway.

"Oh, and Zach?"

She always did this. He turned but continued backpedaling toward Rosewood. He was already starting to feel like he was being pulled in a dozen different directions.

She cupped her hands to her mouth. "Would it kill you to do it with a smile?"

You never know, Zach thought. You never know.

Keys jingling and clanking, Grant Winkler opened Rosewood's front doors. The smell of rotting plaster and dust was a stale belch into the warm day.

Winkler casually strolled into the asylum while the paranormal groups ventured in behind him. Beyond a modest foyer, the lobby expanded upward taking up two floors. Strewn with cobwebs and littered with garbage, what had once been the asylum's reception area did not serve Rosewood's haunted reputation. It looked like any other ill-kept vacant building. The lobby was absent any furniture, although a few dust brambles the size of rodents rolled across the dirty wood floor, no doubt gathering mass as they did so. First order of business would be cleaning the place, the lobby at least, so that the dust didn't foul up their electronic equipment.

On the opposite side of the lobby from the reception area, a curved staircase led up to the second floor. Its white marble steps swept up and around, encircling half of the dingy lobby like a waning moon. The wooden railing appeared relatively new and had no doubt been a product of one of the stalled reconstruction efforts.

"Can we get a shot from inside of you opening it up?" Sara asked Winkler. She pointed a location to one of the cameramen. "Everyone, back outside please."

"What?" Winkler appeared dumbfounded.

"Please, sir?" Sara's wink and smile had worked on tougher men.

"Alright, but make it quick."

They repositioned and filmed the reenactment. Sara made sure that Bryce and Zach followed Winkler through the double doors together into the building. This time when Winkler entered the foyer, it was with an attitude—even more of one than he'd thus far displayed. He started talking before most of the people had caught up with them.

"Up there's most of the rooms, some of 'em's locked, most not," he shouted pointing at the staircase. "Down this hall here, if you go about a hundred feet, is the cafeteria. Down that one is the infirmary.

"You *are* taking us on a tour, right?" Zach asked.

"Tour? What's this look like, Disneyland?"

"Not exactly," Zach said. "But we were led to believe we'd be shown some of the spots where hauntings were said to have occurred."

"Nobody told me nothin' about no tour. All I was instructed to do was to let you's in and show you the place."

Zach sighed. "Wouldn't that be—"

Sara stepped in. "Mr. Winkler, couldn't you just walk us through Rosewood and point out the specific places *you* might think might be haunted? You know, your friends and family would probably like seeing you on TV..."

Zach knew what she was attempting. If she could manipulate her way into at least getting a cursory walkthrough, she'd get video footage and use voiceovers during the clips.

"Well, I don't have friends or family that would watch a show like this." He cocked his head as he'd done earlier. His inflection was sarcastic to the point of being patronizing. "I'll tell you what? You explain to all three of my bosses why I wasted my whole morning walking you through an abandoned property. Then, I'll show you where some asshole cut the fence last week. Or maybe you'd like to see the door jam I had'ta replace yesterday from some young punks prying their way into the administration building? Yeah. Yeah, then I can show you where I cleaned up the vandalism. Oooh boy, won't that be a hootenanny!"

The echoes of his tirade faded to a dull hum and then were gone. Despite hosting a lobby full of people for the first time in over a century, Rosewood had never been more silent.

Then came the Grant Winkler *coup de grâce*. "Besides, I don't believe this place is haunted none anyways."

By the time Zach convinced Winkler to leave a set of keys so that he could open locked rooms and close the main door at night, the early-day promise of Indian summer had delivered in spades. Unseasonably warm autumn temperatures in Chicago typically brought gaiety to those not wanting to release summer's carefree days, but as the groups realized how much equipment would need to be put in place, the heat brought only anxiety.

Zach walked up the driveway after having seen Winkler out. He passed the *XPI* and the *Demon Hunter* equipment vans parked near the front door. They faced outwards and, had they been any closer to the building, they could have been gargoyles. Sara and Bryce were chatting behind the *Demon Hunter* van.

"Is *any* of it usable?" Bryce asked her.

"No. It's horseshit."

"Let me guess," Zach said. "Old Man Winkler?"

"It's not funny." Sara put her hand on her hip. "We wasted most of the morning here, and we don't even have a client walkthrough."

"What the hell was the state thinking sending us a schlock like that?" Zach asked.

"Follow the money, my friends," Bryce said. "Follow the money."

After less than twenty-four hours, Bryce's arrogance had worn thin, but Zach was curious as to his theory. "What do you mean?"

"Okay. It's like this. They can't tear this place down because of this landmark status or whatever, right?"

He waited a second for confirmation, but Zach said nothing. Sara merely twirled her hand for him to continue.

"So like, they want to sell this place," he said. "They give a shit if it's haunted or not. All they need is the publicity. From what I've heard, Illinois is one of the more 'ethically casual' states in the country right?" Bryce was one of those people who used his fingers as quotation marks around words when he spoke.

"Go on, please," Zach said.

"Dude, they need the publicity. That's where we come in. If we show that it's not haunted...Boom! They sell it off or can justify reopening it as some hospital or something. Hell, probably somebody's brother-in-law gets the construction contract to gut the place and—"

"And if it is?" Zach asked.

"And if it is, what?"

"And if it's *haunted*?"

"If it's haunted, and we can prove it..." Bryce's face took on a smug satisfaction.

Zach looked at Sara; she wasn't getting it either.

Bryce sighed and rolled his eyes. "This isn't 1905. Do you know how many people out there are into the paranormal? Dude, why do you think *we* and a dozen others like us have TV shows in the first place? You know how many rich people would love to own a 'verified' haunted asylum built in the 1800s? I bet there are tax benefits up the yin yang to owning a federally protected landmark. They come in and give tours of the place. Or they turn it into some damn bed and breakfast. I dunno."

"A bed and breakfast?" Zach echoed. "Seriously?"

"Okay, maybe not that, but they could turn it into something....something cool."

Zach hated to admit it, but Bryce made sense—at least a little. "So why send us Winkler, then?"

Bryce shrugged. "He's the perfect guy for the job. Whoever's pulling the strings knows how he feels about this place, how he'll come across on TV. What better person to represent their official nonchalance? This way, they don't look pushy or desperate. We're practically their real estate brokers. All they have to do is sit back and field offers!"

"So, come on guys," Sara said. "What difference does it make? We've got a show to do. We need to film a tour of the grounds. Ideas? Suggest—"

"I've got one," Bryce said.

"Go." Sara pointed as though they were on camera.

"Well, Patrizia is a bit put out." Bryce eyed Zach. "She didn't get any air time earlier and she helped Wendy with the historical research until the wee hours of the night. I say we have her host a tour of the place based on her research. We explain on the air that there's no guide from the state because we couldn't get anyone willing to brave the infamous Rosewood Asylum."

Zach wondered how Bryce had done it. In one fell swoop, he'd gone from numbskull to white knight. He'd not only rescued Patrizia, but had restored balance to Sara's show. Worst of all, he'd slyly introduced a slightly dishonest spin that not only seemed justified but entertaining. Sara said nothing, but by the way she gazed at Bryce, she could have been about to say, "My hero."

Chapter Nine

Even with the doors open an hour, they hadn't completely aired out Rosewood's stale air. Angel had managed to sweep a full box worth of dirt and dust out of the lobby with a broom procured from the nearby *GrocersMart*. Pierre and Matthew had unloaded a slew of equipment cases from the trucks and were investigating the hallways for logical spots to place cameras.

Patrizia was pacing the length of the lobby when Zach walked in. Her rugged boots clomped across the wood floorboards. Her fingers pulled through strands of her long dark hair in slender groupings as she again retraced her steps.

"Hey," Zach said, as he approached. "Sorry we didn't get you on camera this morning. I'm looking forward to your tour."

"Yeah." She absentmindedly flicked her hair from her hand and put both arms down at her sides.

Her nose slightly hooked, Zach guessed she was of Greek or Italian descent. Equally as tall as him, her boots gave her a few inches height advantage. He found himself sweating under her glare.

"Are you about ready...ready to begin?" He ran his hand through his hair.

She didn't answer and was intently staring at his wrist. It was as if she were about to dissect him. "I like your tattoo," she said, pointing to the *Chi Rho*. "You have more, don't you?"

"Like these?" Zach was unable to hide his surprise.

How had she guessed?

"Just—any?" she asked, and then quickly added, "I've got— here I'll show you."

She slipped off her white leather jacket exposing a black sleeveless shirt and slender but toned arms. Covering her right bicep and triceps from her shoulder to her elbow was a sepia-toned tattoo of a buff angel. Dressed in warrior garb, his wings extended up on both sides of her shoulder, beneath her shirt. His arms crossed over the handle of his downward-pointed sword, and disappeared into clouds drawn near her elbow. His jaw was determination incarnate—a badass, guardian angel in repose.

"Michael?"

"*San Michele Arcangelo.*"

"Huh?"

"Yes. Michael the Archangel."

"So you're Italian?"

"*Si.* At least my parents were."

As though the question had inspired her, she untucked her shirt and pulled it up to just below her chest. Exposing more than her spandex top had shown the previous day, she revealed, just below her left breast and close to her sternum, a red heart with a gold dagger running through it. Dripping off the tip of the dagger was a single drop of crimson blood.

"That's for love," she said. "I have one other that I cannot show you."

Zach blurted the first thing that came to mind. "A tramp stamp?"

It was probably the stupidest thing he could have asked.

Her jaw clenched and her eyes narrowed. "No."

Considering the look made him slightly lightheaded, he didn't follow that line of questioning. The faint scent of *Sailor Black* tobacco was his first indication that he was getting overly excited. His fingers went numb, and his feet lost some of their feeling.

"Show me yours," she said.

Zach's heart skipped a beat. "I can't."

She rolled her eyes and scowled.

"No, I mean there's nothing really to see. They're like these." He flashed his wrists, "Only they're bigger and I'd have to…"

"I understand," she said, and then added a pout.

Zach relented and reached for the top button of his shirt. "Okay I'll—"

"Hey you two!"

Saved by the Wendybird. Showing Patrizia the tattoo on his side would have led to questions he didn't want to answer.

"What's up?" Wendy asked, looking completely disinterested in an answer. "Zach, I need to tell you something before I leave."

"Oh, right. I'll walk you out." He turned toward Patrizia. "Can you give me a second?"

Patrizia merely turned and walked away.

"God, she's such a bitch," Wendy said.

Zach watched Patrizia make her way down the hallway. Feeling returned to his fingers and toes. His legs felt more stable than when he'd been talking to her. Patrizia was something of an enigma; in his mind, she was anything but a bitch.

He motioned Wendy toward the front doors. "Okay, shoot. Whatcha got?"

"First, thanks for waiting until the last minute to give me that information last night. I had to pull all kinds of strings to get what I got at that hour and I'm still nowhere near finished."

"The fires? I told you, it was a last-minute tip."

Wendy appeared all the more peeved that Zach was ignoring her *prima donna* act. She wasn't used to boys not falling over themselves for her when she batted her crystal blue eyes.

"Anyway, I found something."

"What?"

"Well, I discovered something *late* last night after I'd written my presentation and after you told me to focus on events relating to fires."

Zach nodded. "Okay?"

"I knew you and Sara wouldn't want me to divulge this right up front in the historical section. It's creepy as shit."

"Okay, spill it already."

"So, on July 4th 1899, on the site of the female quarters destroyed by fire earlier that year, some guy doused himself with kerosene and set himself ablaze."

Zach realized his mouth was ajar, but quickly composed himself. "Lit *himself* on fire? Who?"

"They didn't have the technology back then to determine his identity, but there had been an ongoing investigation into series of fires including the *original* Pullman Market Hall that burned down in 1892—"

"Wait, Market Hall? Same location as the one that burned in '72?"

"The one and only," Wendy said.

"1892 was the same year that the hospital opened?"

"Yes, sir."

"Are they connected?"

"That's what I need to research today. There were a lot of fires around that time, including the White City in 1894."

Evelyn had mentioned the White City the prior night. Zach had looked it up online. "The site of the 1893 World's Fair?"

"Well technically, it was called 'The World's Columbian Exposition,' but yes."

Zach ignored her anal retentiveness, and motioned for her to continue.

"But here's the kicker," she said, "from everything I gathered, after the suicide by fire here in 1899, high-profile buildings in the area stopped being torched, the arson case was closed and — "

"And the haunting here at Rosewood started full force."

"Aren't you a smart one?"

"Good work, Wendy."

"Well," she said donning her on-air flirtation. "Is that all I get?"

"You come up with a connection between all this and our haunting, and I promise you'll get a lot more time in front of the camera."

By the glee on her face, he might as well have just told her she'd won the lottery. She batted her eyes at him. "Well in that case," Wendy said, "it might be a coincidence, but that incident with the Lovecroft girl?"

"Yes?"

"It happened one year *to the day* from when that man set himself on fire."

Chapter Ten

Bryce spoke in dramatic tones for the cameras. "In a moment, giving us the opening tour of Rosewood Asylum will be *Demon Hunters* very own *DemonHistorian*– Patrizia!" He extended his arm toward her. "You may be asking yourselves, why is Patrizia leading the tour? As most of you know both *Demon Hunters* and *XPI* typically have the property owner give us a tour and point out the hot spots. Well friends, we couldn't find one person working for the State of Illinois who was brave enough to walk us through Rosewood!

"But first, Zach wanted me to remind all you amateur Demon Hunters and *XPI'ers* why a tour is so important."

Zach had done no such thing. He set his jaw and attempted to feign ambivalence.

"Knowing the 'hot spots,'" Bryce continued, "is necessary to document evidence of an intelligent haunting."

No, Zach thought, they weren't. It helped to know where to look, but it wasn't necessary. Even if Bryce's facts *were* accurate, this kind of speech was the type of spoon-feeding the audience that Zach often butted heads with Sara about. Next, Bryce would be telling the audience the most basic of ghost hunting facts like that Electromagnetic Field meters, or EMF meters, were used to detect the presence of spirits.

"Residual hauntings refer to the residue attached to places and things a spirit had been connected to during their life. They are like looped reruns of activity the ghost had participated in during their lifetime—things like laughter, speaking, giggling, music and singing. In comparison to these snippets of paranormal activity, intelligent hauntings are very rare. Intelligent hauntings are when spirits attempt to contact or interact with the living."

Zach's reaction to Bryce's speech was being filmed, so he nodded. He had to admit that Bryce had pretty much nailed that explanation. Typically, there were important reasons for a spirit to conduct an intelligent haunting; they weren't always logical motivations, but uncovering them was what Zach did best, thanks to his special gift.

Bryce's monologue was drawing to a close. "Now, without further ado, here is Patrizia."

Patrizia smiled at the camera, and then led the group down the long hallway toward the cafeteria. They peeked in each room taking pictures and EMF readings just in case a daytime apparition lurked naked to the visible eye. Angel needed to unlock a few of the rooms but most were open. Many of the doors had long been removed, perhaps ported and used in other hospitals.

They approached the doors of the cafeteria. "Hey," Shelly yelled out. "My EMF meter just leapt from .04 to 1.8. Did anybody else get that?"

"I caught it," Rico said.

"Me too." Zach's reading dipped back to an ambient .04.

"It would make sense to get readings here," Patrizia said. "With this being the largest inside gathering place on the property, it was also the most active spot for violence."

Zach, Shelly, and Rico scanned the room with their EMF meters. None of them picked up a reading above .05 anywhere in the room.

Rico positioned himself in front of one of the cameras. "That was a definite paranormal spike!"

Bryce turned to Patrizia. "Did anyone die in here?"

"Well, I didn't find any records of specific locations where people died," she said. "It would be likely that those injured in fights here would have passed away after being taken to the infirmary."

"Not just gorgeous, folks," Bryce said into the camera, "but smart too!"

Patrizia ignored the comment. "There were several reports of violent acts here: patients smashing trays into other patient's faces, fistfights, and even a couple incidents of forks used to gouge out fellow combatants' eyes."

She proceeded through the double doors and into the wide-open space. Oversized windows made the room bright, but the bars outside must have provided ample reminder to the long-ago diners that they weren't free. Along one wall, large square openings would have allowed staff to pass food to patients and linked the dining hall with the kitchen.

"I want to see the kitchen!" Shelly said.

They herded through a door and into the adjoining room. Dented and rusted metal cabinetry and countertops adorned the room, but all appliances had been ripped out.

"Yo, you guys, these aren't the originals," Rico said, banging on one of the counters. "I'd say these are circa 1960."

"If they're new, why are they all dented?" Shelly asked.

"Good question." Zach's finger outlined a gash deep enough to have been caused by an angry gorilla. "Were there any reports of suspicious fires in here?"

"As opposed to *unsuspicious* ones?" It may have been Patrizia's attempt at a joke. "No. There were no reported major fires or accidents in the kitchen."

The group soon continued out into the back corridor of the hospital. Rooms on the interior half of the hall had no windows to the outside world. They reminded Zach of prison cells he'd seen while touring Alcatraz—the flaking tan paint and grime on the walls cemented the impression. Conversely, the outer side of the hallway contained what may have once been nicer rooms with windows, large meeting areas and solariums which would have looked out onto the back gardens.

"Generally speaking, the patients kept on the outer main floor were the least violent and safest to the hospital staff and visitors," Patrizia said. "Many roamed the halls with minimal supervision and may have been people today who would be diagnosed with clinical depression. Some were alcoholics needing to dry out. The upstairs rooms housed the more dangerous elements."

"The folks they didn't want decent people to have contact with," Rebecca whispered to Zach. "The ones likely to be haunting this place."

XPI's Occult Specialist maintained a strong connection to the supernatural that had emerged from personal experience. Her mother passed away when Rebecca was a toddler, but her only memories of her mom were from when she'd been six or seven-years old. The discrepancy confused Rebecca; she and Zach had developed a theory that her mom's spirit must have visited her until she'd been old enough to care for herself.

"Are you picking up any psychic vibrations?" Zach asked her.

Rebecca shook her head. "Nothing. Nothing, yet."

Sara and her cameraman swarmed in and out of the group as they proceeded down the long hallway. Zach guessed that ninety-five percent of the tour, absent any drama, would end up on the cutting room floor. Still, it was necessary for them to understand the asylum's layout before wandering these halls in the dark.

"This was the visitor's area," Patrizia said when they arrived at a great room at the end of the hall.

The room, situated at the asylum's back corner, connected the two long hallways that jutted out in 90-degree angles. It would have allowed visitors to meet their friends and relatives in a place with a nice view of the gardens without having to venture inside Rosewood's innards. Devoid of any furniture, the room was large, but felt unthreatening. The group rambled down the hallway that led to the infirmary using thermal cameras to check for cold spots and continuing to look for EMF anomalies. Zach couldn't help but chuckle at Winkler's earlier comment. It *did* look like a field trip.

"Are the hallways this long on the upper two floors?" Angel asked Patrizia.

"Longer. Those floors are all patient quarters. No large rooms on either end. There are also connecting hallways in the middle of each wing."

Angel turned to Zach. "Between the two groups, we've got fourteen stationary night-vision cameras."

"That's cool."

"Yes, but without known 'hot spots,' we're only going to be able to cover a fraction of this place after dark."

"How many mini digital cameras do we have?" Zach asked.

"Six total."

"And we'll have three pairs of investigators each with at least one of those, an EMF meter and a thermal cam."

"Three pairs? Are you going to let Matthew investigate?"

"No," Zach said quietly. He pulled Angel aside. "Patrizia is going to team up with Shelly."

"Ohhhhh. That will go over well, *mi hijo*."

"Don't you worry about it. As soon as we get done with the tour, I want you to set up a technical command post in the lobby, and I want you to take charge of the tech group and make as many of the decisions as you can," Zach said. "No slight to our Australian friend but you're the guy I trust."

"*Gracias, señor.*" He mixed cultures and bowed, Japanese style, at the waist.

"I mean it, Angel. If something isn't right in regards to the set up, I'm going to hold you responsible, and if something isn't sitting well with you, I expect you to come to me pronto."

Angel's acne-scarred face beamed. "Seriously Zach, I appreciate that. I won't let you down."

"Boys. Boys." Sara's voice echoed through the vacant hallway. "Keep up!"

The group had reached the infirmary.

By the time Zach and Angel entered, the rest of the group stared around the series of connected rooms with stark disappointment.

"I thought there'd be...like...stuff," Ray said to a chorus of "Me too's."

The infirmary rooms looked like all the others in the vacant hospital–empty, dirty and bland.

"In here!"

Sara and the camera crew led a stampede into the adjoining room where the shout had come from. Rico and Turk stood next to a row of five-foot tall metal file cabinets. The rest of the group descended on the drawers like starving vultures on a dead wildebeest.

"These aren't..." Rico had gotten a head start and was examining the contents of a folder. He shook his head. "They're court records."

"From the 1940s," Rebecca chimed in.

"Misdemeanors," Bryce said. "Traffic violations and whatnot. What the fuck?"

"The State of Illinois used this building for record storage from the 1920s until the 1960s," Patrizia said. "I'm fairly certain that none of this is from the period of the asylum."

A few uttered growls and groans. Matthew slammed a drawer closed. Shelly continued taking EMF readings that showed no abnormalities.

"Guys, this was the infirmary, so as harmless as it may appear now, people would have passed away in here," Zach said. "We'll want this room heavily video monitored and explored tonight."

"Maybe we pitch one of the tents in here tonight?" Bryce's tone made it clear he wasn't volunteering to sleep there.

Zach noticed that no one leapt at the chance to camp out in the room people had died. "I think we'll want to keep together tonight," he said. "Two groups of tents. One in the lobby where the nerve center will be and a group outside on the front lawn not far from the vans. And while we're on the subject, no one roams the grounds or any building on the property alone after dark. Safety first, people."

Shelly raised her hand. "Hey Patrizia?" She looked around the infirmary. "Wouldn't there have been a morgue around here somewhere?"

Patrizia scoured the map but didn't locate one.

"If I might?" Rebecca spoke up and waited for Sara to get a shot of her. "It's doubtful that in those days there was one. Cadavers were at a premium and would likely have been sold to medical schools."

"All of them? Wouldn't their families want them?" Bryce asked.

"To be realistic, maybe some of them had close family relationships, but they'd have been in the minority. This was a public institution. Visitor facilities notwithstanding, the vast majority of these patients were outcasts, forgotten about and never recovered their mental health. Any corpses not given over to family burial would have been sold. Except those with infectious diseases and maybe..."

"And maybe?" Bryce asked.

"Well, back in that day, the medical schools wouldn't have accepted suicides."

"What would they have done with those?" Zach asked.

"They wouldn't have been entitled to a Catholic burial, so they likely just dumped them in the ground somewhere on the property — probably in unmarked graves."

Although no one's thermal camera detected a cold spot, a few in the room shuddered.

"They probably stored dead bodies temporarily downstairs, in the basement," Patrizia said.

"A basement?" Rico's eyes were ablaze.

"Can we go there next?" Shelly asked.

"Hey guys, c'mon. This is Patrizia's tour." Zach winked at her. To his surprise she flashed him a grateful smile.

"I was saving the basement for last," she said.

"First, I have some stories of patients who stayed on the upper floors."

"Onward," Sara instructed.

They all clodded up a concrete stairwell next to the infirmary to the 2nd floor. Apparently, there had been less salvaging on the upper level. Unlike many of the rooms below, most of the rooms still had doors — most of them barred. To Zach, the second storey more resembled an abandoned prison's solitary confinement holdings than a hospital wing.

"Room 217." Patrizia stopped outside the room and ushered the group into the vacant cell. It was located on the interior side of the hallway. Absent windows to the outside except for the barred door, living in the room must have been hell. "It was in this room, in 1897," she said "over the course of a weekend, patient Kurt Wozniak ate his entire bed. Mattress. Pillows. Wooden frame and sheets."

"Did it kill him?" Rebecca asked.

"No, but later that year, despite attempts to keep a closer eye on him, he managed to sneak a jar of peaches into his room. They found the peaches on the floor the next morning. Wozniak's dead body was lying in here, the glass from the jar, inside his shredded stomach and intestines."

"Eww," Shelly whispered. "I may never eat peaches again."

"So does that qualify as a suicide, or was it just stupidity?" Bryce asked, smirking.

"Mental illness is *not* stupidity." Rebecca's face had ripened with anger. "And it's certainly no laughing matter!"

"Of course not," Bryce said feigning sincerity for the camera. "This poor man's spirit could still be lingering in room 217."

The hypocrisy was more than Zach could take. He turned to Patrizia. "Were there any incidents that involved fire or arson?"

"Yes," she said. She pointed up. "Upstairs a patient set his room ablaze."

The two groups proceeded to the 3rd floor. Sara was repeatedly checking her watch. Either they were overdue for a break, or she'd suddenly become an obsessive compulsive. From behind them on the stairs, Zach noticed how the two groups appeared to be intermingling rather well. They gathered at the door to room 362.

Patrizia cleared her throat. "In July of 1901, a patient by the name of Stanwick Hartwell managed to set fire to his room and suffered second and third degree burns over much of his body. He claimed voices had prompted him to do it and had supplied him with the matches."

"Yo! That sounds like what happened in '98 at the Pullman factory," Rico said.

"Was he ever suspected in the burning of the female quarters?" Zach asked.

"No. He wasn't a patient of Rosewood in 1898."

"Did he end up dying here?" Zach pressed.

"We don't know," Patrizia said. "After the fire, I couldn't find any records of him."

Sara had moseyed over next to Zach. "Legally," she whispered to him, "the cast and crew need a lunch break."

"We haven't seen the basement yet," Zach said. "Can you, me, Bryce and Patrizia go down there with a night vision camera?"

She frowned. "What part of '*legally*' do you not understand?"

Zach surrendered and made the announcement to the group. After a two-hour break, tech guys were instructed to set up cameras and equipment. Others were instructed to pitch tents. A scaled-down group would tour the basement after the break.

"Are you keeping investigative partners the same as normal?" Shelly asked.

"Yes," Zach said. "This investigation we're putting together three teams that will explore and film. Bryce will stick with Rico, Rebecca will investigate with me, and tonight we're going to match up Shelly with Patrizia."

While most happily chatted about what they'd do or where they'd go during the upcoming free time, Matthew spoke to no one and the disappointment on his face was evident. Shelly didn't look particularly pleased either. Was she disappointed at being teamed with a new investigator, or because she'd been matched up with a *Demon Hunter*?

Day one was just getting underway and besides feeling stretched both mentally and emotionally, Zach seemed to be alienating the members of *XPI* one after the next.

Chapter Eleven

"Are you asking about the ghosts?" the blond boy asked.

After gobbling down sandwiches, Zach and Sara, armed with a mini digital camera, had conducted interviews with the residents east of the asylum who lived on what was former Rosewood property. A few on camera, and a few who asked not to be identified, acknowledged ongoing paranormal activity in their homes. They described events from poltergeists opening cabinets and slamming drawers, to hearing mysterious sounds at night.

One, Mrs. Radkey, an elderly woman who Zach thought resembled a younger version of Evelyn, admitted to having seen a shadowy female figure in her kitchen after nightfall. When pressed for details, she clammed up and refused to say anything further.

After walking down one side of the street and back up the other, no one seemed willing to allow them the opportunity to investigate their property—especially after dark. They had approached the final house on the block before the empty lot—the home closest the main asylum building. The boy had been throwing a rubber baseball up against the concrete stairs of the house and fielding it as it bounced back.

"What ghosts do you mean?" Zach asked before Sara could respond and begin filming. Rosewood experience aside, if he was to be a child psychologist one day, an opportunity to interact with a boy currently undergoing a haunting would be an invaluable experience.

"The ones setting the fires?" The kid took a step back.

Zach guessed the boy to be six-years old, maybe seven. He stood with his glove-hand on his hip and wore a Chicago Cubs jersey.

"Hey, you're a Cubs fan?" Zach asked, with enthusiasm. "So am I, but isn't this White Sox territory?"

"My grandpa's a Cubs fan," he said. "Why are you one?"

"Well, maybe like you and your grandpa, I like to cheer for the underdog."

"My grandpa is dead," the boy said flatly.

Sara stifled a chuckle.

"My name is Zach." He held out his hand the same way he would to an adult.

"I'm Joey."

"Nice to meet you, Joey." They shook. "Is your mom or dad home? I'd like to get permission to talk with you more about these ghosts."

"My mom is home, but she don't believe in them."

"Well, can I—"

The front door flew open and a short, stocky woman wearing an oversized gray sweatshirt emerged from the house. Her brown hair was tied back in a ponytail and she looked none too happy.

"What's going on out here?" She bolted down the steps and shielded Joey from them, pushing him behind her.

"Hello, ma'am. I was just asking Joey to get you so that we could—"

"Well, you should have done that even before you even asked him his name, shouldn't you?" She crossed her arms.

"Technically, yes ma'am, I should have, but we're just here conducting some scientific—"

"Scientific, my ass. Science isn't conducted with video cameras." She turned to Joey. "Go in the house, hon. I'll be in in a minute."

"But mom, I didn't tell him about 'Boy,' yet."

"Go in the house, Joey."

He stood there picking imaginary dirt off his baseball glove.

"Now, young man. In."

"Yes, mom." He climbed the steps bouncing his mitt off his thigh the way major leaguers often did. He opened the door and before going in, turned back to Zach and waved.

"What did he mean by 'boy?'" Zach asked.

"He didn't mean anything. Let me be perfectly clear with you, Mister..."

"Kalusky. Zach Kalusky." He held out his hand, but she didn't accept it.

"*Mister* Kalusky, if you or your people at," she peered at the logo on Sara's shirt, "Sci-D TV, use any videos of Joey without my permission, I'll have my lawyer up your network's ass faster than you can say 'child exploitation.'"

She headed toward the house.

"Ma'am, wait."

He turned toward Sara and signaled her to cut the taping just as her cell phone rang. Sara answered it and backed away giving Zach some privacy. He saw an opportunity.

"Ma'am, please, off camera. We're just person to person, now."

She stopped in the middle of the concrete steps.

"Here's my business card. I'm a paranormal researcher. I help people who are struggling with supernatural experiences. If anything weird happens, my cell phone is on here. I'm available day or night."

He gingerly inched toward her with the card extended. She flashed an inkling of vulnerability. "Okay."

He was a bit surprised that she took it.

"What's your name?" he asked.

"Virginia Forster." Again, she crossed her arms across her bosom.

"Virginia, *off the record*, what did he mean by 'not telling us about the boy?'"

She hesitated ever so briefly. "Look, Joey's got an imaginary friend. That's all. It doesn't make him crazy. Now please, get off of my property."

With that, she stormed up the rest of the stairs and into the house. The door slammed. At the apex of Zach's disappointment, Uncle Henry spoke to him for the first time that day.

Joey holds the key.

The key to what? Joey is just a little boy, Zach thought. How is he going to help solve the mystery of a century old haunt?

Behind him, Sara slammed her cell phone shut. "Fuck."

"Now what?" Zach asked.

"That was Bryce. Sashza isn't coming."

"What? I thought he said he talked to her and she'd show."

"Well apparently, she prayed about it and decided she can't tolerate all the 'lies and deception.'"

Chapter Twelve

"Are we awake?" The voice asked.

Zach had known better than to expect a 'hello' on the other end of the phone line.

"I don't know. Are we...black?" Zach responded.

"Yes, we are."

Zach could never recite this part without a chuckle. "Then we're awake. But we're *very* confused."

The exchange of movie lines from the 1974 classic comedy, *Blazing Saddles*, had become a tradition for Zach and Hunter Martin. It was not only fitting since Hunter closely resembled the lead of the film, Cleavon Little, but it also mocked the stereotype that black people, at least those not practicing Voodoo in New Orleans, weren't psychic and never dabbled in the occult.

"Hey buddy, how did you know it was me?" Zach asked.

"I'm psychic, remember?" Hunter spoke with a faint lisp.

"Yeah. You *psychically* looked at your caller ID." Dealing with Hunter was always a pleasure, and with Sashza threatening to no-show, Zach was glad to call on the consultant for help.

Bringing in a professional psychic for cases had been Sci-D TV's directive, and Zach originally had fought the idea. He didn't like outsiders influencing *XPI's* investigations. Hunter proved his worth on the very first case. The entire team was stumped as to why a family was hearing groans and unintelligible words from an upstairs closet. Hunter connected to the spirit—the ghost of a deaf boy who had been abused, thrown into the closet, and neglected during his short life. The lead helped Wendy identify the spirit and *XPI* had been able to release the ghost and successfully solve their first televised case.

There was another reason Zach liked Hunter. They enjoyed an unspoken "don't ask, don't tell" policy in regards to each other's abilities. Hunter had to know that there was something unusual about Zach. But Hunter clearly understood the two shared mutual oddities, and the tone of their relationship had always been light.

"Caller ID? What's that? Zachary, is there a purpose for this call or did you just want to brag to an old man about all your technologically advanced gizmos and toys?"

"Priceless," Zach said. "Hey, what are you doing tonight?"

"I've got three words for you. *Murder, She Wrote.*"

"Seriously."

"Seriously? Okay, I've got an appointment from seven until eight o'clock and after that I'm free. Are you finally setting me up with that Rebecca?" Hunter was mildly effeminate, but he was not gay. In fact, he left no doubt about his feelings for Rebecca—and apparently for Hunter, lust was considered a feeling.

"Something better."

"Better? Rebecca's coming over for *Murder, She Wrote?*"

"Better."

"Oh these games, Zachary. Tell me."

"How would you like to join Rebecca, myself and some more of our friends for a psychic walkthrough of Rosewood Asylum?"

"Riiiiiight. I'm hanging up now."

"I'm dead serious, Hunter."

Silence.

"Cat got yer tongue?" Zach asked.

"Wow. Gee, thanks for the advanced notice. One of the most haunted places in America and you want me there in twenty minutes? Whoever will I get on such short notice to style my hair?"

Hunter was nearly bald.

"I don't need you in twenty minutes. Can you be here around midnight?"

"You're there...you're there now? What's it like?"

Zach looked around at the tents on the lawn and the equipment vans parked in the driveway. The sky was blue; the weather was warm. Robins intermingled with sparrows in the treetops, while cardinals whistled their signature song back and forth. Even in the heat of the Indian summer day, the scent of autumn clung to the occasional breeze.

But something was just not right.

"Get here before midnight," Zach said into the phone. "I'll let you see for yourself."

Patrizia's flashlight beam bobbed and weaved ahead of them in the darkness as they descended into the basement. Already ten or fifteen degrees cooler than the lobby, the underground level smelled of humid earth and sewage. Of course that's while Zach wasn't bombarded by Bryce's beer-stenched breath. Apparently, his co-host and Pierre had consumed quite the liquid lunch.

"This basement was mostly used for storage — cleaning supplies and canned foods," Patrizia said. She waved her flashlight toward a doorway ahead of them.

Zach wondered if the underground corridor had looked any different one hundred years ago. Exposed ducts ran along the length of the ceiling which was only about seven feet high. Bryce seemed uncomfortable with the rusty pipes so close to his head. He crouched as they made their way down the tunnel-like hall. The barren concrete walls may have once bore paint, but Zach doubted the place had ever exuded an atmosphere other than brooding. Unlike the upper stories which had experienced obvious renovations, the basement had never been upgraded.

"One day in 1898," Patrizia continued, "an orderly who was substituting for a missing coworker, discovered a woman living in one of the storage rooms. She claimed that she wasn't insane and had been living there in hiding from her jealous husband."

"Was she a patient?" Zach asked.

"That's where the story gets even more interesting. No one recalled having ever seen her. There were no records of her admittance. She insisted that her 'friend,' an orderly had snuck her in and had taken care of her while she was there."

"Hiding from her husband?" Rebecca asked.

"Yes. But that's not the end of the story. The day that they found her, they also discovered the corpse of Thomas Carter, *the orderly*, in the stables. He'd been stabbed dozens of times."

"She did it?" Bryce asked.

"They assumed that she did. They found bloody clothes down here. The police wanted to take her into custody, but the hospital administrator fought it since she was already committed to the institution. He withheld her identity from the official records."

"Dr. Johansson?" Zach asked. "The one Wendy said died right before the hospital closed?"

"Yes."

"What eventually happened to this woman?"

"Apparently, she stayed at Rosewood and was transferred to the female quarters."

"Did she die in the fire?"

Patrizia shrugged. "This morning, Wendy stated the death toll of the fire was 'more than a dozen.' My research found that it was quite a bit more than a dozen. The actual number was nineteen. Nineteen women burned to death."

The lobby was deserted when Zach and Rebecca arrived. He grabbed a bottle of water from their supplies in the lobby and handed it to her. She had been coughing and wheezing the entire trip up from the basement.

"Allergies?" he asked.

Rebecca coughed. "No. Smoke...did you smell it?"

"No."

"I couldn't breathe down there. I definitely think the woman from the basement died in the fire."

"You felt a presence?"

"Something. I felt something strong."

Shouts echoed down the north corridor that led to the infirmary. Instinctively, Zach bee lined for the commotion.

"Why don't you fucking speak English?" Matthew's voice rang through the cavernous hallway.

"Hey, guys. Guys!" Angel shouted.

Zach entered the infirmary. The three tech guys faced each other in a triangle. Angel looked from Pierre to Matthew.

"Look bloke, belt up. I don't want to hear from a septic tank how to p'form my dodge and shirk!"

"You calling me a septic tank you stupid foreigner?"

"Hey!" Zach yelled. "What the hell is going on?"

All three of them spoke at once—an indistinguishable blather of words. Bryce and Sara had caught up and stood behind him.

Surprisingly, she stayed quiet and waited for him to do the heavy lifting.

Zach held up his hands. "Quiet!" Their word stream tapered off. "Angel, what the hell is going on here?"

"I'm not sure, boss. These guys were laying cables and setting cameras up. I came running when I heard the shouting."

Bryce pulled no verbal punches. "Pierre, I told you to work as a team. What the bloody hell are you doing?"

Pierre seemed as stunned as any of them at Bryce's berating. He ran a hand through his sweaty black hair. "Listen Bryce, do me a bloody Rod Laver and don't blame me until you take a butcher's hook how high up this bloke wants to position the cameras."

"I told this fucking guy to speak English!" Matthew shouted.

"Could say the same about you. You've the IQ of a Joe Blake."

Matthew reached and grabbed Pierre's polo shirt before Angel could pull him back. Sara seemed content to watch how Zach and Bryce would handle things.

Bryce charged Pierre and smothered him in a hug. "C'mon. Let's go. We're going for a beer you and I," he said.

"Beer?" Zach asked. Don't you think —"

"Trust me." Just before exiting the infirmary, Bryce half turned and looked back. "Matthew, I'm sorry about this. Set those cameras up the way you want them."

Pierre cursed and muttered in unintelligible dialect and pointed back. "I'm tellin' you —"

"Quiet. I told you that you and I are going for a drink. That's it." He turned again. "Zach, Sara, set up whatever work schedule you need. I'll take care of this and let's meet back at five o'clock?"

"Okay," Sara responded. "Five o'clock in the main lobby."

Once they were out of earshot, Zach tore into Matthew. "What part of work as a team do *you* not understand?"

"Are you kidding me?"

Angel eased into the space between Zach and Matthew.

"You know I'm not kidding. This isn't funny." Zach kept his tone firm and his emotions in check.

Shelly and Ray rushed up the hallway. Apparently they had heard the commotion from halfway across the property.

"No, what's funny is that I've been in this from the beginning...look, it's bad enough I've got to report to you two,"

Matthew pointed at both Zach and Angel. "But now I've got to kowtow to some foreign idiot? Even the girls don't have to put up with that many bosses."

"Even the *girls*?" Shelly echoed. "What the hell do you mean by that?"

"Okay, okay." Sara finally stepped in. "Let's not escalate this. Matthew's upset and he has a point."

"Gee, ya think?" Matthew seemed hell bent on alienating everyone.

Sara glared at him. "Do you want to take the night off?"

He crossed his arms across his chest. "No. I never said I didn't want to be a part of this."

"Alright, then take a few hours off. In fact, take as much time as you need to calm yourself down. Ideally, I'd like you back here before sundown."

"Fine." He made his way down the hall alone.

"The rest of you," Sara said, looking around. "Where is the Turk?"

"He and Rico went to check out the stables," Angel said.

"Really?" Zach wasn't sure if he was more upset that Turk had left without getting permission or because he'd taken off to investigate with a *Demon Hunter*.

"Well, spread the word," Sara said. "We're all meeting up at five o'clock in the lobby. We've got a long couple of days and nights ahead of us. Let's pace ourselves, people."

"Damn straight," Ray said. He motioned to Shelly and Rebecca. "Come along now, *girls!*"

"You need a good ass kicking don't you?" Shelly asked, failing to keep a straight face. She punched him in the meaty part of his arm.

"Oww." He began shadow boxing Muhammad Ali-style, and then extended his right arm straight putting his palm on her forehead – a move that made it impossible for her to reach him with punches. "C'mon, *girl*. C'mon, *girl*."

Shelly chuckled and played along. They meandered down the hall toward the exit. Rebecca grabbed Zach by the elbow and held him back.

"I need to ask you something." She looked unsure of how to express herself, which for her wasn't unusual. Rebecca often had trouble articulating her feelings and conveying her psychic experiences.

"What's going on?"

"I'm not sure. Do you feel anything here? I mean, when you're inside this place?"

Zach inhaled a deep centering breath. Other than dust and the faint smell of musk, he sensed nothing. "No. But you're more attuned than I am. What do you feel?"

She looked him in the eye, which for Rebecca, was rare. "Something is in this place — something ugly. It's subtly — in this case, not so subtly, affecting people's moods."

He nodded.

"Zach, something evil is roaming these halls."

Chapter Thirteen

That Sashza showed up to Rosewood shocked a few — even Bryce had claimed that her appearance was a fifty-fifty proposition. Sara had gotten the network to apply significant pressure to the transvestite-psychic. Apparently a Sci-D lawyer had told Sashza that if she expected to ever be seen on television again, she had better perform her psychic walkthrough.

When Sashza did appear, it surprised no one that she showed up in dramatic fashion. She strolled up the driveway wearing a pink sequined dress and emitting an attitude as if she'd been pulled away from an Emmy Awards dinner. Her sequins picked up the light of the setting sun and flashed and twinkled. But her hat was what stole the show. A throwback to maybe the 1940s, a faux white rose perched upon a tiny brim from which long thin white feathers sprouted. And of course the *pièce de résistance*, the white veil wrapped around her face as though it could shield her from all harm.

"Hello everyone. Hello!" She waved like she was in a parade. "Thank you for all the calls!"

Her mood seemed to cool to just about frigid when she approached Sara and the camera. With a nervous fluster, Sashza looked away and focused on Bryce. "Darling, I am so glad you insisted I come. This is a once-in-a-lifetime chance at really making contact with souls who need help."

She grabbed Zach's arm and pulled him close, as though she needed both their support if she were to take more than a few steps forward. "And Zach, my dear, I do hope to provide you a first-hand viewing to the effectiveness of my readings."

Zach smiled. "I'm sure it'll be a treat."

"We're going to walk the property," Bryce said to Sashza. "We're going to start at the administration building, move to the old stables, and lastly go into the main hospital building."

"Very good. And it will just be a small group of us, yes? I don't wish to be distracted by conflicting vibratory sensations."

The crew had finished filming Sashza's arrival. Sara walked out from behind the camera. "It's just going to be the on-air talent here and us." She pointed to the two cameramen and herself.

Zach always loved being referred to as 'on-air talent.'

Sashza acted as if Sara wasn't even there. "Bryce dear, could you get me some water? My throat is incredibly parched."

Bryce trotted to the equipment van to fetch her drink.

"Where did you come from this evening?" Sara asked, seemingly intent on breaking the iceberg-sized barrier.

Sashza looked at Zach and then at the sky. As though realizing she couldn't be overt in her rudeness toward Sara she spoke, but without looking at her. "I had an early dinner with a lovely friend in the city."

"Really? Where?" Sara asked.

"Oh, I don't know." Sashza focused on flicking away imaginary lint from her dress. "Downtown. I don't remember the name of the establishment."

Zach glared at Sara. She was enjoying this too much. Fortunately Bryce returned with bottled water which Sashza used as an excuse to wander a short distance away—in the exact opposite direction of Sara.

I'm sensing a little girl," Sashza said. "Why would a child be in this place? She's lonely. Not scared but lonely. She wishes she had...a friend."

Zach, Bryce, Sara and her cameraman stood outside the administrative building near the far southeast corner of Rosewood's property line. Sashza had not experienced any psychic feelings inside the building. Upon exiting, she had meandered around the perimeter in a semi-trance before standing still, closing her eyes and beginning to speak.

"Boy!" Sashza squeaked. Her facial expression took on the innocence of a cherub—her complexion cleared and the wrinkles in her face seemed less pronounced. Zach would never have believed it just an hour earlier, but Sashza actually looked like a young girl.

They waited patiently for her to continue, but she seemed to be far away — in the recesses of her mind.

Bryce broke the silence. "There is a boy?"

"Not a boy. Just Boy."

Zach looked at Sara. Had she told Bryce or Sashza about their experience with Joey? As if reading his thoughts, Sara deliberately shook her head.

"Where are you?" Bryce asked. His eyes never left Sashza's face. He moved close enough to catch her if she swooned, but stayed a safe distance from invading her space.

"I'm here!" Sashza giggled, but the laugh wasn't at all like her.

Bryce appeared confused, and then rolled his eyes.

"*When* are you?" he asked. "What year is it?"

"It's 1900, silly. Don't you remember the big New Year's party?"

"Ohhh, sure," Bryce said. "Did you have fun at the party?"

"Yes, but it also made Mommy and I sad because Father had died."

"How old were you when your father died?"

Bryce seemed very comfortable with Sashza's state – almost too comfortable. Almost *rehearsed*. Had it not been for Sashza's mention of 'Boy' after Joey had used that term earlier, Zach wouldn't be buying any of this.

"Seven. But I'm eight-years old now."

"That's great. So tell me about this boy…"

Sashza's brow furrowed and she frowned. "Not 'this boy,' just 'Boy!'" Her tone had taken that of an insolent child.

"Okay," Bryce said, calmly as ever. "Tell me about Boy."

"He tells me things."

"Like what kinds of things?"

"Secret things."

"What kind of secret things?"

"Boy said not to tell. I can't tell anybody!"

"It's okay," Bryce said, softly. "You can tell me."

"Nooooooo!"

"Why not?"

Sashza's face darkened. "Boy? Who is she?"

"Who are you talking about?" Bryce asked.

"B-but I don't…" she stammered, "but why?"

Bryce appeared confounded. Sashza put her fingers in her ears, as if blocking a high-pitched whistle. The terror in her expression made Zach's abdomen tense and his toes tingle. He considered shaking her out of the trance.

Sashza put her hands down to her sides, and then she inhaled deeply, "Mamma, help! Help me!"

The small group stood in the open expanse in front of Rosewood. The day's unseasonable heat had dissipated at sunset, and the chilly Chicago breezes provided subtle warning to everyone that October approached. Fireflies periodically dotted the darkness, their tiny flashes of yellow light serving as a nostalgic reminder of summer nights.

Considering Patrizia's disclosure of the murdered orderly, Sashza had a surprisingly uneventful reaction to the old stables.

"Okay," Zach said. "Okay. Let's go into the main building."

Angel and Pierre chatted in their constructed, technical nerve center. Shelly was leaning over the bank of video monitors checking out the images. Rather than flooding the area with bright lights, Angel had set up dozens of pillar candles around the lobby. Zach opposed the idea on the grounds of fire safety, but Bryce, Sara and pretty much everyone else vehemently overruled him. Zach usually knew when to pick his battles, so he'd given up his opposition. He had to admit that, with the eerie incandescence, it was precisely how Zach had always imagined Rosewood.

"Take me to the basement," Sashza said.

"Downstairs?" Bryce stared at her.

"It's the only part of this building worth me looking at." The certainty in Sashza's voice echoed throughout the lobby.

Zach led the way. As his confidence in Sashza had increased, his anxiety level had risen—especially regarding the basement. If Rebecca's raw but underdeveloped psychic powers had gotten such a visceral reaction, what kind of experience were they in for with Sashza?

He opened the door, flicked on his flashlight and headed down the steps. He took advantage of the darkness. He breathed deeply to calm his nerves. Sashza wasn't the only one "touched." An inattention to his own emotional state could trigger his condition.

The result would be an episode dramatic and graphic enough to freak out the most hardened Sci-D TV viewer.

An overwhelming urge to say something gripped him. He stopped before reaching the bottom step, turned around and faced up the stairway. Sashza gazed down at him.

"We all, Bryce, Sara and myself, agreed not to taint your impressions of Rosewood by telling you anything that happened earlier today," Zach said.

Eye contact let him know that he had one-hundred percent of her attention.

"If at any time you feel yourself in danger, please let us know so that we can get you to safety."

Sashza solemnly nodded. Behind her, halfway up the stairs, Sara was grousing to the cameraman that he should be filming. Zach ignored them, offered Sashza his hand and guided her down the remaining steps and into the corridor.

"Lies," she said.

Zach flinched. "What?"

The others rushed down and gathered at the base of the stairs. Zach pulled his hand away from Sashza as the cameraman aimed to film.

"Lies and deception. All around us. Especially around you!" Sashza stared at Zach, but her eyes became expressionless, almost vacant. She closed them. "She's lying to you. She means well. But deceiving nonetheless."

Zach swallowed his pride and did his best Bryce impression. "Who's lying?"

"He told her it would be okay. She doesn't understand. She's not letting me. She doesn't belong here."

"The woman they found?"

"Yes."

"Why was she here?" Zach asked.

"She was tricking him. Just like she's tricking him now."

"Who?"

Zach felt lost. Sashza was picking up on something, but he couldn't seem to guide her or to make sense of it. Her face contorted into a countenance gruesome and furious.

Her eyes opened.

"She fucking lied she did! And now, she'll burn!"

"The woman was the reason someone burned down—"

"Someone? You are a liar. How dare you?"

"Dude, that's it. I'm stopping this." Bryce rushed around her and stepped between them. "C'mon honey...Sashza, snap outta it."

Whoever or whatever Sashza had become, lunged for Bryce's jugular. "Oh, you're the reason? You, Carter? You're a fucking joke! I'll kill you!"

Zach grabbed for her, but it was unnecessary. Sashza's half-hearted attack was little match against Bryce's strength. Her large hands kept hold of his throat for a moment, but then seemed to lose their passion. They released and fell to her side. Bryce smothered her in a bear hug. She tried to escape, however he gripped her tightly.

"Shhh. It's okay," he said.

Sashza let out a ghastly wail. "Stay away! Stay away from him! You don't know what you're up against!"

"Sashza, shhh. It's okay," he repeated. "C'mon back to me."

She mustered one final but futile attempt to struggle away from him. Failing, she looked up and screamed. "Dr. Johansson, I don't belong here!"

Sashza passed out in Bryce's arms.

Chapter Fourteen

"This is crazy. Check it out!" Matthew said.

The technical nerve center in the asylum's lobby looked like a broadcast trailer at the Super Bowl. Several video screens, both small and large, monitored rooms, hallways and outdoor landscape all throughout Rosewood's grounds. Matthew, Pierre and Angel were gathered around a video monitor at the lobby's control center. Angel held a camera in his hands.

Sara trailed behind Zach. She instructed her cameraman to film whatever was being discussed. Bryce was escorting a distraught Sashza to her car. She'd taken nearly half an hour to snap out of her trance in the basement, and then had claimed that she felt something from the asylum invade her physical presence. She adamantly swore she needed to leave Rosewood. She had insisted on leaving immediately.

"What's up boys?" Zach asked.

"You're not gonna believe this, *mi hijo*," Angel said. "I saw that the video feed to Camera 3, the one in the cafeteria, had gone out. I assumed it was just some power issue, so I walked down there to see what was up. I find the camera not only lying on the floor but look."

He held it out. There was a huge gash on one of the corners. Angel flipped the camera over and exposed the lens. It was shattered.

"What—"

"Check for yourself," Matthew said. He'd cued up a video recording from Camera 3.

The picture displayed the night vision images of the giant room. Its far corners faded to greens and grays. The image wiggled slightly, and then slowly the perspective changed. It rose from the four-foot shot to perhaps six or seven feet in the air. It paused there only a moment before plummeting to the ground. The picture was gone for a second. Then a still view of the room flashed back on screen through the shattered lens. Then the screen went black for good.

"That's it," Matthew said. "Holy crap. I'd say we got ghosts!"

Zach turned to Angel. "How long was the feed out before you went and found the camera like that?"

"I dunno. A couple of minutes? I periodically eyeball the video monitors to check that they're working. We had people hanging around up here right about that time, so I was distracted for maybe five minutes—at the most."

Bryce walked up. "What's the haps, peeps?"

Matthew explained the situation and reran the video for him.

"That's awesome. That clip's gonna make for an awesome preview for the show!"

Zach sighed. "Yes, but it's still unsubstantiated evidence."

"Unsubstantiated?" Bryce threw his hands up. "And how would you like this authenticated, oh wise one?"

"I'm just saying, theoretically someone could have lifted the camera up and smashed it."

"*Theoretically* who?" Bryce puffed out his chest.

"Theoretically, *anyone*."

"Cut!" Sara glowered at Bryce and Zach. Her command had been to stop filming, but everyone in the room understood the double entendre.

Zach unzipped his tent. He stooped through the opening and plopped down on his sleeping bag. Crazy psychic readings, broken video cameras, infighting between the teams, and it wasn't even midnight.

"I need about a week's worth of sleep."

Ray lay on his half of the tent with his feet crossed. His head was propped up on a gym bag as he worked on a text message. It smelled like he'd bathed in cheap cologne.

"Aww, did poor Zachie pooh have a rough day being on TV? Was it hard hanging out with the hot Asian chick while I pitched our tent by myself?"

"You have no idea, pal-o-mine," Zach said. "Who are you texting?"

He squinted and pursed his lips. "A coworker."

"Raymond Michael Ross, you had better not be chasing after a stripper!"

Ray glared at him. "Are you kidding? I'm texting another bouncer to see about swapping shifts so I can hang here tomorrow."

"Oh. Sorry."

"You better be, ya clown."

"And, seriously, thanks for setting up the tent."

"No problem. You just owe me *another* blowjob."

"Am I interrupting?" The question came from a female voice just outside the tent.

Zach recognized the scent of her perfume—French vanilla with a wisp of honeysuckle. His face went flush. He scrambled toward the tent's opening—toward her.

"Patrizia. Hi. Hello. No."

Her hair was tied back in a ponytail and she'd changed into a spandex bodysuit like Trinity wore to kick people's asses in *The Matrix*.

"Do you have any spare flashlight batteries?"

"Sure, in my car. You need some?"

"I forgot to bring backups and want to be prepared in case they run out while investigating."

"Good idea," Zach said. "I'll run to my car and get them before we start."

"Thanks." She smiled and left.

Ray's bemused face made Zach grin. "Shuddup."

"Oh Zach," Ray said, raising his voice several octaves, "do you think maybe you could shove some of your big powerful batteries into my flashlight?"

"You need a good ass kicking."

Ray smirked. "From you?"

"No, from her. You were already pretty hard on my ass the other day."

"Yeah, I put you over my knee and spanked you. Just like she'd probably do."

"Yeah, like she'd do to you," Zach said.

"Yanno, she's kinda hot in an Amazon woman sort of way," Ray said. "I mean as long as she ain't another one of them transvestites!"

There was the sound of shuffling footfalls outside the tent.

"Shhhhh," Zach said to Ray.

"Zach? Are you in there?"

"What's this, Grand Central Station all of a sudden?" Ray asked, loud enough for whoever it was outside to hear.

"I'm a popular guy," Zach said.

Sara popped her head through the unzipped tent door and gave Ray a snotty look.

"What's up?" Zach asked.

"Well, we're about to get ready to start the investigations, aren't we?"

"I can't relax for ten minutes?"

"Sorry but before we start, I need to talk to you..." She glanced at Ray. "Outside?"

Zach followed her out of the tent. "So? What's up?"

Her lips pursed slightly as they did when she knew she needed to say something delicately. "Well even before the little tiff in there," she tilted her head toward the asylum, "Bryce requested that we even out the airtime a bit."

"You gotta be kidding me. Even out? Really? Did someone already edit the footage from today and not tell me?"

"Zach."

"Did we have a stopwatch timing how long Patrizia's tour lasted and compare it to how long Wendy's introduction was?"

"Za-aaack."

He hated when she said his name that way — it reminded him of how his dad pronounced it.

"Fine, Sara. We've got three teams of investigators and two camera crews. While one team is in the asylum, another team can be checking out the administration building and stables, while a third team keeps an eye outside the front yard area. That third team won't have an HD camera, but their night-vision portable and mini digital camera should be enough. If Bryce wants, he and Rico can take the first shift in the asylum. That's probably the team that will get the most usable footage, right?"

"Good idea," she said.

"Sara, don't do that."

"What?"

They were both silent a moment while Rico and Turk passed by and disappeared into Rosewood's lobby.

Zach still spoke in hushed tones. "Don't pretend like this was my idea."

"Well it was!"

"Okay, whatever." He started back to his tent.

"And Zach?"

He stopped, but didn't turn around.

"Like we talked about, can you stop hanging around with Ray at least another twenty-four hours?"

"What happened to your candles?" Zach asked.

In lieu of candles, there were a few battery-powered lanterns dotting the asylum's lobby.

"I can't get them to stay lit," Angel replied.

"Really?"

"*Si*. I don't know if it's something supernatural or just a draft, but they tend to not stay lit very long. I just gave up."

"That's interesting. We should run some tests on that later." Zach said, inspecting the row of video displays. "Hey, why isn't a camera covering the basement?"

"You wanted one there?"

"We've had a lot of activity downstairs. Why wouldn't we?"

"Because even before losing Camera 3, we were stretched as thin as possible by the thousands of feet of hallway?"

"We need one down there," Zach said. "Figure something out."

Matthew had been leaning on the railing of the main staircase eavesdropping. "We could take one from the hallway on the 2nd floor. Camera 8?" He pointed above the infirmary.

"That one's gotta cover room 217," Angel said.

"What about the one at the other end of the hallway?" Matthew asked.

Angel turned to Zach. "What do you think, boss?"

"That should work. Get it done ASAP. We're going to start filming in five minutes."

Matthew circled up the lobby staircase. "I'll have it done in three minutes!"

Zach went outside and met up with the production crew and all the investigators.

"Anybody ready to hunt some ghosts?"

Chapter Fifteen

Armed with flashlights, a thermal cam, an EMF meter, a digital EVP recorder and accompanied by a cameraman, Zach and Rebecca stood at the doorway to Rosewood's administration building. Splitting into three teams of two investigators made the most sense. That way, they'd be able to cover a good portion of the property all at once, and the different makeup of the teams, one male, one female, one mixed sex, would give spirits a choice of which team they felt comfortable interacting with.

At 9:16 PM, Zach held the two-way radio to his mouth. "Everyone ready?"

"Team One is ready," Bryce's voice transmitted back.

"Team Two, ready," Patrizia said.

"Team Three, ready," Zach broadcast to them.

"Tech Team, ready." Matthew had been given the honor of running the technical team's walkie-talkie. Zach thought it a nice compromise that he utter the show's line to commence their search. "*XPI* and *Demon Hunters*…investigate!"

"Are you ready?" Zach asked Rebecca, already turning the doorknob.

"As long as there's not ants."

"What's with you and ants, anyway?"

"I'll tell you when I know you better."

"When are you going to know me better?"

"Maybe," she said. "Sometime when we're off camera?"

"Ah. *Touché.*"

They crept through the foyer using their flashlights sparingly and keeping as quiet as possible. The cameraman followed, his lights off in favor of a night vision setting. When they reached the first office, Zach whispered to Rebecca. "Talk to them and try to capture some EVPs."

She nodded and clicked on the recording device.

"Hello? Is anyone in here that would like to communicate with us?" She held the EVP recorder up and slowly moved it about her, hoping to pick up digital recordings that were indecipherable to the human ear. "We mean you no harm. We'd love it if you could show yourselves."

Save the sound of crickets chirping, all was silent.

Zach prepared his EMF meter and held it away from the mini digital camera. He spoke. "If there is a spirit here, give us a sign of your presence."

Nothing.

"Knock on something," Rebecca said. "We want to know where you are."

In a room down the hallway there was a knock. They crept toward the sound's origin.

"If that was you," Rebecca called out, "do it again, please?"

"Who are you?" Zach asked. "Did you work here at Rosewood?"

"Come closer to us. We won't hurt you," Rebecca said.

Zach's EMF reading flinched and then spiked. He nodded vigorously to Rebecca and motioned to her to repeat what she'd said.

"We won't hurt you. We promise."

There was a large bang in the foyer. It was as if someone had opened and slammed the door. When Zach and Rebecca investigated, no one was there.

"Team Three, entering the old stables building," Zach broadcast over the walkie-talkie.

"Copy that," Matthew sent back from the technical command post.

An odd feeling washed over Zach as he and Rebecca continued to take EVPs and thermal cam readings throughout the old stables building. He was bored. Other than a slamming door, there had been no activity of note, and certainly no documentable scientific evidence. He'd waited his entire life to investigate this place with the expectation, perhaps unrealistic, that it would be an asylum of horrors, and at the moment, it was just another case. Despite being called "the stables," with the wood stalls removed and any horse smells long disappeared, this could be just an ordinary warehouse. He attempted to distract himself with the historical implications of the building they were investigating. Built in 1892, it would have had a vital use to store and care for the primary mode of transportation at that time.

Wendy had laughed at his ignorance when he'd asked how long it would have been in use during Rosewood's operation. "You don't know much about history do you?" she had said over the phone. "Zach, how many cars do you think were in use back in 1903 when the hospital closed?"

"I don't know. I know the automobile was being produced in the late 1800s."

"Right. And the computer processor was being produced back in the 1950s but that doesn't mean in the 60s every flower child had a laptop!"

"Okay. I get it. So how many people were actually driving cars in 1900?"

"At the turn of the century? Like less than one tenth of one percent of the people, Zach. I mean in 1901, Olds Motor Works was considered the mass producers of automobiles because it churned out about 400 cars."

Despite her quasi-inappropriate dating history, Zach had to concede that Wendy knew her actual history.

"Did you hear that?" Rebecca asked.

"Sorry," Zach said. "I kicked something."

They both trained their flashlight beams in the direction of the noise. Zach's spotlighted it first.

A Coke bottle.

Rebecca hurried over and picked it up. "Hey this isn't one of those replica-retro bottles. This is an old school 1960s, 1970s? Maybe earlier." The wonder in her voice resembled that of an archeologist having just discovered Atlantis.

"Pick an era, any era," Zach said. "Over the years, they tried to convert Rosewood into everything from a museum to a retirement community. I think it was seven times that they started, and then ended up halting rehab projects."

"Because..."

"Something always scared them away."

In a loud voice, Zach addressed the spirits. "Is that what brings you out? Do you not like threats to your...home?"

He waved his EVP recorder in the air hoping it would pick up a voice or a noise. Something.

"Give us a sign that you're here," Rebecca said.

"Is the orderly who was murdered in 1899 still here?" Zach called out.

There was a moment of complete silence except for the discordant hum of crickets. Then, from the far back corner, a high-pitched moan could be heard. It sounded both forlorn and distant. Zach motioned for Rebecca to repeat her question as they crept toward where the noise had originated.

"Hello? Was that you?" Rebecca asked. "Can you make that noise again? As a sign that it was you?"

They were arriving at the back wall when they heard it again. This time, it was louder. The tingling sensation Zach had been feeling turned to disappointment. It was the unmistakable sound of a far-away, but quickly approaching, train horn.

"The three most exciting sounds in the world: anchor chains, plane motors, and train whistles."

"What?" Zach asked with attitude into the phone.

After the disappointing investigation at Rosewood's outbuildings, he was in no mood for riddles. He and Rebecca were making their way toward the backside of the hospital near the old visitor's room when Hunter Martin had called. Zach was filling him in on their investigation.

"Anchor chains, plane motors, and train whistles," Hunter Martin repeated. "Sorry. That's an *It's a Wonderful Life* quote."

"Some angel you are," Zach said, imitating a grumpy George Bailey. "It wasn't a welcome sound at the time. The train tracks run behind the industrial property that borders Rosewood to the south. Between that and the muffling of the thick walls, we'd have to discount any reports of moans."

"Well, there has to be some truth to the reputation of that place. I get a creepy feeling anytime I drive by it." It sounded like Hunter was currently in his car. "So even though you say this

Sashza has already done her psychic tour, you still want me there?"

"Absolutely." Zach was hoping that Hunter could provide clarity from Sashza's readings. Without a clear understanding of why Rosewood was haunted, Zach would be forced to induce one of his episodes.

"Hey, is there a coffee shop nearby there?" Hunter asked.

The question was completely off topic, but Zach answered. "Yes, a *Muses*. Why?"

"*Muses*?" Hunter's voice had risen in pitch.

"Yes."

"Does that place mean something to you?"

"It might. Why?"

"I'm not quite sure. I get the feeling you need to go there. Are you supposed to be meeting someone there?"

"Interesting. Maybe I'll tell you when you get here." Zach hung up without saying goodbye like the way people did in the movies. Hunter would understand—he loved movies.

Zach continued walking with Rebecca. They approached Rosewood's back wall and looked out where the female quarters had once stood. Most of the homes were completely dark. The porch lamp on the house where Joey and his mom lived emitted an amber glow.

"I think I should go and talk to those people," Rebecca said.

The comment caught Zach by surprise. "What do you mean?"

"I need to..." Rebecca gazed at the houses as if transfixed. "Suicides are buried there. I need to go. Tomorrow."

"Sara and I talked to most of the residents earlier. None would allow—"

"Is there a Mrs. Radcliff there?" She shuddered and then peered at Zach.

Mrs. *Radkey* had been the woman who had admitted to having seen a shadowy figure in her house.

"Mrs. Radkey?" Zach asked.

Rebecca's psychic abilities never ceased to surprise him. In the interest of his show, because she wasn't that comfortable on camera, he may have been holding back her talent.

"Yes." Rebecca's voice was calm and confident. "I need to talk to her. She knows more than she's letting on."

"Like what?"

"I don't know. I may be able to convince her to let me investigate there. She may not allow cameras but..."

She stared out at the homes a hundred yards away and slightly downhill from Rosewood. Her eyes were vacant, as though unfocused. "Which is hers?" she asked.

"You tell me."

Rebecca closed her eyes and extended her arm. Her index finger pointed out to the dual rows of homes. It circled in the air a moment and then came to rest aimed at the building on the north side next to the vacant lot. She'd chosen the house across the street from the Foster residence — the home of Mrs. Elizabeth Radkey.

The two-way radio flared static. They both flinched.

Sara's voice came across the transom. "Zach? Come in, Zach!"

He put the radio to his mouth. "I'm here."

"Rosewood Psychiatric Hospital is ready for you and Rebecca."

Chapter Sixteen

"Zachman!" Bryce bounded out of the front doors of Rosewood. "This place is ripe!"

Rico tread out behind him looking stirred but not shaken. The cameraman and Sara followed behind. The lights from the HD camera made it difficult to see for a moment. Bryce dashed at Zach and stopped just a whisker away. He grabbed Zach by the shoulders and shook him with every syllable.

"You are go-ing-to-be-a-mazed-in-there!"

"Really? That's awesome."

"We got some good shit. Didn't we, Rico?"

Rico's eyes got wide and he nodded. "I've not seen anything like this since maybe that case we did back in Atchison, Kansas."

"We smelled peaches in room 217!" Bryce rose up on his toes and then dropped down flatfooted. His eyes were unusually active and his movements were quick—almost cat-like. Zach didn't need the scent of *Sailor Black* nor his godfather's voice to tell him that Bryce was on something.

"Didn't we Rico? Tell them."

Rico pursed his lips. He tilted his head to one side and then the other. He seemed unwilling to confirm but equally unwilling to object.

"Dude, what's it like out in the boonies?" Bryce asked.

"We didn't come up with all that much," Zach said. "But once the spirits start getting activated, who knows what may happen?"

"That's right!" Bryce said. "Boo-yah! We're gonna wake these bitches up!" He strode off toward the administration building with so much bounce in his step that Zach imagined him to be a human version of Tigger. After bounding fifteen or twenty paces, he turned back. "Let's go, Ricooo!"

Rico hurried off to catch up. Zach watched them practically skip across the field of shin-high weeds before he turned back to Sara.

"Have at it," she said, following after Bryce and Rico with her cameraman in tow. The first-night plan was for Rebecca and Zach to cover floors two and three. This is it, Zach thought. The real investigation begins now. I'm finally fulfilling my dream of investigating Rosewood. They rushed through the technical command center and were headed up the lobby's main staircase when Rebecca stopped. "Wait. What happened to the candles?"

"Apparently, Angel couldn't keep them lit."

She emitted a pensive, "Hmmmm."

"Hmmm, what?"

"Something therein that doesn't love a fire," she said, parodying a Robert Frost poem. "Can we go to room 217?"

Zach nodded, and they climbed up and around the lobby to the second floor. Wood floorboards creaked and groaned beneath their feet. The corridor, lined with one doorway after another, stretched on ahead of them. Some of the metal doors were closed, but most remained at least halfway open, as if daring Zach and Rebecca in. As they crept down the darkened hallway using their flashlights as sparingly as possible, Zach reminded Rebecca not to let the setting affect her mood.

"The trick is to experience the place as if the building is a blank slate and not a creepy asylum."

"Easier said than done, but I hear you," she said. "Still, this place doesn't feel right. It's...off—not as bad as the basement, but there is a lot of latent torment here."

"We knew there'd have to be residual effects, but we're hoping for some evidence of an intelligent haunting." Zach flicked on his flashlight as they approached room 217.

"Say 'hi' to the boys," Zach said, pointing his beam at the camera situated to monitor the room's doorway.

"Hi, boys." Rebecca waved.

"Hi back." Matthew's voice crackled on Zach's walkie-talkie.

Zach raised his index finger to his upper lip and made the shush motion to the camera. Once inside the room, they took thermal readings and performed a few EVP questions as they'd done in the administration and old stables buildings.

"Smell anything?" Zach asked.

Rebecca took a series of measured inhalations in various directions. "Nothing but old plaster and dust. You?"

Because the camera was filming, he only replied, "I don't smell or sense anything unusual in here." What he couldn't say was that he thought Bryce was crazy...or worse.

"Something has been bothering me about this case," Rebecca said in hushed tones.

Before heading back down to the lobby, they'd stopped in a few rooms on the third floor, but hadn't experienced anything unusual.

"What's that?"

"The fires and the suicides—spirits of those who've committed suicide are very confused. There have been cases where they've even believed that during their lifetimes they were murderers, even though they weren't."

"Yes," Zach said. "Remember when we first set up *XPI* and we encountered that case in—was it Joliet?

"Lockport," Rebecca corrected.

"Right. That guy had committed suicide and his spirit was inadvertently haunting his wife and child—"

"Yes, believing that he'd killed them too. It's fairly common with suicidal haunts. Their reality becomes a mishmash world of confusion and misunderstanding," Rebecca said. "And there is a greater danger."

"The confused spirits are more susceptible to demons," Zach said.

"Demons and evil spirits, ghosts wishing to be demons who recruit them for some malevolent purpose."

Zach was unfamiliar with that particular phenomenon. "Like what?"

"They're called 'Soul Snatchers' or 'Soul Collectors.' Their aim is to build an army of the dead—sometimes both the living and the dead."

"Why?"

"Sometimes there's a motivation behind it, but usually it's just an obsession to prove they can do it. The power, the control of it."

Zach placed his hand on the cold plaster wall. A century of grime had made it sticky to the touch. The complexity of the case was unlike any other he'd faced. The fires, strong evidence of spirits, Evelyn's information and confusing history, not to mention Sashza's negative forecasts, added up to one inevitable conclusion. If Hunter's reading didn't clarify the situation, Zach would need to induce an episode and utilize its powers. He shuddered. Summoning his visions carried consequences—serious ones, which he'd rather not face during an investigation this large in scale. Precautions would need to be taken.

His wrists throbbed as they sometimes did when he thought about his episodes.

He pressed thoughts of them away. Not only were they making him anxious, the mere act of remembering an episode increased the chances that one could accidentally occur.

"Tomorrow," he said to Rebecca, "before you talk to Mrs. Radkey, could you do some more research on these 'Soul Snatchers'?"

"Sure."

"Maybe prepare a little presentation for the group?"

"Do I have to?"

Unlike Wendy, Rebecca detested giving on-air speeches.

"I think you're the most qualified to present it."

Rebecca sighed and continued panning the room with the EMF meter. It sometimes took a while for her to relent.

Zach had found flattery the best angle to use. "I always enjoy when you share your paranormal expertise with us. I'm sure our viewers learn a lot from you. I'd hate to deprive them."

Sometimes a little bit of guilt did the trick too.

"Okay, I'll do it." She acted as though public speaking might kill her. "You just don't get how hard it is for me."

She had no idea that Zach was preparing to bear his own cross.

Zachary's Past—Age 7

"Za-aach? Zach!"

Gary Kalusky shook his son. Later, he would wonder if he had shaken him too hard.

"Zachary Thomas!"

The boy needed to get to a hospital, but fucking Christ, how would he explain this? Worst of all, he didn't know if these wounds were self inflicted or if his mother had, in one of her states, administered them. And Gary didn't know which scenario frightened him more. He picked up Zach's limp body and cradled him in his arms like an infant.

Crybaby idiots on the radio were always singing about their damn hearts breaking. None of them could ever put into words what it really felt like. He clutched his son, his only son, wrapped him in a blanket and carried him to his car. Gary gently laid Zach on the passenger seat and carefully strapped the seatbelt across him.

Despite driving at faster speeds than he ever had in his life, those first few blocks seemed to last an eternity.

Then Zach stirred.

"Uncle Henry?" he called out.

"Shhhh, Zach," Gary said. "We're on our way to get help."

"Daddy." His son's voice sounded so content, so peaceful, that it helped Gary focus his thoughts. At 95th street he needed to make a decision—an important one. A right turn led him straight to Christ Hospital. A left hand turn would—

"Daddy, take me to church?"

With the vehicle stopped at the red light, Zach had opened his eyes and realized where they were. His drawn, pale face had a death-like quality, but his green eyes were vibrant and alive. At the moment, he looked much older than a boy two weeks away from making his first communion.

"Zach, you're sick. We've got to get you to a hospital."

"No hospital."

"Buddy, church is your mom's thing, not mine. When you're sick—"

"I'm not sick. I'll be okay, Dad. It's happened before...lots of times."

Behind them a car honked. The light had turned green. Gary motioned out the window for the driver to go around them. As the vehicle passed, Gary flicked a one-fingered salute.

"I promise," Zach continued, "I'll be okay."

Before turning left, as though it was a condition for taking him to the church, Gary said, "Zachary, your mother must never, never, never find out about this."

"Don't worry, Dad, I know."

His son understood that his mom wouldn't be able to cope with something like this. Not now. Not ever. That's why Zach had hidden in the garage; he knew his mom wouldn't find him there.

Gary sped recklessly toward Saint Francis of Assisi. He'd take Zach to Monsignor Macginty. Gary didn't attend services, but he'd met Macginty on a number of occasions. The old priest would know what to do; how to help Zach get a handle on this...thing. Some things are better turned over to priests, not spoken of again – buried.

As he pulled up to the rectory, Gary made what turned out to be his final, direct comment about Zach's affliction.

"You need to find a way to control this thing, Zachary."

Chapter Seventeen

Pierre and Matthew seemed to have mended fences and were working together in the lobby. Next to the command center were a number of drained beer bottles. Zach suspected the beer may have contributed to them bonding. Angel was asleep in a nearby tent; he'd be working a later shift.

Zach pulled Matthew out of earshot of the others. "Hey, go easy on the drinking tonight, okay?"

Matthew looked back at the bottles. "Oh, that's all him, boss."

Zach's reaction must have shown doubt.

Matthew got closer and whispered. "Boss, I swear, I haven't had a drink."

His breath was honest—it was bad, smelled of garlic-laden salsa, but sober.

"Okay," Zach said. "Keep an eye on him."

Matthew nodded and went back to the video control center.

Zach walked outside into the cool night air. The fireflies had long since called it a night, but the crickets remained in full harmony.

"Zach to Team Three. Come in Team Three."

"Team Three is right behind you." Patrizia's voice played in stereo on the radio and behind him. She and Shelly had emerged from behind the *Demon Hunter* van.

"Hi there. How's it going?" he asked.

"Kind of boring so far," Shelly said.

Patrizia nodded. "We got some EMF spikes in the administration building but that's about it.

Zach shared his and Rebecca's experiences.

Shelly shrugged. "There's always tomorrow night. Besides, things might pick up when Hunter shows up. You know the effect he has on ghosts."

While unscientific and unproven, there often did seem to be more paranormal activity on their investigations when Hunter was present.

Patrizia inched toward the Rosewood main door. "We should start in the basement. Right?"

"Sure."

They entered the asylum, passing Rebecca who was on her way out. She carried the thermal cam. "Maybe we'll get something with this outside—"

Shouts coming from inside one of the tents cut her off.

"Whoever the hell that is, cut it the fuck out!" Inside, Ray pounded outward on the tent wall.

"You okay, pal?" Zach called out.

"Zach, r'you screwing with me?"

"No. What's going on?"

There was internal rustling and the whiz of the tent's zipper. Ray popped his head out. "Who's out here?"

"It's just me and Rebecca."

Ray stumbled out in shorts and a white tank top. "No one else? This whole time?"

"I've been at the asylum front door for a while. What's up?"

Ray surveyed the landscape. "The tent—someone kept pounding on it. It felt like there were two people—one on each side."

Zach peered around, but there was no one. "You're sure it wasn't just a dream?"

"I know the difference between a dream and someone almost knocking over my damn tent."

"Easy. I was just..."

"I know what you were 'just.'" Ray ran his hands over his face and through his hair. He sighed. "This wasn't a dream. Trust me on that."

"Tell us what happened from the beginning," Rebecca said.

Ray shivered. Zach couldn't tell if it was from the memory or the cool night air, but his friend didn't ask for a sweatshirt. "You're not filming this are you?"

"Do you want me to?" Zach asked.

"No."

"Okay, then tell us before someone else walks up."

"I woke up—I dunno, maybe a half hour or so ago. Someone was tapping on the outside of my tent. I asked who was there and the tapping stopped. No one said anything. I figured one of you guys had mixed up the tents and knocked at the wrong one."

"Did you see what time it was?" Zach asked.

"No."

"Did you fall back asleep?" Zach asked.

"Yes," he said, squinting at him. "I dozed off, but I woke up about no less than ten minutes ago and have been *awake* since then, your honor."

Zach waved his flashlight beam back and forth over the ground where Ray had indicated the activity had come from. "There's some trampled high grass, but that could have happened when you set up the tent."

"Go on, Ray" Rebecca said.

"The tapping woke me again. It was harder this time—less like a signal and more like someone trying to screw with my sleep. I called out a 'knock it off' and that's when it really started. Pounding on one side then immediately on the other—like there was two of them. At first, I thought it was Matthew and Angel or maybe a couple of the Demon Hunters. I hollered for them to stop and when I hit back, that's when the laughing started."

"Laughing?" Zach and Rebecca said it in unison.

"Yes," Ray said. "You guys didn't hear it?"

Both shook their heads.

"It continued right up until I heard you guys calling out for me. The tent hitting kept going until just seconds before Zach asked if I was okay."

"If it was anybody else but you, pal, I'd suspect it was a dream," Zach said.

"Well it ain't anybody else but me."

Ray wasn't prone to either drama or delusions, and he didn't look like he'd just woken up. His eyes are clear, Zach thought. He's focused and alert. Fired up even.

"Look, buddy." Zack cocked his head to the side. "If you believe this was a real experience, go to the cameraman and get your account on tape. There's one inside."

"Where's Sara?"

"She's in the outskirt buildings with Bryce and Rico."

Before Ray could indicate if he intended to go public with his story, Zach's two-way radio buzzed.

"Team Three to Teams One and Two. Come in please," Patrizia's voice called across the radio lines.

"Team Two here," Zach broadcast.

"Team One listening."

"Please report to the Technical Command Post ASAP. Repeat. Please report to the Technical Command Post ASAP. Over."

"Wilco." Bryce's voice sounded official.

"Be right in," Zach said into the radio.

He stared at Ray. "Are you coming with us?"

"If I'm going to be up and alert enough to watch video at five o'clock, I'm gonna have to get some sleep. If I decide to tell my story on camera, I can do it just as well in the morning."

"Aren't you two supposed to be investigating the third floor?" Zach asked upon entering Rosewood's lobby.

"Well hello to you too, Mr. Crabby." Shelly said.

Patrizia snickered and then defiantly stuck her tongue out at him. This behavior was uncharacteristic of them. Something big must have happened—after a supernatural experience, investigators were often giddy.

Shelly continued. "Wait until you hear the EVPs we got in the basement!"

Matthew and Pierre were adjusting sound settings on the computer software program that evaluated the high frequency noises that often were undetectable to the human ear.

"Whatever happened to having our Evidence Review Team conduct an independent analysis?" Zach asked.

"We're just playing the recording they took. We're not altering it any," Matthew said.

Before he could consider the implications of his underlings running the asylum, a blunt force hit Zach between the shoulder blades. From behind, a huge arm closed around his chest.

"Zachman!"

Bryce was panting. Zach smelled something on his co-host's breath, not to mention in his jacket. It was sweet, pungent, herbal. Marijuana.

Zach broke free of his grip. "Did you guys sprint up here?"

"Came as fast as we could, my friend. We came just as fast as we could." Rico's eyes appeared equally as distant but he wasn't as amped up as Bryce. It seemed he mellowed when he smoked weed.

"Dude, we got some *killer* EMF readings down there at the administration building," Bryce said.

"That's great."

Pierre cracked open another beer and offered it to Shelly. She refused it. He left his arm extended with the bottle, but she continued to refuse. After the third refusal, he gulped down a third of the bottle.

Two high. One drunk, Zach thought. No wonder their ratings were so popular.

The pot smell neither dissipated nor faded, but rather was overwhelmed by the familiar scent of *Sailor Black* and Pierre's pipe was nowhere in sight.

Listen to the recordings.

It was a good idea. It might help everyone calm down and refocus.

"Hey," Zach said as loud as he dared. "Let's listen to Shelly and Patrizia's EVP recordings!"

A hearty *Demon Hunter* cheer of pounding fists and wild dog barks erupted around him. Even Shelly joined in. The cameraman was capturing this entire scene and, when the time came to edit the video, it would likely air as a bonding moment between the two teams. Zach had the sudden and terrifying image in his mind as Sara using it as a promo for the show.

"Let's play that clip," Zach instructed.

Matthew connected the laptop that had isolated and digitized the recording to large broadcast speakers that would allow them all to hear. He hit play and the recording began:

Shelly: Is anyone down here who wishes to contact us?

Female voice [series of noises] oooou

[pause]

Patrizia: Can you say something to us?

Female voice: [undistinguishable] eeet me.
Patrizia: Did you hear that?
Shelly: shhhhhh. Is that you? Can you speak?
Female voice: [undistinguishable] kk oooh [undistinguishable] eyre.
[barely audible chime and a loud bang]
Shelly (whispering): sounds like a door slammed.
Patrizia: Are you still there? Talk to us. Tell us who you are.
Silence and static.

"That's it," Shelly said. Her face beamed.

Patrizia looked proud, but a bit lost. Maybe she didn't fully comprehend the recording's significance.

"That's evidence of an intelligent haunting," Bryce said. "Awesome!"

Some of the evidence is tainted.

Tainted, Zach thought. Tainted with what? His uncle's warning was rather cryptic and he didn't know what to make of it.

"I want to listen again," Zach said. "Did anyone pick up what she was saying?"

Rico raised his hand. "At one point I think she said, 'Eat me,' didn't she?"

There were a few giggles and snickers.

"She didn't say 'eat me,'" Bryce said. "She said, 'feed me.'"

Rebecca and Patrizia were the only ones besides Zach who apparently didn't understand that quip. The rest laughed heartily.

"What's so funny in here?" Sara with her cameraman in tow strolled into the lobby. "What are you clowns up to now?"

"Careful who you're calling a clown, ya clown," Bryce called out.

Zach knew before Sara got close enough to see it in her semi-vacant eyes. She was trying too hard to act casual, but still remain professional. It was as though she were attempting to play the part of herself instead of just being herself. He didn't even need confirmation from the voice.

She smoked with them.

His godfather's voice served as apt reminder for Zach to calm his emotions. He breathed deeply through his nostrils hoping to disguise his sigh, instead the exhale sounded like a horse's snort.

"Can we listen to this recording again?" Zach asked, hoping to get things on track before Hunter arrived. He was looking forward to guiding the psychic through the asylum.

Bryce whispered something to Sara and then explained to her what they were listening to. Matthew cued up the audio for a second listen:

Shelly: Is anyone down here who wishes to contact us?

Female voice (very faintly): h-hoo ar oooou

[pause]

Patrizia: Can you say something to us?

Female voice: -eeet me.

Patrizia: Did you hear that?

Shelly: shhhhhh. Is that you? Can you speak?

Female voice: --akk --ooh -- they're.

[chime and bang]

"We didn't hear that first sound, did we?" Patrizia looked at Shelly.

"No. Not when we were down there. It sounds like she's saying 'who are you?'"

Most agreed, but the other phrases were up for debate and argumentation. Matthew postulated that the second EVP said "see me," while Shelly suspected it was "meet me."

Although it was only mildly humorous the first time, Rico repeated his "eat me" joke.

"Can we please," Rebecca said, "show some respect for the dead?"

For a few minutes the group maintained a somber attitude, but soon enough flippant guesses and quips were flying. Sara seemed intent not to make eye contact with Zach. Conversely, he caught Patrizia eyeing him guardedly a few times.

Zach interrupted the fun and guesses by announcing a two-hour break for cast and crew. He planned on making a coffee run before Hunter arrived. He quickly took everyone's order.

"Wait!" Wendy marched through the Rosewood lobby wearing high-heeled boots. Her hair and makeup looked impeccable. With such a grand entrance, she obviously was planning on additional airtime.

"Zach, I have an update on my research!"

Sara ordered both cameramen to film her presentation. "Go!" she called out to Wendy.

"On July 4, 1899, approximately five months after the female quarters were destroyed in a suspicious fire, a man doused himself with kerosene and set himself ablaze on that very site." She paused for dramatic effect and then waited for the group's murmurs to die down. "Ironically and perhaps not coincidentally, it was July 4, 1900 that nurse, Abigail Lovecroft, and her daughter, Amelia, experienced a paranormal event that caused Abigail to quit her nursing post."

"Did you find a connection between those two events, Wendy?" Zach asked.

"Well, late this evening," Wendy said. "I may have uncovered historical documents which can provide that link. At the very least, it will give us an eye-witness account of both of them."

"What kind of documents?"

"Doctor Louis Johansson was the Physician-in-Chief of Rosewood Psychiatric from 1896 until his death in 1903. He kept detailed records of each patient and the happenings at Rosewood in a professional daily record."

"That's great!" Zach said, not even needing to amp up his enthusiasm for the cameras. "Patrizia, would you mind helping Wendy go through those records tomorrow?"

She hesitated, but then nodded and flashed a thumbs-up sign.

"From everything I gathered," Wendy said. "If we can figure out the identity of the 1899 suicide, we'll solve several high-profile arson cases. In 1892, the original Pullman Market Hall, the one used by all Pullman employees to purchase their goods, was destroyed by fire. In 1894, at the height of the Pullman strike, much of the World's Columbian Exposition fair grounds were destroyed in a fire."

"The site of the 1893 World's Fair?" Zach asked. "Known as 'The White City'?"

"Correct," she said. "And in 1895, the hotel known as 'The Castle' which was built and used by H.H. Holmes, the serial-killing physician who murdered many during the Columbian Exposition, burned down under mysterious circumstances."

"Then in 1899, the female quarters at Rosewood were torched." Zach said. "Great work, Wendy."

"But Zach, I haven't told you the most exciting news of all!"
She'd gotten him again.
"Yes, Wendy?"
She clutched his arm. "This is something that holds the potential to throw enough light on the mystery surrounding Rosewood's haunting to forever solve the case!"
"Tell us!" Sara called out.
"Just before Rosewood Hospital shut down forever in 1903, an attending physician noted something odd in Doctor Louis Johansson's professional record. Doctor Johansson had passed away earlier that year of heart failure." She reached for a water bottle and took a sip. Wendy was milking the attention for all it was worth. Zach supposed that she had practiced the timing of her presentation for hours.

"It was a mention of a *personal* diary that he'd begun keeping in order to, and I quote, 'keep certain delicate and private matters of certain patients and their families extremely confidential.' Doctor Johansson indicated that he'd hidden this diary somewhere on the Rosewood grounds — a personal diary that to date, has never been found."

Chapter Eighteen

Unlike their Pacific Northwest rivals, *Muses Coffee House* insisted that every store remained open until midnight every night. Allegedly, in the early days, the policy had been a bone of contention since malls closed at either nine or ten and wouldn't allow a midnight closing time. *Muses'* CEO had held firm to his conviction that decaf coffee and teas would serve as the perfect nighttime drink, and would not launch a store unless it could remain open until midnight.

Muses advertised heavily in schools to students needing after hours caffeine jolts, so many were located near college campuses. Typically, during the later hours, people wrapping up dates and students in the midst of pulling an all-night cramming session populated the stores. However, when Zach arrived, *Muses* was completely deserted—no sign of Evelyn.

There were still a dozen cars in the lot when Zach had pulled in just before 11:00, so apparently, *GrocersMart* stayed open late as well. Zach enjoyed the aroma of ground coffee and attempted to keep his mind off the case by reading *Muses Coffee House* marketing material while the young guy behind the counter prepared his Café' Americano.

The Muses of Greek mythology were goddesses who inspired the creation of literature. Daughters of *Zeus* and *Mnemosyne*, the goddess of memory, they have aroused the process of creation through song, writing and dance. The Muses were the physical embodiment of performed speech of all types. Today, the word "muse" is implicit in words and phrases such as "amuse," "music" and even "museum."

Muses Coffee House specifically recognizes and honors in their logo, five of the Muses:

Clio—the muse of history and writing; the desire to find truth and knowledge.

Calliope—the goddess of eloquence and storytelling.

Polyhymnia — the muse of oratory, poetry and symbolism.

Melpomene — the muse of tragedy.

and —

"Hello, handsome," a seductive voice said.

Zach flinched and whirled around.

"Evelyn."

She wore a similar dress to the one she had the last time they'd met and had wrapped a simple white shawl around her shoulders.

"I'd hoped to run into you here again," she said smiling.

If Zach didn't know better, he'd think she was flirting with him. Then again, maybe he didn't know better. "As did I," he said. "Your leads were quite impressive."

"Café' Americano."

Zach motioned to Evelyn to wait one moment as the apron-adorned kid behind the counter handed over his drink.

Zach gave him a written order for the desired beverages of cast and crew. "Can I get these to go?"

The kid appeared confused. "You want *all* these?"

"Yes, is that a problem?" After a long day, Zach was annoyed at the barista's attitude.

"I need you to pay in advance." The barista glanced towards Evelyn, and then cast Zach a suspicious look.

"Fine."

As they concluded their business at the cash register, a bell signaled the arrival of more customers, a group of boisterous teens.

"You can make my drinks after theirs," Zach said.

The barista rolled his eyes. Zach led Evelyn outside and made sure to hold the door for her. She picked a corner table not far from a propane heater.

"I'm sorry, Evelyn, did you want something to drink? Water even?"

She shook her head.

"Are you going to be warm enough out here?" Zach asked.

"Oh, you're such a gentleman," she said. "Yes. I'll be fine. Thank you."

"No. Thank *you* for the information."

"You learned of the fires that destroyed the female quarters on this acreage back in 1898 — and the others?"

Zach nodded. "Unfortunately, there's only so much we've been able to verify, and I want to ask you about some specific things we've discovered."

"Yes, of course."

Zach read from a list he'd made in his journal. "Did your mother ever say anything about room 217?"

"No. Not that I recall."

"How about the man who lit his room on fire?"

"No."

"Do the names Abigail or Amelia Lovecroft mean anything to you?"

"No."

"Did your mother ever mention anything about a lady found living in Rosewood's basement?"

Evelyn's mouth twitched as it had a few times during their first visit. "No."

Zach no longer believed it to be a nervous tic. There was something untruthful about the way that she'd answered. Should he press the issue or move on? He decided on the latter. "Does the name Doctor Louis Johansson ring any bells?"

She squinted and looked into the night sky. "That name sounds familiar, but I just can't place it, although it is a rather common sounding name."

"It is. Here's one," Zach said, not exactly sure how to phrase it. "Have you ever heard anything about 'Boy'? Not 'a boy' or 'the boy' but just Boy?"

Evelyn's jaw dropped. Her eyes widened and she likely realized that there was no use in trying to hide her reaction. "How do you know about Boy?"

"C'mon now. I'm the one asking the questions tonight. Tell me what you know, please."

She said nothing. It looked as though she couldn't speak.

"Evelyn, pardon the expression, but you look as white as a ghost. Please tell me, and I promise to keep what you say in confidence."

"Zachary." Her face was somber. "I promise to tell you what I know. First, I need you to tell me who has seen Boy."

He debated his options. Don't tell, offend her and probably learn nothing. Tell her and risk her not keeping her promise—unlikely. Tell her and trust that she would open up more to him. He didn't need upper level psychology to make his decision.

"Alright. I'll tell you, but I need your word…"

"You have it."

Zach relayed first the odd responses of Sashza. He expected more of a reaction from Evelyn, but she seemed nonplussed. However, when he mentioned what Joey had said, the elderly lady became visibly distressed.

"Which house does this Joey live in?" she asked.

"The one closest the street on the far— Hey! You're supposed to be telling me what you know."

"You'll research this without telling anyone where you got the information?" she asked.

"Yes. Of course."

"John Paramour was born on the afternoon of April 14, 1865."

Zach was no historian, but even he knew that to be the day of Abraham Lincoln's assassination. The fact that someone connected to this investigation was born on that day amazed him.

"You may wish to take notes, Mr. Kalusky?"

He opened his journal and began jotting the information down. "Yes, of course. This John is the spirit of 'Boy?'"

"John's mother, a woman of Russian decent, adored President Lincoln and--"

"And this John," Zach said. "Who is he to your mother? Was this your dad?"

"Mr. Kalusky—"

"Zach. Please call me Zach."

"Alright Zach, this is extremely difficult for me to speak about," she said. "Please just let me tell you in my own way."

"Yes, ma'am. Go ahead."

"Ma Paramour, Mrs. Paramour suffered from some sort of mental affliction. She likely would have been considered as a patient of Rosewood had she lived long enough. In any event, she was cruel to him and somehow, because of the day of his birth, blamed him for the loss of the president."

"Just because he—" He'd interrupted again already. "I'm sorry. Continue."

"Who knows why? She was a very ill woman and evil to the core. Her condition and John's punishments worsened after her husband left. Of course she blamed John for that. He was only four." Evelyn peered up at the stars, as though she had tried to banish these stories from her mind and the night sky was helping her recall them. "He was beaten often, but her favorite punishment involved scraping burning embers from the fireplace and using them to scald his feet. She told him that wicked people were burned at the stake. She insisted if he continued in his evil ways, he'd burn for his sins, and she threatened to sacrifice him in a fire."

"Good Lord." Zach made the sign of the cross.

"Then, in October of 1871 —"

"Oh!" Zach couldn't stay quiet. "That was the Great Chicago Fire!"

Evelyn appeared on the verge of tears. "Yes. John was six years old. I shudder to imagine what that woman must have done to him during that time. Whatever it was, it scarred him for the rest of his life and led him to…"

"He was the arsonist, wasn't he?"

She said nothing.

"Was he the one who set himself on fire in 1899?"

As though on cue, the bell on the door to *Muses Coffee House* tinkled. The young barista came out with a box neatly packed with caffeinated beverages and set it on the table in front of Zach. "Anything else for you, tonight?"

"No, thanks," Zach said. "We're fine with this."

The barista looked at Zach as if he had the bubonic plague. Was he new? How unusual was it for someone to get an order to go?

"Okay, have a good evening," the barista turned and stormed back into the store. Maybe he was just pissed at having to make such a large order so late or maybe because he didn't get a big tip? As he slammed the store door, the bell rattled harshly. Zach made a mental note to mention the behavior to a manager the next time he came in.

"Hey Zach!" Matthew approached from the direction of *GrocersMart* carrying a large paper bag.

Evelyn's back was to him. She looked horrified. "I cannot be seen with you," she said.

Zach held up his index finger. "Hey Matthew, could you give us a second?"

Matthew stopped dead in his tracks. "Yeah. Sure."

Zach sensed his time with Evelyn was drawing to a close. "Please," he said. "Tell me the rest of the story."

She stood up and brushed by him. "Meet me here tomorrow, anytime after sunset. I'll tell you everything then."

"Wait a second." Zach stood up and took a step toward her, but she quickened her gait and did not look back.

"What did you say, Zach?" Matthew called out.

"Just a second, Matthew."

By the time Zach trotted after her, Evelyn had zipped around the corner of the building and was gone.

Chapter Nineteen

"What's up, boss?" Matthew asked.

"Nothing," Zach said. "What brings you here?"

"Sara sent me out for snacks and things. Anything specific you want?"

Zach retrieved the box of coffee drinks and peered at the array of junk food pouring out of the bag. "Nacho Chips, Pretzels, Cheese Doodles and Barbeque Potato Chips."

Probably half of it would be consumed by Bryce before 3 AM's Spirit Hour.

Zach shook his head. "Nah. That should cover it."

They made their way to the parking lot. The traffic on 115th Street had all but ceased for the night, however the distant hum of the 94 freeway to the east and the closer chirp of crickets was nearly loud enough to fill in awkward gaps in the conversation.

"Thanks for giving me more of an active role tonight," Matthew said. "I think you'll see that I really am capable of much more investigative work than you give me credit for."

"That's not been the issue," Zach said. "It's just that there are only so many investigative roles possible on the show. Had we needed to cover this place on our own, that would be a different story, ya know?"

"Yeah. It's just...yeah. I get it."

He struck Zach as someone who was never satisfied with what he had. Zach could identify with his ambition, but there had always been something about Matthew that seemed a bit too aggressive—in a passive aggressive way.

"Oh, hey," Zach said. "Before I forget, I don't want a lot of questions being asked, so please do me a huge favor and don't mention that you saw me here with that woman tonight?"

Matthew smirked. "What woman?"

Zach grinned. "Exactly. Thanks."

"One thing, though, on a serious note," Matthew said. "Can I ask you a question?"

One of Zach's biggest pet peeves was people asking permission to ask a question, but he shrugged it off. They'd reached Zach's white Ford Focus and he hoped the question didn't require a lengthy answer. Hunter was due at midnight. He looked at his watch—11:56.

"Sure, but I have to hurry back to meet our psychic."

"This woman..." Matthew's eyes widened at something behind Zach. "Holy Christ!"

Zach turned around and almost dropped the whole box of drinks. Beyond Lincoln Avenue, a fire raged. One of the massive oak trees standing near Rosewood was completely ablaze.

They drove around to the front gate where fire trucks and squad cars were already pulling up. Their sirens blared only until they reached the property and then were turned off. The red and white lights continued to flare in circular orbits.

A group huddled well outside the area under the care of the fire team.

"What happened?" Zach asked to no one in particular as he walked up.

Sara had one cameraman filming the fire extinguishing. "We don't know yet. Rebecca smelled smoke, we came outside and saw flames at the base of the tree and called the fire department. That's all we know at this point."

The flames were contained to just the one tree and were doused with seeming ease. Fortunately no one was injured, but aside from losing a century-old tree, the blaze was terrible news for conducting a quiet investigation. News teams most certainly would follow up on a fire at the infamous Rosewood Asylum, and finding both *Xavier Paranormal Investigators* and *Demon Hunter* crews was certain to cause a stir.

The Fire Chief came over and shouted for whoever was in charge. Both Zach and Sara approached him. Bryce laid low, apparently not wishing to tempt fate with his marijuana scented overcoat.

The firefighter could have been a lifeguard with a slick backwards hat. "Are you two's the ones in charge here?"

Sara answered first. "Yes, we both are."

"Well everything here appears to be taken care of. Since no structures were damaged, we don't conduct a formal investigation, but do you folks happen to know how this fire started?"

"No," Sara said. "Of course not."

"Well, we didn't find any cigarette butts in the vicinity. There was no accelerant used, no gasoline or nothing, I can tell ya that. I don't suppose any of you kids smokes a *pipe*, do ya's?"

Zach didn't like the tone and implication of the way he said "pipe." Sara was staring at Bryce. Zach glanced over at Pierre who was slugging down a beer. For the first time in a long while, he and Sara seemed to be on the exact same wavelength.

At the same time, they both answered, "No, sir."

"The psychic is a'near!" Hunter shouted as he meandered up the Rosewood driveway. "Although I practically had to pull my 'Obi-Wan Kenobi' on the guard at the gate in order to get through."

"Don't film this yet," Zach said to Sara before rushing to greet Hunter and embracing him in a hearty hug. "I'm glad to have you here, buddy."

"This is really happening, eh? Rosewood Asylum."

"Yes it is." Zach pulled away from the hug and called back to Sara. "Are you guys about ready to film 'The Talent's' entrance?"

She flashed him a thumbs up.

Before they began shooting, Hunter grabbed Zach's forearm. "Hey brother, is your dad okay?"

"He's doing alright," Zach said.

Hunter scrunched his face. "Does he have...fleas?"

"What?"

"I don't know I picked up something strange...like he has fleas or something."

"Oh!" Zach got it. "My dad has *termites*."

"Ah. That's it."

"Too funny. You were close, but you might want to hone the focus of those psychic talents."

"Hey, I was close," Hunter said. "A bug is a bug."

"Ready to roll!" Sara shouted.

In order to film the psychic's "arrival", Hunter and Zach parted about ten paces from each other as if they were starting a duel.

"Rolling."

Zach and Hunter approached each other and shook hands warmly.

"Welcome, Hunter. Have I told you anything about this case?"

"No. Absolutely nothing."

"Have you conducted any research on your own or do you have any prior knowledge of this case?"

"Only what I read in the funny papers."

Cute. Zach had gone on autopilot and asked Hunter the question he did before every case. Of course, Hunter knew *something* about Rosewood. He introduced Hunter to Bryce and the other Demon Hunters. *XPI* members greeted Hunter.

"So, there's been a fire here tonight?" Hunter asked.

"Wow!" Bryce exclaimed. "Did you pick up on that psychically?"

"No, I can smell the ash, I saw fire trucks leaving as I pulled up and," he pointed towards the burnt oak, "one of these trees is not like the others."

The quip elicited a chuckle from the group and seemed to endear Hunter to the Demon Hunters, except perhaps Bryce.

They proceeded to the fire site where the burnt scent of wood and leaves left traces in the night air. It wasn't an unpleasant smell, but the knowledge that an ancient tree was gone—had died, made the scent unwelcome. Both groups of investigators crowded close to Hunter. Plans were for his Rosewood tour to be conducted only with Zach and Bryce, so everyone seemed eager to experience this psychic reading. The Demon Hunters especially appeared interested in what he had to say.

"Give Hunter some space," Zach ordered.

The circle around him expanded; some stood under the blackened branches. Hunter closed his eyes. His chest heaved in slow regular breaths. There were no passing vehicles on 115th Street, and with traffic on the 94 having tapered off, it was quiet. Not silent but city quiet.

Hunter's arms hung at his side. His right hand jerked forward. His left hand pointed in one direction and then another. The spastic movements gained in rapidity. His eyes opened, but they seemed focused on something a thousand miles in the distance. "This fire was started by something paranormal."

Zach knew and had experienced Hunter's psychic skills on other cases. He glanced around at the group. *XPI* members stared with interest at every word. Demon Hunters seemed mesmerized.

Hunter's eyes closed again. His nose scrunched as though not understanding the psychic message he was receiving. "It was not only done to get our attention, but to serve notice to other spirits here at Rosewood." His arms jerked at his side. "This won't be the last fire."

Chapter Twenty

"That was impressive, bro," Bryce said to Hunter once the group's ranks had thinned.

Bryce's demeanor had mellowed considerably since earlier in the night, and the whites of his eyes had taken on the hues of a sunset. Zach wondered if his co-host would even make it until the 3 AM festivities. The three of them, accompanied by Sara and the cameraman, entered the administration building.

"Yes," Hunter said. "Yes, I feel a presence in here."

"Female or male?" Bryce asked.

"Male. Definitely male."

"How old?" Bryce asked.

"Shh. Quiet. Let him do his thing," Zach said. Interruptions annoyed Hunter and Bryce's interruptions were annoying enough to upset just about anyone.

Underfoot, the floorboards creaked. Their instruments' gages exuded faint light in the darkness.

"He's a doctor." Hunter's arms flinched at his side. "He's upset. Upset at what happened in the stables." He pointed toward the other building. "Yes. Yes. I feel him in here."

"Who?" Zach asked.

"The doctor." Hunter inched through the darkened administration building. His hands extended out from his torso but not as though trying to avoid bumping into anything; it was more like he was wading through waist-high waves. Unlike Bryce's directed questioning of Sashza, Zach knew to allow Hunter's psychic feelings to wash over him.

"Doctor..." Hunter looked around as though trying to feel for the name. "J-something."

"Johansson?" Sara asked off camera.

"Yes! Dr. Johansson," Hunter said.

Zach glared at her. He knew she'd splice out her hint and air the episode as if he'd guessed it right off. Hunter didn't need help to make his readings appear accurate.

"Was Dr. Johansson the spirit who burned down the tree?" Zach asked.

"No. He didn't start the fire, but he seems to know who did."

"Who?" Zach and Bryce asked at the same time.

"Over here," Hunter pointed and crept toward a nearby room. They followed him in. "This is where he found...a fingerprint. It was too large."

"Too large for what?" Zach asked. "Does this have to do with tonight's fire or does it deal with past events?"

Hunter's eyes were glazed over. "They were new. Fingerprints were. Not used like today. He realized though. Too large he said. Not hers. He's scared now. Scared and angry. Scared of them both. Upset too. Upset over what happened in the stables. And afterwards. He's concerned now about the fires, but he doesn't venture out much anymore. He just protects....protects Rosewood as best he can."

Hunter wasn't making any sense, and his reading didn't at all connect with the reading that Sashza had given.

"Tell us about the fingerprints," Zach said softly.

Hunter's arms went spastic, his eyes fluttered and his entire body shook. He opened his eyes.

"What happened?" Zach asked.

"Dr. Johansson said to go to the stables."

As the hour grew nearer to 3 AM, the irresolute Chicago weather shifted dramatically toward colder temperatures. The unseasonable heat of the day had vanished as though sucked by the escalating winds into the stygian sky. As the group approached the stables, debate began regarding the upcoming activities.

3 AM was known commonly as the "Witching Hour" because it was the inverse time from when Jesus was said to have died on the cross. Many claimed that while spirits were always active and just noticed more at night, actual demons used 3 AM to mock God. In the industry, it had been called various nicknames. Some

used "Lights Out," others referred to it as "Dead Time." The *Demon Hunters* called it "Demon Hour." *Xavier Paranormal Investigators* invented and used the term "Spirit Hour." Sara enjoyed her own double entendre "Power Hour."

"If we're going to start on time," Sara said. "We've only got forty-five minutes to decide and plan it out."

"What do you mean, 'if we're going to start on time'?" Zach asked.

"We could always do it later and just claim it was 3 AM," Bryce said.

Zach and Hunter glared at him. Sara judiciously said nothing.

"What?" Zach said, harsher than he meant to.

"There were a few times where we —"

"Look," Zach said. "I don't need to know that. This show does *Spirit Hour* on time."

"Oh. You mean *your* show. I thought this was *our* show."

"Boys..." With that tone, Sara didn't need to say any more.

They'd reached the old stables building. Hunter approached the building and put his hands on the wall. Intuitively, the others stayed back to give him room and finish their conversation.

"Fine," Zach said. "We call it 'Demon Hour' tonight and 'Spirit Hour' tomorrow, but we start promptly at 3 AM both nights."

"Dude...whatever. Fine."

"So now that the pissing contest is over," Sara said. "What are we actually going to do?"

"We power off all lights, cell phones, electrical devices and film with only the hand-held cameras like always. Then we could —"

The conversation was interrupted by Hunter's muttering. He was at the door and jiggling the knob to get in. "It doesn't make sense though," he was saying.

Zach trotted over and unlocked the door. The cameraman had fortunately displayed initiative and had been filming Hunter the whole time.

"Here you go," Zach said, guiding Hunter into the darkened structure.

Hunter proceeded to an area in the distance and to the right. "A man in a dress. A knife with a broken tip. Blood. But it doesn't make sense."

Zach paused a moment to ensure Hunter needed prompting. "The murder doesn't make sense?"

"No. It's not murder. Stabbing, but not murdering. But...he was murdered."

"You're right. That doesn't make sense. Is there anything else?"

"The broken-tipped knife. It led to all this. The fingerprint. All three of them were alive here together."

"Who?" Zach whispered.

"Doctor. Patient. Cop."

Before Zach could clarify, there was buzzing and activity behind him. He spun preparing to give Bryce an earful. Instead it was Sara's cell phone causing the noise.

"You've got to be shitting me." She grumbled at presumably a text message. She pressed a button and raised a finger letting Zach know it was urgent. She spoke into the receiver. "Matthew, are you joking?"

She grimaced and slammed the phone closed.

Hunter had snapped out of his psychic state, so it was no use keeping quiet.

"What is it?" Zach asked her.

Sara looked as upset as he'd ever seen her. "Grant Winkler is up at the main building. He's demanding to see you and is threatening to shut us down tonight."

Chapter Twenty-One

"The state has us out here to investigate mysterious fires and you're blaming us for this one?" Sara managed to brave the stench of whiskey on Winkler's breath and get in his face.

"All of them fires wuz just weeds. That tree was a hundred years old!" He waved in the general direction of the burned oak, but it caused his body to tilt. He almost lost his balance and stumbled, but then righted himself. "And I bet you kids had something to do with it!"

"You've got no proof—nothing at all to back that up—"

"All's I'm saying is that if I say you're gone, you pack your shit and go 'cuz you're gone!" His eyes flared. Unfocused as they were, its effect was muted.

"And all I'm saying is if you do that, pack *your* shit 'cuz I'll see to it that my network costs you your job!"

The confrontation had escalated over the course of the previous few minutes. Sara hadn't even bothered to flirt with the custodian this time and she had been all business at the start.

"Yeah. You just try that, missy!" Winkler moved his face even closer to hers but it was clear he was neither thinking nor seeing straight. He might well have been kicked out of his neighborhood bar and had shown up merely to throw his weight around.

"Hey now, come on," Zach said moving between them. It was obvious Bryce wasn't about to play the role of peacemaker this time.

"'Hey now c'mon' is fucking right!" An animalistic voice shouted.

Zach's eyes widened. He'd known that voice since the sixth grade and at this hour, its owner wasn't likely to be a calming influence. Before Zach could shoo him away, Ray was towering over Winkler.

"That's how you talk to a lady?" Ray's massive hands struck Winkler's boney shoulders simultaneously. "That's how you wanna be?"

"Fuck you!" Winkler staggered backwards. His body language spoke louder than his vulgarities.

Zach and Sara each grabbed a Ray Ross arm. Bryce had faded into the background and the cameraman was still clearly filming. Should Ray get out of control with Winkler, a lawsuit could cripple the network.

"C'mon, big man. Let's go!" Ray stepped toward him.

Zach and Sara trailed like two ribbons on a kite.

"Yeah. You think you're so tough," Winkler said. He glanced behind him as if he hoped an army had materialized to intercede on his behalf or at least save his pride by pretending to hold him back.

"Tougher than you, old man. You wanna piece of me or are you gonna go home to your nice warm bottle of booze?"

"Yeah? Fuck you!" He raised a finger and waved it until it looked like it might topple him. "I'm warning you. One more fucking problem here and I'll have the cops out to send all you punks home!"

Zach pulled as hard as he could on Ray's shoulder. "Shhh. It's over," he whispered. "We won. Let it go."

"I'm serious. Try me one more time and it will be bye bye!" Winkler backpedaled until he nearly tripped and then swung around and strode toward the main gate.

"Night night, crazy man!" Ray called after him.

"Hey, cool it," Sara said. "Enough."

"What? I just—"

"Go back to bed, Ray," she said, turning and walking away.

"Hey." He grabbed her arm. "I did that for you."

She shook free and was walking away when she said it. "Men..."

"Ray," Zach said. "Go back to bed. Let things calm down."

Zach put his hand on his friend's arm. "I appreciate what you did."

"Thanks." Ray barely looked at him and stormed off for his tent.

Hunter must have sensed it a safe time to approach Zach. "Nice quiet little hangout you have here, brother."

With only fifteen minutes before the commencement of "Demon Hour," a decision needed to be made on what to do from 3 AM to approximately 3:30.

"We could just go lights out and see if anything happens," Zach said.

"Ugh, that's so pussy, dude," Bryce said. "No offense, Sara."

"None taken."

"Seriously, Zach, we've only got two nights here and we're gonna waste one sitting around twiddling our thumbs and staring into fucking candles?" Bryce seemed to be getting his second wind, although he may have had pharmaceutical assistance. "We know this doctor is lingering. He worked his whole career here and somehow got caught up into the place. Let's set him free. Tomorrow night we've still got the peach-smelling room, the basement and who knows what else to exorcise in the main building."

Zach hated when Bryce made a series of good points. He looked at Hunter for his opinion.

"Well boys, I don't know. I don't sense that the doctor is a threatening presence, however I don't know that we're going to get a clearer picture from him as to what transpired here."

"So we've gotten from him what we need," Sara said. "Look, the state of Illinois called us in here to solve the haunting. The state is our client, and the state wants these spirits gone. Our job is to clean this place up one spirit at a time."

Waiting for direction on their final activity of the night, both the members of Demon Hunters and *XPI* looked like death twice baked. Young people or not, most of them had been up at the crack of dawn and except for short breaks, they had been on the go the entire day.

Zach's head felt more and more like a bowling ball every minute. His eyelids seemed ready to betray him. Worse yet, and what he couldn't divulge to anyone, the confusing nature of the two psychic readings had made him realize he would need to induce an episode of his own in order to gain clarity. It would have to wait until the following evening and he would need to be well-rested for it.

"Fine. Let's do it, then," he said. "Rico, Bryce, Shelly, and Hunter, head to the administration building for 'Demon Hour' and the spirit release ceremony. Sara can film it. Patrizia, Rebecca and I will man the main asylum building and especially monitor the basement."

"Yeah, pun not intended," Patrizia said. "We'll 'man' it."

"You knew what I meant." Zach frowned. He was too tired to be politically correct.

"Rebecca could come with me," Hunter said, attempting way too hard to sound casual.

Zach flashed him a "not tonight" look. Psychic or not, Hunter responded by nodding his head in agreement and then bowing it.

"Okay people," Sara said. "Get moving to your positions. I know you're all tired, but we've just one last scene to film, and then you can sleep."

"Yes," Zach called out. "And lastly, remember to stay in groups of twos at all times. No one wanders off alone at night!"

As the groups scrambled to get ready for Demon Hour, Bryce nodded at Zach and motioned him off to the side of the activity.

"Brah, you looked wiped," he said.

"I'm pretty tired but no more so than anyone else."

"Do you maybe," Bryce whispered, "want something to help you stay awake?"

"You mean like...what?" Zach thought he understood where this was going but wasn't certain.

"Like, whatever." Bryce looked away.

"No. Thanks though," Zach said, wishing to avoid both conflict and complicity on this topic. "I'll be okay."

"Suit yourself," Bryce said.

Zach wondered if any, and how many, Demon Hunters and XPI members had taken Bryce up on his offer.

Before the group heading to the administration building departed, Zach called everyone together for a prayer circle. He held hands with Patrizia. Just inches away from his own arm, under her jacket, a Michael the Archangel tattoo stood guard—they were about to say his prayer.

After a moment of silence, Zach's voice echoed in Rosewood's lobby with both confidence and humility. "Saint Michael the Archangel, defend us in battle. Be our protection against the wickedness and snares of the devil. May God rebuke him, we humbly pray; and do Thou, O Prince of the Heavenly Host—by the Divine Power of God—cast into hell, Satan and all the evil spirits, who roam throughout the world seeking the ruin of souls. Amen."

Many in the circle repeated, "Amen."

While there were words of well wishes being exchanged between various people, Zach called Hunter aside.

"Stand your ground down there," he said. "Don't let them push you around."

Hunter smiled and nodded. "Ditto to you and good luck up here."

Nearby, Patrizia chatted with Rico, while Bryce gathered his equipment and supplies from his tent which had been constructed in the cavernous lobby. He pulled out an empty water bottle and sauntered over to Zach.

"Do you have any holy water?"

"Yes, with my stuff. You didn't bring any?"

Holy water was as necessary to a ghost hunter as a wrench was to a plumber.

"No. They wouldn't let us bring any on the plane."

"Plane?"

"Yeah, from California. Where I live. Patrizia's from there, too."

Something about that comment didn't sit right with Zach, but he shrugged it off. Later, he'd blame his obliviousness to the lateness of the hour and the urgency of the task at hand.

"Sure. I have some with my stuff," he said. "I'll get it from the van on the way out."

"Coolio. Thanks." Bryce turned and walked away. Zach was as sure as ever that he was hiding something.

Preparing for the 3 AM shutdown of all nonessential electrical equipment, Matthew changed out DVDs and swapped disk-drive tapes.

"Where's Angel, anyway?" Zach asked.

"Sleeping. He's got the last shift," Matthew said.

Pierre was nowhere to be found either—likely passed out in his tent.

Rebecca and Patrizia could be seen clearly on the video monitor. Zack raised the walkie-talkie to his mouth. "Ninety seconds until lights out. You ladies ready down there?"

"Ready, Freddie." Patrizia's voice sounded chipper, maybe too chipper. She waved excitedly at the camera. After Bryce's offer of something to help him stay awake, almost everyone's behavior seemed, to Zach, suspiciously upbeat.

"Ready out there at the administration building?" he transmitted.

"We is ready, sire," Bryce replied.

"All cell phones, pagers and flashlights off," Zach commanded both teams over the radio.

"Roger that."

"They're off."

"Rico's turning off his vibrator now," Bryce quipped.

"Come on," Zach broadcast. "Let's get serious now."

Matthew began shutting off the video screens that displayed various hallway scenes around Rosewood.

"You're just shutting off the monitors?" Zach asked. "Those cameras will still be recording though, right?"

"Yes, boss." He powered off the last couple. Only a few remained on; one displaying the basement, one operated by the cameraman at the administration building and of course, BryceCam.

"Okay, people," Zach transmitted. "It's 2:59. Lights out. Radios to be used only in an emergency."

The monitors now displayed black and green night vision scenes. All other lights in the lobby were off. The candles that Angel had laid out that evening, continued to resist remaining lit. Moments earlier, Zach had fired up a few and placed them in various points around the lobby. For a while they remained lit, casting wispy flickers of orange light into the darkness. Once again, a draft had seemed to have come from nowhere and had blown them out.

"Would you like to do the honors?" Zach asked Matthew.

He hesitated, but then grabbed the two-way and put it to his mouth. He looked at his watch and paused just a few seconds. "Here we go, folks. Demon Hour commencing."

One of the screens displayed the images of Bryce, Rico, Shelly and Hunter sitting cross-legged on the floor facing each other. In a moment, they'd begin attempting to exorcise Dr. Johansson. By trying to observe both locations, Zach had removed himself from the action. Sitting on the sidelines wasn't a comfortable experience, but he tended to avoid exorcisms.

On another video screen, Patrizia and Rebecca each squatted holding a candle. They'd chosen that position rather than sitting on the grimy floor. Their job was just to observe, record and report.

Hunter began rocking back and forth, a signal that he was in contact with a presence.

"I wish we had audio," Matthew whispered.

"You read my mind."

The girls in the basement remained stationary, although they clearly seemed to be nervous. Patrizia glanced to her left, but then refocused her attention on Rebecca.

On the other screen, Bryce stood up and inched his way around the perimeter of the seated trio. He was speaking and waving his arms about dramatically. Another monitor displayed the view from BryceCam. As Bryce moved around the circle, the camera panned crazily about. Sara would have a difficult time using any of its footage. Zach hoped Bryce wasn't preventing Hunter from locking in on the doctor's spirit.

"Look," Matthew whispered.

Rebecca had stood and was looking toward the ceiling. Patrizia eased to a standing position and it appeared they were taking turns speaking out to whatever paranormal activity they were encountering. Both looked terrified. Zach wished that he could pan the static camera in the basement. Off camera something was happening.

"I shouldn't have sent them down there alone," Zach mumbled.

On the other screen, Bryce was shouting. Hunter responded. Bryce said something and both Rico and Shelly stood up.

The other monitor showed Patrizia duck suddenly. Her hands were around her face. Rebecca was flailing about, her arms extended and her hands groped for the wall. It looked like she was crying. He realized that neither was holding the two-way radio.

Zach stood up. It was time to break one of his own rules. He leaned over to Matthew. "You going to be okay here on your own?"

"Um, sure."

He put the two-way to his mouth. "Rebecca, I'm coming down. Over and out." He tossed the radio to Matthew. Zach grabbed a flashlight and headed through the darkness toward the door to the basement. Not wanting the light to scare off whatever entity was downstairs, he turned the flashlight off before opening the door. He opened it, but was unable to prevent the creak that, due to the stillness of the asylum, seemed to echo louder than normal.

The first couple steps were easy to descend; he held the door open as he went down them. Once he let it ease closed, the pitch of black surrounded him. The scent of mold seemed to thicken in his nostrils and only the railing provided any sense of direction.

Below and some distance down the hall, Rebecca's voice seemed to be reassuring Patrizia. Zach couldn't make out the words. He took a step and then followed with his other foot.

Another step and he started hearing whispers. He first thought they were echoes of Rebecca or Patrizia but they seemed closer. Faint, but closer.

He stuck his foot out and searched for the next stair. It seemed farther than the others had but he found it. He clutched the railing with one hand and even crossed the hand holding the flashlight over to it. His lead foot went down another step. He decided to go down sideways. One stair at a time.

Rebecca's words floated up. "What you do here," she said. Or maybe it was, "Do you hear?"

Regardless, having heard her, it was obvious that the next sound he heard wasn't coming from that distance away.

"Zach," the voice whispered. Raspy. Upset. Undead.

What the hell, Zach thought. Rules were not made to be broken. Why had he ventured down here alone?

This experience would end sooner if he moved faster. He stepped down and trailed with his back foot. He repeated it. There couldn't be that many more steps.

Something crawled across his hand. It may have just been a cobweb.

Sailor Black invaded his senses. His hands were becoming numb. This wasn't merely a caution. It was last-minute notice that an episode would occur unless he calmed down. And quickly.

"They're everywhere!" Rebecca's voice from far away.

Zach thought that adrenaline would propel him forward in circumstances like this; instead, exhaustion washed over him wave after wave like a fire hose drenching a flaming house. His heart rate was plummeting.

He took another step. His feet were numb and a tingling sensation moved up his shins.

"Zach," the voice whispered. It was close. Not his godfather's.

His legs froze and his hands bore into the railing.

"Zaaa-aack," It was right in his face. "Zach, whyyy?"

The smell of pipe.

"You're making a mistake. Leave me alone," the voice hissed.

He couldn't wait it out any longer. He flicked on his flashlight and whirled the beam all around him. He stood alone on the staircase.

Chapter Twenty-Two

"Ants," Rebecca said. "I'm sorry I dropped the radio. There were ants all over it."

"There were like two of 'em." Zach had already brushed them away. The walkie-talkie was clean.

"It's not her fault," Patrizia said. "There were other things going on, too."

"Like what?"

"Like..." Patrizia chose her words carefully. "Voices. Movements."

"Yes," Rebecca said. "There was a presence here. Stronger, way stronger, than this afternoon."

Zach looked at his watch. It was 3:30. "You mean 'yesterday afternoon.'"

"Did you sense anything coming down here?" Rebecca asked.

"Let's head upstairs," he said. "It will be interesting to see if anything shows up on the audio."

They made their way toward the staircase. Just shining his flashlight up it gave him a tiny shiver. Going up would be easier than venturing down.

"You okay, Zach?" Patrizia asked.

"I'm fine."

Using their flashlights, they trudged up the stairs and headed toward the lobby.

"Welcome back," Matthew said upon seeing them. "The other team radioed in. They're on their way in, and they think they released the spirit from the administration building."

"That's good," Patrizia said flatly. "I can't wait to see and hear our stuff."

"No. No, no," Zach said. "We need rested investigators tomorrow. The audio and video evidence isn't going anywhere. Ray and the Turk will be up in a couple of hours to start reviewing it. They can edit it down for us and we can watch it tomorrow."

Rebecca and Patrizia appeared disappointed but too exhausted to object.

"I mean it," Zach continued. He handed the equipment to Matthew. "No one watches anything more tonight. Patrizia, we need you to research the hell out of the records about that patient found in the basement. Rebecca, you're going to need to be peppy to deal with Mrs. Radkey."

They pouted like children being sent to bed Christmas Eve after being told there was no Santa Claus.

"You're right," Rebecca said finally.

"I know I am. Go and get some sleep. Once I see Hunter off, I'm on my way to bed myself."

Patrizia and Rebecca bid their adieu.

Zach turned his attention to Matthew. "And you, too. Isn't it about time for you to turn in?"

When Matthew delayed his answer, Zach added, "I need you rested tomorrow. It's going to be a long day. It's Pierre's turn at the helm, right?"

"Yeah. Yeah," Matthew said. "I'll wake him."

"Okay, g'night. Zach was already heading toward the front doors.

"Goodnight, boss."

Outside, the temperature continued to drop. It was as though it had gone from July to November in a few short hours.

"Zachman, we got him!" Bryce trotted over with his hand held up for a high five. Zach weakly obliged.

"I've told the others and I'd appreciate your support on waiting until morning to review the Demon Hour activities. Everyone needs to be rested tomorrow."

Bryce looked at his watch. "Wow. Crap. Yeah. Sometimes I forget."

Rico moseyed up to them. "Yeah, jerkoff. Try being on New Jersey time. It's almost 5 AM in my time zone."

"Wait," Zach said. "When did you guys fly in?"

Rico froze and then acted like something behind Zach had caught his attention.

"Just today," Bryce said. "Or like yesterday now, I guess. We found out about this gig two days ago. Same as you did."

Interesting that Zach hadn't asked him *that* question. Nor did he believe Bryce's "answer." Before he could pursue the topic, Hunter, Shelly, Sara and her cameraman rambled up. One look of that group made it clear that he'd get no argument from them about turning in for the night. It looked like the only thing keeping Shelly and Sara awake was the cold.

"How'd it go?" Zach called out, hoping for Hunter's report rather than Bryce's.

"Very good. Good stuff," Sara said.

"I'm exhausted," Shelly stated. "G'night all."

Sara echoed Shelly, and a series of goodnights were exchanged. Everyone made their way to their respective tents except Zach. He motioned to Hunter who wasn't staying. "I'll walk you out."

They headed down Rosewood's driveway.

"Well? How'd it go?"

"I don't know," Hunter said. "Something about it bothers me."

"You don't know if the doctor was released?"

"I'm just not sure it was a good idea."

"Why not?"

"Balance."

"What do you mean?"

"I don't know what I mean. The word came to me during the exorcism. It was as if it was the doctor's final warning."

"Final warning?"

"I don't know how to explain it."

Hunter was behaving strangely. Zach wasn't used to him acting sketchy like this. Upon reflection, everyone seemed already affected by the case — or perhaps by Rosewood. Zach himself felt overwhelmed and needed sleep. It promised to be a full day tomorrow.

"Let's talk tomorrow. You're coming back, right?"

"Only if you'll have me." Hunter smiled weakly. "I booked a hotel room just down I94."

They'd reached the security car that was parked just inside the locked main entry point. The engine was running, but the vehicle was dark. Zach tapped on the glass. The guard at the wheel stirred and opened his door issuing a string of apologies. He unlocked the gate and let Hunter out.

"Drive safe," Zach said. "See you tomorrow."

Hunter waved.

Zach trudged back towards Rosewood. No one was around and the grounds were silent. Overcome with fatigue he stumbled to his tent, spilled in and crawled into his sleeping bag. He slipped off his pants but left his shirt on. Also, unlike Ray, Zach wore his scapular to bed; even in his dreams, he needed the Lord's protection.

Unfortunately, the scapular didn't guarantee a night of restful sleep.

"Knock. Knock," Uncle Henry said, reaching up and rustling his parka. "Breakfast is served."

He reached under his chin and tugged a zipper from his jugular down his sternum to below his belt. The scent of *Sailor Black* transitioned to fresh ground java beans. Evelyn emerged from inside his godfather. As she climbed out, Zach calmly noted that her body was that of a skeleton.

"Wakey. Wakey," she said. "Your Café Americano is here."

Zach stared at the inside wall of his tent and at Ray's crumpled sleeping back. It was light out.

"Your coffee, my liege."

Ray was standing at the entrance to their tent holding out a tall, *Muses* to-go cup. Zach sat up and pretended his head wasn't filled with remnants of dream world material. Eyes half closed, he reached for the cardboard Café Americano. Its heat focused his mind. Steam surrounded the cup and his hands around it.

"Don't like the weather in Chicago?" Ray said, quoting the oft-heard, local expression. "Wait a minute, it will change," His breath brought a stream of mist.

"Time is it?"

"Seven thirty-ish."

Zach grunted. "Shouldn't you be reviewing video?"

"Yes, sir. Just bringing you your coffee, *sir*." He saluted using one inappropriate finger.

Zach rolled his head on his shoulders. It felt like he'd slept on a bed of frozen peas. "Sorry."

"Ahhh," Ray waved off the apology. "This case is so off the charts that even your morning grumpiness can't get to me."

"What's so off the charts?"

"Well, I mean in the past, we've captured doors closing on their own and images and voices, but we've never had one interact so boldly as last night—to burn down a tree?"

Zach understood what Ray meant, and after hearing Hunter's warning and considering how destructive fires could be, he didn't welcome this powerful of an interaction with this particular spirit.

"Hey, c'mon," Ray said. "We've been reviewing for a couple of hours. Turk's already found something."

Zach sipped his coffee. Without it, he'd certainly have retreated back into his sleeping bag. Ray exited and closed the zipper of the tent reminding Zach of his bizarre dream. He tried to recall what had transpired before Evelyn had emerged from his uncle but it was lost to the ether. Any hope of retrieving it was gone when from outside the tent, Ray hiss-whispered Orson-Wells-style. "Rosewood!"

The dusty odor of Rosewood's lobby had taken on, but not been completely taken over by, the musky smell of unwashed men.

Angel sat at the command point. His head propped up by his fist.

"Well, good morning, stranger," Zach called out.

Angel stirred.

Zach slapped him on the back. "You missed all the excitement last night."

"So I heard."

"Anything fun or exciting happening this morning?"

"Bryce and Rico are doing a sweep of the building. They radioed down that Room 217 is filled with the smell of peaches. They want you to get Sara and a camera crew and go up and take a look."

"Cool. Actually, could you get Sara and tell her I'll meet her up there? I've gotta check something out with the video review guys."

"You talked to Ray?"

"I did. I guess Turk found something?"

"Supposedly." Angel sighed and pointed down the hallway toward the infirmary. "They set up a video review center in room 111."

"Thanks."

Zach bounded down the hall clutching the remnants of his Café' Americano. Caffeine began coursing through his veins. Even with only a few hours of sleep, his excitement in solving Rosewood's riddles had replenished itself—or had at least been jumpstarted by the java bean.

By the time he passed room 107, he could hear them rumbling around in the room up ahead.

"When's he gonna get his ass here?" Turk was saying.

"I told you, he's coming," Ray said.

Good ole Ray The Protector.

Zach reached room 111. "Hello, ladies. I hear you have something to show me."

"Zach!" Turk said. "Wait'll you see this!"

Already cued up on a monitor was a video display of what, by now, Zach recognized as the basement. In the upper right corner of the screen, a digital clock kept the recording time, as well as a counter of total minutes filmed. It currently read 11:22 PM. Turk clicked the remote and the video began.

It ran about a minute before Zach noticed what the commotion was about. In the greenish darkness, an image formed and swirled. It seemed to manifest out of the ether. At one point, it appeared to be the form of a woman. Then it vanished in a puff that went straight into the ceiling.

"This was right before the fire," Turk said. "Maybe this activity caused it?"

"Replay it," Zach said.

Turk clicked the rewind and the video reversed back to murk. He hit play.

"Here it comes," Ray said.

"What the..." It was even more impressive the second time Zach saw it.

"Play it for him frame-by-frame," Ray told Turk.

They examined the footage in that manner and froze it when the form had reached its largest. There on the screen, right before their eyes, was a young woman with shoulder-length hair. With the picture stilled, they could even make out features of her face—nose and lips.

"She's a looker," Ray said.

"No thanks," Zach and Turk responded in unison.

"Screw you's," Ray said.

"Hey, seriously," Zach said. "Let's get this to our digital analyst, pronto. Maybe he can enhance the image."

"Will do, boss," Turk said. "Are ya proud of me?"

"Hell yes," Zach said. "If this holds up to digital enhancement, I'll freakin' name her after you!"

"Turko's Treasure," Ray said.

Something told Zach that the nickname might stick. "Hey, get through the footage as quickly as you can to see what happened down there during Demon Hour," he said to Turk.

"You mean, 'Spirit Hour.'" Turk winked at him. "Will do."

"Did you hear about what Bryce and Rico found in Room 217 this morning?" Ray asked.

"Yes, I'm headed up there now," Zach said. "Do me a favor and review the footage from Camera 8 outside that room?"

Ray looked a bit put out. "What do you think I've been doing since I heard the news?"

Chapter Twenty-Three

"We discovered it this morning doing a quick walk through," Rico said.

Even having arrived skeptical, Zach had to admit that standing inside Room 217, it smelled strongly of peaches.

"I told you I smelled something last night." Bryce posed as though he'd just climbed Mount Whitney.

Sara and her cameraman filmed them examining the floor and walls for evidence of the scent.

"Check this out." Rico crouched near the far corner of the room and pointed to a puddle of clear liquid the size of a silver dollar.

"Don't touch it." Zach rushed over. He got on all fours over the spot and eased his nose closer and closer, careful not to inhale too deeply. Sometimes even odorless liquids could be harmful. This was not odorless. It smelled like peaches.

"Maybe it's ghost ectoplasm!" Bryce's enthusiasm was even more annoying in the early morning than it was late at night.

"I think it's just peach juice."

"Are you sure?" Bryce asked.

Zach scooped some of the liquid into a tiny sealable container used for such purposes. "We'll take it in and have it analyzed of course, but I think we're gonna find it's a natural fruit juice. How it got here is anyone's idea."

"Maybe," Bryce said, pacing the room, "the ghost of the man who died eating the peach jar has returned to warn us of something."

"Anything is possible," Zach said to the camera. What he didn't say was that this whole thing stunk more of planted evidence than it did of southern fruit.

"Let's walk through the rest of the asylum with the camera crew," Rico said.

Zach's cell phone buzzed notification of an incoming text message. It was from Ray: Need 2 see u. Private.

"You guys go on up ahead. I'm going to get this to a safe place," he said lifting up the container. "I've got to look into something. I'll catch up with you in a few."

Sara glared at him but didn't say a word.

"Patrizia," Zach said into his cell phone as he walked down the hallway. "Do you have anything more on that mysterious patient from the basement?"

"Hello Zach," she said. "I've isolated many of Dr. Johansson's notes on this woman. After they found her in the basement, they treated her in the infirmary and then held her in room 11 for close observation for over a week. During that time—"

"Wait." Zach tap-stepped down the marble stairs of the lobby's staircase. "Did you say room 111?"

"No. It just says here room 11."

"There isn't just an 11. There's a 111, 211 and probably a 311."

"Oh. Well, yes. I guess *now* it would probably be room 111," Patrizia said.

Pierre and Matthew had joined Angel at the command post. Matthew looked tired; Pierre appeared seriously hung over. The three of them were gathered together speaking in hushed tones. They suspiciously broke apart and started making small talk as he circled towards them while descending the stairs.

"What do you mean, 'now it would be 111'?" He nodded at the Tech Team as he passed by. They seemed far too interested in his presence. Something was afoot.

"Well, reading through this," Patrizia said, rustling papers on her end of the line, "I found out today that in July of 1900, Dr. Johansson changed the room numbers at Rosewood. Apparently there had been confusion about the numbering having two digit numbers on the first floor and three digit ones on the second and third floors. There was something about people confusing one of the offices outside the infirmary with room 101, a patient's room."

Zach stopped dead in his tracks. "So until July of 1900 rooms on the second floor had three digits that started with a 1?"

"Yeah. Why would that matter?"

"When did that guy, Wozniak, eat that jar in his room?"

"Before that, I believe. Yes, yes. 1897."

"Right!" Zach tried to keep his excited voice down. "So that means that room 217 today used to be called room 117 and room 317 is actually where Wozniak was kept."

"Okay, yes. Is this relevant information?"

Zach had forgotten that she hadn't been privy to the discovery that morning in room 217. "No, it's not vital, but could you keep this info between you and me just for today?"

"Sure." Her transmitted voice wasn't all that convincing.

"Thanks, I really appreciate your help with this. Keep up the good work."

Across the cell transmission Patrizia seemed to ignore the kudos. "Hey, Wendy wants you to call her in like ten minutes. Apparently she has something *vital* to tell you."

As soon as Zach popped into room 111, Ray told Turk they were taking a fifteen minute break and asked him to make a *Muses* coffee run.

"Didn't you just have coffee like an hour ago?"

"That," Ray said, "was a cappuccino. And I'm thirsty. Go."

Turk mumbled and complained, but eventually disappeared out the door and down the hallway. Zach punched his friend in the thick part of the arm.

"What's up, pal-o-mine?"

Ray didn't appear to be in a joking mood. His brow remained furrowed and he was plucking at his lower lip with his thumb and index finger. He turned back to the video monitor. "You need to see something."

"What's wrong?"

"I'm not sure, but I don't like it."

This wasn't Ray's normal video review demeanor. When a baffling issue arose, he'd typically be lighthearted and almost comical in his approach to solving the mystery. He pointed to the monitor. "This is from Camera 8."

That particular night-vision camera had been placed about fifteen feet away and across the hallway from room 217, the now infamous peach-smelling room. The angle had allowed the picture to show about twenty-five feet of darkened hallway with the room's doorway prominently displayed. As with the video of the basement and all other recordings, a clock kept the time in the upper right hand corner of the screen. Ray clicked the remote and the video began.

It ran between a minute and ninety seconds before Ray paused it. "You didn't notice either. Good."

"What did I miss?" Zach asked.

Ray raised his eyebrows. "I didn't see it the first time through either. Try it with the audio."

He handed Zach headphones, rewound the tape and replayed it. With the exception of a couple of faint clicking sounds that could have been anything from the building settling to plaster falling from the walls, he stared at a darkened hall and doorway with zero activity.

Ray paused it again.

"There's nothing there." Zach removed the headphones and handed them to Ray who was grinning broadly. "Look buddy, I know your sleep got interrupted a couple times last night, but still...you might be losing it."

Ray nodded and smirked. "You are correct, sir. There's nothing there."

"What the —"

His friend smiled and held his index finger up. "Keep watching." He sped the video to twice the normal speed for almost a minute peering at the clock. When it apparently was at the right spot, he clicked the remote to resume normal play.

"See that?" Ray pointed to a small white orb that moved on the left side of the screen.

Zach examined the object as it flickered a bit in the green night-vision light. "Ray, that's a fucking moth!"

"I know," he said. "Well, it's a moth. It's not a fucking moth because it would take two of them to mate, but it's a bee-u-tee-full moth!"

Best friend or not, Zach didn't have time for games. "Soldier, what is your major malfunction?"

Ray beamed as though he had anticipated Zach's doubt. "Watch," he said confidently. "Watch the moth."

Zach attuned to its movements the way he would follow the moving light during an eye doctor's glaucoma test. It flew up toward the ceiling and then darted back down. It disappeared to the left of the screen for just a second, and then whizzed onscreen and upward. Just as it was about to disappear from the camera's view, the moth froze in midair.

"Ray!" Zach glared at him and then realized that his friend had *not* paused the video. "I don't get it. The tape froze? What—"

Ray pointed to the stopped onscreen clock as he mumbled. "One thousand three, one thousand four, one thousand five, one thousand six and…action!"

The picture continued to display the green tinged hallway. The moth had disappeared.

"The recordings paused. Could it have been a system technical glitch?"

"That's what I wondered at first," Ray said. "If other cameras stopped, they would have been the ones on the same floor right? But no. I cross checked the time with cameras 9 and 10. They didn't freeze."

The previous night's warning from his uncle came back to Zach. *Some evidence is tainted.*

"Someone or something paused this particular recording."

"I'd guess 'someone.' 'Something' sounds a bit too dramatic there psychology boy." Ray rewound the video and handed Zach the headphones again. "Now watch it again with the sound."

As the moth disappeared from to the left of view there were two distinct clicks, similar to the ones he'd heard while listening to the earlier footage. They sounded mechanical.

"It's a signal," Zach said. He removed the headphones.

"A signal to pause the tape just a few seconds…"

"…while someone slips past the camera and into the room." Zach completed his friend's thought.

"I'll rewind and show you the first segment you watched," Ray said. "You'll see that about one second after those clicks, the tape pauses just like this for about six seconds!"

"That's okay, buddy. I trust you." Zach smiled widely at him. "In fact, if you weren't so ugly, I'd kiss you."

"Yeah, and if you weren't such a big wig TV star, I'd break your nose just for thinking about it!"

They both laughed, but the gravity of the discovery was hitting Zach hard.

"Have you watched the tape from Camera 6 yet?"

"Yeah. With all my spare time."

"Seriously," Zach said. "Forward to about ten minutes earlier than the first pause of Camera 8. If someone snuck up behind this camera, they must have come from the stairway outside the infirmary."

Ray nodded. "And they'll either be on that video or, more likely—"

"That tape will be paused in the same way."

Ray scribbled something in his notebook. Zach made a mental note of the time that the video was paused. He remembered Angel, Pierre and Matthew huddled together. As he'd done thousands of times playing poker, he envisioned their faces at that moment, froze them like the video had done on the moth. Zach saw their faces clearly. Pierre—embarrassed. Matthew—confident. Angel—afraid.

"So you've got two people involved working as a team," Ray mused aloud. "And one of them is certainly a tech guy."

"But who?" Zach asked.

As though on cue, Pierre's accented voice echoed down the hall. His words were unintelligible. The smell of coffee drifted in and there was rustling in the hallway.

"I heard that. 'But who' did what?" Turk asked, rushing in with their drinks.

"You're back in a hurry," Ray said. "Why the short break?"

"I already made pals with the kid at Muses, so he gives me jiffy service." Turk looked from Zach to Ray. "Besides, I didn't want to miss anything."

Ray pulled a cup from the carrying tray and handed it to Zach. They made and maintained direct eye contact. At that moment, Zach knew he and his best friend were sharing the exact same thought.

Trust no one.

Chapter Twenty-Four

As Zach walked the long hallway toward the Rosewood lobby, his phone buzzed notice of an incoming call. He did a double take at the identification. He hadn't yet changed "Mother & Father," to just "Dad."

He flicked his cell open. "Hello."

"Za-ach, it's your da-ad." Despite being a simple tradesman, the way his father pronounced Zach's name sounded like a disappointed English actor performing Shakespeare.

"I know who it is, Dad. Have you ever heard of caller ID?"

"Ah," he said, "I don't believe in that stuff."

"The 1970s called, they want your rotary phone back."

"Uh huh. Okay. So did I wake you up?"

"No, I've been up for a while. I'm working on a case."

"Oh." Dad sounded confused. Zach knew his father loved him, but he wasn't sure his dad understood anything he'd shared with him about his TV show. Dad wasn't at all interested in the paranormal. "So, did you talk to Ray about the deck?"

"Yes, Daddy Dearest. We'll be out there this weekend for sure."

"Okay. Because you know these little buggers are—"

"I know. I know," Zach said, even though he had no idea what his father was about to say.

"Okay. So do you have a few minutes to talk?" Dad asked.

Zach's dad relished long phone conversations the way the pope approved of fornication. Not at all.

"I'm working a case, Dad. Is there something you need to talk about?"

"Oh, yeah, that's right," he said with a sigh. "Well hey, I figured I should let you know before you got here that...well, I had to take your mom's rose trellises down."

"You did?"

"Yeah, they were completely infested and the termite guy said that the queen and the colony are probably out there in the garden. Whatever that means."

Gary Kalusky was neither a vengeful man, nor one who believed in symbolic gestures. If he had removed his dead wife's rose trellises, it had been for practical reasons. Zach was glad though that his dad had given him a chance to mentally prepare—to anticipate seeing the remnants of his mother's favorite pastime demolished.

"Okay, thanks for letting me know." Zach had arrived at the command center in the lobby and needed to speak with Angel. "Hey, I've got to get something taken care of. I'll call you tomorrow to confirm everything."

"Okay, all right. b-bye."

"Love you, bye."

"Your boyfriend?" Angel snickered.

"Funny." Zach knew what he needed to do, but the phone call had thrown him off kilter. "Angel, what was the Tech Schedule for last night?"

Angel became serious. "Is there a problem, boss?"

"Don't give me that. I asked you a question. I put you in charge and I need to know who was working here when."

Angel saluted and then chuckled, but his casual demeanor seemed false—forced. "Matthew worked the first shift. Pierre was scheduled to take over after 'Spirit Hour' or whatever you guys called it last night. I was to relieve him around 6 AM."

"And that's how things shook out?"

"Pretty much, *si*." Angel was one of the worst liars in the world. He not only couldn't hide his nervousness, he perspired rapidly when stretching the truth.

"Good," Zach said. "That's what I thought."

"Is there a problem?"

"Nothing that I can't handle."

Zach exited Rosewood. The fresh air helped clear his head. Rebecca's comment the previous day about something evil roaming the halls had stuck with him. Zach wasn't sure about an evil presence, but there was something about Rosewood.

Something beyond the stale air and dusty floors that didn't quite sit right. Long periods of time spent inside the asylum made him feel out of focus, not centered, watched. The feeling of being observed, of constantly being evaluated was, perhaps the most uncomfortable, and he couldn't seem to shake it.

Not while he was inside Rosewood.

Zach flipped open his cell phone and called Wendy.

"Just a sec," she said. Her hushed tone indicated she was in a library or somewhere she couldn't talk.

Echoed sounds came through the earpiece, indicating that Wendy had reached an outer hallway of some kind.

"Hey, before I forget," Zach said, "Could you research a name for me today?"

Even over the phone line, Wendy's sigh conveyed frustration that bordered on contempt. He usually used the proverbial stick with Wendy, but occasionally the use of a carrot was in order.

"Please?" Zach made his voice as sweet as he could. "This lead has the potential to blow the case wide open..."

"What is it?"

"Find out everything you can about a John Paramour. Date of birth, April 14, 1865."

"Are you serious?"

"Yes. And *yes* I know why that date is significant."

Her end of the line was silent a moment, but he could almost hear her mind racing. "That name seems familiar," she said finally. "I can't put my finger on where I know it from though. She sighed again, but it contained less angst. Then, she grunted. "Okay, I'll find out who he was."

"Thank you, Wendybird. Hey, Patrizia told me you had something to tell me?" he asked.

"Yes. Remember in my opening pitch how I mentioned that suicides had increased at Rosewood?"

"Sure."

"Well, I hadn't known the extent of it. Apparently, between July of 1899 and Rosewood's closure in 1903, there were *thirty seven* of them."

It sounded like a lot, but Zach didn't have anything to compare that number to. "Do you have the number prior to —"

"Of course I do. Between 1892, when it opened, and July of 1899—a span twice that of the other timeframe, there were only *eleven* suicides. Zach, that's like a six hundred percent increase."

"Hey Zach, can I talk to you a minute?" Shelly asked. She approached him from the area where the tents had been set up.

"Yeah, sure. What's up?"

Her furrowed brow and frown told Zach that she was upset with something. Oh no, he thought, here it comes. Due to the inclusion of the Demon Hunters, Shelly, his most trusted investigator, had been pushed into the background of this case. He'd paired her with Patrizia, the least-experienced partner possible, and he expected she was upset about it.

"I found something," she said. "I found something very...odd."

"What? Where?"

"In the administration building. It would be easier to show you. C'mon." She turned back in that direction.

They trekked across the weed-strewn lawn to the far southeastern end of the property. Zach should have known better than to doubt Shelly's team-first attitude. She was a terrific investigator—able to intuitively know where to focus her efforts.

"I'll be honest," she said, as they approached the outskirt building, "it looks like someone might be trying to falsify evidence."

Might be, Zach thought. Shelly didn't know the half of it. "Show me," he said.

She led him into the building and through to one of the small rooms that used to be an office. The prior night, all the teams had experienced dramatic EMF fluctuations in the room. Shelly stood in the center, not pointing anything out. "I think it's more obvious now," she said. "I may have slightly discolored it while investigating it. Or maybe it just seems more visible because I know it's there."

Vacant and dusty, Zach didn't notice anything unusual. The walls were eggshell. Perhaps they had once been white and yellowed over the years, but Zach suspected based on the continuity of color that they'd always been—he saw it. In the far corner of the room, just above the baseboard, a square the size of a cocktail napkin was slightly discolored from the rest of the wall. Zach approached it and knelt down.

"Yep, you found it." Shelly stood behind him.

"What is it?" Zach lightly tapped the area with his finger. "It's sticky."

"Yes. Something was taped up there and recently too, otherwise the adhesive would have attracted more dust."

Zach peered closer. All around the outside of the cubed area in question, tiny brush strokes blended with the wall's color. It even appeared that a darker layer had been applied over it to appear dirty. "Someone painted whatever it was to match the wall so that it wouldn't be detected."

"Look closely at the wall," Shelly said. "In the center of where the patch was, there's an imprint."

She was right. Something the size of a matchbook had been pressed into the wall and had left behind very small scratches.

"It was probably something metal." Zach touched it with his fingertip. That spot wasn't sticky. "A transponder of some sorts? A bug?"

"With all the crazy EMF activity in here last night, I wouldn't be surprised if it was something designed specifically to give us false readings." Shelly held up her EMF meter and pointed it throughout the room. I've gotten no spikes at all since we've been here. Last night this room was nuts with EMF fluctuations."

"I need you to keep completely quiet about this, Shelly. Can you do that for me?"

She nodded.

"Seriously," Zach said, "No one can know."

"Okay. But do you know who's responsible?"

Zach didn't know for certain, but he was getting a pretty good idea.

As Zach approached the asylum, Matthew stood outside on the Rosewood driveway. It was quickly approaching noon, but the overcast wasn't showing signs of dissipating. A cold wind from the north had kept it below sixty degrees all morning, and they'd be lucky to keep the temperatures in the fifties until nightfall. The air contained the autumn scent of decaying leaves.

"Glorious day, huh boss?" Matthew said.

"I need to speak with you," Zach said, softly.

Matthew's grin disappeared. "What's up?"

Zach glanced back at the asylum and ventured down the drive toward Rosewood's main gate. Matthew obviously knew to trail along. Once they were safely out of earshot, Zach spoke.

"There's no easy way to say this. Angel has betrayed us."

Matthew almost stumbled. "What? Oh my God."

"I know," Zach said. "It came as a shock to me, too."

"What do we do? I mean, what has he done?"

Zach's nose tingled from the cold, but he refused to rub it. "I need you to keep an eye on him. I need you to tell me if you see or have seen anything suspicious."

Matthew adjusted the brim of his baseball cap. "Okay. I will. I'm not sure I know what to look for though."

"Keep on the lookout of anything suspicious with the Demon Hunters. Pierre, Bryce, even Rico."

"Sure. Did they find something suspicious with the video review?"

"No. Not exactly," Zach lied. "I know he's hiding something from me, lying to me."

"Okay, so there is something you should know." Matthew rubbed his chin. "But you have to promise not to let on that I told you."

Zach knew in circumstances like this it was wiser to say nothing. He nodded.

"Pierre drank too much last night and passed out. When I went to wake him for his shift, he was just flat out. So I worked a bit longer. Maybe another hour or so and then was ready to pass out myself."

"That's late. You musta been wiped. What time was it?"

"I didn't look at my watch, but I think it was about 4:30. I figured that Angel had already gotten some sleep. Why not let him take over? I figured he would wake Pierre when he needed to."

"Angel's the lead. You should have woken him up as soon as you couldn't wake Pierre."

"I know, but I didn't want anyone to get in trouble, and I was still pretty amped from Spirit Hour."

"That's understandable," Zach said. "So what happened with Angel and Pierre this morning?"

"I dunno. I just know when I woke up, Angel was still on duty...I suppose he could have gotten Pierre up at some point, but I doubt it based on how Pierre looked this morning."

"Agreed. Matthew, I need you to keep this strictly between you and me. I'll let you know the next move and I wouldn't be surprised that if this time next week, you're the Tech Lead of XPI."

Matthew's face brightened and he grinned. "Yes, sir! Although, I mean, it would come under rather awkward circumstances."

"You let me worry about that."

As though Zach didn't already have enough to worry about, he began feeling massive pangs of guilt. During the course of that conversation, he had not been entirely truthful.

Chapter Twenty-Five

"Bless me father, for I have sinned," Zach said, once the confessional's partition opened. "It's been three days since my last confession."

"Zachary?"

"Yes, Father."

"Why are you in *here*, boy?"

"There are still a few people waiting. I figured I'd take care of business the old fashioned way and then we could talk face-to-face after you're done working."

"I'm never done working, son." Monsignor Macginty chuckled. "Go ahead with your confession."

Zach admitted to having had angry thoughts about people throughout the week, especially Bryce Finman. He shared minor infractions such as laziness for not having attended an early morning class, to showing subtle disrespect to Mr. Winkler and others. Lastly, he confessed to telling a major lie to a member of his team.

"And why'd you do that, son?"

"It was about someone else on the show—a well-intentioned type of ruse. It's kind of hard to explain—it may all be a bit too self serving."

"Who was this canard about now, Zachary?"

"My Technical Lead, Angel."

Behind the partition, Macginty sighed. "So you lied about an Angel, son?"

Zach hadn't really thought about it that way. Pondering it on his knees in the dark, he realized it was pretty damn ironic.

"Yes, Father. At least I think so. It's a rather complicated situation, actually."

"I see." Macginty's calm voice seemed neither detached nor judgmental. "Okay son, I want ya'ta say six 'Hail Marys' and one 'Our Father' out there."

"Yes, Father."

"And Zach...you're going'ta have 'ta make things right with this Angel fella. You're going'ta need to be honest with him."

"I understand, Father."

"And Zach? Would 'ya please stop callin' me 'Father?' I'm a *Monsignor*. I work for a living."

It was one of their running jokes.

"Of course, Father."

Macginty mumbled a series of sacramental words that ended in "go and sin no more," and closed the partition. Zach exited the confessional, knelt in a pew near the statue of the Virgin Mary and said his prayers.

For Zach, absolution was Catholicism's single coolest feature. Provided he completed his penance as instructed by the priest, the sin was no more. It wasn't like an erasure in a ledger; it was as if the mistake had never taken place. Still, setting things right with Angel was likely going to be awkward, and Zach still wasn't one-hundred percent sure his suspicions were correct.

After reciting half a dozen Hail Marys, Zach was breezing most of the way through the Lord's Prayer when the ambient smell of candles was replaced by the scent of cheap deodorant and even cheaper aftershave. Macginty had sidled up on Zach's left.

Zach completed the prayer aloud. "And lead us not into temptation, but deliver us from evil."

"For Thine is the Kingdom, the Power, and the Glory ferever'n ever," Macginty added, pulling Zach into a bear hug.

Approaching seventy-years old, Macginty kept his white hair in a short crew cut. He had not, as long as his photographs were to be trusted, lost an ounce of muscle since he was in his thirties. He'd been an army chaplain in Vietnam. Prior to that, as long as a priest's word was to be trusted, he'd been a local boxing celebrity of sorts—in the early 1960s he'd lost the bout, but had gone the distance with Sugar Ray Robinson. Macginty claimed the judges "robbed" him of the victory, but if they had not, he might have gone onto a professional fighting career and missed his calling as a priest. It had been Monsignor Macginty who first encouraged one young Ray Ross to put on gloves and climb into the ring. When Ray threatened to take on the nickname, "Sugar Ray," Macginty had anointed him "The Railroad." And that was that.

"Can I trouble you to make me some holy water, Father?" Zach asked, holding up a couple of already full water bottles.

"I told 'ya. Holy water is holy water, is holy water. Help yourself whenever you need'ta, son."

"I know, father, but it's hard to get it out of baptismal and besides, I think it works better when you bless it specifically for me."

"Aren't you a charmer?" Macginty said. "C'mon. Let's us go up'ta the altar."

From the elevated position, Saint Francis of Assisi brought back a slew of memories for Zach. He'd been an altar boy for a number of years, which had afforded him an excuse to spend an inordinate amount of time with Macginty. It was in the sacristy of this church that Zach had finally gained control of his special talent.

Macginty stood at the altar, passed his hand over the water bottles and blessed them.

"I don't like this particular case yer workin' on, son."

"But I haven't told you anything about it."

"I know. Imagine how I'd feel about it if 'ya did?" Macginty handed him the water bottles. "You know I don't like lies, Zachary, and if yer speakin' untruths, then that means others must be doin' the same."

It wasn't anywhere near as dramatic as Sashza's proclamation on the quad, but it was just as spot-on accurate.

"The case is baffling, Father. There are so many divergent puzzle pieces, and I don't know who I can trust."

"Ya trust yourself well enough though don'tcha, son?"

Zach shrugged. "I'm thinking of inducing an episode tonight. I need to understand what's going on there."

Monsignor Macginty crossed his arms across his broad chest. He never scolded Zach for using his powers to solve paranormal cases, but just like a concerned parent, he usually expressed reservations. He had helped Zach gain control over his affliction, but it had taken Zach years to tell the priest about the voice, the visions and the spirit living inside him. Upon finding out, Macginty suggested excising it. Zach protested that his godfather's spirit helped him with his affliction. The monsignor cajoled, debated and lectured, but he never threatened or judged.

And Macginty had always made it clear that he'd never given up hope of such an outcome.

"Ya think that will solve it, then? Ya suppose a century of Rosewood's mysteries'll give themselves up ta'ya?"

Stunned, Zach couldn't answer but attempted a question of his own. "Ha-how'did you..."

It's my job'ta know, son." He walked to the tabernacle and pulled out a vial of holy anointing oil. "Besides, it was all over the TV. *Good Morning Chi-Town* did a story about a tree burnin' down there last night."

"Are you shi—" He caught himself. "Are you serious?"

"I am serious, boy. I make it'a point not to shite while standin' at this altar."

"What did they....did they say if..."

"It's TV, son. They didn't say nothin'. Now c'mere. C'mon. Before I change my mind." He motioned Zach closer. "Bow yer head."

Zach did.

"Most holy God, bless this oil and he who wears it. May it strengthen, consecrate and preserve so that he may resist contagion with the sins of the world and may it fill him with grace so that he may be Your dear disciple and faithful witness now and forever. Amen."

"Amen," Zach repeated. "Oh, Father, what about Ray? He's working on the case, too."

"Ugh," Macginty sighed. "That lug'll be fine. Here's hoping that somethin' happens'ta force him away from that den of sin he's workin'in."

"You know about that?"

Macginty grinned. "It's my job'ta know, son. Now off with ya before I decide'ta put you ta work around here."

Zach flipped open his cell phone. He had turned it to silent mode before entering Saint Francis. There were two missed call notifications from Rebecca and three text messages—one from her, one from Ray and one from Sara as well.

Ray: Camera 6 as u thought. Was an 8 sec pause b4 & 6 sec one after cam 8.

Rebecca: Radkey said no, but call me asap for amazing news!
Sara: G'Mrning Chi-Twn was here. Others likely to follow.

Zach skipped down the concrete steps of Saint Francis and hit the "call back" button.

Rebecca didn't even answer with a hello. "She said I could come over tonight! I can bring my own camera and someone to film it and set up equipment."

"Radkey agreed? I thought you said that she said 'no.'"

Rebecca let loose an uncharacteristic giggle. "I'm way ahead of myself," she panted. "I did my best to convince her, but she just wouldn't have any part of us coming over."

Zach had gotten to his car and stopped dead in his tracks. "I thought you just said she said—"

"Wait, listen," Rebecca transmitted. "Radkey said 'no.' I got really weird vibes from her. Didn't she come across to you as creepy?"

Zach thought about the elderly lady. He recalled that she had vaguely resembled Evelyn, and that their mannerisms were similar. But that was it.

"Creepy? No."

"Okay, well anyway, I left Mrs. Radkey's and just before I got into my car, the other woman stopped me. Mrs. Foster? I guess she goes by Ginny. She told me you'd be shocked."

Zach couldn't believe Joey's mom had pulled a one-hundred and eighty degree turnaround. "Shocked doesn't begin to cover it..."

"She said to tell you sorry for being such a biotch yesterday. She said after you left, she researched who we were and felt bad. Then, last night, I guess she had a pretty traumatic experience."

"What happened?"

"She wouldn't say. Well, I didn't press her for it because I didn't have a camera. I told her we'd talk tonight. I didn't want her changing her mind on me, so I made her promise I could come with one person to operate a mini digital camera. Wanna hear the funniest part?"

"Shoot."

"It was *Good Morning Chi-Town* that got us the gig?"

"Get out."

"Well, in a roundabout way, I guess. Ginny said that things got so bad last night that she prayed for the first time in years. She said she prayed for a sign. Then, the first thing she did this morning was flick on the TV and—"

"And there we were, both across the street and on TV."

"Stranger things have happened," Rebecca said. "Anyway, who should I bring over to help me?"

Without hesitation the name spilled from Zach's lips. "Angel."

"Okay. Really?"

"Yes. Please tell him I said so, and that I'll be back there in about an hour to speak with him about it."

"Okay!" she said. "I've got a really strong feeling something good is going to come of this."

"Speaking of something good," Zach said into the phone, "before you go tonight, I'm looking forward to your presentation on Soul Snatchers."

There was a moment of static.

"You sure know how to put a damper on a girl's good news."

"Sorry but—"

"I know. I know. And I'm already collecting information."

"Cool."

"And Zach, if this is the case of a Soul Snatcher, we may be encountering something more powerful than anything we've ever dealt with."

Chapter Twenty-Six

Need 2 talk 2 u offsite. Meet @ muses @ 1?

Zach had gotten the text message from Angel just minutes after hanging up with Rebecca.

Young people packed *Muses Coffee House*. There wasn't an empty table. Chicago State University was just a mile or so up the road, and south Pullman was the trendiest area within a quick driving distance.

Zach hoped to also catch Evelyn there early, but as neither she nor Angel were anywhere to be seen, he placed an order and waited out on the deserted patio that overlooked Rosewood's backside. He'd just taken the first sip of his delicious beverage when Angel rambled up.

"Yeah, that's one of the reasons I wanted to meet with you offsite. To warn you and accompany you back through the 'crowd.'" Angel made quote signs in the air using his fingers. "Looks like maybe some of our fans have made their way here for coffee."

Zach motioned towards the door with his cup. He led them outside and around the corner to the deserted patio that overlooked Rosewood's backside. Before Zach could speak, Angel tore into him.

"All due respect, Zach, why am I being cast aside on this investigation? I can understand your placating Matthew with more airtime last night, but tonight I'm banished from my own control center to cover some side project? What gives, *mi hijo?*"

Zach focused all of his attention on Angel's eyes. Childhood advice from Monsignor Macginty ran through his head: First, make sure you're right, son, and then go full flurry ahead.

"What gives?" Zach repeated. "What gives is that there is a traitor on my show. *My* show! The show I put blood and sweat and tears into. The show my PhD studies depend on. A traitor. Someone tampering with equipment and planting false evidence!"

Zach had managed the entire speech without smelling a warning of *Sailor Black*. Angel's mouth opened and clicked closed. The glossy sheen of his eyes resembled that of billiard balls.

"And I think," Zach continued, "you know who the traitor is."

Angel's mouth agape, he managed only to waggle his head in denial. That's when Zach hit him with the zinger. "I told Matthew it was you."

"What? No way...boss, it's not—"

"I know it's not you," Zach said. "It's him."

"Who? Matthew? No, it can't be."

"Why not? You saw how drunk Pierre was last night. Do you think he was in any kind of condition to plan or execute a scheme to falsify evidence?"

Angel's lips pursed. He put his hand on his thick neck. He wiped from the base of his throat up over his pock-scarred face to his forehead. "Could that have been an act?"

"An act? Why would you say that?"

Angel began to perspire. Considering the temperature was only about sixty degrees, either he was about to lie or admit to one. "Boss, remember how I told you I came on at 6 AM?"

"I do."

"That's not exactly how it happened."

"*Exactly* how did it happen, Angel?"

"Pierre passed out. Matthew couldn't wake him when it was Pierre's turn to stand guard, so Matthew covered most of his shift."

Zach knew the important question. What time had Matthew passed the torch? Instead, Zach chose to wait and dig for more information first. "Why did Matthew cover for Pierre?"

Angel shrugged. "Those two had seemed to make their peace last night."

Zach considered it. Was it possible that Matthew had been ordered to mend the fences? Or were they working together and their argument had merely been a diversionary tactic? "So Matthew woke you to take over."

"Yes. He told me that he'd covered Pierre's shift as long as he could and was falling asleep. This morning, the three of us talked and agreed to not say anything about Pierre's passing out."

"Why?"

"Pierre claimed that he'd been drugged."

Zach hadn't expected that. "Drugged?"

"Yes. He said that he drinks a lot. He admitted that he *always* drinks a lot and that last night he drank no more than normal."

"Did he smoke any pot?"

"Not that I know of."

"So why did he suspect he was drugged?"

"He said he never passes out after consuming that amount and that in the middle of the night he woke up and puked violently a few times."

Zach was incredulous. "So he drinks a lot, passes out and then throws up. This is his rationale for claiming he was drugged?"

"No."

"What then?"

"He had a headache. He claims that he's one of those people who never has them...or had them. He said, and I believe him, that this morning was the first headache of his life."

Even if Zach believed that, something wasn't ringing true. "So let's just say that he was drugged. Wouldn't that give you more reason to report it rather than less?"

Angel frowned. "I wanted to tell you. I almost did," he said. His face darkened as though for the first time realizing he'd been manipulated. "Both Pierre and Matthew convinced me that it would be an unnecessary distraction to the investigation. So..."

"So you covered it up."

Angel's head hung so low that it looked like he expected Zach to lop it off with a sword.

"All will be forgiven," Zach said, "if you answer the God's honest truth to this question."

Angel looked up, his face brightening.

Zach glared deeply into his eyes—so deeply that after a moment of intense focus, a whiff of *Sailor Black* filled his nostrils. "What time?"

"Huh?"

"What *time* did Matthew wake you?"

"Just before 5 AM." Angel's voice was unwavering and there wasn't a drop of sweat anywhere on his broad forehead.

"I need you to be more specific."

"I looked at my phone once I was fully awake," Angel said. "It was 4:48."

"Are you sure?"

"Yes. I was confused as to why Matthew was waking me and pissed it was so early."

Zach stared at Rosewood's backside. The time of the pause on Camera 8 had been at 4:37 AM. Seven minutes after Matthew claimed to have woken Angel and twelve minutes before Angel claimed Matthew had woken him. One was lying. If Angel was to be believed, Matthew was a traitor. If Zach took Matthew's story as gospel, no pun intended, Angel was guilty. Zach stared deep into Angel's eyes reading him for any sign of doubt or dishonesty. There was none.

"I need to tell you something else important, boss," Angel said. "This I wasn't hiding from you. I just found out this morning and was waiting for the right time to share it."

"Okay."

"The Demon Hunters have known about this gig for a lot longer than we have."

"How do you know that?"

"Pierre slipped up this morning. It's one of the reasons I believed the other parts of his story."

Zach wasn't following, and his facial expression must have shown it.

"While Pierre was lamenting his missed chance to man the control center last night, he made the comment that 'he'd been looking forward to Demon Hour at Rosewood for a week.'"

It took a moment for the implication to sink in. Then, Zach remembered Bryce mentioning taking a plane from California. Of course. *Demon Hunters* had known about this investigation for longer than just a couple of days.

"He said it so casually, so off-handedly," Angel continued. "I don't think Matthew even picked up on it, but I did. How could he have been looking forward to it for a week if —"

"If Sci-D just got permission for the investigation a few days ago."

"Right." Angel ran his hand through his hair. "So boss? With all this going on, wouldn't it make sense to keep me at the control center tonight?"

Zach smiled. "Haven't you ever heard the axiom, 'Keep your friends close and your enemies closer'?"

Angel nodded. He still wasn't exuding enthusiasm over his assignment. "Last thing. What's on your forehead, boss?"

Zach had almost forgotten about the oil. "Don't worry about it," Zach said to Angel. "It's just something that helps me focus."

Maybe it was the anointing oil or maybe mere intuition, but Zach knew with certainty that Angel was innocent. He was just as certain that Matthew was guilty.

Chapter Twenty-Seven

Angel had walked over from Rosewood, so he rode back with Zach. Once Zach spied the mini-crowd that congregated around the main entrance, he was grateful for the company. He pulled up and honked at the security guard who took his sweet time unlocking and opening the gate.

With the commotion outside, Zach almost didn't hear his cell buzz. It was Wendy.

He answered. "I could really use some good news."

"Well hello to you too," she said. "Whatcha doin'?"

"Angel and I are trying to get back into Rosewood. Apparently the fact that we're investigating it was on TV today."

The cell transmission couldn't hide her excitement. "I know, right? *Good Morning Chi-Town!*"

"Yep. Yep. So, what do you have for me?"

"Are you someplace you can focus?"

He was pulling up the Rosewood driveway. Sara stood near the *XPI* van and was already glowering at him, likely for having taken too long to get the holy water.

"Of course not. But go ahead anyway."

"Okay, well our historical research revealed something rather...well, rather disgusting."

"Great."

"Remember how Rebecca suggested during the tour that suicides might have been buried in unmarked graves on the Rosewood grounds?"

"They were?"

"Not only that. Zach, the burials were done on the site of the old female quarters."

Zach was exiting the car when the news hit him. He felt ill. Suicide corpses buried under the homes—under *Joey's* home?

Angel headed towards the Rosewood lobby command center. Zach put his phone against his thigh to muffle the sound. "Angel, wait. Hold up a second."

"Sure, boss."

He apparently hadn't muffled it enough.

"Zach," Wendy said, once he'd put the phone back to his ear. "Tell Angel I said hello. Please."

When Zach did so, Angel's face glowed. Why Wendy liked to torment him so, Zach would never understand.

"Anyway, back to the burials..."

"All right," she said. "Dr. Johansson's notes were pretty specific regarding those. Patrizia and I are going through all of the patient records to find out how many were buried back there, but the number is certainly in the dozens."

Playing a hunch, Zach blurted out the question before it fully made sense in his mind. "Are you counting them forwards or backwards?"

"Huh? What do you mean?"

"I mean go through the records backwards. From the closing of Rosewood until the suicide."

She sighed. "Okay, we can do that."

"Did you find out the name of the woman found in the basement?"

"Oh sure, in our spare time."

"Wendy..."

"Dr. Johansson was rather peculiar about that information. I've looked through several hospital records, but the only reference he made were the initials, P.M.E."

"It would really help to have a first name in order to try and communicate with her tonight. 'P' doesn't help much. Could it be Paula? Pamela? Patricia?"

"Penelope, Petunia, Ptolemy..."

"Wendy."

"I know. I know. It's just you've got us going in so many different directions, Zach. We're trying to read a thousand pages of a nineteenth century doctor's scribbled notes."

"I know," he said. He repeated it attempting to convey more empathy. "I know. Your work is going to be greatly rewarded."

"I hope soooo..."

"So, is there anything else?"

"Oh, yeah! I almost forgot...again. That name you mentioned to me that sounded familiar? Paramour?"

"Yes, John Paramour," Zach confirmed.

Wendy spoke, but her transmitted words didn't even register in his brain when she uttered them. It was as though she'd said something in a foreign language.

"Could you repeat that?" Zach asked. Evelyn's chilling biography of John Paramour had led Zach to suspect that he had been, at minimum, the serial arsonist, if not also the man who set himself on fire months after the female quarters burned to the ground.

This time when Wendy said it, she slowly enunciated each word. *"John Paramour was the Pullman Chief of Police."*

"You okay, boss? Angel asked.

Zach hung up with Wendy and needed a moment to collect his thoughts. It felt as if all the blood had drained from his head. He surveyed the Rosewood grounds. There were no shadows, but the gray sky and cool temperature led to a feeling of gloom. It appeared the sun wouldn't be breaking through the overcast. Dusk would come early. Even in this light, he could hardly see beyond the first row of trees at the far end of the property. Once the sun set and the sky darkened, it would provide the perfect cover for him to induce an episode and call on his visions. It was the least likely spot on Rosewood's property where he could be interrupted or discovered. As though on cue, the scent of *Sailor Black* invaded his nostrils.

Now you're onto something, godson.

"Boss?" Angel's voice contained concern.

"I'm okay," Zach said. "Listen. That 'side project,' as you call it, with Rebecca...it's just taken on much more importance. I'm going to need you to be very watchful of her and the entire situation."

"Why? What's going on?"

"Nothing to worry about. Just be mindful and pull the plug over there if things get out of hand." The more Zach talked about it, the more he wished he could send more people to Joey and Ginny Foster's with them, but a request like that might cause her to cancel the investigation entirely. "And Angel, before you leave?"

"Yes."

"Pull some of the hallway cameras and put them in and around room 317. Also, let's get a couple more cameras and recording equipment in the basement."

"Sure. Hey..." Angel lifted an index finger. "What about if I put some of those 'Whistling EMF-EVPs around?"

Angel had developed a revolutionary gadget that was comprised of a combination of ghost-hunting devices typically used independent of each other. They'd tested it with decent results on their season-ending episode. The "Whistling EMF-EVP" operated exactly as named. It entailed using a standard EMF meter which was connected to a device that emitted a variable-pitched siren, or whistle, depending on how quickly and how high the EMF meter spiked. The simple genius of Angel's idea was to then connect an EVP to the device set to VOX mode. This would start and stop it when there was a noise. Thus, the recording device only turned on at the sound of the siren and when paranormal activity was most likely to be occurring. Additionally, the noise could alert the team of the EMF spike even if they were in another room.

"Good call!" Zach said. "How many did you make?"

"I've got three standard ones and four that I've modified slightly."

"Modified how?"

"Basically, one of the things I've played with since we last used them, was to insert a tiny vocal chip to activate in conjunction with the siren mechanism, so that when — "

"In English, please," Zach said.

Angel smirked and wagged his head from side to side. "Okay, okay. The modified ones both whistle and emit random questions. You know how you can squeeze certain dolls or stuffed animals and they 'say' something?"

"Sure."

"These lil babies I made are rigged to ask questions like: 'Who are you?' 'What do you want?' 'Who goes there?' stuff like that."

"That's awesome. So not only will we know where the EMF activity is, and record any EVP activity in the area, but the device will ask questions *we'd ask* if we were in the area!"

Angel shrugged, grinned and seemed to be attempting to squelch a blush.

Zach continued. "Okay, put a couple of them in the basement—one on the staircase going down there. Put one in the hallway outside of room 111 and put one in room 317."

"What's with room 317 all of a sudden?"

"Don't worry about it, *mi hijo*." Zach slapped him in the arm. "But move quick. Rebecca's giving an important presentation before you two leave."

Chapter Twenty-Eight

"Soul Snatchers," Rebecca began, "are a rare and rather insidious paranormal breed."

Unlike Wendy, Rebecca had never mastered the art of public presentation without reading from a script. She continually looked from the camera to the notes she clutched with both hands and back to the camera. *XPI* and Demon Hunters intermingled on the Rosewood front lawn. As Zach gazed out at their faces, he couldn't help but equate it to a police lineup. He smiled at Matthew and quickly looked away, fearful that his suspicion might be betrayed in his eyes.

"A Soul Snatcher is purported to be an entity of power and extreme evil." Rebecca appeared to have lost her place in her notes and froze.

"Take your time," Sara called out.

In contrast to her demeanor with Wendy, Sara either remained silent or gently encouraged Rebecca during her speeches. Later, all Sara's skills as an editing genius would be needed to splice Rebecca's presentation into a TV-ready monologue. Zach wondered if either Sara or Rebecca could be the other person tampering with evidence. Sara had acted strangely on this case, but he rejected any thoughts of her sabotaging their results. As for Rebecca, he couldn't imagine either a motive or an opportunity for betrayal.

Rebecca coughed. Standing next to her, Zach sensed her trembling. He put his hand on her back and gave it a quick rub. She flashed him a weak smile.

"Soul Snatchers often start as misguided people who've lived ugly and dysfunctional lives. Individuals whose existence is characterized as egotistical and self-serving. After death, they remain attached to our realm and use their powers to sway the will of living people in order to gain their souls. It seems that a Soul Snatcher's skill in manipulating others is where his true power lies. They supposedly persuade the innocent and or sick to do their bidding with promised lies."

To his left, Bryce and Rico stood side by side. Both appeared to be focused intently on Rebecca's presentation and were overlooking her herky-jerky style. Had one of them made promises to Matthew to manipulate him to do their bidding? Certainly if Bryce had been in the know about the investigation for a week, he would have had ample opportunity to try and taint the results. And his motive? Who knew what motivated him? He seemed the type that would put on a pay-per-view Ultimate Fighting bout against his mother if it would promise big ratings.

Rebecca's speech continued. "Any willing or manipulated victim can offer their souls to a Soul Snatcher and he will collect them. As a Soul Snatcher collects, or snatches souls, he gains in power. As he gains in power, he can use his powers to do many things, such as manifest himself in the world of the living or infiltrate people's subconscious."

Not far from Rico's hip, as was now usual, Turk appeared more interested in the incoming messages on his cell phone than in Rebecca's presentation. At least he'd turned it to silent mode. Zach wondered about Turk's "buddy buddy" relationship with Rico. If Zach wasn't pretty sure that Matthew was involved, he might suspect Turk and Rico being in cahoots. But would Turk team up with Matthew? Or was Rico's budding friendship with Turk merely a cover for his established alliance with Matthew?

Next to them, Pierre puffed on his pipe as though he didn't have a care in the world. This was a guy who was claiming to have been drugged less than twenty-four hours ago? The words that had played in Zach's head when he'd run into Pierre at Rosewood came back to him. *One may smile and smile and be a villain.* But did Pierre have the wherewithal to plan out a distractive argument with Matthew and feign being drugged? And if so, why? What benefit would two tech guys get from creating more dramatic results?

"A Soul Snatcher's purpose is to collect the souls of the dead and gain in power and force as he does so." Rebecca stood awkwardly in front of the camera. "Often that increase of power can be felt in the living world more acutely. Although Soul Snatchers are sometimes confused with biblical demons or the

Devil, there appears to be no firm connection. Soul Snatchers, however, model themselves after the Devil and apparently lust after power."

Shelly and Patrizia stood next to each other. He knew Shelly, and the odds were long that she'd tamper with evidence. And moreover, why? She'd never shown any discontentment with being exactly what she was—a quality investigator. Patrizia was more of an enigma. Zach didn't know her well, but she seemed trustworthy. Besides, anyone with a massive tattoo of *San Michele Arcangelo* on her arm got the benefit of the doubt in Zach's book—unless evidence pointed toward her.

"Most Soul Snatchers model themselves after the Devil's lust power." Rebecca paraphrased herself looking at her notes. "In death, their dreams of power and glory still unfulfilled, they set themselves on collecting souls." She shuffled her papers and looked up apparently finished.

Shelly raised her hand. "How can we tell if we're dealing with a Soul Snatcher here?" The team knew that Rebecca did better answering questions than making a presentation.

"One sign is suicide. A Soul Snatcher first drives the victim to despair, then encourages him or her to end his life. After death, the Soul Snatcher will convince the lost soul that he has no choice but to join the Soul Snatcher's world, and the Soul Snatcher's power grows. The more souls it collects, the greater its influence in our world—from what my research suggests."

"Could the Soul Snatcher be this famous female ghost of Rosewood?" Ray asked.

And finally there was Ray, Zach thought. Not a chance of him tainting evidence and then calling Zach's attention to it, right? Not his best friend. Never having been in the position of trying to root out a traitor, from Zach's vantage point, even the obviously innocent bore the outlines of potential guilt.

"It could be. You never know." Her formal presentation over, Rebecca became visibly less nervous.

"Are there any other telltale signs?" Shelly asked.

Rebecca took a deep breath. "Typically good spirits remain to oppose Soul Snatchers and protect people from evil. That is kind of why I'm concerned about our releasing the spirit of the doctor last night, he may have been providing balance."

"Balance?" Bryce said. "Dude, there have been all kinds of haunts here. What kind of balance is that?"

"Well, no one has ever been killed or injured on the property," Rebecca said. "At least since it closed down."

"True dat." He adjusted his belt buckle so that BryceCam panned to Rebecca.

Really? Zach thought. Could this clown be responsible for a conspiracy to taint evidence? Zach knew that as he continued to be distracted by these ruminations, time was running out on the opportunity to solve Rosewood's haunting.

"How many suicides can a Soul Snatcher be responsible for?" Zach asked.

Rebecca scoured her notes. "Well, I mean, there's no...set number," she said. "The highest *reported* case apparently involved a Soul Snatcher which was exorcised from a castle in Germany in 1987. Throughout the centuries, over thirty suicides were attributed to the entity."

"Earlier today, Wendy told me that there were thirty seven suicides here at Rosewood between 1899 and 1903."

Rebecca's eyes widened. "Thirty seven in four years? That's an unbelievable rate. Soul Snatchers are often discovered after four or five. Ones who have claimed ten lives are extremely powerful."

"So, if this thing claimed the majority of those suicides," Shelly interjected, "it's pretty safe to say that we're dealing with the most powerful Soul Snatcher ever."

"I could stay," Ray said. "Really."

He was nearly fully dressed for his bouncer job. In the low ceiling of their tent, he sat on his rolled up sleeping bag and put on socks.

"Nah, we'll be alright," Zach said. "Besides, you put in, what? Four, five hours of video review today?"

"Screw you. I've been at it since 5 AM."

Zach looked at his watch. It was going on 3 PM. "Okay, so a *couple* more than five hours."

Ray saluted with his middle finger and left it extended. He smiled but only for a second. "You sure you're going to be okay?"

"We're—"

"I didn't mean the plural 'you,' or the 'royal' you."

"I know what you meant and I appreciate it."

"You better." Adorned in a white tuxedo shirt and black dress slacks, Ray looked pretty spiffy. Not that many patrons of *Wine, Women & Thong* would be noticing him unless they decided to harass one of the dancers. "So why the long face, buddy?"

Zach grunted. "I'm pretty sure that Matthew's one of the guys tampering evidence."

Ray paused midway through tying his shoe. "Yeah, I could see that."

"One of our team?" Zach whispered.

Ray leaned forward and spoke in hushed tones. "Yes, but show business is cutthroat. You held him back from being an investigator. Maybe he thought this would somehow benefit his career."

"I can't believe you're being so matter-of-fact about this."

"He tried to manufacture drama on a TV show. It's not like he killed someone."

Ray always had the ability to put things in perspective.

"No, he's not a murderer, but how much of this other evidence we're uncovering is planted or tainted?"

"Don't get me wrong..." Fully attired, Ray shoved the rest of his stuff in his gym bag. "If I were you, I'd be pissed. You want me to kick his ass?"

"No," Zach said and then added, "Not until I find out who he's working with."

"Prolly Rico, or Bryce...or Shelly."

"Shelly?" He'd said it way too loudly. If someone were lurking around the tent, they may have heard him. "Let's talk on your way out."

Ray grabbed his gym bag; Zach nabbed his friend's sleeping bag. They exited the tent and headed down Rosewood's driveway.

"So why would you suspect Shelly?"

"It would seem more logical if both parties were from the same team. Of any *XPI*, she'd be...I mean, Angel is too loyal, I don't see the Turk having a motive. Rebecca or Wendy? Nah."

"I guess I agree with you on that," Zach said.

"I mean, I initially suspected Bryce or Rico and Pierre. I suppose it could be Matthew and one of the Demon Hunters." He shrugged. "It would just be way harder to coordinate."

"They knew about the investigation about a week before us."

"How do you know that?"

"I just found out."

"Well, that would give them the opportunity to try and set something up. Maybe Bryce wanted to ensure drama for the ratings? Maybe Rico has an axe to grind that we don't know about? It's not like those guys are the most ethical anyway. Don't forget about that frozen-beer-can cold spot."

"Trust me, I haven't."

They'd reached the front gate. The security guard, this one an elderly gentleman, pried himself from the car to open the lock for them. A few people stood outside. One of them, a tall middle-aged man, whistled and waved at Zach who sheepishly returned the wave. It appeared Ray would be able to leave without a media swarm descending on him.

"Hey," Ray said. "I made copies of those video stoppages. I'm taking one copy with me and I left a DVD in with your clothes...just in case, ya' know?"

"Thanks." Zach handed him his sleeping bag.

Now that both of Ray's hands were full and he couldn't defend himself, Zach whisked his index finger into the oil on his forehead and, before Ray knew what was happening, wiped it on his friend's brow.

"What's this?"

"Holy anointing oil from Monsignor Macginty. It'll keep you safe."

"You saw him? How's that old coot doing?"

"Good. Good. He doesn't exactly approve of your night job."

"That guy," Ray said, shaking his head. "Once you tell him something, he never lets you live it down."

Zach's own experience with the priest differed, but he said nothing.

"Anyways," Ray said. "You know where I'll be if you need me. The club is only twenty minutes away. I can be here right quick."

"I know. Thanks pal-o-mine. Either way, I'll call you later and fill you in on the evening's activities."

"Okay. My shift ends at three," Ray said. "I should be back here before three-thirty."

Holy oil or not, Zach couldn't suppress the inexplicable feeling that Ray wouldn't be completing his shift.

Chapter Twenty-Nine

As Zach meandered back up the Rosewood driveway, Rebecca and Angel were headed out in her gray Toyota. Angel was behind the wheel and stopped alongside him.

"You two look low key."

"We've got the equipment in the trunk and are going to drive around for a while to make sure no one sees us going over to the Foster's," Angel said.

"Good call. Hey, Rebecca, I want to know what's going on over there. Call me as soon as she tells you what happened last night."

"Will do," she called from the passenger seat.

Zach turned back to Angel. "You set up those whistling EMF-EVPs where I asked?"

"Absolutely, boss." Angel smiled. "Oh, I had one extra and put it on the main staircase in the lobby."

"Why there?"

Angel chuckled. "I want to be sure the guys at the control center are warned if there is a ghost nearby," he said with mock concern.

"You hope there's an EMF spike on those stairs at some point, and it scares the *bejesus* out of them..."

Feigning innocence, Angel shrugged.

"I guess," Zach said, "rank doth have its privilege."

With waves and nervous smiles, they recommenced their journey down the driveway. Zach proceeded in the opposite direction.

He needed to talk to Sara and didn't have to search long for her. She was leaning up against the *XPI* van, apparently waiting for him.

"I haven't seen much of you today," she said. "Everything okay?"

"Not really. We need to talk."

"What's wrong?"

"There's no one around?" Zach craned his neck and checked both sides of the van.

"Not that I know of."

"I need this to stay between you and me."

"Sure." She brushed hair away from her face.

"Sara, I need you to promise."

"Okay, okay." She raised her right hand as though being sworn into office. "I promise. What's up?"

"Not all the evidence in this case is legitimate. I, actually Ray, found something on the videos that proves two people conspired to plant that peach juice in room 217. I learned that room isn't even the one that the glass-eating guy killed himself in."

"Do you know who it is?" she asked. "Who planted the evidence?"

"I have my suspicions, but I want to keep it to myself until I have concrete proof. I'd appreciate it if you kept your eyes peeled for any suspicious behavior and let me know right away."

She put her hand on her hip and appeared ready to argue.

Zach preempted further debate. "Sara, that's all I'm willing to tell you right now." He said it firmly.

"Okay, alright. Fine," she said.

"And Sara?" Zach had long pondered how to word this. Sara's marijuana smoking was so out of character for her that he knew she'd be defensive when it was brought up. "I'm not judging you or anything, but could you *please* refrain from any herbal-like 'supplements' tonight?"

Later, when armed with more evidence, Zach would replay her initial reaction in his head over and over. It lasted only a flash of a second before she returned to her cool demeanor and casual confidence. Unmistakably and without exchanging a word, Zach caught it all at once. Shock. Embarrassment. Confusion and guilt. At the forefront of all the emotions was, of course guilt.

"Agreed," she said flatly.

He smiled weakly hoping to express gratitude. He turned and started away from her but intended on turning back all along. In boxing terms, as Ray had taught him, after stunning your opponent, it was sometimes best to back away for a fraction of a moment to let them hope that another flurry wasn't imminent.

Zach knew this tactic would work with Sara. He'd get a natural and unabridged reaction doing it this way.

On this subject, he *needed* the truth.

"Oh yeah." He threw his hand in the air, index finger pointed. He spun around. "Why did you notify the Demon Hunters about this investigation a week before us?"

Her face told him all he needed to know about the validity of the claim. Unlike before, she couldn't quickly fling a veil over her reaction. Her eyes widened and her lips parted slightly. Her expression couldn't have been more telling had he shot her with truth serum.

When she finally managed an answer, she didn't even bother to deny it. "I-they just needed to have more time in terms of arranging their travel stuff."

It may not have been a complete canard, but it was hardly the entire truth. Sara's voice betrayed her.

"Sara. C'mon..."

"Zach, there are things that I just can't tell you right now."

It didn't matter. He'd nodded and walked away. Zach had gotten the information he needed. Bryce, Rico, Patrizia or Pierre would have had plenty of time to plan something with Matthew.

Zach lay in his tent atop his sleeping bag, his head propped up on a pile of his clothes. He was twiddling his thumbs over his stomach as if the action would cause his weary brain to grow sleepy. It hadn't worked for an hour, and as it got closer and closer to dusk, Zach realized the time had nearly arrived for him to induce an episode.

He had spent the previous couple of hours checking the technical set up and reviewing video with Turk. Nothing else had shown up on video that equaled his female ghost image. Turk promised he'd have it digitally enhanced and independently evaluated. When it looked like Turk's eyes were about to fail him, Zach had sent him home for a shower and a good long break. Fortunately, they would have plenty of time to review video evidence in the coming days.

Outside, a stiff wind buffeted the tent as color slowly faded from the ceiling. Daylight was surrendering to dusk.

During the better part of the afternoon, Pierre had manned the control center all by himself, perhaps feeling guilty for the previous night's disappearing act. He was extremely pleasant, but didn't volunteer any information or suspicions to Zach about why he'd passed out and missed his shift. Angel must have kept quiet. When Zach asked about Matthew, Pierre had told him he was in the tent asleep.

Bryce and Rico spent quite a bit of the afternoon napping as well. It promised to be a late night and everyone wanted to be fresh and energized once it got dark. Zach had also decided to nap, but his churning mind had another plan. Rumination.

This was by far the most complex case he'd ever worked. With most, the clients would report on the paranormal activity, they'd study the history of the haunted place and pieces of the puzzle would fall into place. Sometimes quickly, sometimes slowly, with attention to details, it always got solved. Rosewood's pieces weren't falling into place at all. Years ago, he had seen a special on the JFK assassination. A conspiracy theory expert had postulated that with most murders, as evidence comes in, it slowly but surely points to one solution. One assassin. One culprit. With the JFK murder, it was reversed. The longer time passed, the more disparate the evidence and theories became. The expert had seriously questioned if we'd ever solve the conspiracy question.

Rosewood was the Dealy Plaza of haunted places.

Perhaps because it had been the home of so many with emotional problems and mental issues, there seemed to be so many dramatic events, but they weren't connecting. No overall story of the haunting was becoming clear and it needed to be thoroughly understood. If they had erred by releasing the spirit of Dr. Johansson, there was now no margin for mistakes.

The tree line is dark enough.

The voice of his godfather had been silent for a while. It was no coincidence that Zach had been in his objective investigator mode the past couple days. That was all about to change. Inducing an episode was a highly emotional and intense experience.

Godson, it is time.

The smell of *Sailor Black* was so strong that Zach's sealed tent may as well have been a pipe smoking lounge.

Wait, he thought, let me center myself. Let me focus.

The visions during his episodes weren't self directed. Zach wasn't sure how his uncle guided him, but often, perhaps seventy percent of the time, Zach would view on the topic he requested. Tonight, Zach was conflicted between solving the mystery of Rosewood and figuring out both the reason and the details of the evidence tampering. As he normally did when torn between two paths, he chose the more difficult one. He closed his eyes and submitted a silent intention on solving the haunting of Rosewood Asylum.

He sat up and gathered towels and blankets he'd earlier transferred from the trunk of his car to the tent. Slowly and silently as possible, Zach unzipped the opening of the tent. Glancing out and seeing no one, he slipped between the folds. He reached back inside for a small gym bag and then swiftly moved toward the line of trees.

Chapter Thirty

Zach took off his shirt, but left his scapular on. During his episodes, he especially needed the Lord's protection.

He rolled up his pant legs and sat down on the tattered navy blue blanket. Better to be old and best to be a dark color Zach had found. He'd procured a number of these types of blankets from garage sales and flea markets and kept them in his trunk—likewise with the towels. He spread one over his lap careful to favor his right side where blood would flow down. Many years ago, Zach had experimented by binding his wrists and feet prior to an episode but was blocked from any visions. The flowing blood was apparently required for him to connect to the higher plane of consciousness.

He leaned back against an oak tree, its rough bark felt good on his shoulder blades—scratchy but centering. His heart rate was already slowing naturally. Soon, his hands and feet would tingle and then go numb. He inhaled deeply smelling the fresh air, dirt, leaves and wood. Soon those smells would fade from his senses and be replaced by the smell of his uncle.

The low murmur of crickets soothed him. Zach placed his hands palms up on the cloth and began to quietly pray:

"Lord, make me an instrument of your peace,
Where there is hatred, let me sow love;
where there is injury, pardon;
where there is doubt, faith;
where there is despair, hope;
where there is darkness, light;
where there is sadness, joy."

The Saint Francis Prayer didn't induce an episode, but it prepared his mindset for one. In addition to accidentally inducing an episode by becoming overly emotional, the power of the prayer's words centered Zach to a point of religious and spiritual fervor. He did wish to be of service to others. He badly wished it.

The desire was his life's calling. In this state, the priorities in his life became clear.

"O Divine Master, grant that I may not so much seek to be consoled as to console;
to be understood as to understand;
to be loved as to love."

As a teenager and as he became more in control of "The Curse" as he'd then called it, Zach had, with the suggestion from Monsignor Macginty, discovered the power of this prayer and had became determined to use his gift in the service to others. That day, unbeknownst to Macginty, Zach had gone to the tattoo parlor and gotten the *Chi Rhos* on each location of Christ's wounds. There had been five tattoo artists on duty that day. Zach commissioned one tattoo each. Kyrie, the woman with photographs of her daughters dressed up as angels had worked on his left wrist. Barbara, she of the purple hair and nose ring had worked on his right. Hollister, a raspy voiced guy with at least three days of growth on his face worked on his left foot. Mark, an emaciated guy with long blond hair who didn't talk much, had worked on his right.

The four of them had done the hands and the feet at the same time. At first they fiercely resisted, but Zach paid extra to have it done the way he wanted. They were instructed not to look at the others' work as they drew. The *Chi Rho* on his side had been completed later that day, by Martin, a tall black man with a shaved head. Martin had but one tattoo himself, a teardrop beneath his left eye. Zach knew the significance of that mark: Martin's grief over having taken a life. Zach had chosen him specifically to tattoo the location on his body where the spear had pierced Jesus's side after his death.

"For it is in giving that we receive;
it is in pardoning that we are pardoned;
and it is in dying that we are born to eternal life…"

He closed his eyes and repeated the prayer. Most people knew that stigmatics bled from the wounds of Jesus. What most didn't know, or didn't care to know, was that when bleeding from those wounds, on some level, stigmatics experience the pain and anguish of Christ during the crucifixion. The pain came not as a cutting sensation, more of an explosion on his wrists and feet. His side felt an intense cold as though a frozen hole had been created there.

There was only so much pain Zach could take, but having worked for years with Monsignor Macginty to control and channel it, Zach could remain semiconscious during his episodes and experience the gift of vision that they brought.

Before he finished the Saint Francis Prayer a third time, blood began to ooze, first from his wrists, and then from his feet and his side. The scent of pipe tobacco surrounded him. The *Sailor Black* during an episode wasn't jarring or uncomfortable like it was in waking life. It felt wispy and pleasant. Welcome. The voice of his uncle came to him.

Welcome back, Godson.

Zach never saw Uncle Henry during his visions, but felt his godfather's presence and was guided by his soothing voice. As jarring as the voice could be in waking life, it gave him great comfort during an episode.

You need to see things.

The picture in Zach's mind focused. At first, Rosewood was sepia-toned, more so than it had been during sunset the night before the investigation. Colors seeped in. As they did, as the picture appeared real enough to walk into, people in the vision began moving. As though on fast forward, they zipped past. Zach couldn't make out faces, but could tell by their attire, the derby hats and flowing dresses, that the time period was near the turn of the twentieth century.

On his left, led by two horses, a closed black buggy pulled up. The images slowed to normal speed. A man dressed as a policeman, possibly a police chief, exited the driver's side and walked, no shuffled, around to the passenger's door. He looked from side to side as though nervous of being observed. From Zach's vantage point in the vision, he could have reached out and touched the man's square jaw. The policeman stood six-feet tall, large for that time period, Zach noted. He had broad shoulders and a barrel-shaped chest. The brim of his police cap hid his eyes in a shadow; his pug nose crooked to one side as though once broken and never healed. He opened the door, exposing a large bundle wrapped in a navy-colored rug. He slung the rolled carpet over his shoulder and headed into the stables. Seconds later, several horses whinnied.

"This is John Paramour? I don't understand," Zach said.

Keep watching.

It was as if his godfather knew what Zach needed to see and provided him images that Uncle Henry himself could *not* see—or perhaps could no longer understand. Maybe Uncle Henry could perceive Zach's reaction to them, but not the visions themselves?

The image morphed, and Zach was inside the stables at an elevated position. The policeman had taken off his hat and covered up his uniform with an off-white piece of clothing. It's a patient's garment, Zach realized—a dress?

Based on Hunter's psychic reading of a dead body being repeatedly stabbed, the policeman's intent was clear before the corpse and kitchen knife were revealed from inside the rug. The cross-dressed cop hunched over the body, then he raised and lowered the knife repeatedly. Zach's visions were silent, but he couldn't help imagining the repeated sounds of pfft. pfft. pfft...

The policeman took backward steps revealing the ravaged corpse. There were a few slashing wounds to the torso, but they appeared to have been incidental. The brunt of the attack had been inflicted on the face. It had been flayed beyond any recognition. The eyes were mere bloody sockets, the nose was completely gone and the cheekbones revealed protruding bones. The neck had been ripped apart and blood had stained the dirt and hay beneath and around the head and shoulders of the victim. The sight of blood...

Blood! Zach remembered that in real life he was slowly bleeding from five wounds.

Yes, godson, be mindful.

"Show me more, please," Zach said.

The scene sped up. Again as though on a preview setting of a DVD, it quickly displayed the discovery of the body, a flurry of people coming and going and then the vision slowed again to regular speed.

Directing two other uniformed officers, the policeman from the previous scene was now clean-shaven. A man in a white coat, presumably a doctor, looked on. He halted the police chief as he reached for the knife. It must be Dr. Johansson, Zach thought.

Presuming it was, Dr. Johansson had a thin face, high cheekbones and a pointed chin. He wore spectacles, and age was turning his blond hair to white. He appeared to be giving the police officer a lecture of sorts, and then a conversation ensued. At first, the policeman appeared puzzled. Then, a more heated discussion took place with hand gestures and pointing. After a moment, uncomfortable resignation formed on the officer's face. He shrugged and waved at the knife on the ground. When the doctor turned away, the policeman's face betrayed a look of hostile disgust. A look that would kill? Zach wondered. Presuming this was Paramour, and there was every indication he was, had he killed Dr. Johansson to cover up this murder? No, Zach remembered, Dr. Johansson had died of heart failure.

The doctor moved to the bloody knife, withdrew a hanky from his pocket and used it to lift the knife by the blade. He lifted the handle near his face and examined it. After a moment, and without looking back at Paramour, the doctor exited the stables carrying the knife in a hankie near the blade's broken tip. Paramour walked, no—shuffled away. Zach wondered if the childhood abuse, the burning of his feet that Evelyn had informed him of had left permanent damage. Or, Zach wondered in horror, as he'd gotten older, had Paramour *continued* to punish himself for his sins in the same manner his mother had?

Without an answer, the scene morphed.

A doctor's office. The administration building? Zach was at eye level with the doctor who was taking measurements of the knife's handle and portions of the blade. He applied a powdery substance to the blade and with tape lifted what appeared to be a partial print from an index finger.

Fingerprints, right? Why didn't the cops...

Keep watching.

The doctor compared the print with a set of smaller ink fingerprints on a pad. His face scrunched into a puzzled scowl. His lips pursed, and he searched his desk for something. Finding a small black book, he opened it and made several notations. His private journal, Zach thought, can I see where it is now?

The doctor's office wiped away like chalk on a board. Another vision took its place.

An emaciated and aged Dr. Johansson stood among thick tree trunks. With a shovel, he painstakingly lifted clumps of earth from a small hole and piled them next to a tin can. It was obvious to Zach that the black diary must be inside.

That tells me nothing. Zach's thoughts were cloudy and he was lightheaded. Even the visions were becoming blurry.

"Is there more?"

Yes, but you've not got time.

"One more!"

Quickly, and then you must go back.

The scene returned to the doctor's office, but time had shifted. Surprisingly, it had shifted backwards. Dr. Johansson was younger—the same age as in earlier visions. An attractive but haggard young woman stood in front of his desk. Her blonde hair was chopped very short. The diary was nowhere in sight, perhaps put away? Hidden?

Dr. Johansson said something to the woman. In response, she pounded her fist on his desk. Obviously upset, she unleashed a torrent of silent accusations or insults. She pointed at him. Her right hand was smeared with black ink. He had fingerprinted her.

The already blurry scene became even more hazy, smoky. Wait, one more, Zach thought.

No. It is enough.

The scene faded amidst an overwhelming stench of *Sailor Black*.

The pieces will fall into place. But be careful.

And, with that, the presence of his godfather was gone. The smell of tobacco abated, Zach fluttered his eyes open, but he couldn't see. It took a moment before Zach realized that his eyes were adjusting and there was nothing really to see. It was night.

He sat cross-legged in full darkness. Bark from the oak dug into his back, and the blood's warmth on his flesh was already cooling. More time had passed than he had planned on.

Much more.

Typically, he'd get one or two scenes during an episode. This had been what, four or five? Six, he thought, six scenes. He wanted to rest, but knew that he couldn't yet. He pulled a small vial of holy water from his bag and began pouring it on his wounds. The bleeding slowed and stopped, but based on how weak he felt, he suspected he'd lost more blood than ever before.

He reached inside the bag and felt for the gauze. The strain of such a simple movement nearly caused Zach to pass out, but he fought it off. Slowly, deliberately and methodically, he wrapped his wrists and then each foot with gauze. As his heart rate increased to normal levels, the feeling in his extremities returned. It made the pain worse, but Zach didn't mind physical pain. He rested a minute before retrieving a large bandage from his bag and slapping it onto his side.

He reached for his long-sleeved shirt. He was shivering—he needed a nap to recharge, but he didn't think he'd have the time. They'd be looking for him.

He wrapped the shirt around his shoulders and slipped his arms through. Before he could button it up, two figures emerged from Rosewood headed in his direction. Even at a distance and even lightheaded, he knew the silhouette with the baseball cap to be Matthew. The other, more than half a foot taller, was clearly that of Bryce Finman.

Chapter Thirty-One

"How the hell should I know where he is?" Little more than a whisper, Matthew's voice cracked.

Bryce said something in low tones that was too garbled for Zach to understand.

"No, he never just takes off like this. He suspects something," Matthew said.

They stood at the edge of the tree line, close enough for Zach to hear their hoarse argument. Far enough away that he remained hidden in the shadows. Or so he hoped.

"Dude, you're just paranoid. Don't fall for the trick where he pretends to know more than he does in order to get you to admit to something. That's one of the oldest tricks in the book."

"No, he suspects something. I'm telling you," Matthew said. "I know this guy."

"Yeah," Bryce said, "you know 'this guy' well enough to know he's never going to make you an investigator on his show."

"What does that have to do with it? I'm not backing out, I'm just sayin'..."

There was the flash of a lighter. Bryce lit a cigarette—from the initial smell of it, a regular cigarette. "Sayin' what? It sounds like you've got cold feet, like you're tempted to not go through with it."

"Hey, fuck you," Matthew said. "I'm the one taking all the risk."

"Yeah, right. Whatever, dude. C'mon, let's do this."

Upon further sniffs of Bryce's secondhand smoke, the cigarette was laced with marijuana. His head already woozy and his stomach empty, the odor nearly made Zach pass out.

"Put your weed out," Matthew instructed. "People will be able to see the light all the way to the asylum."

"Yeah, right. They'd just think it was a firefly." He gurgled out a laugh.

"Shhhhhhh." Matthew was staring in Zach's general vicinity. "Did you hear something?"

Zach resisted an urge to duck and flatten his body on the ground. He tried his very best not to move one muscle lest he make a sound. He kept his breath shallow as he could without blacking out. If they discovered him in this weakened condition, he'd be completely at their mercy. Something Zach had learned at the poker table and had observed ever since in real life: desperate men take desperate actions. Not only can't those actions be predicted with any regularity, they're usually harsher than the situation calls for. Zach didn't want to test this theory tonight.

"Yeah, I heard something" Bryce said, "a fucking ghost." He raised both hands and waved them wildly around Matthew's face.

"Fuck, asshole. You just burned me. Put that fucking thing out now or I *will* call it quits."

Zach resisted another urge — to relax. He couldn't let his guard down. He closed his eyes and remained as calm and meditative as he could.

"Okay. Okay." There was a rustling as Bryce presumably snuffed out his joint.

"Alright," Matthew said. "Let's go get the stuff."

The leaves rustled beneath their feet. Zach kept his eyes closed. Opening them meant taking the chance they'd catch a shine or a glimmer. Or that he'd think they'd seen him and make a noise that would give him away.

They'd either see him or they wouldn't. He'd hear their response if they did. Not many people could stifle a reaction when stumbling upon a half-clothed, bloody man in the woods.

Still, his heart raced. More rustling. Were they farther away or was it his wishful imagination? A small branch snapped behind him...but a safe distance behind him. They'd passed by.

He opened his eyes and, seeing no one, he reached for his jeans. Slipping them on without disturbing the sticks and leaves under and around him posed a problem. Even the slightest exertion made his vision blur and his heart pound. He needed rest. He needed nourishment. But most of all, he needed fluids. He reached into his bag and pulled out a water bottle and guzzled it down as quietly as he could. After the massive blood loss, it wasn't nearly enough.

He stared at the remaining holy water.

"Holy water is water, son." Macginty's voice in Zach's head was a modification of the Monsignor's earlier words. Macginty had never uttered that actual phrase, nor would he. Or would he? In an emergency he might, then again—

Zach caught himself passing out. From his sitting position, he'd nearly tipped all the way over on his side. He stared at the container of remaining holy water. There was about a liter of it and, in his state, it looked so enticing.

Holy water is water.

Was it his godfather's voice? No smell of *Sailor Black,* thank God, or he'd have passed out for sure. Zach chugged the entire container of holy water. Some of it spilling on his cheek and chin. It helped. A little. He wished he could eat a protein bar he'd packed in the bag, but unwrapping it now was not an option. His head wasn't so woozy to think that Matthew and Bryce wouldn't hear wrappers crinkling in the haunted forest. Zach almost laughed but caught himself—then centered his emotions with a silent deep breath. He grabbed the protein bar and slid it into his back pocket.

He stood. He took two steps and stubbed his toe on a stone. The pain rang through the bones of his bloodless feet. Out of nowhere, he recalled cymbals throbbing with tone the last time he was at a jazz club. Focus. Focus. Shoes.

He heard voices and a hushed "Psst. Here."

He looked about wildly, but no one was there. The sounds had come from near the back fence line maybe twenty yards away. It sounded closer, but the breeze must have carried it. Zach backtracked and tried to slip on his shoes while standing. Couldn't. He sat down and pressed them onto his aching feet. Evelyn's voice rang in his ears. *"She punished him by scraping embers from the fireplace and scalding his feet."*

He shivered. Poor John Paramour—the man who went on to stab dead bodies and commit arson...

Zach caught his head bobbing, his eyes half closed. Both shoes were on. Sockless, it felt like wood planks across his toes—the pressure grated the gauze over his wounds. He tried to stand. Couldn't find his balance. Decided to crawl. One arm and knee forward after the next. Like in Kindergarten. His palms and wrists now ached worse than his feet. A smell invaded his nostrils. The smell of wet leaves and urine? Had Bryce and Matthew pissed back here? Was this a dream of some sorts? A nightmare? Shhhh. One deliberate movement after the next. He'd crawled twenty-five yards or so, and was within spitting distance of the tree line. Voices drifted from the far corner of the property. He inched toward them stopping once to recoup energy.

He reached a row of waist-high, boxwood hedges that ran like a mini barricade just past the outer trees. About five feet separated them from the back fence. Zach double-timed his crawl the remaining distance. His woozy, throbbing head sobered when he saw that he was lying about six feet away from Bryce Finman's feet.

"C'mon, before somebody sees us," he was saying.

"Don't worry. See how dark it is? I shot out both of those streetlights."

Zach imagined Matthew pointing over the fence. Were they going to climb it? It's barbed wire, Zach reminded himself. Not impossible but...

"Fucking bankrupt State of Illinois and City of Pullman," Matthew continued. "It'll probably take 'em months to replace those bulbs."

"Just, *come on* already," Bryce said.

"There. There it is. It's open."

"Holy fuck me, dude," Bryce said, moving farther from Zach's hiding place. "I gotta admit, that's fuggin' brilliant."

"I told you I was good," Matthew said. "I cut the fence down that way to give Old Man Winkler something to distract him."

"Distract him? For what?"

"Hello? What do you think?" Matthew sounded annoyed. "When I broke into the administration building, I had to leave another hole for him to discover so he wouldn't find this one."

"Winkler'd never notice this." Bryce grunted. "Fuck, I knew it was here and didn't see it."

Zach couldn't resist a peek. He raised his torso off the ground and settled into a wobbly crouch. His eyes adjusted, but he couldn't believe what they saw.

Matthew stood on the other side of the fence holding a net-like contraption. A modest triangle segment had been cut from the fence's corner pole to the ground. The hole was wide enough that Bryce could crawl through it.

"Careful. Careful. Don't touch the side or the top if you can help it," Matthew said. "Lean against the pole." He stretched the net-like contraption up and away from where Bryce passed through.

Zach wondered if he was hallucinating.

Once Bryce had cleared the fence, Matthew stretched the net-like apparatus across to the post and fastened it back in place. From Zach's vantage point, even knowing there was an opening in the fence, he couldn't see it.

Apparently, the work was just as impressive up close. Bryce stood with hands on his hips and was shaking his head. "Fucking amazing."

"Yeah, it won't last," Matthew said. "We were lucky not to get any rain the past couple days. First good downpour will crack the paint all to hell."

"Who gives a fuck." Bryce stated flatly. "Come on. Let's get outta here and get the stuff."

They made their way up Lincoln Avenue. When Zach was certain they were far enough away to be able to see into the darkened corner, he stood. Perhaps Bryce and Matthew had been able to leap over the boxwood hedges, but in his weakened condition, Zach would have to press through them. At full strength, the task would barely have slowed him down. However, short of blood, dehydrated and weak, he ventured only halfway through the bushes before he had to stop and rest. His heart pounded against his chest. His head swam and tiny lights flashed in the corners of his eyes. Anxiety that bordered on panic reared its Medusa-like head. He couldn't pass out halfway through the bushes. The noise. They'd come back. He couldn't pass out at all. Certain that his willpower alone would sustain his consciousness if he only wished for it hard enough.

I wish I may, I wish I might, have the wish I wish tonight.

He had to follow them—find out what they were planning and figure out what they'd done. Zach pushed through the hedges, ripping leaves away from their branches and breaking dead twigs. He tried to press through despite his fatigue. Determined not to fail.

When you wish upon a star, makes no difference —

It was happening again. He was losing his thought stream. His heart was pumping too fast for too little blood, which meant his head would get less and less of it.

Be careful what you wish for, you might just get it.

They were his mom's words. His mom's old warning. When she had said it to him as a boy, he'd had no idea what it meant. Mid-shrub, the meaning was very clear. Get your wish, cross to the other side of the bushes, pass out, and let Bryce and Matthew find you when they return.

Zach strained to reverse his course. He didn't have much time to get back to the safe side, the darker side.

He teetered a second, his head swimming and his vision failing. Against his will, for the first time in a long while, Zach blacked out.

In fact, he was completely unconscious before his head hit the ground.

Chapter Thirty-Two

8:02 PM - Rebecca

"How many times are you gonna call him?" Angel asked. "There must be something wrong with his phone. Call Sara. She'll know what's up."

"I called her already," Rebecca said. "She hasn't seen him for hours."

An intuitive feeling had been running through her since about 6 PM. Where was Zach? For just a flash, in her mind's eye Rebecca saw him, envisioned Zach covered in blood. She shook free of the mental picture. She banished it far away.

The Foster's modest front room contained cheap oak furniture and smelled vaguely of spoiled milk. The walls were decorated with country prints and pictures of Joey.

Ginny joined them. "He's asleep. He was tired and cranky all day. He didn't sleep very well after the thing last night. He kept having nightmares."

"So are you ready to tell us what happened?" Angel readied a video camera.

Ginny looked between him and Rebecca, then she nodded and sat on the edge of her couch. She sighed. "Yeah."

"Let me light some incense?" Rebecca asked, hoping to cleanse the air.

"Um, sure."

Ginny didn't look thrilled about the idea, but Rebecca lit it anyway.

"Okay, so the thing is, there's what Joey did, and then there's the creepy thing."

Rebecca glanced at Angel to make sure he was filming. He flashed her a thumbs up. "Go ahead," she said.

"Last night after dark, after Joey was in bed sleeping—or so I thought, I looked out the front room window across the street. Mrs. Radkey was standing in her yard with her hands on her hips and her hair in curlers. I didn't think anyone still wore curlers or that Mrs. Radkey had anyone to curl her hair for, but that's beside the point."

"What was she doing exactly?" Rebecca didn't see how the story was important.

"She was staring. Just staring at something along the side of my house. Of course I ran outside to see what was there." Ginny looked at the wall.

"What was it?"

"I stormed out and sprinted to the side of the house. There, just around the corner was my son...playing with matches—not just playing with them. He was trying to set the house on fire."

"Oh my gosh."

"I know, right? Anyway, I grabbed him hard and I scolded him bad. I even spanked him. It's the only time I've ever spanked him in public. But he looked so...lost, so confused. It was like he'd been sleepwalking. I was still angry and put him to bed."

"What about Radkey?" Rebecca asked.

"By the time I'd taken Joey back inside the house, she'd disappeared, presumably back into her house. I'm telling you though. She was watching him the entire time. Staring as though she'd *known* what Joey was doing. Something's wrong over in that Radkey house."

Rebecca could feel it. She had felt something drawing her attention there the prior night. Talking to Radkey earlier in the day had creeped her out.

"Joey was raised better than that. He's a sweet boy, but he's been radically different since his dad died."

"Aw, his dad passed." Rebecca said.

"What happened?" Angel asked.

Ginny looked composed as she said it. "Seven months ago, my—I mean Joey's dad committed suicide."

8:37 PM - Sashza

Bryce hadn't called and by now, she was sure he wouldn't call. And that was that for Rosewood. She was done with it. Solve the mystery or not, release the spirits or not, she wasn't even going to tell him what else had come to her. Bryce Finman wasn't interested in anything but ratings anyway. She knew that. It used to bother her, but accepting reality had its own reward. Accepting the reality of what the *Demon Hunters* really were, a television show and nothing more, allowed her to focus on her private practice. Her private clients who, once fame had been established on the show, were willing to pay three and four times what they were before she was "famous." It was for her, the end justifying the means. Sashza wished to begin a series of operations which would transform her from what she had been created as, to what she knew at heart she was meant to be.

But these visions, or "after-visions" as she'd come to refer to them, were like nightmares with tentacles attached to her soul. She couldn't shake the thoughts or the memories of the little girl. Amelia was her name. Had something from her psychic reading at Rosewood stowed away in her subconscious? Had it been ported home with her? She wondered if anguish over having been denied a female childhood had attracted something in Rosewood's haunted residue. Memories, although not Sashza's memories, had lapped over her throughout the day like bathwater slowly turning cold and cloudy.

"No," Boy had said, looking up, "this is my place."

That one caused her to shiver every time it came back. Not so much what he said, but how he'd said it. Not so much the icy resolve in his eyes, but the hate that lay just behind it. Not so much who he had been in life, but what she sensed he had become — was becoming in death.

No. She would not tell Bryce Finman anything about it.

Sashza traipsed through the living room of her North Shore home in slippers. She would make a spot of tea, turn in for the night and shake this evil from her. She grabbed the teapot from the stove and trinkled it full with water. She closed the lid and placed it on the stove's back burner, where she placed it most nights. Turned the knob, as she did most nights. The flame for the back burner took a moment longer than it did most nights to light. Click. Click. Click.

There was a cold draft. Click. Click. Click. It caught and lit — as did three other burners simultaneously. There was a flash of fire.

The blaze caught her robe. With a wisp of air, the flames attacked her. She could feel them tearing at her chest, like vicious little mouths. They were singeing her eyelashes. They ran up her nostrils.

She turned her face away, but she couldn't hide. It had come from nowhere. It had come all at once.

This can't be happening, she thought amidst the blaze.

But it was.

8:49 PM - Ginny Foster

Something was wrong. Call it women's intuition, mother's intuition or whatever. Ginny knew it. She had trusted these kids in her home, and had told them about the previous night's activities. Now, Rebecca and Angel were like workers at the DMV making her wait, and wait.

And wait.

Enough had gone on the last twenty-four hours that Ginny was ready to pack her shit up, as her father used to say, and drive the keys to her landlord. If he wanted, he could chase her ass down for the rest of her rent. Screw the security deposit.

Exhausted and cranky, Joey had been put to bed an hour ago. He fussed and even cried as he often did when overtired, but within three minutes of his head hitting the pillow (and after Ginny tickled his back), he was asleep. Now, she sat on the edge of his bed listening to his rhythmic, sleep-drenched breathing as she played with his matted blond hair. Nothing would hurt her Joey. Not on her watch.

Nothing.

Ginny knew he'd been put through a lot during her rocky marriage to his dad. Joey's father, ass that he was, never learned not to scream at her in front of little Joey. When she'd finally convinced him she was serious about throwing his ass out and divorcing him, what was his final legacy to his son? To kill himself.

How does someone explain suicide to a six-year old? Joey, your dad loved you very much but not enough to stick around to watch you grow up? Honey, your dad was really just sticking it to your mommy by ending his life? Buddy, your father was a sick man and his self-prescribed cure was boarding up the garage and running the car inside until the carbon monoxide put him to sleep forever?

That fucker.

She'd let Joey's dad off the hook for all the things he'd done to her during the marriage, but she'd never forgive him for the suicide—doing it *on the property* and trapping her in this damn house with nine months left on an ironclad rental agreement. And the emotional trauma it would stick Joey with for life? She'd never forgive that bastard.

Never.

In the adjoining room, incense burned coiled rings of odor toward the ceiling. The smell reminded Ginny of India (although she'd never been to India) and she generally didn't care for the scent. Rebecca had suggested it and despite everything to this point, on an intuitive level, Ginny liked Rebecca. She hadn't judged or scoffed at Ginny as the previous night's events had been shared. Neither had Angel. But they seemed frozen and confused as they awaited word from their leader, Zach. Ginny could feel the anxiety beading off of them even from a room away. And she wasn't typically into all of that "hocus pocus" stuff.

Joey sighed and shifted from his right to his left side facing away from her. He mumbled something that sounded like "grewer." Ginny wondered what he was dreaming. She considered the thoughts that ran through his head and the anger mixed with fear flooded back when she considered what he must have been thinking to play with matches. It wasn't like matches were laying around her house. She didn't smoke. She'd maybe understand better if he had seen a pack on the coffee table and decided to play with them. But that's not what had happened. He must have scoured the drawers (or had watched her put them away the last time she'd had to relight the oven's pilot flame). She remembered doing that just two days prior. Had Joey intentionally blown out the pilot light?

Ginny looked at her son. At his age, he couldn't be diabolical. At six-years old, he didn't even have the ability to plot such a complicated set of intentions. There had to be someone or something else propelling him towards these dangerous acts. Fast asleep, Joey curled into the fetal position and popped his thumb into his mouth. She hadn't seen him do that in over a year — since well before his father had died.

She plucked out his thumb hoping he'd give it up for the night. Instead, just before he slipped his thumb back past his lips, she heard Joey say something. He said it clearly. Subconsciously, she'd heard him say the same thing just before she rushed around the corner of the house and caught him.

"Okay, Boy."

Ginny made a mental note to tell Rebecca and Angel that tidbit. She couldn't wait to get the hell out of this house — out of this neighborhood. Only two months remained now on her lease and Ginny had already begun packing shit up, preparing for the move.

She played with Joey's hair fanning out blond clumps that perspiration had matted together. Even on the cool night, while he slept, Joey was sweating.

8:57 PM - Mrs. Elizabeth Radkey

Very few people called her "Elizabeth" anymore. Her doctor did during check ups, as well as her dentist. The elderly florist (she'd forgotten his name, but he always wore a name tag) smiled and called her by first name when she stopped in on Sundays to get flowers for George's grave.

To most, she was "Mrs. Radkey." To a few, who she never saw except for weddings and funerals, she was referred to as "Aunt Liz," even though she technically was no one's aunt. Her special friend called her "Elizabeth," and he was the only one since her dear departed husband, George, had passed away who pronounced it perfectly.

Elizabeth.

He, her special friend, had never tried to hide what he was. Not that he would have been able to deceive her; yes, she was an elderly lady, but she was not a stupid woman. For the first few years, she'd merely enjoyed the presence of his company. He commanded a strong presence, yet he never aged. It took a long time before she was comfortable enough to engage him in conversation, but once she mustered the courage, they'd had some delightful chats.

It was nearly time for what they'd discussed the previous night. She shuffled to the basement door, opened the door and called down. "Boy?"

She listened a moment for him to whisper her name the way she loved to hear it said. When she didn't hear his voice, she called down again. "Are you here, Boy?"

Zachary's Past—Age Fifteen

Monsignor Macginty cradled the back of the boy's head against his chest and rocked him to and fro. Zachary was more a young man than a boy, but Macginty sang to him a song that long ago and a continent away, Mrs. Macginty had used to comfort her weeping children. If someone should walk in and see them now, let them be damned for thinking somethin' other'n holy thoughts. Besides, the blood would give 'em a scare now, wouldn't it?

After several minutes, Zach came slowly back to his senses. As always, his head was cloudy at first. As always, he felt guilty and ashamed. And as usual, Macginty would talk him back to sanity. He'd help'ta right him on his path, he would.

Macginty wasn't above getting to his knees when he needed to. Wiping the boy's blood from the marble floor made him thankful. Even more, he was amused at the irony. When he'd been a young priest, he'd wanted to, had prayed for and been obsessed with, witnessing a miracle. Now, for almost a full decade, he'd been cleaning up after dozens of Zachary's little miracles.

"Let me help you with that." Zach started to rise and then lost his balance.

"You just rest yourself there for another couple'a minutes. Besides, I'm not doin' ya no favours."

"Yes, you're – "

"Don't interrupt me, son. I wasn't finished."

"Sorry, Monsignor."

"What I was going'ta say, 'I'm not doin'ya no favours because I plan on savin' up all this blood and sellin' it at a profit when you're good'n famous.'"

Zach laughed. It was good to see the color returning to his face. This hadn't been a bad one, but it was his third in less than a month. The poor boy's heart must be doing more work than Mother Theresa.

By the time he'd done cleaning up both the floor and the boy with holy water (it only seemed appropriate), he could tell Zachary was good'ta go.

"C'mon, son, help me set up for the five o'clock mass."

The boy looked at his watch but didn't even complain that the mass wasn't for several hours. He was a good one, that Zach. They passed through the sacristy and out onto the church's apse. Macginty stood behind the altar and fiddled with the chalices there.

"Are ya' ever going'ta tell me where this stigmata of yours comes from?" He tried to make the question sound casual. As if merely rephrasing it would be enough to get the boy to spit out the answer to a question he'd been asking all these years. As if the stigmata's origins meant nothing at all.

The boy was quiet for a good couple of minutes before speaking a word. For years he'd been claimin' not to know how he'd gotten his gift. Sometimes, he even called it "his curse."

Zach finally spoke. "How do ya' know I know?"

Macginty chuckled. "Zachary, you're a good kid. You're a smart kid. And fortunately for me, you're a terrible liar."

"Are all lies bad, Monsignor?"

The boy also had a gift for changing the subject when he didn't want to talk about somethin'.

"Not all of 'em..."

"Really? But you being a priest, I'd think — "

"What is this?" Macginty questioned. "Interrupt Monsignor Macginty Day?"

Zach shook his head.

"What I was going'ta say was that 'white lies,' ones that keep people safe from harm or save 'em from hurt feelings, can sometimes be excused. They still need'ta be confessed, don'tcha be misquotin' me." He checked if Zach's eyes displayed the clarity of understanding. They did. "Now, ya don't really think I'm going'ta get any money by sellin' yer blood, do ya, son?"

The boy pursed his lips together tightly to try and hide a grin, but the corners of his mouth betrayed him.

"Ya just hav'ta come clean and take care of it in yer head, before the lie becomes the truth."

Zach was trying to stifle a giggle but apparently could not.

"What's so funny, son?"

"You're quoting Michael Jackson songs now, Monsignor?"

"I don't know what'cha mean, son. C'mere now and fetch me that incense dispenser."

For an instant, Zachary looked as green under the gills as he had when he'd first come out of the trance. For some reason he wouldn't admit to, the boy hated the smell of incense and certain types of tobacco. But it wasn't like the thing'd been lit. He shuffled slowly to the dispenser, picked it up and started singing the lyrics to Billie Jean just under his breath. He brought the incense to where Macginty was standing.

"And don'tcha get started by singin' songs about lies, now son," Macginty warned.

"What? I thought you just said you didn't know that song."

Macginty looked at him as if the boy's intelligence had shrunken to that of a termite. "C'mon now, son. I was dancin'ta that song at weddings before you'wuz born."

Zach's face was marred with incredulity. "You dance, Monsignor?"

"Of course I do. 'Tis the only benefit'a havin' been a boxer."

Zach laughed and laughed.

They continued to pretend to prepare Saint Francis of Assisi for a mass that was hours away from starting. Not many people knew that Saint Francis was the world's first recorded stigmatic. Macginty thought it was no coincidence that the boy had been called here — brought to him. No coincidence at all.

Chapter Thirty-Three

Zach opened his eyes with his cheek pressed to the grass. Was this the backyard grass, he wondered. He must have slipped and fallen off the pile of milk crates again. He'd better get up before mom saw him laying there or she'd pitch a fit. No, wait. It was dark...and he wasn't a child. He must have drunk too much at a fraternity bash? For being a Catholic fraternity, *Phi Kappa Theta* really knew how to throw a party. His ears were ringing and he felt weak. From throwing up?

He lifted his throbbing head and pushed his torso off the ground. It smelled of dried grass smothered with oak leaves and sprinkled with honeysuckle. Guilt at having passed out clung to him even though logical faculties had begun to usher it away. It wasn't his fault. Was it?

The gauze bandages on his wrists prompted his memory. Zach knelt up and looked around.

Rosewood.

His head hurt and he was still weak, but not as bad as immediately after his episode. He looked at the bushes he'd fallen from. He'd not crossed all the way through them and had made it back to the safe side. If Bryce and Matthew had returned, they'd likely passed by without noticing him under the umbra of the hedges. Had he successfully gone through the boxwoods and they'd returned, no doubt they would have seen him. He'd have been a sitting duck.

Zach moved to a sitting position and slumped against the boxwood hedges. He pulled out his cell phone to check the time. Instead, there were a slew of missed calls: three from Sara, three from Rebecca, two from Wendy, one from Hunter, one from Angel and interestingly enough, one from Matthew. The most recent one was from Ray at 9:01. There were eight text messages waiting, but Zach clicked "view later," so that he could see the current time. The screen cleared.

It was 9:08.

A bitter chill ran through him. He was letting his team down. He'd broken his own rule about being alone on a case in the dark. He could lose his show. The hint of *Sailor Black* warned him to calm down. This was no time to panic.

The protein bar. He pulled it from his pocket, unwrapped it and munched on the flattened fake-chocolate meal replacement. The more gulps he swallowed, the more his head cleared. He needed to slip out Matthew's secret entrance. Zach hoped that he hadn't missed Evelyn tonight; his intuition told him that either she'd wait for him, or she'd somehow know when he arrived. First, he needed to know for sure that Bryce and Matthew had returned.

He opened his text messages. The last one he'd received was from Sara—the one he needed to contact. Semi-ignoring her message which stated that if this was his way of getting revenge, he'd better get his ass back, he clicked reply and typed out: Not playin games - got somthn big. Back in 35 mins. Need to know if mtthw & bryce r back there. Txt dont call!

He kept his phone on silent mode and waited for the display to light up. Her reply flashed almost immediately: Thyre here. Where r u????

"Im close," he typed. He chuckled at the irony and then continued. "35 mins. Will expln evrythng."

He hit send.

Zach scrolled to a group folder that would mass text all of *XPI*: Sorry 4 disappearing. Im ok. Wrking on something big...back in 35 mins. Please don't txt or call! Will expln l8r.

He'd risen to a crouching position when he remembered that, because Hunter was a consultant, Zach hadn't entered him into that *XPI* text group. In any case, Zach wanted to send him an amended message: Im ok. Pick me up @ muses in 30 mins? Please txt if yes. Will expln l8r.

Zach stood as carefully as he would have aboard a train on rickety tracks. His legs were weary but not wobbly; his head throbbed with warning of dehydration. It was dark; it was quiet. It was time to get through the boxwood hedges. He glanced around to make sure nobody was around. No one was but, looking east toward Lincoln Avenue, Zach realized that the hedges only ran along the back fence. In his woozy state earlier, he hadn't even noticed that by walking, or likely crawling, another thirty feet, he could have merely snuck around them.

Be careful what you wish for, godson.

His uncle's voice was as clear and loud as a church bell. As was his meaning. In the divine plan, Zach hadn't been meant to follow Bryce and Matthew. Something bad would have happened.

Stealthily, he circled around the boxwoods and approached the corner of the fence where earlier the guys had snuck through. From up close, he could see Matthew's handiwork on the fence. A scene from Saint Xavier Theater's production last year of *Southside Story* flashed through his head. It had been Matthew's first in charge of set design, and he'd invited Zach and other team members to attend. There were tall fences set up on stage made of this very material.

He'd used stretchable cords similar to, but thinner than, the webbing contraption used in place of a tailgate on the back of pickup trucks. He must have gone through painstaking lengths to match the size and color of the actual fence with such precision. Tiny hooks latched to the actual fence and the corner post. As Matthew had admitted to Bryce, it wasn't built to last, but the forgery was invisible to the unknowing eye. He'd probably planned on coming back next week and cutting it off, maybe slashing up more of the fence to look like vandalism.

Zach unhitched the hooks on the post, slid through the opening it created and emerged on the other side. As he reattached the hooks as they had been, a thought struck him—what else had Matthew designed and planted? No doubt he had concealed a device on the administration building wall, a contraption designed to create false EMF readings. The peach room was bogus, but what else?

He strode up Lincoln Avenue as quickly as his legs would take him. At one point, he attempted a trot, but the pain precluded it. Each step felt as though he were walking on skeleton feet. The chilly night air nipped at his nose and his ears. The breeze carried with it more than a suggestion of burning wood. Apparently, people who just the previous afternoon may have run their air conditioners, were now blazing fireplace logs to prevent having to prematurely light their furnaces.

Zach's mind wandered back to the visions he'd experienced. The cop had been Paramour, of that he was certain, and there'd been a cover up. Paramour had tried to frame the woman living in the basement of murder. But why?

Zach called Wendy, who answered on the first ring.

"Zach, where are you? We're all wor—"

"Shh," he hissed into the phone. "Don't worry. I'm fine. Hey quick. Tell me something, when did fingerprints get discovered?"

She sighed. ""Generally, Henry Faulds is considered the 'Father of Fingerprinting,' but there is some controversy surrounding—"

"When, Wendy? When?" Zach had cupped his hand over his mouth to muffle his voice.

"Oh, like late 1800s, like 1890s."

Zach was passing the empty lot that adjoined Ginny Foster's house. Fortunately, there weren't many windows along the home's west side. Why would there be? There should have been another house right next door.

"And when were they used by police?" Zach whispered into the phone.

"I think Scotland Yard used fingerprints as early as 1901, but they weren't used in court until like 1905. First in England and then—"

"That's all I need," Zach said. "I'll talk to you—"

"But Zach, don't you want to hear what I found out about Paramour today?"

He considered Wendy's tendency to go on and on, but his curiosity outweighed his need for brevity. "Only the very most important part," he said. "The rest can wait. I can call you in an hour."

"Aren't you going to be back here at Rosewood before that?"

"You're at Rosewood?"

"Yes, I am. Anyway, about Paramour. He disappeared in early July of 1899. At his home, he left a brief note saying that he was following a lead on his missing wife's whereabouts and that he'd return."

He limp-walked up the middle of Lincoln. On the opposite side of the street from the Fosters, Mrs. Radkey's house was completely dark. Odd at this hour for her to be either asleep or out and about. Maybe it was bingo night. Zach continued past the house. There were tiny trinkets of light that danced with the shadows in the back windows.

A sure sign of lit candles.

"His wife had gone missing?"

"Yes, a couple years earlier."

"And what happened?"

"Well, the first part of Paramour's note *may* have been true," Wendy said. "Who knows? But, in the end, the second part proved to be false. He was never seen nor heard from again."

It all fit! Paramour killed the orderly, Thomas Carter, and then tried to frame "PME," the woman living in Rosewood's basement. Being a doctor and a scientist, Johansson would have known about the theory of fingerprinting. He'd have read about it at least in medical journals if nothing else. Police weren't using the technology yet and so Paramour hadn't bothered to take precautions when stabbing the body. Dr. Johansson may not have been able to match the fingerprint on the knife to Paramour, however he'd known it didn't belong to the patient in the basement. Johansson's findings threatened Paramour.

How was the woman connected to Paramour? Was it in Dr. Johansson's buried journal?

She scraped embers from the fireplace and scalded his feet.

It was his godfather's voice, but they were Evelyn's words. Hunter had been right. Dr. Johansson hadn't been responsible for the fires. John Paramour, the police chief who tried to frame a woman for murder, the boy who had been punished by his mother by having his feet burned, had to have been the arsonist.

"Wendy, you're the best!"

"Tell me something I don't know, Zach."

They said their goodbyes. The fireplace scent in the air melded with the odor of ground coffee beans the closer to *Muses* that Zach got.

Before he could put his still-silent-moded phone back in his pocket, a text message flashed on his display screen. Without slowing his limped gait, he opened it.

A message from Hunter: R we awake? Will pick u up @ muses but Lucy, u got some 'splainin' 2 do!

Zach's wallet contained just enough money for three overpriced, 20-ounce, bottles of water and an extra-large Café Americano. If he had more money, he'd have ordered more water. The hot drink would be used to warm his hands until his body rehydrated. Then, he'd trade a tinch of dehydration for the energy jolt the caffeinated beverage would surely provide.

Except for one overweight man, his laptop open, drinking iced-coffee topped with whipped cream, *Muses* was empty. The late-night crowd hadn't yet arrived, and the post-dinner folks had already departed. The snotty barista who'd given Zach the dirty looks the previous night was again on duty. He looked at Zach with contempt. Zach suspected that, covered in dirt and leaves, not to mention dehydrated and short of blood, he must look an utter mess. And, considering he'd guzzled two water bottles before even paying for them, Zach would cut the kid some slack.

"It's nice to finally see you." It was her voice.

Zach turned around. Evelyn was standing near the door.

"Evelyn. I'm glad to see you, tonight."

"Well," she said, with a decidedly nervous grin, "it's nice to be seen."

"Café Americano," the kid shouted out. "Any 'to go' orders for your friends tonight?"

"Maybe later," Zach said.

"Riiiiiight."

With an attitude like that, Zach thought, I still may be reporting your behavior to your boss.

Zach felt obliged to apologize to Evelyn for the kid's behavior, but before he could say anything, she spoke. "With the exception of you, I just don't understand most young people today."

Zach chuckled and motioned toward a table near the front window. It was too cold to sit outside, and he wanted to be in a position to see Hunter as soon as he arrived.

Once seated, Evelyn looked Zach up and down. "You look like you're neither here nor there."

Zach wasn't sure what to make of that, but he wasn't about to waste time. "Evelyn, I need answers."

"Answers for what?

"On John Paramour. On Dr. Johansson. On his journal."

"I've told you, I don't know a Dr. Johansson." Her mouth twitched.

Zach decided to try and catch Evelyn in a lie. "We made contact with and released Dr. Johansson's spirit last night."

Evelyn put her hand to her mouth. "Oh dear."

The ruse had worked perfectly, but its effectiveness did nothing to dull his disappointment in her. "You did know of him. Why did you lie? Why did you claim you'd not heard of him."

"Zach, please," she said. "I don't mean to lie. It's just that the truth for me is sometimes hard to identify."

Zach had no idea what that was supposed to mean. "You also know more about John Paramour than you're letting on."

She sat without movement or sound. Zach had already decided to let her sit until she spoke, until she told him what he needed to know. She held several of the pieces to the puzzle he was trying to complete. One silent moment stretched uncomfortably into another. When she did speak, Zach thought she was joking.

"Oh, no. Your friend is here. The negro one."

"What?" Zach peered outside. Hunter's white Lexus had indeed pulled up to the no parking zone in front of Muses.

"I told you," Evelyn said, "I can't be seen with you." She rose from the table.

"But I *need* to know what you know about this case."

"Meet me back here later. I'll wait for you and I'll tell you everything." She inched away from the table toward the back of the shop where the restrooms were located. "But Zach, come alone."

Chapter Thirty-Four

Zach's strength wasn't one-hundred percent, but he hurried outside. Hunter stood next to his car, and took a few steps towards Zach. "The psychic is near— Christ, pal you look..."

"I thought I asked you to pick me up in thirty minutes," Zach said his tone almost accusatory.

The smile was gone from Hunter's face. "Zach, what's wrong?"

"I don't feel really well, but I'll be all right."

"Have you heard about Sashza?"

"No. What now?" Zach said more cynically than he'd intended.

"She's at the hospital," he glanced at Zach and continued. "She has second and third degree burns over much of her body."

A flash of anger seized Zach. *Sailor Black.* Just a hint of it. Just enough to remind him of his weakened state and the implications that might arise out of him slipping out of control. Zach had never lost so much blood during an episode; accidentally instigating one now would most certainly cost him his life.

"What happened?" he asked.

"Get in. I'll update ya on the way back to Rosewood."

Zach got in the car. Hunter sped through the parking lot and onto 115th Street. By the time Hunter finished explaining what he knew, which wasn't much, they'd pulled up to the Rosewood entrance. More lookie loos had shown up since dusk, and Zach felt grateful that none had decided to encircle the property and caught him going through the back fence. As they waited for the security guard to unlock the gate, the faces outside his window mostly blended together. One old black man stood out from the rest. He was tall, had a white-stubbled beard and wore a brimmed hat. He held a sign that read: Jesus is NOT a ghost!

Zach had no clue what that message hoped to convey, but he had an irrational desire to hop out of the car and ask the man what he thought of the Holy Spirit. He realized he still must not be thinking with perfect clarity.

Hunter passed the security checkpoint and roared his car up toward the conglomeration of vehicles outside the Rosewood lobby. He stopped far short of them. He put the car in park and turned to Zach.

"Brother, I picked you up early 'cuz there's somethin' I need to tell you."

"Shoot," Zach said.

"I didn't release Dr. Johansson."

Zach couldn't believe his ears. "What? How?"

"You never reviewed the film of the exorcism did you?"

"No," Zach responded. "I haven't had time."

It was partially true, but Zach also had obvious personal reasons for avoiding exorcisms, even taped ones. Better to be safe than sorry in regards to Uncle Henry.

"Well, I did it in Latin," Hunter said. "I knew a doctor from the nineteenth century would understand me."

"And Bryce and the others wouldn't."

"Correct."

Hunter's eyes had taken on a faraway stare. "At a crucial moment, at the very last minute, rather than ordering the entity from the premises, I asked him to hide."

"To hide?"

"Yes, to make a bit of a scene to both impress and fool the others, and then to hide for twenty-four hours."

"And why didn't you tell me this last night?"

"It was so late, and my reasons for doing it weren't clear in my head. I planned on telling you first thing this evening. I didn't expect not to see you 'til ten o'clock!"

"And now that your head is clear," Zach said. "What were your reasons for doing it? Or rather not doing it?"

Sara peered from the steps of Rosewood out toward them.

"Hurry," Zach said, with as much urgency as he could muster. "Tell me!"

Short of having it wrung out of him, Hunter seemed reluctant to speak the reason out loud. Sara had started down the driveway towards them.

"C'mon!"

Finally, looking Zach squarely in the eyes he said, "Because down deep, I knew we'd need him to fight the evil here."

Sara walked up to the passenger's side door just as the car stopped.

Zach had only halfway emerged from the open door when Sara pressed him back into the vehicle.

"We need to talk," she said, sternly. "Hunter, do you mind if we use your car a minute?"

Hunter, who had already taken a few steps up toward Rosewood, shook his head.

"Move over," she said to Zach squeezing in. In his weakened condition, it took great effort to hop over to the driver's seat. "So what's up?"

"Sara, I'm sorry for disappearing, I assure you—"

"Assure me later," she said. "We don't have time now, Zach. What's going on?"

"I'm not exactly sure, but I know who planted evidence and may be planning on something bigger tonight."

"Who?"

"Matthew and Bryce."

She looked doubtful. "Are you sure?"

"I'm sure, Sara."

"How do you know?"

Zach explained the conversation he overheard and detailed Matthew and Bryce's exit through the false fence.

"Did they bring anything back through the opening?" she asked.

"I don't know. What time were they back here?" he asked, hoping to deflect.

"It's hard to say since everyone was on break and, I *thought*, taking naps." She shot him a look undoubtedly intended to make him feel guilty.

Considering what he'd done for the benefit of the show instead of napping, it didn't work.

"I saw them," Sara continued, "before eight o'clock."

"So before the thing happened at Sashza's?"

"You don't think they had something to do with that, do you?" Her face expressed incredulity, her eyes, fear.

"I don't think Bryce would...but I don't know the guy. Obviously."

She appeared uncharacteristically befuddled. "What should we do?"

"Well, let's just get through tonight without anyone else getting hurt. Tomorrow, we can confront them and hopefully get them to admit what evidence is false. I already know the peach juice thing is bogus."

She nodded in agreement. "Sounds good. Let's both keep our eyes open and no more secrets, okay?"

"Sure," he said.

"I mean it, Zach...oh," she said, "have you talked to Rebecca?"

"Not yet," Zach said. "I planned on calling her first thing after checking in here."

"She's waiting on you."

"Okay," Zach said. "I'll call her now."

"The little boy over there apparently was playing with matches last night."

"Really? Did she say if he's still talking about Boy?"

Sara's face expressed horror.

"What? Is it something about Boy?"

"No," Sara said. "Look."

He followed her gaze toward the back of the Rosewood property. At first, he couldn't believe his eyes. The sounds of Sara dialing 9-1-1 and reporting it, shook Zach from his daze. He opened the car door and stepped out. The stench of it overwhelmed him. A few *XPI* and *Demon Hunter* members spilled out of Rosewood to see what was going on.

The old stables building was engulfed in flames.

Chapter Thirty-Five

The next half hour was a blur to Zach. Members of both *XPI* and Demon Hunters spilled out of the surrounding tents and from Rosewood's lobby. Some came up to him to ensure he was alright. Many asked where he'd been. He told them they'd meet when all the commotion died down and he'd explain. Firefighters arrived on the scene. Cameramen from the show followed their efforts as swarms of firemen vainly attempted to save the building.

There was no chance.

Many of the lookie loos from outside the main entrance must have slipped by the lone security guard while the gates had opened for the fire trucks. A few onlookers attempted to blend into the show cast and crew, while others ran wildly through the property waving their hands and screaming like banshees. Within a few minutes, security back up arrived and rounded up people who didn't belong, transporting them to whereabouts unknown.

Amidst the chaos, Zach's godfather spoke to him.

Clear out of Rosewood.

Uncle Henry's tone sounded concerned.

Zach dialed Angel's number. It hadn't even completed a full ring.

"Hey boss, you okay? Are you back?"

"Yes, I'm back," Zach said into the phone. He looked over at the Foster house. Because of the incline, he couldn't tell if they could see the old stables building. "Can you see the fire from over there?"

"No, but we can sure smell it. The wind is blowing this way."

It was then that Zach noted the stiff easterly breeze had shoved a thick fog of smoke through the night sky toward the neighboring homes. The smoke cloud mostly held together as it floated over their rooftops like a slow-motion umbrella.

It reminded Zach why he had called. "Angel, I need you to get back here and start rounding up the equipment lickety-split."

"Huh?"

Zach hollered into the phone. "Get back here and get as much equipment out of Rosewood as fast as you can."

"Yes, bos—"

Zach clicked his phone closed. Calm, stay calm, Zach reminded himself.

A steaming gray billow of smoke had emerged from the remnants of the old stables building. It was nothing more than a smoldering skeleton now. Some firefighters sloshed across the wet grass making sure all embers were doused. Others continued to make sure the cameramen and show members kept a safe distance. However, most firefighting activity appeared to be finished.

Scanning the tree line, Zach realized that he'd conducted his episode only about fifty yards from the old stables building. He hoped that their investigation didn't uncover his bloody blanket and towels. Although nothing immediately would link him with them, he'd have a hard time explaining why the Sci-D TV water bottles he'd used for holy water were out there...not to mention, nearly one-hundred fluid ounces of his spilled blood.

A whiff of *Sailor Black* and his godfather's voice gave him a chill.

They won't find it, but someone will.

Zach could hardly traipse over there now and retrieve the stuff. He had planned on getting it later when everyone was asleep. If someone found it before then, good luck to them in trying to figure out what it meant.

From afar, he reexamined the charred remains of the old stables. He hardly thought the fire was a mistake. A premeditated action most likely, and he suspected foul play rather than paranormal activity. Is this why Matthew and Bryce had slipped out the secret hole in the fence? To get materials to commit arson? Was this their way of distracting attention from the hospital building so that they could plant more bogus evidence? And lastly, where were they?

Hunter sidled up next to Zach. "Something there is that doesn't love a fire."

"Where did you get that from?" Zach peered at him.

"Rebecca said it to me at some point," he said. "It's kind of eerily catchy."

"And, in this situation, appropriate."

"Someone or something is starting these fires in the hopes of damning these spirits to hell." Hunter said, in a matter-of-fact tone.

"Do you believe fire cleanses a place of them?" Zach asked.

"In certain cases, I believe it does." Hunter said. He was silent a moment. "You're thinking about leaving, aren't you?"

"I'm thinking I might need to beat up both Bryce and Sara but I'd say it's time to pack up our stuff and get the hell out of here before someone else gets hurt."

Hunter made a guttural noise that sounded a cross between a growl and a "hmmm." His lips scrunched off to one side and it looked as though he was biting at the inside of his cheek.

"What's buzzing through your head?" Zach asked.

"The doctor," Hunter said. "I feel responsible for him now. It feels as though things here aren't yet finished."

"What do you mean? You still feel his presence?"

"No," Hunter said. "I mean, yes I sense he hasn't left, but no, it seems as though he's still in hiding. It just feels like our work here isn't done."

"It may not be," Zach said. "But it's done for tonight. I'm putting my foot down before someone else gets hurt...or worse."

Hunter nodded absently and peered out at the line of trees in back of the property. "So do you want me to stick around then?"

As tempting as it was to ask Hunter to stay, as much as Zach missed Ray and wanted someone who he knew was firmly in his corner, Zach didn't want Hunter involved with whatever negativity would certainly come of what he was about to do.

"No. You head out now," Zach said. "Let's talk tomorrow."

"Yes, we sure will," Hunter said still gazing far away. "Yes, we will talk tomorrow."

"What are you planning to say?"

Most of the chaos had subsided. The fire engines departed, and only the fire marshal and a couple fire inspectors remained to poke through the rubble. Angel and Rebecca returned from the

Foster residence. Zach ordered him to leave the control center intact, but begin taking down cameras from the third floor and work his way downward. He asked her to spread word for everyone to assemble in the lobby. That's when he noticed Patrizia staring at him.

Maybe it was the insanity of the situation, possibly it was his exhaustion, but Zach finally recognized the expression on her face as she gazed. Her head slightly cocked, her eyes set and her lips slightly parted. She was looking at him with an expression of *longing*. Sara had approached and Zach pushed thoughts of the implications of that to the back of his mind.

"*Zack*, what are you planning to say?" Sara repeated.

"Just keep the cameras rolling—no matter what. I've got a plan."

Sara rolled her big brown eyes but said nothing. She darted off to coordinate with the cameramen.

Zach stood outside Rosewood's front door encouraging team members into the asylum, Patrizia approached with a look of determined intention. She gripped his forearm. "We need to talk."

Zach hustled along as she dragged him down the long Rosewood façade and pulled him around the corner of the building. Did she have some important piece of evidence that would further implicate Matthew and Bryce or someone else? Before he could think through the implications, Patrizia pressed him up against the brick wall. He didn't even put up a fight when she pulled up his shirt sleeve.

Her dark eyes looked down at the gauze bandages and then glared at him. She only needed to utter one word. "Why?"

The tingly pinpricks of embarrassment attacked his torso, especially his back. He muttered the first thing that came to mind. "It's not what you think."

"I know you're not suicidal," she said. "But you're a cutter?"

Zach knew of the practice. He actually understood why people might put themselves in physical pain to release emotional suffering. Still, he had never cut himself, nor would he ever. She gazed at him with such concern, such nonjudgmental interest that he felt the need to show her.

He unwrapped the gauze; they'd be healed by now. He could feel her penetrating glare as he wound it around and around in counterclockwise circles. When he'd finished, he held out his wrists for display. There was some spotting of blood on and around his *Chi Rho* tattoos, but as she undoubtedly could see, there were no cuts.

"I-I don't understand," she said. Her fingertips caressed the insides of his wrists in tiny S-shaped patterns.

"It's okay," Zach said. "No need to apologize and I appreciate your concern."

Still with his back pinned up against sharp bricks, he wasn't sure that he fully appreciated her concern, however...it seemed the right thing to say at the time.

"Do you?" she asked. "Do you really?"

His heart cranked into double time, and with the shortage of blood in his veins, he needed to be careful, very careful.

"I think that I do." He needed to look up at her because of her heeled-boot advantage. "Patrizia, we should—"

"Go in," she said, completing his thought. "I know we should. I know we need to. I just needed you to know that I care. I've watched all your shows and I know that you're for real. I care a lot."

Her face inched closer to his. If not for the brick-wall supporting his spine, Zach might have fallen over. As her lips gravitated towards his, Zach thought of her tattoo and the lithe arm that bore it. Their lips met. There was a creamy taste of lipstick and softness. At first, her nose tickled his cheekbone, and then pressed into it as he moved deeper into her mouth. His tongue lightly caressed hers in slow rhythmic circles. She emitted a soft whine of desire. It was a sound he'd never expected to hear from her, but it was unmistakable.

From seemingly another dimension, Sara's voice was laden with sarcasm. "Za-ach, we're all waiting for youuu."

Patrizia pulled away and stared at him. Zach knew he should say something witty or clever or romantic, but he was too stunned to process. Given the circumstance, anything that he would have uttered may not have made sense.

"Well, anyway, I just thought you should know," she said. She turned and walked away leaving Zach alone.

He expected Sara to come prancing around the corner of the building and, in a knowing voice, ask what had been going on. She didn't, and it allowed him to consider his next move.

Playing poker, Zach had learned that sometimes it was necessary to talk your opponent into or out of calling your bet. In this situation, with a lot of bravado and bluster, Zach could accuse Matthew and Bryce of deception and fraud, but getting at least one of them to admit guilt would be far better. Besides, if someone other than the two of them were involved, he'd only know for sure if that party was fingered by one of the other two culprits.

He turned the corner and caught a glimpse of Patrizia approaching Rosewood's entrance. Before she slipped from sight, she glanced back. Even from that distance he could see that she was grinning at him. Only then did he realize it was the first time he'd seen her smile.

Chapter Thirty-Six

"What's the John Dory wif you chaps pullin' down the cameras?" Pierre asked, before Zach had a chance to address the *Demon Hunter* and *XPI* teams.

Bryce stood on the far side of the lobby away from the group by several feet. Everyone was present or accounted for. Angel could be seen occasionally on the video monitors hauling down equipment. It looked like he'd finished removing the cameras from the third floor and was taking them down on the second level. The rest of the team stood around the lobby waiting for explanation to what was going on. The only member missing, and the one member Zach really wished could have been there, was Ray.

"Yeah, boss," Matthew said, "What gives?" His voice seemed tentative, although it may have been Zach's knowledge of Matthew's guilt being amplified.

"We're packing up and heading out before someone else gets hurt on this investigation. I take it you've all heard about Sashza?"

Heads nodded throughout the room.

"You think her accident had something to do with Rosewood?" Wendy asked.

Leave it to Wendy to ask the question most likely to make it onto the actual show. Sara zigzagged around the room with a handheld video cam; two regular cameramen also were filming the meeting. The whole scene ultimately might not make it into the final cut of the Halloween Special, but if it did, Sara would edit it to provide maximum drama.

"To be honest, Wendy, I don't know if they're connected or not." Shelly and Rico's eyes bulged at the mere possibility that they could be. Others maintained their somber mood. "But with this place's history of fires, and a fire here both last night and tonight, I'm not willing to take that chance. Something at Rosewood likes fire."

Sara momentarily dipped her camera. She was possibly already visualizing the shot, with that line as a commercial.

"Dude, you've *got* to be shitting me." Bryce strode from the far end of the lobby towards him. "You're going to run away now? Whatever. That's fine. But I think I speak for my entire team when I say that we're staying."

The Demon Hunters appeared either uncertain or unprepared to pound their fists together and bark. Zach had counted on precisely this reaction from Bryce.

"In fact," Bryce had moved closer, but maintained a safe distance. "The *attack* on her has us even more determined to solve the mystery of this place. We shall exorcise each and every evil spirit here at Rosewood!"

At that, the Demon Hunters erupted in their signature cheer.

"Bryce, I understand your frustration and desire to avenge your fallen team member, but I need to tell you something and I need to say it right to your face."

Bryce obliged. He towered over Zach. Like a ruffled-feathered peacock, Bryce puffed. His chest and shoulders swelled in a posture that suggested he was not about to back down.

But he'd never expect this.

Out of the corner of his eye, Zach spied Angel at the top of the lobby's circular staircase. He must have noticed Bryce in Zach's face and treaded down the stairs, as a sign of support—perhaps to lend physical support if needed.

"Man to man," Zach said, looking up at Bryce. "I need to apologize to you."

Apparently expecting an insult or an argument, Bryce reacted almost as though Zach had slapped his face. He opened his mouth and closed it.

Zach put his hand on Bryce's arm. His cohost's already tense muscles further constricted into stone-like bulges. "I need to look you in the eye and say 'I'm sorry' because one or more members of my team have sabotaged this mission and put us all in danger. Worst of all, he may have rigged an explosive device in Sashza's stove as retaliation for her having tried to warn us."

The group's murmur was loud enough to echo through the asylum's lobby. Bryce's glare softened for just a second. He cleared his throat. "Who?"

Zach so wanted to say, "You know who, you bastard." Instead, in dramatic fashion, he extended his arm, finger pointed, directly at Matthew. In silence, members of both teams turned and stared at the accused.

Before Matthew could deny it, Zach advanced on him. "Before we all arrived here at Rosewood, he cut a hole out of the back fence so that he could get onsite to plant evidence. I've seen the net-like contraption he devised to cover up the opening. At some point, he planted a device in the administration building which caused the wild EMF readings. After we went to bed last night, he removed it. Then, he paused the filming of two different video cameras and allowed his accomplice to sprinkle peach juice in room 217, which Patrizia's research has uncovered, wasn't *even the room* the peach jar patient killed himself in." The last part seemed to provide more credence to the accusation.

"I didn't..."

"You did!" Zach's anger level rose but was cut off by the smell of *Sailor Black*. He stopped four feet shy of where Matthew stood and took a deep calming breath. He would need to stay centered during this speech. "I gave you an opportunity and you betrayed me. Worse than that, even if it wasn't intentional, whatever you planted in the old stables building may have caused the fire!"

Matthew shook his head.

"Yes," Zach said. "I know for a fact. You organized and led someone else to stab me in the back. Who?"

Matthew said nothing. For a moment, Zach wondered if his plan had failed or worse, would backfire.

"How could you do this to me, Matthew? *How?*"

"I'm sorry," he said.

When he admitted it, everyone froze. The silence was so complete that even a tiny piece of plaster falling on Rosewood's third floor would have sounded like thunder.

"Who, Matthew? Who else did you recruit? Who else did you *poison?*"

Matthew's eyes lowered and his head drooped.

"I didn't," he said again. "I didn't recruit anyone."

"What do you mean?" Zach asked.

Matthew looked up, but didn't make eye contact. He was looking past Zach. Please say it, Zach thought, please say it.

"It was Bryce. He called a week ago and asked me to help him ensure a good show. That's all we were trying to do. Make sure this case got us results."

That was it. He'd gotten Matthew to say it!

"Whoa, dude!" Bryce said. "You got caught with your hand in the cookie jar. Don't go trying to smear my good name."

"Stop lying. It's over!" Matthew turned to Zach. "I broke the camera, yes. I planted the device and I paused the videos so Bryce could sprinkle peach juice in the room, but I did *not* do anything to the stables building or to Sashza. I had *nothing* to do with the fires."

"I don't believe a word you say." Angel rushed toward Matthew. "I trusted you—we trusted you. Screw Bryce Finman, *you're* the damn traitor."

He pressed his face close to Matthew's. Before Zach could step in, Matthew pushed Angel away. He attempted a punch which Angel mostly dodged. It hit him in the meaty part of the shoulder. Turk and Rico grabbed Matthew at the shoulders. Zach pressed both hands to Angel's chest and struggled to hold him back. Rebecca and Shelly stepped into the middle of the fracas. Zach wished they hadn't but they did.

"Calm, calm," Zach said in Angel's ear. "I've got this."

Angel eased up some, but it felt tentative.

"Bryce," Zach shouted. "I know Matthew's telling the truth. I saw you two leave out of the hole in the fence together!"

Bryce looked like he had taken a punch on the chin. "Dude, that's bullshit. What are you talking about?"

An extremely unwelcome figure stood behind Bryce.

"I don't give a rat's ass what any'a ya's are talkin' about. Git yer shit asses outta here!"

Flanked by two state troopers, he wasn't a phantasm, although, at that point, Zach wished he would have been.

"Don't even pack yer shit up neither," Grant Winkler shouted. "I don't get paid no overtime, and I ain't even on the clock. You can come back tomorrow during the day. At *my* convenience." He cackled as if they'd been sentenced to a chain gang under his command.

The only one in the room who moved was the state cop on Winkler's left. Tall and uniformed, he strode over to Matthew. A buzz cut of blond hair could faintly be seen under the trooper's brimmed police hat.

"Do you want to press charges?"

"Huh?" Matthew appeared stunned.

"I saw that," he pointed to Angel, "*gentleman* get up in your face. He can be charged for that."

"Hey!" Angel said. "He pun—"

"Quiet, *boy*. I wasn't talkin' to you."

He turned back to Matthew. "Do you want to press charges, sir?"

Demon Hunters and *XPI* alike stood motionless.

"Excuse me, *officer*," Sara called out. "Would you mind saying your name on camera for our *television* show?"

His attitude likely wouldn't have changed more if she'd proclaimed that she was the Queen of England.

"Yes, ma'am. Officer White, ma'am."

"How *appropriate*," she said. "Oh, Matthew, I'd answer the officer correctly, or else I'm *sure* the network will most certainly be pressing criminal charges in this matter."

Matthew shook his head. "No officer. No charges."

The cop nodded and looked relieved that this incident may not make the airwaves.

"Look children. The party here is over. Git out now!" Winkler wasn't as sauced as the prior night, but it was early. He still had time.

"Let's go people," Sara called out. "Grab what you can and throw it in the trucks. Pronto!"

Both teams started moving. They unplugged monitors and packed their ghost hunting equipment into metal cases.

"No grabbing your playthings. I said to git out now!"

Everyone froze.

"Oh I'm sure the policemen won't mind if we grab just a few expensive items on our way out. Would you, *Officer White*?"

He made eye contact with his partner and turned back to her. "No, ma'am. We'll wait outside, but we can only give you five minutes. Grab what you can and contact Mr. Winkler tomorrow for the rest."

Sara smiled. "Thank you, sir!" Without moving her lips, and under her breath, Zach could have sworn she added, "Fucker."

"Hey, no!" Winkler screeched. "I said widdout their shit!"

"Outside, sir." Officer White pointed to the door. "Now."

Apparently state cops didn't take orders from state custodians. Winkler reluctantly stumbled towards the door. As the threesome exited, the other state trooper turned to Winkler. "You're not planning on driving home tonight, are you, sir?"

"Zach and Bryce," Sara called out. "Tomorrow morning. First thing. Sci-D headquarters. The rest of you, I'll text you if and when we'll need you to help us clear out the rest of this equipment. For now, grab the small stuff. Detectors and gadgets. Anything that people could walk away with."

If Sara could possibly have known what would happen at Rosewood shortly after midnight, she'd never have allowed anything to be left behind.

Chapter Thirty-Seven

Welcomed by *Muses* door chime, Zach spotted Evelyn sitting at a table in the back. It appeared they'd have relative privacy. Four teenage girls sat a few tables away chatting and laughing, their movements and sounds resembling a gaggle of geese.

After having been escorted out Rosewood's gate by Winkler and an ever-growing number of Illinois state troopers, Zach knew he needed to get back to *Muses*. Afterwards he'd catch Ray before he got off work. Sara and Rebecca had chosen to call it an early night and headed home. When Angel heard that Zach was going to the strip club, he decided a few drinks would do him well. Turk agreed and it hadn't taken much convincing to get Shelly and Wendy to tag along. Then again, they were so shocked that Angel and Turk *agreed* on something, they could hardly object. Matthew, obviously, wasn't invited. He slunk out without saying anything to anyone and his fate, according to Sara, would be decided at the following morning's meeting with Dr. Benz. Zach had sent his friends on ahead and had stopped to rendezvous with Evelyn at *Muses*.

Being denied access to Rosewood didn't mean the case was over. For Zach, a paranormal investigation was over, not just when most of the mysteries were solved, but when *all* elements of the haunting were set straight.

He sat down. "Evelyn, no more fooling around. I need answers." Zach's adrenaline was flowing and pleasantries with her had gotten him nowhere.

"I'll do my best."

"Do you know what was written in Dr. Johansson's journal about John Paramour?"

"I didn't know Dr. Johansson kept a journal." Her mouth twitched.

"You're lying!" Zach slammed his hand on the table.

Loud whispering came from the teenage girls. One looked over her shoulder at them, whispered something to another and they'd all giggle. Considering their age group was dead smack in the middle of his new demographic base, they were likely fans.

"Cut the crap, Evelyn. Why have you been so secretive?"

"I was instructed to withhold information from you."

"By whom?"

"By your...patron."

"My *patron*?"

"Yes," she said, softly.

Was she referring to Sara? Dr. Benz? Or was this merely a diversionary tactic? Zach decided to ignore it and bear down. "Paramour was a relative of yours, wasn't he?"

"No."

"You're lying. I know you're lying!" Zach slapped the table again out of frustration. Evelyn's mouth hadn't twitched, but Paramour *must* have been a relative.

Tables away, the teens' whispers and giggles had transitioned to full-fledged laughs. Embarrassed, Zach lowered his voice. "He's too old to have been your father. Was he an uncle? Your grandfather?"

"No."

"Who was he?" Zach whispered. "Who?"

"He was an arsonist."

"C'mon, Evelyn, I figured that much out. He was also Pullman's Police Chief and he killed the hospital orderly, Thomas Carter, too. But why? "

Her lips pursed and her eyes filled with tears before she fluttered them and looked away. "Honestly, I'm not certain."

"Why try and implicate the woman living in the basement of the crime?"

Her teary eyes cleared with what looked to be amazement. She peered at him. "Wait, how did you know that?"

"John Paramour was the man who burned himself alive, wasn't he?"

She appeared perplexed. "I don't...he did?"

"But who was he to you? Your mother's first husb—"

One of the teenaged girls, one with long dark hair and wearing braces, had taken on the role of The Leader. She approached cautiously and stood halfway between her table and Zach's.

"You're the guy from that show, right?" she called out.

"I just might be." He tried to make his smile as pleasant as possible, given the circumstances.

"Do you talk to ghosts?" she asked, inching closer.

Behind her, the friends grabbed each other and embraced in giggles. Zach thought he heard one whisper, *"He talks to dead people."*

"From time to time, I do," Zach said, still smiling.

"Oh," she said. "'Um, 'cuz my friends were wondering — are you talking to one now?"

"What?" Zach asked shaking his head and flashing an apologetic look at his companion.

Evelyn wasn't smiling. Since the girl had approached, Evelyn had sat there staring with a blank expression — she seemed frozen, as though on pause waiting for him to resume their conversation. The unmistakable scent of *Sailor Black* tobacco had enveloped them.

"Well, like, we don't see you with a headset or an earphone and," the girl looked back for support at her two friends who, at that point, were doubled up with silent laughter. "And if you're not on the phone, then..."

"Then, what?" Zach asked, trying to hide his annoyance. What were girls this age doing out this late on a school night in the first place?

"Then, who are you talking to?"

This time, the voice in Zach's head was his own.

The store was completely deserted.

The secretive old girl kept some late hours.

Evelyn snapped out of her trance-like state. Her eyes grew wide, as though she was offended but afraid to say anything. Things other people had said replayed in Zach's mind.

"Anything for your friends tonight?"

"What's up, boss?" "What woman?"

Evelyn's wrinkled face had changed, transformed. Her skin looked hard, scorched. And then, as overwhelming as the pungent bouquet of *Sailor Black* during one of his episodes, it hit him.

Evelyn had zipped around the corner of the building and was gone.

"I cannot be seen with you."

Evelyn's skin continued to transform — into charred, black flesh. Her hair burned away leaving ragged, uneven stalks. Some peeled from her skull. In addition to the *Sailor Black*, Zach now smelled soot and ash.

In his head, he replayed the EVP recording in the basement. His subconscious mind finally supplied the missing parts:

Female voice: Meet me.

Female voice: Zach go there.

Charred flesh covered Evelyn's face. The smell of *Sailor Black* hit Zach so strongly that he wanted to vomit. He heard the voice of his godfather; however the words had been Wendy's. *"The only reference we have are the initials, PM.E."*

Her figure morphed again — blonde hair chopped short, delicate features, an impeccable complexion and those same kind eyes — the face Turk had discovered in the video footage of the basement! Evelyn's right hand was smeared with black ink. She was the woman who had been in Dr. Johansson's office — the one he'd fingerprinted. The one hiding in the basement and accused of murdering the orderly.

The only reference we have are the initials, PM.E.

"Paramour, M-something, Evelyn," Zach mumbled.

"Evelyn Marie Paramour," she whispered, almost apologetically, and then smiled as though noting the recognition in his eyes.

She vanished.

Behind the counter, a tray of glasses rattled seemingly of their own accord. The bell on the store entrance chimed as the door opened and then banged close.

"OH MY GOD," the leader girl said to the others. "Did you see that? Did you see her?"

"Yes!" they screamed in unison. They waved their hands around in staccato tempo, as their yells filled the coffee shop.

One of them screeched, "There was a woman sitting there."

In a teeming flailing bunch, they rushed outside; a chime marked their departure. Only then did Zach recall that the door had never chimed when Evelyn had entered *Muses*.

He sprinted towards the door. Before he could exit, the snotty barista tossed out a feeble semi-warning. "Dude, if you come in here again..."

"Don't worry," Zach said, storming through the door. "I won't be back."

He knew he wouldn't find Evelyn outside, but he knew where she'd be — the basement of Rosewood. He couldn't get to her there. Or could he?

But it wouldn't be alone.

As Zach sped down the 94 freeway to catch up with the others at Ray's club, the shock of Evelyn being a spirit wore off. He'd seen spirits before, however they were typically only passing glimpses or apparitions. He'd never interacted with one like that. Except for his Uncle Henry.

But that was different.

With Evelyn, he'd had no idea that she was a spirit. Still, the pieces fit and on some level, maybe he'd known subconsciously all along. What plagued him were the whys. Why did she contact him? Why had she been so secretive?

The vacant freeway offered no answers, and the hum of the road seemed almost to be mocking him. Zach flicked on the radio, but with his thoughts racing, he barely paid attention to the noise.

Why hadn't he pressed her on what she meant by "his patron"?

In everyday language a "patron" referred to a regular customer. However in the past, perhaps Evelyn's time, it was common to use the word for someone who supports or champions someone. Used in the term "patron saint" by the Catholic Church, it meant a saint who advances a particular cause or group. Evelyn could have only referred to one person with that term.

Zach's godfather, his Uncle Henry.

Ironically, the word patron came from the Latin, "patronus," meaning "father." Before he was able to ruminate on his godfather instructing other spirits to withhold information from him on cases, Zach arrived at the club.

Standing in the side parking lot was the pared-down group of XPI: Angel, Turk, Wendy and Shelly.

"It took you long enough, *mi hijo*." Angel said.

Wendy elbowed him in the ribs.

"Sorry, I had to make a stop first," Zach said. "Let's go find Ray."

He led them around to the front of the building.

"What the hell happened?" Ray yelled out to them. He was standing under the black awning of *Wine, Women & Thong.* He had positioned himself behind a purple velvet rope that connected two gold plated poles not quite waist high.

Zach shrugged. Behind him, the others remained silent.

"Nice to see you too, buddy," Zach said.

"Everything okay?" Ray asked, opening the velvet barrier to their admission.

"If by 'okay' you mean, 'holy fuck-me crazy,'" Angel said. "Then yes. All is okay."

"You got alcohol in there or what?" Turk asked.

Ray nodded, held open the door and waved them in. Shelly passed through first, pausing at the ticket window just inside the doorway. She pulled a bill from her purse. Ray leaned in, peered at the heavyset girl in the booth and held the side of his index finger in front of his lips. "Shhh, Gigi, we're forgetting to collect a cover from these guys."

She flashed an okay hand gesture and went back to reading a magazine.

The group received the news with an approving woot. As Wendy passed by, she ran her fingers across Ray's chest. "Thank you, Rayyy."

To which Angel, behind her muttered, "Free shit rocks!" He slapped Ray on the arm. "Thanks, man."

After Turk passed through the entrance, Ray turned to Zach. "Let's get these clowns settled in and then I want to hear everything."

Feeling somewhat weak and out of sorts, Zach leaned in and gave Ray a man-hug—a one-armed lean with a couple slaps to the back. "Let's go," he said.

Ray quickly caught up to the group and guided them through the glitzy chaos to an elevated table off to the side of the club. Zach had only been inside *Wine, Women & Thong* one other time and it had been his very first adventure in a strip club. The week after Zach completed his undergrad degree, Ray took him out to celebrate. The strip club was Zach's second-to-last stop on his graduation "celebration tour." The final stop having been a glamorous close-up view inside his toilet. It had been an experience Zach was eager never to repeat and certainly not one, as a good Catholic boy, he wanted to become habitual.

The club teemed with young, thin girls scantily dressed. Most wore miniscule underwear bottoms and skimpy halter-tops. During his previous visit, Ray laughed when Zach had expressed his expectation that the girls would wear more clothes before going on stage in order to prolong the experience of getting naked. He'd laughed even harder when Zach had asked if *Wine, Women & Thong* only served wine.

"I don't think I've ever seen anyone drink a glass of wine in here," Ray had said.

Of course the girls did not get completely nude on stage or anywhere in the club. They stripped to merely topless in a skimpy thong. It had been more than enough excitement. The admission of his activities had resulted in a good chuckle, and then a half-hearted lecture from Monsignor Macginty during Zach's next confession.

"What's behind there?" Wendy pointed to a purple velvet drape that covered a door near the back of the club. Above and below the curtain, only mirrors and black lighting could be seen.

"That's *restricted* area back there," Angel said, with a wave of his hand. "And it's *heaven!*"

Wendy didn't seem to know what he was talking about, but laughed anyway before sipping her margarita. Apparently Angel's machismo had made him, temporarily anyway, her favorite. Turk didn't seem to mind. He guffawed at Angel's quip and held out his fist for him to knock. Angel obliged and followed up with a sarcastic and mocking version of the *Demon Hunter* cheer.

"Yeah, what assholes they turned out to be," Turk muttered.

Considering Bryce's part in falsifying evidence, the Demon Hunters had not been invited along for drinks, and it had been an odd parting. Rico and Pierre shook hands and said goodbye as though nothing unusual had happened. Bryce got into the van without saying a word. Patrizia was solemn and cast Zach one longing goodbye glace. She hadn't said anything.

"Okay, kids. You all behave. No touching the performers. If they—"

"Performers!" Shelly chuckled and then snort laughed. "Sorry, Ray..."

"Anyway, if they touch you it's okay, but no touching them." He grabbed the nearest cocktail waitress. She probably wore less clothing than ninety-nine percent of women in ninety-five percent of all bars. Yet at *Wine, Women & Thong,* she seemed overdressed. "Maria, first round of shots and drinks is on me. The rest, these lowlifes can buy on their own."

The group cheered. Angel instigated the mock *Demon Hunters* cheer and the others immediately chimed in with gusto.

Zach's thoughts turned back to Patrizia and the kiss. It had come from nowhere. Seemingly nowhere, yet looking back the tension had been building between them since they'd first locked eyes. And now, considering how *XPI* and the Demon Hunters had left things, she might be out of his life forever.

"Hey, buddy-boy." Ray grabbed Zach by the neck with both hands and pretended to strangle him. "Come help me out up front a few minutes."

"Oh sure," Zach said. "You're just trying to get out of buying me a shot and drink."

"Tell ya what," Ray said. "You down a shot'a tequila and guzzle a margarita, and I'll get up there and dance." Ray thumbed the stage.

"Alright. Alright," Zach said. "I'll help you out up front!"

"Hooooo!" Angel shouted out.

Again they pounded fists *Demon Hunter* style. Zach pitied their waitress.

"Then let's go, son," Ray said, grabbing Zach by the collar as though he were going to toss him out on his ear.

They backtracked through the club. It was crowded for just past eleven on a weeknight. Ray navigated them towards the front door, and they arrived unscathed having survived flirtation attempts from several strippers.

"How do you deal with this every night?" Zach asked.

"Oh, I manage." Ray carded a group of college aged guys who were patiently waiting outside. They entered, and he turned to Zach. "Okay, buddy. C'mon, spill it. Tell everything."

By the time Zach updated Ray on the night's events—most of them at least, and returned to the table, it was clear that the foursome had imbibed far more than just one round of shots and drinks. Empty glasses cluttered the table. Zach looked at his watch. 11:25. He'd been away for a little less than half an hour, but it appeared as though he'd missed at least three rounds of shots. Apparently Rosewood's tension wasn't cut with a knife; it was drowned with a bottle of tequila.

Wendy was pressed up against Angel and—practically sitting on his lap. Even though she wasn't wearing a slave outfit, Zach couldn't suppress thinking there was a faint similarity to Jabba the Hutt and Princess Leia.

If Wendy had intended on making Turk jealous, it didn't appear to be working. He sat talking to Shelly; his opposite arm was casually draped around a "performer" who had nestled up to him. She'd rested her dyed blonde head on the front of his shoulder and was indifferently stroking his chest. As Zach walked up, he could have sworn he heard Turk talking about some girl he'd been dating less than a month whom he knew he was destined to marry.

"Zachman!" Turk lifted a nearly empty glass of something on the rocks. Upon realizing Zach didn't have a drink, he returned it to the table. "I got the last round. Whose is its turn?"

"Whose is its turn?" Wendy repeated.

They all laughed.

"I insist," Shelly shouted. "My's is its turn!"

They all laughed even harder.

The dancer who was sidled up to Turk must have seen this as her opportunity to escape. She slipped past Zach with a mere, "Excuse me..."

Turk didn't even seem to notice her absence. "Zach, whatcha havin'?" He put his arm over Shelly's shoulders. "My confidant and advisor's is its turn to buy."

Even though their third round of laughter was little more than a chuckle, Zach knew he would scream if someone made the same joke a fourth time.

"How much have you all had?" Zach asked. When there was no response, he added, "Did any of you eat dinner?"

"I did," Angel admitted, raising his meaty arm.

Shelly and Wendy exchanged glances that suggested they were colluding to not answer the question.

"Dinner's fer pussies," Turk said.

Considering Zach hadn't eaten anything since that protein bar since lunch, he wasn't one to lecture. Besides, unlike him, none of them had lost several pints of blood.

The waitress came and collected empties from the table while the group went through extensive machinations to essentially order another round of the same. Clink. Clink. Clink. She stacked shot glass upon shot glass. Mesmerized, Zach stared. She clunked the group of them into Angel's empty pint glass. Just like John Paramour, Zach thought, *collecting souls.* The more the waitress stacked, the easier the group of glasses was to manage. And if she dropped them? Imagine the impact.

Zach now knew that Evelyn was a spirit. However, was she the infamous female ghost of Rosewood that scared people away? And if she was, why? Zach gazed across the club at the strippers putting on false faces to attract customers, and the answer came.

Evelyn keeps putting on false faces to repel people.

XPI had been banned from Rosewood, but this case was far from over. John Paramour needed to be stopped; otherwise he and Evelyn would continue their haunting indefinitely.

"Zach, it's time..."

"Huh?"

"Time to order?" Wendy said.

"Oh yeah."

"Boy oh boy," Angel said, "if dat's what sobriety does to ya', git me an'udder round!"

Zach ordered his beer as the others laughed. "A bottle," he told the waitress. "Anything domestic."

He wasn't even sure why he'd bothered to ask for it. He didn't need his godfather's voice to confirm what his intuition had already told him. Zach would never get the chance to sip from that beer.

Chapter Thirty-Eight

"Did *who* call me?" Zach shouted into the phone as he darted towards the exit. "Rebecca, calm down. Hold on a sec."

He trotted past the girl in the ticket booth. She barely glanced up from her magazine. Zach burst through the door and outside to the cool night air and quietude.

"What's up?" Ray asked.

Zach held up a finger and whispered, "It's Rebecca."

Ray's brow furrowed. Like Zach, he knew she wouldn't have called at this hour except in an emergency.

"Ginny." Rebecca's tinny voice could finally be heard. "Foster. Joey's missing!"

"Missing? How? When?"

"She said he woke up screaming. Blabbering nonsense about his dad. And Boy."

"What?" Zach must have shouted it louder than he'd intended. Ray peered over and mouthed the words, "What's up?"

"Yeah, right? She said she calmed him, but he was both clammy and feverish. She went and got him a drink of water and he was gone. Like 'poof disappeared' gone. Ginny didn't know we'd gotten kicked out of Rosewood. She thought we were still in the neighborhood, so she called me." Rebecca was out of breath. "I'm getting in my car now but I'm forty-five minutes away. Can you go?"

"Rebecca, wait."

He's inside Rosewood.

Over the phone, Zach heard noise in the background—a car door slammed, keys jingled and dummy dings notified a driver to buckle the seatbelt.

"Wait, what?" Rebecca asked.

Zach reconsidered his instinct to try and convince her to stay home. It would be futile, wasted time. Precious wasted moments. Zach looked at his watch—11:33.

"Rebecca, call Ginny back. Tell her...tell her, I'm on my way. I'll be there in twenty minutes and to meet me at *Muses*. You meet me there, too."

"*Muses*? Why?"

"Rebecca, listen. They're open for another half hour. So is *GrocersMart*. Maybe someone down there saw Joey."

"Okay. Okay," she said, sounding a bit relieved. "I'll call her. I'll meet you there." She hung up.

He's inside Rosewood.

Zach knew Joey was inside the asylum. He knew no one near *Muses* or *GrocersMart* had seen him. It was nothing more than a fool's errand, and it wouldn't be the last Zach would need to conceive.

He's inside Rosewood. His godfather's voice said again. Despite the cool autumn night, Zach was sweating. His heart rate was dropping. And of course, there was the *Sailor Black* thick as coastal haze at dawn. Then, Uncle Henry's voice spoke again.

Zachary, you must go in there alone.

Ray had taken up residence within a foot of where Zach was standing. "Whatever it is, I'm going with you."

"But work?"

"Screw work."

"But R—"

A Ray "the Railroad" Ross hand waved in Zach's face. It would be no use arguing. Precious wasted moments. Ray opened the door, leaned close to the ticket booth and mumbled something to the girl. All Zach heard were the first and last words. "Tell" and "emergency."

Zach remembered the pairs of night vision goggles in the *XPI* truck and trotted to the parking lot to retrieve them. For a brief moment, he considered leaving Ray behind. He hadn't told him where Matthew's secret entrance was. By the time he'd gathered three pairs of goggles and locked the van, Ray was already there.

"C'mon, buddy. I'm driving." Ray pointed to his truck.

You must go in there alone.

"Shit, what about the others?" Zach asked. If he could get Ray to go back inside, he could make a break for it.

"Nah, we'll call them from the road. Time's a wasting."

Zach stood motionless.

Ray was already hoofing it to his pickup. "C'mon, buddy. Let's go. We'll make this an adventure. Find the kid and be heroes."

Becoming a hero was the furthest thing from Zach's mind. A gnawing fear ate away at him that not everyone that went into Rosewood would get out alive.

"Pull up there." Zach pointed to a spot flanked by an SUV and a late model Oldsmobile. Two letters, the "s" and the "i" on the Olds had long since fallen away leaving, "Old mob le" sprawled across the trunk.

"I don't think I can squeeze..." Ray peered across. "Ah, screw it."

He pulled in cockeyed with the back end of his pickup hanging out into the street. "I get a ticket, buddy, you're payin' for it."

"Deal," Zach said.

They were three-fourths down Pine Avenue, a good one-hundred and fifty yards past Rosewood's entrance. The location would give Zach the perfect opportunity to go left to the back fence and follow it to the far corner where the opening was. During the ride, he and Ray had discussed circling Rosewood separately, and then meeting up with Ginny and Rebecca in the *Muses* parking lot.

"So what's the plan?" Ray asked.

"We talked about it, you go one way I'll go the other and — "

"Yeah, yeah. I know. Which way should I take?"

"Oh." Zach looked right and then left. "Uhh, you go right. Rebecca should be getting there by the time we meet."

"Sweet," Ray said. He looked toward the main Rosewood gate. "Although I notice you're giving me the security guard to slip by. Or should we let him know about Joey?"

"We'd better not. We don't want to alert him in case we do need to go in there later."

"So what if he asks me what I'm doing poking around?"

Zach winked and grinned. "Hey, you're the boxer. Knock his block off if you need to."

"Roger, Dodger," Ray said with a smile. "So where is this secret entrance?"

"Around on Lincoln Avenue, near Ginny's," Zach lied. "Once we're all together, if we haven't found Joey, we can sneak in there and look. Although I'd have no idea how he'd have gotten in."

"That's true," Ray said. "Well, let's get cruisin'. Race you to the other side!"

They took off in separate directions. Zach's feet still ached from earlier, but he had at least managed to slip a pair of socks on to dull the chafing. The chilly night air smelled much as it had when Zach had walked from Matthew's fence hole to *Muses*. At the late hour, fewer people were keeping their hearths active, but ash from the fire at the old stable building lingered in the smoky air.

Zach passed by the administration building which was just thirty yards from the fence. No sign of Dr. Johansson; Hunter had asked him to lay low for twenty-four hours, and they were just about expired. Zach wondered how adept the ghost doctor was at tracking down missing kids.

Before turning the corner of the back fence line, Zach looked behind him; however the darkness had eclipsed Ray. The thought spooked him and he began jogging. The sooner he got inside Rosewood, the more time he'd have to locate and retrieve Joey before Ray and the others came looking for him. He had no plan of action. He hadn't had much time to think of why Joey would be in Rosewood or what Paramour wanted from him.

He ran parallel to where, earlier that night, the fire had been. Through the trees, the remaining framework of the old stables building seemed to glare at him as he passed. It was almost as if it was warning him off, telling him he was crazy for returning. And he well might be at that. He sprinted on, increasing his speed hoping that the cool breeze blowing past him would cleanse him of all insecurities and fears. Panting, Zach stopped running thirty yards short of the corner of the fence. He didn't stop out of fatigue. It was surprise.

Shock.

The netting constructed by Matthew to hide the opening had been pulled back. Someone else had crawled into Rosewood. There was a hole in the fence to prove it.

"Joey?" Zach called hoarsely into the night. "Joey? Are you here, Joey?"

The night vision goggles helped him navigate through the wooded vicinity beyond the fence. He figured he should swing through that area before heading up to the asylum itself. He'd also hoped to stumble upon his deserted belongings. They weren't in the location where he'd initiated his episode.

"Joey?"

He's inside Rosewood. Uncle Henry's voice repeated for the umpteenth time.

There was no use wasting any more time. The voice wouldn't lie about something like that. Combing the grounds had been a wish, a hope. A fantasy. If Joey had somehow found a way into the asylum, Zach would have to discover how, and then follow him in.

Zach trudged up toward the asylum. It appeared ever more ominous through the green hue of the night vision goggles. He tried to keep panning from side to side as he advanced towards Rosewood, but each glance toward the streetlights lining the asylum's property, turned the green images to a white haze.

Joey was inside Rosewood, but why? To what end? To serve what means? Had Paramour disguised as "Boy" lied to him? Worse, could Paramour be attempting to lure Joey into a dangerous situation, see to his death and steal his innocent soul? Or had Paramour been patient all these years, gaining power until the right child came along to attach himself to—reincarnate himself with?

As Zach had learned, possession was an uncomfortable situation, far unlike that portrayed in the movies. Possessions by spirits were far more common than the more dramatic demon possessions that fascinated people. Ghost possession, spirit possession while not immediately harmful to one's soul, contained many dangers. The accompanying spirit at times could be an unwelcome and insidious force. In Zach's case, it had proven helpful if not necessary. His godfather, Uncle Henry, had loved him, still loved him. However, people's souls changed when they die. At best, they stagnated. At worst, they decayed. Souls weren't meant to stay in this realm. Over the years, that had become more and more clear to Zach. Another thing that was obvious—neither John Paramour, nor the thing he had become, loved or cared for Joey. The havoc Paramour would wreak on that boy's soul would destroy it.

As Zach reached the asylum's brick wall, the scent of *Sailor Black* came to him.

Watch your eyes.

His eyes? What did his Uncle Henry mean by that? Zach took off the night vision goggles. From this point, he could navigate by moonlight. No sooner had he rounded the corner of Rosewood, than a powerful light blinded him.

The intense beam remained on his face. Zach raised a hand to shield his eyes from it, and it doubled as an attempt to protect himself from whoever was blinding him. His eyes struggled to adjust, but Zach could see nothing beyond the light.

"I knew y'az would come back. Knew it!"

It was the voice of Grant Winkler.

"Listen, Mr. Winkler, I know how this looks, but you've got to believe me, a boy is missing and —"

"Oh no. A boy is missing. Oh boo fucking hoo. Your boys and girls can kiss the ripe part of my ass!"

"No, sir. I mean a little —"

"Oh, don't worry. I closed and locked the door to the old visitor's area that you clowns left open."

He cackled at his own brilliance. He was blind stinking drunk, and with what Zach knew of Grant Winkler, that meant he'd be belligerently drunk. Who had left a door to Rosewood open? Bryce? Matthew? Had somehow Paramour's ghost opened it? And why?

So the boy could get in.

"And what in the mother of fuck me, is this?" Winkler diverted the beam to an area on the ground. Illuminated there were Zach's bloodstained towels, the blanket and his gym bag. "You kids kill some animals out there? Some initiation or somethin? Whad'juz go runnin' around cutting each other up?"

Zach felt numb from his toes to his chest. "No, sir. I assure you no one and no animals were —"

"You fuckin' kids think your shit don't stink. Ya' comes in here all high and mighty and think you're gonna fuck with my property? Well fuck you. Fuck them, too. You're goin' to jail ya' punk."

Reasoning with this bastard wasn't going to work. Zach stared directly into the flashlight's beam, and then looked away. He peered into the dark space above the flashlight hoping to be able to catch a glimpse of the man's figure.

A figure he could take aim at.

Zach sessions in the ring with Ray might come in handy after all. Zach was going to clock Winkler and he was going to clock him good—knock the bastard out.

One. Two. One Two. One two. Ran through his head. The first punch would hopefully stun him; the second would really do the damage. God forgive him, but this was a necessary and justified action. He crept closer.

"Please, Mr. Winkler, if you'll just listen a second." He inched closer still.

"Stay back ya' shitter," Winkler growled. "I'm callin' the cops now!"

Beyond the flashlight's glare, the soft emanation of light from a cell phone illuminated Winkler's jaw line ever so faintly. But it was enough.

One. Two. One Two. One two.

Zach charged.

Chapter Thirty-Nine

Winkler must have seen Zach coming because the flashlight wobbled. Its unsteady beam bounced and weaved as he tried to move away. The cell stayed lit long enough for Zach to hone in.

One. Two. One Two. One two.

"Stay back!"

Zach cocked his right, his jabbing hand.

"Stay—"

The flashlight wavered and lowered. Zach swung at the Winkler's darkened face.

One. Two!

There was a beast's growl. A thunk of body on body. Zach's fist sailed harmlessly through the air. Connected with nothing. Winkler was down.

Whatever it was that attacked had barely grazed Zach, but already off balance from the missed punch, the contact threw him to the ground.

Hit by a beast. Winkler had been knocked over by a beast. Zach thought it might be a wild dog. Fear toyed with his mind. A bear? A werewolf?

Beside him, in the darkness, Winkler whined in vain. "Noooo!"

There was a smack of flesh on flesh.

"Ah, fuck!"

It was quiet except for heavy breathing. His own and whoever or whatever else was there. On his knees, Zach scrambled away fast as he could.

"Zach, you all right?"

"Ray? Is that you?"

His eyes were still adjusting to the darkness. The flashlight lay ten yards away pointing to a dull spot on Rosewood's brick façade.

"Yeah."

"What the hell are you doing here?"

"I think I broke my hand."

Zach crawled closer. His friend's features appeared from the darkness. He was holding his right hand. *His* power punch hand. Next to him, Winkler was lying like a dead cowboy on a dusty main strip. Arms spread out. Head turned to the side. Instead of a soiled brim hat, Winkler's White Sox cap slanted off his head.

Zach stared at his friend. "Are you okay? How'd you get in here?"

"I'll live. It might be broken, though. Maybe just the pinky if I'm lucky. Crap."

"What? How..."

"Buddy, you're a great friend. You're a helluva ghost hunter," he said. "But you're one of the worst liars in the world."

It became clear. Ray'd doubled back and had been following him the whole time.

"When you turned the corner and I saw the beam, I ran around Rosewood quick as I could. Sorry it took so long."

And he was barely panting.

"What the heck is this shit?" Ray asked peering at the bloody accoutrements near Winkler.

Having just been told he was a terrible liar, Zach chose a version of truth. "Winkler had 'em when I got here."

"Weird! Hey, is that a Sci-D water bottle?"

"Hey, listen," Zach said, hoping to change the subject. "I've got a feeling Joey is in Rosewood and my intuition tells me I need to go in there alone in order to — "

Footfalls approached them in rapid succession from the same direction Zach had come. Before either could stand, a deep voice called out. "It's after midnight — technically that means it's 'tomorrow.'"

"Who's there?" Ray growled.

"Are we awake?"

Upon hearing the *Blazing Saddle's* quote, Zach took a deep breath and stuck his arm out to hold Ray down. "That depends," Zach whispered, unable to stifle a smile. "Are we black?"

"Yes, we are and *I'm* very confused! What are you white boys doing nappin' on the job?" He twanged the last line in a Slim Pickens drawl, a parody of a *Blazing Saddles* movie quote.

Hunter emerged from the pitch. He was fully clothed in black. "You boys wouldn't be able to see me at all except for the full moon," he said.

In the commotion of the night, Zach had never noticed the moon at its apex. Hunter was probably right. Even with ample moonlight, it was hard to see him. "What the hell are you doing here?"

"I felt called to come back tonight. I intended merely to stand on the back fence line to try and contact the doctor. I saw the hole in the fence and came on through. When I saw you two clomping through the trees, I figured I'd better tag along. Just in case."

"Yeah, you're just in the nick of time, thanks," Ray said. He and Zach stood. Ray still cradled his right hand in his left.

"Is he alive?" Hunter cocked his head and peered at Winkler in an odd sort of way.

"He'll survive," Ray said. "Prolly wake up with a hell of a headache."

"He was a whiskey shot away from passing out anyway," Zach said. "With any luck we'll find the kid and be gone before he wakes. With a lotta luck, he won't even remember this in the morning."

Hunter continued to stare down at him. "No. He's no threat to us. To himself, maybe, but not to us. Better take his cell phone just in case."

Zach did and also located the custodian's keys.

"Okay, are we ready to go in?" Ray headed towards Rosewood's entrance.

"Hold on guys," Zach said. "I really feel strongly that I should go in there alone."

"And I feel really strongly that I should get sex from Natalie Portman any time I want," Ray said. "But ain't gonna happen...neither of 'em."

"No," Hunter said. "Hear him out."

"Listen, I can't explain it. I just feel it. And I know you guys will try and protect me at all costs..." He sighed. "What if, what if you just give me ten, maybe fifteen minutes in there? Hunter, you go try and make contact with the doctor. Try and solicit his help over here. Something big is going down tonight. More than just a little boy missing. Do you feel it?"

"I feel it, brother."

"Ray, call Rebecca and tell her there was a change of plans. Sneak out and around to the security guard at the main entrance and meet her and Joey's mom there. Tell them that we're getting permission to come in and look and stall them there as long as you can. Ginny's presence here will only hurt things."

"Yeah, but—"

"But what if it takes longer?" Zach didn't even wait for him to nod. "I'll give you Winkler's keys, so you can break ranks and barge in whenever you feel you need to. You could even get away from those guys and sneak back through the fence hole. Just give me fifteen minutes. *Please.*"

Ray reluctantly agreed.

"And Ray? Get some ice for your hand. You're of no use to us long-term with a maimed paw."

They shared a chuckle, albeit nervous and brief. Zach retrieved the custodian's wayward flashlight, clicked it off and decided to bring it along as a backup to his night vision goggles. He unlocked the front door and tossed the keys back to Ray who snatched them with his good hand.

They stared up at him, waiting to leave once he entered. It seemed something should be said. It felt like *he* should say...something. But all that he wanted to say, all that needed to be said was too much. Anything spoken would come across as trite. So he said nothing to his friends, and they said nothing back.

Zach turned and journeyed into Rosewood's murk. Behind him, the door shut.

Chapter Forty

Zach had no idea where Joey would be, but he knew the first place he'd look. Also, he hoped to contact Evelyn. He needed to solicit her help.

Zach passed through the lobby. Through his night vision goggles, the scattered electronic equipment in the ancient vestibule gave the impression that the past had somehow smashed into the present, or perhaps vice versa.

He thought he should at least make a half-hearted attempt to avoid a prolonged search. "Joey? Joey are you here?" He thought of adding, "It's the guy from TV," but did not. He was especially grateful he didn't when the echo brought his words back at him. Hearing something that stupid in his own voice repeated back to him would have caused him to lose all self-respect. He stifled a chortle. What was it about libraries and terrifying, deserted, haunted asylums that brought out the giggles in people?

"Joey?"

No such luck. Zach would need to look for him and for Evelyn in the basement. That meant going down the basement stairs. He'd nearly put his last experience on them in the dark, out of his mind. He opened the door that led down, took a deep breath and tried to put it out of his mind again. This time, he told himself, he had night vision goggles. Still, he was having difficulty making out the stairs, but taking his second step, he had the thought of throwing caution to the wind and sprinting down them. Then the low battery indicator flashed urgently in his field of vision. They'd been fully charged earlier in the evening and the battery should have lasted several more hours. A phantasm had obviously sapped it. Was draining it.

Zach was taking his third step down when he heard an echoic voice. "Turn back!"

Zach wasn't afraid of Evelyn—however, on the staircase, it was difficult not to wonder what other spirits haunted Rosewood's basement. At night. During a full moon.

Quickly, he took another step down. And another while the night vision picture flashed. Another as it faded and was gone. He stood in complete blackness. He took off the goggles and placed them against the wall.

A shriek whistle emanated from somewhere on the staircase. It rose in pitch until Zach's ears hurt. "Who are *you?*" a voice boomed.

It was one of Angel's Whistling EMF-EVPs. Seemingly a lifetime ago, but it was only hours, he had told Angel to place one there. It must have been forgotten in their rush to leave Rosewood. The siren continued to signal paranormal activity. "Why are you here?" Angel's recorded voice asked.

The hair on Zach's arms stood straight up. His whole body tingled.

At the bottom of the stairs, a faint light came into view. Zach used the glow to locate the EMF-EVP on the steps and switch it off. He looked back and saw an apparition. It was a little girl. She was hazy at first, as though emerging from fog. Dressed in rags, her hair was unkempt. She took a step up toward him.

"Evelyn, is that you?" Zach yelled.

As if in response, the girl pointed up at him. Her mouth opened exposing a swollen tongue. Her lips never moved as the words came. "Get out!"

A chill ran through Zach. It was as if ice water crept up his legs and once it reached his waist, shot up his spine. He took a chance and stepped toward her. "Evelyn, a little boy is missing. We need to find him. We need your help."

The image wavered. It flashed and disappeared. In its place stood the skeletal remains of a burn victim. Flesh, sparse and charred, hung off the bones. There was a black-light glow that emanated from its core. It stood there glaring at him. Zach hoped this was Evelyn. He couldn't be positive that it was her, but he knew it was not John Paramour. Of that he was certain.

Zach's leg trembled as he inched forward to the next step down. "No," he said, softly. "You'll not scare me away. I need your help."

It, the thing, screeched. It was a terrible ungodly sound of pain and suffering. Zach thought of the air trapped in a balloon squealing as it escaped through a clamped opening. This noise was misery escaping through a stretched portal.

Zach took another unsteady step towards it. He stood just three or four stairs away. The thing vanished. Its scream continued in echoes off the walls down the basement's hallways. Again it was pitch black.

Zach considered pulling out the flashlight, but that had an extremely limited battery source. A spirit could drain it with very little effort, and then he'd be stuck with no way to flee in case of real threat. He pulled out his cell phone and used the soft glow from the display to light his way. He continued down the stairs one at a time. The interaction with the entity left Zach more convinced that it was Evelyn. It was she who was the mysterious ghost woman of Rosewood. It made sense. She tried to scare people away using her own abilities in an attempt to keep them safe from John Paramour, the real danger.

He made it to the bottom of the stairs and headed down the hallway where she'd been found over a century ago. Was she even hiding back then? Hiding from him? Zach suspected she was.

"But why hide now, Evelyn?" He meant it to be a question but, echoed over and over, his words sounded more like an accusation.

"We can fight him. Fight him together." The repeating echo of "together" sounded encouraging. "Help me find the little boy and stop John from hurting him!" The reverberation of those words jumbled together. Zach was approaching the area they'd caught her both on camera as a female form on her way to meet him at *Muses,* and on EVP recordings made by Rebecca and Patrizia.

"Evelyn, please?" Zach let all the fear and worry and concern get expressed in his voice. "I need your help. Please talk to me."

"Leave this place. Leave!" It came from all around and echoed meekly off the concrete.

"I'll not turn back. I'll not leave," Zach said.

"You're not afraid?"

"No, Evelyn, I'm not afraid of you." Zach said, softly.

The basement air, already stale and chilly became ice cold. She materialized out of the darkness about twelve feet away. She looked like the elderly lady he'd originally met. Taking a few steps toward him, she regressed in age—grew younger. A pretty lady not much older than him—her age at her death. It was hard to think of her as this age—so young. Her hair chopped short had, during that time period, helped her look crazy. By modern day standards, it was in style.

"You're in danger," she said. "You need to keep your friends away from here. I'd hoped that perhaps..."

"That we'd solve the case and get rid of him?"

"No, no. Not like that at all."

A long ago lesson had stayed with Zach, mostly because he thought of it every time he heard the song, *Billie Jean*. Zach considered the advice of Monsignor Macginty.

Take care of it in yer head, before the lie becomes the truth.

Dead over a century, it must be difficult for Evelyn to distinguish between the truth and what she wished was reality. She lived in the shadows between the living and the world of her past. From what Zach knew of her short life, it had been filled with deceit and intrigue. He needed to know the truth; Joey's life might depend on it.

"Evelyn, once this is over, we'll stay away. Everyone will. I promise."

"It would be best that way," she said.

"First, I need to know what happened—an innocent boy's life is in danger. Please tell me the truth."

"What would you like to know?"

"Why did you come to Rosewood?"

"It started one day when John was at work, I accidentally came upon his plans. They were terrible, terrible writings of hate and power. He wanted to be a god. He wanted to be *the* God. He wanted to be a demon. He was insane. I knew I had to hide, not run."

"Why run or hide?" Zach asked. "Why not report it to someone? The Mayor or someone big?"

"Think about it," she said, her voice cracking. "A young woman alone standing up to a powerful man, a police chief? In Chicago? Let's be realistic, these kinds of things just don't happen, Mr. Kalusky."

Zach considered Evelyn being raised a full generation prior to women gaining the right to vote. It would be difficult enough in modern times to bring down a police chief with unsubstantiated accusations of demonology, back then it would surely have been scoffed at. Then a thought really hit him hard. *Who knows what he would have done to her.*

Zach shuddered.

"In any case," Evelyn continued, "with John's resources in the police department, he'd find me if I ran. I bought a train ticket to Springfield. I boarded the train with my packed luggage. I got off the train at the first stop without my bags, without virtually any possessions. Thomas picked me up and brought me back to Pullman. He brought me here to Rosewood."

"Thomas Carter?" Zach verified.

Evelyn's eyes welled with tears. "Yes, dear Thomas."

"You two were lovers?"

"Oh no!" She raised a translucent hand to her mouth. "Not at first anyway. That was only much, much later."

Zach wanted to ask a question but hesitated. It involved Thomas's murder and he knew it would upset her.

"At first, I thought that I'd only stay at Rosewood a short time. I'd let John either get caught for his crimes, or for him to give up on trying to find me. I knew Rosewood would be the very last place he'd ever look. Because of his mother, he feared and despised 'the insane' as he called them. Besides, who would have ever suspected?"

"And Thomas?" Zach asked. He hoped she would give him the information he needed without having to ask her about it.

"Thomas was very kind to me and he provided me with everything that I needed. During the daytime, I was free to stroll the grounds. The nurses and other orderlies knew I wasn't *their* ward and assumed me to be a visitor, a do-gooder that liked to visit the infirmed. I did so enjoy getting to know some of those people."

Her face clouded, darkened. Evelyn looked more pale than when she had first appeared. Her skin wasn't just whiter, her entire image appeared to be losing color, fading.

"When Thomas ended up dead and John tried to frame me for the murder, I knew that if I stayed, it was a matter of time before he got to me. I pleaded with Dr. Johansson to let me go. He knew from something called a fingerprint that I was innocent of the crime, but I couldn't convince him that I didn't belong here. I knew that if I made too much of a fuss, or told him what I knew of John, not only would he really think me insane, but that John would..."

"Have you done in?" But she'd skipped over something important, Zach thought.

"Yes. Now, with the strength he's acquired over the years, over any period of time he cannot be endured, he cannot be resisted. He manipulates people to do his will. Other crimes, he commits himself. Hiding and flight are the only options."

"What about defeating him?" Zach asked. "What about getting rid of him for good?"

"I don't think it's possible," she said. "It's all I can do to keep him away from the hospital building. Look at what he did to your group. His subtle manipulation influenced them dramatically over just two days."

"My group?"

"Well yes, the Mexican boy lighting candles all over the place. The Asian girl, smoking drugs. The tall guy with the weird haircut waiving his funny cigarette around where one loose ember could light the whole property on fire. Do you think these are accidents? Coincidences? He puts ideas into people's heads. He promises them things."

Zach said nothing.

"Think what he can do over time. Imagine his affect on the young, the lonely and the feeble minded."

Zach thought of Wendy's description of the 1998 arsonist. He was homeless, bipolar and he was hearing voices — voices that told him to burn down the Pullman Factory.

"Usually, John preys on women. Before I came to Rosewood, John burned down the Pullman Market Square because he claimed two female spirits were haunting it. His writings stated that he burned down the H.H. Holmes 'castle' to purge it of lingering female spirits."

Zach was familiar with the concept that fire burned and incinerated human spirits. It was a hotly contested debate in the paranormal circles. Zach had once asked Hunter his opinion. "Better to be safe than sorry," he'd said. "If I'm ever a ghost, take care that I'm exorcised and sent to the light before anything burns down my haunting site."

Evelyn's figure continued to lose color. The glow about her was diminishing.

She continued. "I need not mention John's motive for burning Rosewood's female quarters. To murder his wife, yes, but to kill as many women as he could."

The matter of fact way Evelyn spoke of herself in the third person and glossed over her own death didn't surprise him. Many lingering spirits confused the details of their passing. She was rambling now. Sharing everything that had been bottled up in her for over a hundred years. But this was information that Zach might need to do battle with John Paramour.

"Even his final act of arson,' she said, "setting himself ablaze, which to some might appear an act of weakness or surrender was a deliberate and planned act. What the official history doesn't report, what decent people of those times would never print in an official record, was that he first marked the spot with a pentagon. He surrounded himself with grisly souvenirs, trophies, if you will, of his crimes. He wanted — still wants to become a demon god."

Zach sensed that his time with her was growing short. With every passing moment, she seemed to be more and more translucent.

"Before Thomas's death," she continued, "I assumed Rosewood would be the last place John would look for me. After the fire at the female's quarters, I hid quietly here in the basement again. I let John think that I'd departed. I had no intention of leaving and letting him completely take over. Someone needed to thwart his destructive schemes. Could you imagine the havoc he would wreak if they'd made a school or museum of Rosewood? All those children. Oh, my heavens no. I did what I could. I frightened people away. I limited his damage."

"Evelyn, did you and Dr. Johansson work together to keep John at bay?"

"No. Yes and no, really. Dr. Johansson never completely accepted his death. When Rosewood closed, he continued fighting for its survival. He didn't quite understand but regardless, his actions helped keep John away from the administration building."

"Evelyn, why did you withhold this from me for so long? Why didn't you just tell me this that first night we met?"

She answered so matter-of-factly, but her response caught Zach completely by surprise. "Your uncle told me not to."

"What?"

Her voice was becoming more and more faint. "He said we needed to wait and let you figure most of it out on your own."

Zach didn't have time to consider the implications of *that* information. Evelyn's shape was little more than an outline. At the rate she was dissipating, he might not even be able to hear her final response.

"I have one last question." It was the question Zach didn't dare ask earlier. He suspected the answer; however, he needed her reaction, if not her words, to confirm it.

"Hurry Mr. Kalusky. I'm so very tired."

"Did Thomas go to your husband and tell him you two wished to be together?"

Her outline flickered as though the question startled or upset her.

"Oh, no. Thomas would never have done that. We'd talked about running away together. Moving west or south or east but, no. Thomas would know better than going to John. He'd never do that. Thomas will return for me one day. This I know."

The last thing Zach could see of Evelyn before she completely vanished from sight was her mouth twitching.

Before the lie becomes the truth.

Invisible now, Evelyn's voice was fading as though she was moving away through a very long tunnel. "I need to go lie down now, Mr. Kalusky. I hope you don't mind. I believe that little boy is here, wandering the halls. He's not working for John. I suspect he doesn't believe John's lies. The little boy is trying to fight him. I tried to frighten him and his mother away. I doubt he'll..."

The rest, assuming there was any, was inaudible to Zach's ears.

Chapter Forty-One

Zach heard them shouting before he was halfway up the staircase. He used the flashlight to locate the night vision goggles, and then kept it on while he scrambled the rest of the way up.

"Joey! Zach! Hello? Where are you?"

He hurried into the lobby where Ray, Hunter and Rebecca stood. Their flashlight beams swarmed throughout the darkness.

"Hey, you guys were supposed to give me at least fifteen minutes alone!"

"Hey moron," Ray said. "It's been over twenty-five minutes. Which floors did you cover?"

"I got hung up," Zach said. "But he's not in the basement."

Ray growled and surveyed the lobby. "Where the hell is this kid?"

"He's in here somewhere. Hey Hunter, any luck on contacting the doctor?"

Hunter seesawed his hand in a "maybe yes, maybe no" motion. "I felt a presence, but he didn't talk. Hopefully he listened."

"Rebecca, aren't you supposed to be with Ginny?"

"Nice to see you too," she said. "We were waiting with her at the main gate. The cops have to report missing children to the national database within two hours of a report, so Ginny wanted to check in here before making this a federal issue. We left her with the security guard up front. Ray made up an excuse that he needed to show me something in his car. If she finds out we're in here and kept her out of the loop, she's going to throw a conniption fit."

"Hey, we're wasting time here with pleasantries," Ray said. His right hand had swelled to the size of a small water balloon.

"Okay." Zach pointed up the staircase. "Hunter and Rebecca, start at the top and work your way down. Ray and I will cover the first floor. If we don't find him, we'll likely meet up on the second floor somewhere. Partners stick together. No one breaks off alone."

"Live together, die alone," Hunter said.

Zach didn't bother asking what that line was from. "Call or text message if you find him. Let's go!"

They broke off in pairs. Hunter and Rebecca trotted up the circular main staircase. Zach started down the hall toward the back of the building. Ray followed along.

"Where are we heading?" he asked.

"Winkler said something about a door being left unlocked in the visitor's area. Let's start there."

"So what held you up in the basement?"

"Don't worry about it," Zach said. "I'll tell ya later."

They arrived at the old visitor's room and shone their flashlights around it. There were a lot of footprints across the dusty floor, however they looked like they'd come from the ghost hunter's tour their first day at Rosewood.

"What's that?" Ray whispered.

His light beam trained on something on the floor that looked vaguely like a spider. He crept to the far side of the room. He bent, picked it up and held it near his face. Zach sidled up next to him and illuminated the find. It was a fuzzy red piece of lint. The kind that would scrape off a child's pajamas.

"I've got the eyesight don't I, buddy?" Ray asked.

Zach said nothing, but rewarded his friend with a thumbs up signal.

Following the line from the outside door to where the lint had been, the two of them trekked into the hall leading to the infirmary. They left no room unchecked.

"Did you hear that?" Zach asked, hoarsely.

Ray extended his nose in the direction the noise had come from. It had sounded like a child's sigh. After investigating the infirmary, they checked every room and were heading back towards the lobby. Since the tiny evidence of red pajamas, they had found nothing.

"I know where he is," Ray said. "Room 111."

It made sense. In addition to the tables the video equipment was set up on, there were packing pads and a number of equipment cases. The perfect hiding spot for a kid. In hindsight, they should have looked there first.

They entered but didn't see him. "Joey? Are you in here?"

There was rustling behind the cases beneath the table.

"Joey?"

"Go away. Leave me alone!"

Zach turned and flashed Ray a thumbs up. Ray looked as relieved as Zach felt that they'd found the boy. "Joey, your mom's very worried about you."

"Well, I'm worried about her. That's why I'm hiding."

Zach motioned to Ray to call Hunter and Rebecca.

"Joey, it's not safe to hide here. We've got to get you home."

"No!" he skittered away until his back hit the wall. "He told me he'd burn it down if I didn't help him. It's the only thing he said that I believe."

"Who?" Zach asked, already knowing the answer. He inched closer to the boy while the question distracted him.

"The boy who isn't a boy. He promised that he'd bring my daddy back. He wanted me to help him burn this building down. I told him to do it himself."

Zach gently but firmly gathered the boy in his arms. "What did he say to that?"

"He said there was a lady ghost living here who he was afraid of."

It hadn't struck Zach before that John Paramour, or whatever he had become, might not know the spirit in the asylum was Evelyn. With her ability to shift forms, maybe she had been able to disguise herself to him all these years.

"Good. I'm glad he's afraid. I promise. I won't let him hurt you or your mommy. I promise. Let's get out of here, okay?"

Joey didn't respond, but his eyes were already half closed. He put his head down on Zach's shoulder.

"Let's get the puck outta Dodge," Ray said.

They shuffled through the hallway towards the lobby. They were twenty yards away when it lit up. No doubt originating atop the main staircase, a flashlight beam illuminated the crooked figure of Grant Winkler. From Zach's vantage point, it looked like the custodian was in a spotlight at the end of a tunnel.

"Yeah, I seen you up there," he said pointing toward the top of the steps. "And what the hell are you guys doing in here with a little kid?"

Winkler wasn't looking at Zach and Joey; he was looking up the stairs at someone they couldn't see.

Hunter's voice echoed through the lobby. "That's not a boy. Stay away from it."

Winkler stumbled out of view toward the staircase.

"Last fuckin' thing I need, is some nig—. Excuse me, some *person of color*, to tell me what is and what ain't no boy!" He cackled as though he'd just told the funniest joke in the history of late-night TV.

Zach eyeballed Ray and signaled that they move forward.

He whispered in Joey's ear. "Be very quiet, okay?"

Hiding his eyes on Zach's shoulder, Joey nodded. Zach's shirt felt wet as it rubbed against his skin. He wondered if it were Joey's snot or his tears.

They crept forward toward the lobby.

"Look Mr. Winkler..." It was Rebecca. "We're trying to warn y—"

"No, you look here, missy. I'll be the one doin' the warnin'. This is my place. You take your kid and get the fuck out!"

His footfalls plodding up the steps echoed throughout the otherwise silent lobby. Then, from that direction, there came a high-frequency screech.

"Who are you?!" An electronic version of Angel's voice screamed above the increasing blare of a siren. "Who are you?!" It repeated.

It was another Whistling EMF-EVP. Any doubt as to whom or what was lurking on the staircase was erased. It could be none other than John Paramour.

Ray darted into the lobby and looked up. The flashlights from above were steadily dimming—being drained of power.

Zach moved out of the hallway shielding Joey in his arms. He couldn't help but look. For years, no matter how Zach tried to forget it, some random event would trigger a snapshot of the scene. The etched memory would replay with such crystal clarity, that it would cause Zach's heart to race.

At the top of the stairs, Hunter stood with wide eyes. Rebecca bore a similar look of horror. Halfway up the staircase, Winkler was turning around, and was off balance searching for the sound of the siren. Maybe he'd already spotted the device, maybe he hadn't.

And in between Winkler and the top of the staircase stood Boy.

Dressed in a brown suit like those worn in ancient photographs, his haircut looked as if his head had been placed in a bowl. His part left an upside-down V in the middle of his forehead.

It appeared Boy may have been blocking Hunter and Rebecca's descent when Winkler had shown up. His attention, like Winkler's seemed focused on identifying the source of the noise.

From that snapshot things happened all at once. Later, Zach's perception slowed everything down to a crawl, but that was likely a trick of the memory.

Boy glanced in Zach's direction. He didn't make eye contact, but it had been close enough to run Zach's blood cold.

Boy was staring at Joey.

He began to transform, started to grow, not into the burly blowhard police officer John Paramour had been in Zach's visions, but into something else, something different. His legs grew first, or perhaps that's just what Zach noticed. They sprouted both up and out shredding his brown slacks. Boy's upper body erupted, splattering fragments into the air, but the bits of flesh disappeared into nothingness before they traveled more than a few feet. His chest, massive and hairy, expanded outward until it was the size of four men's torsos.

It all happened silently.

Winkler began to turn back. As though if watching a frame-by-frame video, Zach could see it happening—knew what would occur. There had been time to shout a warning—plenty of time. But he didn't.

He couldn't.

He would justify it to himself later with mentally constructed excuses that revolved around the assumption no one else had said anything—an assumption that Zach never could be sure of since, except for his uncle's voice, he heard nothing until *after* the dreadful sound.

You cannot save him.

Winkler had begun to turn back. The Paramour thing's face was in a state of transition. The crooked, pug nose and facial features of the John Paramour that Zach had seen during his episode were briefly visible. Then, the nose and ears elongated. Its pointed chin jutted out even further. Ram horns sprouted from its forehead. It stood nearly nine-feet tall. By the time Winkler turned back, it had already started descending towards him. He looked up and flinched.

The flinch caused him to slip backwards.

His head struck the steps at the same time as his shoulders. At least in Zach's recollection there was still no sound. The head trauma alone might well have killed Winkler. But it was the tumble that did him in—not the somersaulting tumble as seen in movies—more an awkward backward sprawl. He slid down a few steps before his head hit the side of the staircase wall at an unnatural angle. When Winkler's neck broke, Zach heard the snap—and he'd never forget that sound. At first the mind denies—tricks itself into thinking that everything will be okay. But soon enough, awareness sinks in—the man is dead. Zach didn't delude himself into thinking that he liked Winkler. Had the man lived, Zach would likely have continued to dislike him. But there was something about witnessing his death that would link them together forever.

The thing that had been John Paramour, descended the steps. He swept past Winkler's corpse both avoiding and ignoring the body's convulsing limbs.

He moved toward them. Even with his broken hand, Ray stepped in front to protect them.

"Wait," Zach tried to say, but it eked out weakly. He wanted to tell Ray to run. Zach wanted to flee himself, but he was frozen.

Paramour approached with brash indifference. His black eyes—there was an emptiness to them. It suggested that John Paramour ceased to be just a spirit. Over one hundred years of evil—a century of collecting souls had given him power. Paramour barely paused to flick Ray aside as if he were an insect.

Ray flew across the lobby, smashed against the far wall and lay still.

Paramour drew closer to Zach and Joey. A century ago, when Rosewood still housed patients, Paramour had caused as many as thirty seven to commit suicide. Since then, who knew how many lives he'd destroyed, how many fires he'd caused others to light? He'd become so powerful that he could now ignite them on his own in our realm. He wasn't merely a soul snatcher, but as Rebecca had surmised, he was the most powerful soul snatcher on record.

And he wanted Joey.

Ray's spilled flashlight, lying halfway across the lobby, was the last to die. It was pitch black.

The Paramour-thing spoke. His breath stunk of expired beef — his voice toned with contempt and hatred. *"I want you to watch."*

A candle atop the video control panel lit. Then, one after another, each wick of every candle that Angel had laid out the first night in the lobby took fire. It was like a falling domino string of flames.

"I want you to watch *me take him."*

"He doesn't want to be with you!" Zach shouted.

Paramour stopped short of where Zach stood. *"What makes you think he has a choice?"*

From the top of the staircase, Rebecca and Hunter recited familiar words. "Saint Michael the Archangel, defend us in battle. Be our protection against the wickedness and snares of the devil."

Although safe where they had been, they advanced on the entity.

"May God rebuke him, we humbly pray; and do Thou, O Prince of the Heavenly Host."

Paramour glared at Zach. *"Leave the boy. I have no need of you."*

Ray had recovered and joined Hunter and Rebecca in the prayer. "By the Divine Power of God — cast into hell, Satan and all the evil spirits, who roam throughout the world seeking the ruin of souls."

In unison they all shouted, "Amen."

Its mouth opened and emitted a noise that seemed to be comprised of many voices — thousands of discordant screams.

Never had Zach imagined a noise so disturbing. And yet it did not advance on him and Joey. Something was protecting them.

But what?

Hunter and Rebecca continued down the staircase. In unison they shouted, "The power of Christ compels you. The love of Christ commands you!"

With Joey clutching tightly to his neck and shoulders, Zach peered around the room. Ray's strength. Rebecca's intelligence. Hunter's sense of humor. Joey's innocence and his own powerful intuition. They represented so many of the positive qualities of human nature — things John Paramour detested. But they still lacked something. The host and hostess — the keeper and the kept — Evelyn and Dr. Johansson.

He yelled as loud as he could. "Hunter, summon the doctor! Do it now!"

Hunter closed his eyes. His dark face twitched and his lips moved.

Zach called out. "Evelyn, we need your help! We *can* get rid of him. Please!"

At first, the room gave no sign of her, then the candles flickered. He could feel her there, watching, waiting for something. Zach couldn't tell if the doctor was present.

"The power of Christ compels you. The love of Christ commands you!" Ray, Hunter and Rebecca closed in, yelling. They lacked only holy water to cast the demon to hell. Zach remembered Macginty's comment.

"Holy water is holy water, is holy water. Help yourself whenever you need'ta, son."

But how did that apply to this situation?

Holy water is water, son.

The voice was at once both his uncle's and the monsignor's. *"Help yourself whenever you need'ta, son."*

He *had* helped himself to holy water. After his episode, he drank holy water. It was inside him. It had blended with his body, but was still a part of him nonetheless — contained in the microscopic makeup of his cells. Zach imagined it in the blood coursing through his veins. Holy water was present in his sweat. Holy water was lubricating the fluids in his eyes. Hell, it was even part of his —

Zach spit at Paramour. Then, in one fluid motion, he spun and slid Joey across the wood floor away from him so that he stood between the boy and the entity.

Paramour screeched, but held his ground. The anguished cries echoed throughout Rosewood's lobby.

"John," Zach said, calmly. "You're not a demon, John."

Perhaps he shouldn't have — maybe Zach should have merely trusted, however he spit at him again. Paramour seemed to wince, but that might have merely been Zach's wishful thinking.

From his open mouth, a thousand voices cried. *"This is my place. My place!"*

"Saint Michael the Archangel," Zach began. The others, all of them, joined in. "Defend us in battle. Be our protection against the wickedness and snares of the devil."

Evelyn and Dr. Johansson stood side by side — their translucent figures wavered and glowed. She looked young, but her hair was long. Dr. Johansson, spectacles resting above his high cheekbones, appeared healthy and determined.

The voices of his friends rose. "May God rebuke him, we humbly pray; and do Thou, O Prince of the Heavenly Host."

It was time. Time for Zach, filled with holy water, to make the leap of faith onto John Paramour — the wicked man who wanted to be a god. Onto the evil spirit that wished to become a demon.

The police chief version of John Paramour stood just a few feet from Zach.

Confidently Zach said to him, "You're not a demon, John, but you're going to hell."

Paramour's eyes blazed. "You don't have the strength."

"This is not your place," a female voice said. "You must leave."

"It is time for you to go," a male voice confirmed.

Zach sensed Evelyn and Dr. Johansson now flanking him on each side. Between their strength as spirits and Zach's physical body infused with holy water, Paramour didn't stand a chance.

Zach took a few quick steps and dove headlong onto him. There was a deafening squeal. High pitched and rancid to the ears, it masked the sizzle of flesh. Zach hoped it was not his flesh; he felt warmth — not a burning sensation, but it seemed all the moisture was being drained from his body. He thought of his dying mother, he recalled her sadness and pain. He remembered her confusion and anguish as her illness insidiously stripped away all remnants of the person she had been. Her good part. Tears poured from his eyes. Holy water tears.

The Paramour thing dropped to his knees.

"This water is holy water," Zach said, although he couldn't hear his own voice. "Now go to hell."

From seemingly far away, voices cried out, "By the Divine Power of God—cast into hell, Satan and all the evil spirits, who roam throughout the world seeking the ruin of souls."

Despite his emotional and physical pain, with all his might, Zach screamed, "Amen!"

A tormented cry, presumably from the souls that Paramour had collected, arose around them—woeful resignation and wasted rage tainted the voices as they faced damnation.

Sounding far away, Hunter and Rebecca yelled, "Be gone!"

Chapter Forty-Two

It was over.

The lobby of Rosewood was dark and silent. It vaguely smelled of sulfur. The candles had all been extinguished, and Zach's face felt sunburned. Hair had been singed from his arms, and he could tell that he was dangerously dehydrated. There were vague worries that he might be badly burned, but he felt his face and arms. No charred flesh. Everything else seemed intact.

The first face Zach saw was Dr. Johansson. His thin countenance bore an approving smile. Then, his blond white hair took on the hues from a radiant glow from where Rosewood's ceiling should be. Bright and yellow, it felt warm as the late-morning sun. Slowly, Dr. Johansson melded with the light beams. Evelyn stood just a few feet away gazing while the apparition evaporated upward. When he was gone, and as the light receded, she turned to Zach.

She smiled too, but it was an odd, sad smile. When she began slipping through the floorboards into the basement, Zach waved at her to wait. "Evelyn, you don't need to stay at Rosewood now. You can leave, depart."

Evelyn grimaced. "Oh, no. I'm glad to have helped make things right for Dr. Johansson, but I'm not going just yet," she said. "Thomas will come back for me one day."

She vanished downward.

Ray knelt beside him. "Are you okay?"

"I think so."

Who were you talking to?" he asked.

"Evelyn, the ghost who's been protecting this place."

"I didn't see anything."

"I did. A woman." It was Hunter. He and Rebecca were making their way down in darkness. "I saw the doctor depart into the light after that...that thing was abolished. The woman though, she went downward. She's waiting for a lover who is never coming back."

Zach pulled out his cell phone and opened it up. It lit up more of the lobby than he expected. Fortunately, spirits rarely drained lithium ion batteries. He crawled toward the stairs and moved up a couple of steps providing light for their descent.

They met at the spot where Winkler lay.

"He's dead isn't he?" Rebecca asked.

He swore there was a trace of *Sailor Black* in the air as he somberly inspected Winkler's body. While probably pointless, Zach checked for a pulse. There was none.

Next time, it will be one of your own.

Zach was far too drained to deal with premonitions of that sort. Later, he'd question if it had even been his godfather's voice at all. He just wanted to get out of Rosewood and help his friends out safely as well.

Rebecca noticed him using his cell phone as a miniature lantern and she started doing the same. Ray's good hand fumbled for his cell with Joey wrapped awkwardly in his other arm.

Zach approached and reached for Joey, who at first resisted. Once he saw who it was however, he stretched his arms out and clung to Zach's neck.

"C'mon little man. Let's go find your mom."

Chapter Forty-Three

Without Mother's rose trellises, the Kalusky backyard looked barren, stripped naked of character. Once they cleared away the remains of the deck, the yard would be almost empty. Dad planned on building a wide and sweeping back porch in the spring. The way his father procrastinated and worked in bits and spurts, Zach doubted it would be constructed before July 4th, maybe not until Labor Day weekend.

"I'll be able to sit out here and read," Dad said, describing the imaginary porch. Short but stocky, Gary Kalusky had big ears and a round face. "I might even take up smoking a pipe."

"Why would you do that?" Zach asked.

"Why not? Your Uncle used to smoke one. I kind of liked the smell."

"Why didn't you ever start?" Ray asked.

"Okay there, funny guy. If you think the wife got hysterical when I drank, you should have seen her the time she caught me smoking."

Ray assisted Zach in lifting long white wood planks that had once been rose trellises and laying them onto the bed of his pickup truck. The other stuff could be thrown in on top.

"I *hate* the smell of pipe smoke," Zach said flatly.

"Another country heard from," Dad said. "It must run in the family."

The three men worked in silence for a long time. Although that reference to Zach's mother had been the first, it would also turn out to be the last. Regardless, the deck destruction project had a somber undercurrent. It felt like somehow a level of closure was slowly being achieved.

Zach hadn't needed the reference to his godfather to awaken thoughts of him. He'd been ruminating over little else since Evelyn's words: *"He said we needed to wait and let you figure most of it out on your own."*

When he was a youth, his godfather's voice brought comfort to him and helped him deal with his stigmata, that thing Zach sometimes referred to as a curse. Over the years, Uncle Henry had provided Zach so much support that the two things, the religious miracle and the spirit possession, *felt* indelibly linked—but they weren't.

They couldn't be.

The stigmata and the visions it gave Zach, bettered him. He'd not only learned how to cope with the condition, but had learned to use it in conjunction with his talents. It had been an uncomfortable affliction at first but, like any other positive human quality, practicing it worked to his betterment.

It was a something good.

The possession, Zach wasn't so sure about. Uncle Henry's spirit had remained to help Zach cope with the stigmata—he knew that. Before his godfather passed away, he too may have experienced the bleeding. He too may have experienced some sort of visions attached to them. The condition may be a sort of generational family legacy. His uncle had died prior to bearing any children. He had no one, for lack of a better word, to heir the stigmata to. He'd passed away before Zach was old enough to have the condition explained to him. Zach's mother, Uncle Henry's sister, was too mentally unstable to deal with the details of the gift, if she'd ever known about it in the first place.

Regardless, Rosewood had served as ample reminder to Zach what happens when spirits remain in this dimension instead of passing on. Uncle Henry's spirit, not to mention his eternal soul, was in jeopardy. He was trapped in Zach much like Evelyn was attached to Rosewood.

"Hey, Mr. Popular TV Guy," Zach's dad said, his tone lighthearted. Zach fully expected to be the butt of some joke. "All your friends, all those fans, I ask you to bring me one person to help with construction and you bring me a cripple?" He nodded in Ray's direction.

"Ah, Dad, don't worry about it. This is quality time, right Ray?"

Ray frowned and rolled his eyes.

"Besides," Zach continued, "look! He hammers with his left hand."

"Today I do," Ray called out. He knocked a plank of wood away from the other boards with a mallet. "And in the boxing ring, whenever I'm able to get back."

Ray had broken both his pinkie and ring finger of his right hand. He didn't need a cast but instead, wore a metal splint that kept the fingers together and held them in place.

While Ray wasn't looking, Dad flashed Zach a facial expression that clearly communicated the idea Zach shared, but would never say — *how long will he let this delay him from turning pro?*

Zach discreetly shrugged and went back to working. And thinking. The words of his uncle haunted him. *Next time it will be one of your own.*

Not "next time it might be one of your own," or "if you're not careful, next time it will be one of yours. No. *Next time it will be one of your own.*

Zach stared at Ray banging away at the deck and then tossing wood scraps into his pickup truck. He did all the work with one hand and never complained. Zach thought of the other *Xavier Paranormal Investigators.* They were all good people — young people trying to make a positive difference. To lose one conducting the type of paranormal work that they did would be a tragedy.

What did the voice of Uncle Henry mean? Next case? Next time they encounter an evil spirit? Next time they investigate an asylum? Next time they set foot into Rosewood? Perhaps they were just rationalizations, but what was he to do, cancel the show? Tell *XPI* they all had to quit because of a premonition? That wasn't going to happen. Why worry about things he had no control over?

Exactly. So then, why did his godfather say it? It went back to the heart of the matter. Uncle Henry's spirit was playing games — causing stress. He could warn Zach when a flashlight was to be shone in his eyes, but not which member of his team's life was in danger?

Then again, as much as Zach knew of ghost hunting, he knew nothing of what it was like to *be* a spirit. It was possible that feelings, intuitions and fleeting visions came to this godfather and only so much of it could be communicated. Regardless, the longer

Uncle Henry's spirit possessed Zach, the harder it would be to live without him.

But worse, the more his spirit, his soul would deteriorate.

And then there was the matter of Evelyn. With all the terrible visions and experiences the case of Rosewood Asylum had left him with, two things kept him awake at night: Uncle Henry's warning and Evelyn's final words.

"I'm not leaving just yet," she said. *"Thomas will come back for me one day."*

She wouldn't depart. Her perception had become so clouded over a century of deception and deceitful acts. Evelyn Paramour—the young woman who, with high hopes had married a policeman, but had instead gotten a monster. The lady whose lover was murdered, and who was eventually killed by the evil husband she'd wished to escape. Well intentioned as it may have been, her haunting of Rosewood had weakened her awareness to a point that she likely couldn't move on without assistance. If she didn't move on, if she couldn't pass over to heaven, or the other realm, the great beyond or whatever one wished to call it, she would unwittingly have made herself John Paramour's final wasted soul.

Zach couldn't let that happen. After having discussed options with Hunter, Zach had ruled out fire as a means of destroying Rosewood. Not only was there the chance that fire destroyed spirits, Evelyn's death by fire and century-long battle against it had earned her a better fate. Zach hoped to begin a chain of events that would slowly set things right. He intended to enact the plan that very afternoon. In fact, he had already set the wheels in motion.

"Hey Ray," Dad called out. "You want something to drink?"

"Nah, I'm okay for now, Mr. Kalusky."

"Well keep yourself hydrated. The pace my son is keeping, you two are going to be here until after dark."

"Subtle hint delivered, Daddy Dearest," Zach called out.

As Dad and Ray continued to remove plank by plank of the termite-infested deck, Zach set to digging up huge chunks of his mother's old garden and carrying them to Ray's truck. His dad just stared.

Dad had made nearly an identical expression when Zach had asked for the garden dirt as a return favor for helping tear down and haul away the deck.

"What the hell do you want it for?" Dad asked.

Zach was tempted to say, "A science experiment of sorts," with the "of sorts" having inserted a sliver of truth to an otherwise white lie. Instead, he had just shrugged and said, "If it's all the same, I'd rather just not say."

"So you think we're gonna be okay just driving right up in broad daylight?" Ray asked as they drove down 115th Street past the two century-old oak trees that towered on Rosewood's front lawn. One still clung to its brown leaves despite the upcoming winter; the other was barren and blackened with soot. Zach imagined that at some point soon, a tree care crew would cut it down and haul the trunk away.

"Yep. The more you look like you belong somewhere, the more people just assume that you do. Why do you think I told you to wear both gray pants and a gray shirt today?"

They turned onto Pine Avenue, and pulled up to Rosewood's main gate. Zach exited and swiftly unlocked it. They'd been fortunate, or blessed, that the cops hadn't thought to get Winkler's keys from them. Of course the Rosewood custodian's death had been "sold" as an accident. They had reported to the police that he'd been helping them search for Joey when he slipped on a mysterious wet spot on the stairs. Ironically enough, the only drama had come when a detective called to grill Zach about the "bruise and swelling" on Winkler's jaw that appeared to have been a punch. Zach was grateful that he didn't need to answer in person, lest his stretching of the truth be detected. He told the cop that Winkler might have been in a bar fight since his jaw was already swollen when they entered Rosewood.

Later, he confessed all his white lies and told the whole truth to Macginty. The monsignor had ordered him to say more rosaries than he ever had before.

Ray roared his truck up to the Rosewood front door and swung it around so the bed of the truck faced the asylum. "You really think this is gonna work?" he asked.

"I believe it will. Once the asylum begins to crumble, and more so once it's torn down, Evelyn will move on to the other side."

"No, I meant will this termite thing work?"

"Oh. It should," Zach said. "Chlordane treatments used to protect old buildings like these from termites up to twenty years at a time, but it was really bad for the environment and outlawed in 1998."

They began unloading a number of the pieces of infested wood to carry into Rosewood's vacant lobby.

"Yeah, and?"

"And the new stuff they use only protects up to five years at a time."

They made their second trip.

"So it protects up to five years at a time," Ray said. "When was the last time this place was tented?"

"Five years ago last month."

"Well then, won't they be doing it again like any day now, brainiac?"

Had Hunter been present, he would have been impressed with Zach's paraphrased quote from the movie, *Die Hard*. "You ask for a miracle? I give you the State of Illinois."

"I don't get it."

"Well, apparently the "Insecticide Unions" don't have much power in the Illinois State Capital. During the budget wars a few years back, the geniuses in Springfield voted to save money and only spray deserted buildings for termites every seven years. Our little termite friends may have up to two years of an 'All you can eat' buffet."

"Why do I ever doubt you, pal-o-mine?"

"Because you're stupid?"

"Brave words while my hand is broken."

"Aw, does yer poor little pinkie hurt?" Zach teased.

"I've got a finger for you," Ray said, with fake contempt.

After spreading planks of wood throughout the first floor of the asylum, Zach slid the rose trellises down the basement steps. Symbolic he was. Ready to go back down there, he was not.

"You can leave whenever you're ready," he called down. "Goodbye, Evelyn."

Zach pressed the basement door closed.

He and Ray quickly unloaded the chunks of earth and placed them up against Rosewood's façade. Tiny gray termites could be seen in and around the dirt. Zach hoped the little buggers were really hungry.

"Hey, we'd better go wash and disinfect your truck. I'd hate to have you bring termites with you to *Wine, Women & Thong*."

Ray laughed. "Alright. Let's wash it and then we can swing by the club so you can buy me a beer."

Zach sighed. "I'll buy you a beer, but let's go somewhere else — somewhere more...sedate. The strip club just wouldn't seem right after doing this." He glanced at Rosewood.

Ray followed his gaze up at the old structure. "I hear ya." He surveyed the surrounding property. "Hey, while we've got the shovels, think we should go digging for Dr. Johansson's diary?"

Standing in a makeshift gray uniform, and sporting a toothy grin, it wasn't hard to imagine Ray as a gravedigger. Zach nearly blurted out a few quotes in a fit of Hamlet.

Instead, he surveyed Rosewood for what might have been the final time. "Not today. Some things are better left buried."

Epilogue –Zach's Post Production Notes:

I helped Ginny and Joey Foster move to Tinley Park, Illinois, a Chicago suburb farther southwest of Pullman. Joey (or 'Joe' as he now prefers) is thriving at his new school. Depending on which day you talk to him, he intends on becoming either a scientist or a professional baseball player when he grows up.

Bryce Finman didn't show up to the scheduled meeting at Sci-D TV headquarters. At that meeting, Dr. Benz allowed Sara to reveal that she had known Bryce in Hollywood. Apparently he had gotten his start in show business on her show "*Yada, Yada or Yada?*" She admitted to having conceived the plan to combine *XPI* and *Demon Hunter* forces, and had plotted to keep me in the dark as long as possible before the commencement of filming. She felt if I had been given too much time to dwell on working with the Demon Hunters, I'd have not agreed to it. And she might be right.

Sci-D TV declined to renew *Demon Hunters* and no official explanation was given for the cancellation. I've gotten wind that *Demon Hunters* (including a recovered Sashza) are attempting to get a new version of their show (*Demon Hunters International*) picked up in Australia or Germany, but as of yet, they have been unsuccessful. I still keep in rather close contact with one particular Demon Hunter.

Neither Matthew nor Bryce has faced any criminal charges. Sci-D TV didn't want to risk bad publicity for exposing their fraud, and there isn't any evidence to link either of them to arson.

Due to the death of Grant Winkler, the *XPI* Special, "*Rosewood Asylum*" was not aired on Halloween. The network is waiting an "appropriate" amount of time to broadcast the program. Rumor has it that when it does air, because of the buzz generated in the press, it will be the highest-rated show Sci-D TV has ever had. I understand, as a gesture to his friends and family, the episode will be dedicated in the memory of Grant Winkler.

Xavier Paranormal Investigators is becoming (for better *and* for worse) one of the most popular shows on Sci-D TV. Only able to investigate a fraction of the cases that we're now presented, Sara and I engage in "healthy debates" over which ones to select.

Rosewood Psychiatric Hospital continues to remain a vacant, federally protected landmark. As far as I know, it continues to rot from the inside. The only thing now that would save Rosewood from the insidious destruction of termites would be a catastrophic fire—which my newly made friends at the Pullman fire department assure me will *never* happen.

Since Ray and I made our "wood donation" to Rosewood, there have been no sightings of the infamous female ghost. I trust that Evelyn has made her way to the other side where, I'm sure her beloved, Thomas Carter, has been patiently awaiting her arrival.

Please stay tuned for a preview from the next episode of *Xavier Paranormal Investigators*...

The Atchison Haunting
December 26, 1981 – Atchison, Kansas

Glenn Razzovich didn't consider himself a career criminal—just a successful one. He glanced around to verify he wasn't being observed by a nosy neighbor, but at three o'clock the morning after Christmas, *that* was highly doubtful. Most good people were fast asleep dreaming of sugarplums—whatever those were. He crept up the alleyway and through the light dusting of snow toward the darkened house. He didn't care if he left tracks—he planned on burning the old pair of jogging shoes along with his gloves after he was done with the job.

"Good King Wenceslas looked out," he sang under his breath, "on the feast of Stephen."

Glenn had no idea who King Wenceslas was, but years ago he'd stumbled upon the fact that December 26th was the Catholic's feast day of Saint Stephen. He never understood why a holiday song celebrated not Christmas itself, but rather, the day after. In fact, Glenn didn't much believe in Christmas other than one conviction—that he could profit from people who celebrated the long-ago birth by taking trips out of town.

"When the snow lay round about." Glenn casually unlatched and opened the back gate. "Deep and crisp and even."

Houses in either direction remained dark. It was a mature neighborhood outside the center of town and not far from the Missouri river which snaked along the Kansas/Missouri border just east of Atchison. He advanced toward the target, an old Victorian two-story which had been unlit the previous two nights. No tire tracks marred the snow in the long driveway next to the house. He swiftly mounted the back steps and slid into the porch shadows.

"Doo-do doo do doo, that night," he sang, while his hands worked as though operating of their own accord. The lock clicked. "On the feast of Stephen."

Glenn couldn't suppress a wry smile. He opened the door a crack, slipped his wry body out of the frigid air, and then in one smooth motion, twirled and then pressed the door silently shut behind him.

A warm stench invaded his nostrils. It reeked of spoiled meat and rotten cabbage. Did Mommy leave hamburger out? Could Daddy have forgotten to take the garbage to the alley? Many people would have gagged at the wicked odor, but to Glenn it was the sweet smell of an empty house. No human being could live in a home with such a stench — especially not during the holiday season.

Before hunting down the stink's origin (more out of curiosity than any practical reason), Glenn noticed the under-the-counter TV in the kitchen.

"Jackpot," he murmured. "Mommy gets a small television in the kitchen, and Daddy gets bigger toys somewhere else."

Tap.

The noise came from upstairs. He instinctively froze and listened intently. There was the distant rumble of a train, a sound so common to Atchison it was rarely noticed unless one's attention became alerted to it. For a solid minute more, he heard nothing else. Better to be safe than sorry — Glenn crept silently through the house to the front room. A 27" TV sat in the middle of an entertainment center which also housed a stereo and top-of-the-line VCR. Glen noticed the brand names of the electronic equipment and smiled. But something wasn't right.

Dozens of presents were piled under the Christmas tree. Nicely wrapped too — silver ribbons and bows that refracted the moonlight from the front window and sent shards of white light throughout the room. The gifts were stacked in a dramatic fashion around the tree reminiscent of a shopping mall display. Why hadn't anyone opened them? Or taken them on their trip?

Distant mumbling came from upstairs.

And a tap.

Pictures of a man, a woman and two young girls decorated the ascending wall of the staircase. Had one of the kids left a toy going? From deep in the pit of his stomach, a feeling told him to just leave, scrap the couple of nights staking the place out and just cut bait. Ridiculous. No one was home.

No one alive anyway. For all he cared, the rotted stench could be a whole dead family poisoned by Christmas cookies the week before. He'd feel even less guilty about cleaning them out. And the wrapped presents would be a bonus.

The soft speaking again. This time it sounded vaguely familiar — like a quiet chant.

Tap.

It had come from upstairs. Looking up, Glenn climbed the steps. The foul odor became more pungent and more putrid. Glenn wasn't a hardened criminal and had never encountered a dead body, but this reeked how he'd imagined one left for days inside an abandoned house might smell.

He reached the top stair, listened intently, and then headed down the hall towards the far end where he assumed the sounds were coming from. Through the room's open doorway, a picture window let in the moon's blue light. Glenn heard nothing. No talking. No movement. Not even any breathing. He inched closer — a few feet from the door.

"When she'd seen what she had done..."

Tap.

Recognition didn't click right away. Glenn peered into the room. Sitting cross legged on the floor, a girl no older than nine-years old wore pigtails and a white nightgown that glowed in the moonlight. In her hands was a large kitchen knife. Was this one of the daughters from the photo on the stairs?

"She gave her father forty one."

She drove the blade into the wood floor where a wide deep hole had been carved.

What in the love of hell, Glenn thought.

Her unlikely appearance. Her vacant expression. She seemed more an apparition than real.

Glenn slowly backed away. Through the cracked door, he caught a glimpse into the next room. An arm extended at an unnatural angle from a lump on the bed. Even in the half light, he could tell that the sheets were stained with dried blood. There was no doubt that at least one murdered body lay in there.

"Lizzy Bordon took an axe..."

Tap.

Glenn almost puked. He rushed to the staircase.

Before he took his first step down, a floorboard creaked. Not underfoot, but behind him.

He whirled and heard the "Pfffft" before he felt the stabbing pain in his thigh.

"She gave her mother forty whacks."

Her eyes. Wildly insane — inhuman.

Glenn pulled the knife from his groin. Some blood spewed out the hole in his jeans, but most gushed down his inseam.

He staggered down the stairs and clawed at the front door. He clutched his leg remembering to press on the wound. The blood was slippery, warm and wet.

Christ, don't let it end this way!

He fumbled with the locks. He flung open the door and glanced over his shoulder.

She stood atop the staircase. "And when she'd seen what she had done!"

Glenn stumbled outside, across the porch and down the first two steps before tumbling into the cold dusty snow. He frantically gathered a handful of it and pressed it to his wound. He was already lightheaded. Too much blood lost.

Or was this shock?

He tried to stand and couldn't manage. His trail of blood extended from where he was laying, up the front steps through the doorway — the warm red liquid melting the white powder.

He just wanted to live.

He cried for help. But it came out more like a gasping croak. Even to him, it didn't sound very loud. So he inhaled deeply.

And then, as forcefully as he could, Glenn Razzovich screamed.

Acknowledgements

Those who either know me or appreciate the novel writing process, understand that this book is my baby. We've all heard it said that it takes a village to raise a child, and practically the population of a small town deserves credit for helping my work breathe life.

Thanks go to Beta Readers of this novel: Maria Crisman, Susan Prosapio, Judy Popp, Trevor Myers, and Zach's first fan: Rachel Love. The ever intrusive Tammy Szkolny deserves credit to my presale line edits. And to Lynn Calvert for believing in the story.

I owe a huge debt to many writing friends and colleagues: the North County Speculative Fiction Writer's Group, whose suggestions and camaraderie helped make Ghosts of Rosewood Asylum the book it is today...at least the good parts. Special thanks to Nickolas Furr, Meghan Muriel, and of course Irina Ivanova for both help with the writing as well as her amazing cover design. Much gratitude goes to Lisa Brackmann for sharing the journey.

Thank you to everyone at National Search Associates—my second family. Special thanks to Robert Rossi for his photo and logo work.

Those to whom a mere "thanks" is woefully inadequate: Dave Knopp and Joe Prosapio were nothing short of lifelines during the writing of this novel.

No amount of accolades could express enough gratitude to my incredible agent Taryn Fagerness who, for all her ideas and suggestions, might well deserve a writing credit for this novel.

Many people have helped me grow the XPI group on Facebook thanks to all of you, with special gratitude for Liz Nichols, Gayle Bedwell, and Sonya Alarcon, Joe Evans, Lorna Collins, Robert White, Angela Morrell Arnold, and everyone else!

As XPI expands to the world at large, I hope all of you share in my joy.

About the Author

Stephen Prosapio received his Bachelors of Arts degree in Political Science from DePaul University in Chicago. After reporting for one of the nation's largest fantasy football websites, footballguys.com, Stephen wrote his first novel, *Dream War*. Competing against 2,676 other novels, it won a Top Five Finalist award in Gather.com's 2007 First Chapters contest. *Dream War* was released as an eBook in July of 2010. Articles about him and his writing have been featured in the San Diego Union Tribune, The North County Times, Today's Local News, San Diego Magazine and the DePaul University Alumni magazine.

Stephen works as an executive recruiter and resides in Oceanside, California. He is currently crafting a sequel to *Ghosts of Rosewood Asylum* that chronicles the Xavier Paranormal Investigators next case — *The Atchison Haunting*.

Contact the Author:

email: steve@prosapio.com

website: www.prosapio.com

XPI website: www.xavierparanormal.com

http://www.facebook.com/stephenprosapio

http://twitter.com/stephenprosapio

DATE DUE

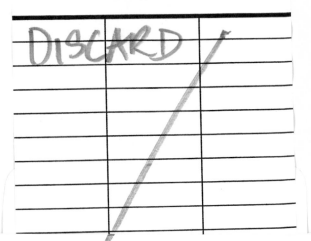

DISCARD

Wells Village Library
5 E Wells Rd
PO Box 587
Wells, VT 05774
802-645-0611
www.wellslibrary.com

CPSIA information can be obtained at www.ICGtesting.com
Printed in the USA
BVOW062142060312

284595BV00004B/2/P

9 781936 593101